THE SIGN
OF THE BOOK

*Also by John Dunning
in Large Print:*

The Bookman's Wake

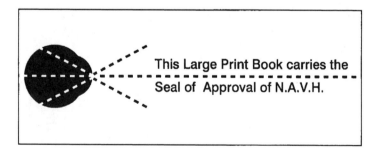

This Large Print Book carries the
Seal of Approval of N.A.V.H.

THE SIGN
OF THE BOOK

A CLIFF JANEWAY NOVEL

JOHN
DUNNING

Thorndike Press • Waterville, Maine

Published in 2005 by arrangement with
Scribner, an imprint of Simon & Schuster, Inc.

Thorndike Press® Large Print Basic.

The tree indicium is a trademark of Thorndike Press.

The text of this Large Print edition is unabridged.
Other aspects of the book may vary from the original edition.

Set in 16 pt. Plantin.

Printed in the United States on permanent paper.

ISBN 0-7862-7547-2 (lg. print : hc : alk. paper)

To Susanne Kirk of Scribner.

Without you there would be no Janeway.

ACKNOWLEDGMENTS

Thanks yet again and a tip of the fedora to Wick Downing for heroic and persistent advice on legal and practical matters. If I made mistakes, they weren't his doing — just my own dogged determination to get things wrong.

And to Sarah Knight, the world's best assistant editor, for her good cheer, her rapier wit, her frightening intelligence. I trust her with my life.

BOOK I
DEATH OF AN OLD FLAME

1

Two years had passed and I knew Erin well. I knew her moods: I knew what she liked and didn't like, what would bore her to tears or light up her face with mischief. I knew what would send her into fits of helpless laughter, what would make her angry, thoughtful, witty, playful, or loving. It takes time to learn someone, but after two years I could say with some real confidence, I know this woman well.

I knew before she said a word that something had messed up her day. She arrived at our bookstore wearing her casual autumn garb, jeans and an untucked flannel shirt.

"What's wrong with you?"

"I am riding on the horns of a dilemma."

I knew she would tell me when she had thought about it. I would add my two cents' worth, she would toss in some wherefores, to which I would add a few interrogatories and lots of footnotes. I am good with footnotes. And after two years I was very good at leaving her alone when all the signs said *let her be*.

She picked up the duster and disappeared into the back room. That was another bad sign: in troubled times, Erin liked to dust. So I let her ponder her dilemma and dust her way through it in peace. Since she now owned part of my store, she had unlimited dusting privileges. She could dust all day long if she wanted to.

Two customers came and went and one of them made my week, picking up a $1,500 Edward Abbey and a *Crusade in Europe* that Eisenhower had signed and dated here in Denver during his 1955 heart-attack convalescence. Suddenly I was in high cotton: the day, which had begun so modestly ($14 to the good till then), had now dropped three grand in my pocket. I called The Broker and made reservations for two at seven.

At five o'clock I locked the place up and sidled back to check on Erin. She was sitting on a stool with the duster in her hand, staring at the wall. I pulled up the other stool and put an arm over her shoulder. "This is turning into some dilemma, kid."

"Oh, wow. What time is it?"

"Ten after five. I thought you'd have half the world dusted off by now."

"How's the day been?"

I told her and she brightened. I told her about The Broker and she brightened another notch.

We went up front and I waved to the neighborhood hooker as she trolled up East Colfax in the first sortie of her worknight. "Honestly," Erin said, "we've got to get out of here. How do you ever expect to get any business with that going on?"

"She's just a working professional, plying her trade. A gal's gotta do something."

"Hey, *I'm* a *gal*," she said testily. "I don't gotta do that."

"Maybe that lady hasn't had your advantages."

The unsavory truth was, I liked it on East Colfax. Since Larimer Street went all respectable and touristy in the early seventies, this had become one of the most entertaining streets in America. City officials, accepting millions in federal urban renewal money, had promised a crackdown on vice, but it took the heart of a cop to know exactly what would happen. The hookers and bums from that part of town had simply migrated to this part of town, and nothing had changed at all: city officials said wow, look what we did, now people can walk up Larimer Street without stumbling over drunks and whores, but here they still were. I could sit on my stool and watch the passing parade through my storefront window all day long: humanity of all kinds walked, drove, skateboarded, and sometimes ran past like bats out of hell. In the few years since I had opened shop on this corner, I had seen a runaway car, a gunfight, half a dozen fistfights, and this lone whore, who had a haunting smile and the world's saddest eyes.

"You are the managing partner," Erin said. "That was our deal and I'm sticking to it. But if my vote meant anything, we would move out of this place tomorrow."

"Of course your vote means something, but you just don't up and move a bookstore. First you've got to have a precise location in mind. Not just Cherry Creek in general or some empty hole in West Denver, but an actual place with traffic and pizzazz. A block or two in any direction can make all the difference."

She looked around. "So this has pizzazz? This has traffic?"

"No, but I've got tenure. I've been here long enough, people two thousand miles away know where I am. And not to gloat, but I did take in three thousand bucks today."

"Yes, you did. I stand completely defeated in the face of such an argument."

I went on, unfazed by her defeat. "There's also the matter of help. If I moved to Cherry Creek, I'd need staff. My overhead would quadruple before I ever got my shingle out, so I'd better not guess wrong. Here I can run it with one employee, who makes herself available around the clock if I need her. What more could a bookseller want? But you know all this, we've had this discussion how many times before?"

"Admit it, you'll never move." Erin sat on the stool and looked at me across the counter. "Would it bother you if we didn't do The Broker tonight? I don't feel like dressing up."

"Say no more."

I called and canceled.

"So where do you want to eat?"

"Oh, next door's fine."

I shivered. Next door was a Mexican restaurant, the third eatery to occupy that spot since I had turned the space on the corner into my version of an East Denver fine books emporium. In fact, half a dozen restaurants had opened and closed there in the past ten years, and I knew that because I had been a young cop when this block

15

had been known as hooker heaven. Gradually the vice squad had turned up the heat, the topless places and the hustlers had kept moving east, and a series of restaurants had come and gone next door. Various chefs had tried Moroccan, Indian, Chinese, and American cuisine, but none had been able to overcome the street's reputation for harlots and occasional violence. Some people with money just didn't want to come out here, no matter how good the books were.

We settled into a table in the little side room and I ordered from a speckled menu: two Roadrunner burritos, which seemed like pleasant alternatives to the infamous East Colfax dogburger. "What's in this thing we're about to eat?" Erin asked.

"You'll like it better if you don't know."

The waitress brought our Mexican beers and drifted away. Erin reached across the table and squeezed my hand. "Hi," she said.

"Hey. Was that an endearment?"

"Yeah, it was."

I still didn't ask about her trouble. I gave her a friendly squeeze in return and she said, "How're you doing, old man? You still like the book life?"

It was a question she asked periodically.

16

"Some days are better than others," I said. "Today was a really good one on both ends of it. Sold two, bought one — a nice ratio."

"What did you buy?" she said, putting things in their proper importance.

"The nicest copy you'll ever see of *Phantom Lady* — Cornell Woolrich in his William Irish motif. Very pricey, very scarce in this condition. I may put two grand on it. That wartime paper just didn't hold up for the long haul, so you never see it this nice."

"You're getting pretty good at this, aren't you?"

"It doesn't take much skill to recognize that baby as a good one."

"But even after all this time you still miss police work."

"Oh, sure. Everything has its high spots. When I was a cop, I loved those high spots like crazy, I guess because I was good at it. You get a certain rush when suddenly you know *exactly* what happened. Then you go out and prove it. I can point out half a dozen cases that never would've been solved except for me and my squirrelly logic. There may be dozens of others."

"I'd have guessed thousands."

"That might be stretching it by one or two hundred. A dozen I could dredge up with no effort at all." I took a sip of my beer. "Why do you ask, lovely one? Is this leading somewhere? It's getting fairly egotistical on my part."

"I know, but I asked for it. Please continue, for I am fascinated."

"I was *really* good at it," I said with no apologies. "You never want to give up something you have that much juice for. When I lost it, I missed the hell out of it. You know all this, there's no use lying, I *really* missed it, I always will."

I thought of my police career and the whole story played in my head in an instant, from that idealistic cherry-faced beginning to the end, when I had taken on a brute, used his face for a punching bag, and lost my job in the process. "But I was lucky, wasn't I? The book trade came along and it was just what I needed: very different, lots of room to grow, interesting work, good people. I figured I'd be in it forever."

"And indeed, you may well be. But nothing's perfect."

I mustered as much sadness as I could dredge up on a $3,000 day. "Alas, no."

"If you had to give this up, how would you feel about it?"

"Devastated. You mean I get lucky

enough to find two true callings in one life-time and then I lose them both? Might as well lie down in front of a bus. What else would I do? Be a PI? It's not the same after you've been the real thing."

"How would you know? You've never done it: not for any kind of a living."

"I know as a shamus you've got no authority. You don't have the weight of the department behind you, and where's the fun in that? You're just another great pretender."

A moment later, I looked at her and said, "So why are you here on a workday? How come you're not in your lawyer's uniform? What's going on with your case? And after all is said and done, am I finally allowed to ask what this problem is all about?"

"The judge adjourned for the afternoon so he could do some research. I think we're gonna win, but of course you never know. Right now it's just a hunch. So I've got the rest of the day off. And let's see, what was that other question? What's this all about? I need your help."

"Say no more."

"Something's come up. I want you to go to Paradise for me."

"You mean the town in western Colorado or just some blissful state of mind?"

"The town. Maybe the other thing too, if

you can be civilized."

"Tough assignment. But speaking of the town, why me?"

"You're still the best cop I know. I trust your instincts. Maybe I'm just showing you that if you did want to do cases, you'd have more work than you've got time for."

"The great *if*. Listen, being a dealer in so-called rare books leaves me no time for anything else anyway. Why do you keep trying to get me out of the book business?"

"I'm not! Why would I do that? You could do both, as you have already so nimbly demonstrated."

Our food came. The waitress asked if there was anything else and went away. Erin took a small bite, then looked up and smiled almost virginly.

"Let's say I want you to go to Paradise and look at some books. You should be able to do that. Look at some books and see if they might be worth anything. Because if they're not, the defendant may lose her house paying for her defense."

"It would be damned unusual for any collection of books to pay for the exorbitant fees you lawyers charge. Is there any reason to think these might be anything special? What did she say when she called you?"

"She didn't call, her attorney did. Fine time to be calling, her preliminary hearing's set for tomorrow."

She didn't have to elaborate. The most critical hours in any investigation are always the ones immediately after the crime's been committed. "Her attorney says she mentioned selling her husband's book collection," she said. "But she's afraid they aren't worth much."

"Trust her, they aren't. I can smell them from here, I don't even have to look, I can't tell you how many of these things I've gone out on. They never pan out."

"I'm sure you're right. Do this for me anyway."

I looked dubious. "Do I actually get to touch these books?"

"Take your surgical gloves along and maybe. You did keep some rubber gloves from your police days?"

"No, but they're cheap and easy to get."

"Kinda like the women you used to run with, before me."

"That's it, I'm outta here."

She touched my hand and squeezed gently. "Poor Cliff."

She took another bite of the Roadrunner. "This really isn't half-bad, is it?"

I shook my head and slugged some beer.

"Oh, Erin, you've got to get out more, you're working too hard, your taste buds are dying from neglect. I'll volunteer for the restaurant detail. I promise I'll find us a place that'll thrill your innards."

"When you get back from Paradise."

I ate, putty in her hands, but at some point I had to ask the salient question. "So do you ever plan to tell me about this thing?"

She didn't want to, by now that was almost painfully clear. "Take your time," I said soothingly. "I've got nothing on my plate, we could sit here for days."

"The defendant's name . . ." She swallowed hard, as if the name alone could hurt. "Laura Marshall. Her name is Laura. She's accused of killing her husband. She wants me to defend her, but I've got two cases coming up back-to-back. Even if I took her on, which is far from certain anyway, I couldn't get out there until sometime next month. That's it in a nutshell."

"I thought you said she had an attorney."

"He's her attorney of the moment. He sounds very competent, but he's never done a case like this."

She gave me a look that said, *That's it, Janeway, that's all there is.*

"Well," I said cautiously, "can we break open that nutshell just a little?"

I waited and finally I gave her my stupid look. "What is it you want me to *do*, Erin? This isn't just an appraisal job. I get the feeling it's something else."

"Maybe you could talk to her while you're there. Take a look at her case."

"I could do that. I'm sure you don't want me to advise her. The last time I looked, my law degree was damned near nonexistent."

"Go down, talk to her, report back to me. You don't need a law degree for that. Just lots of attitude."

"That, I can muster. In fact I'm getting some right now. So tell me more."

"I'd rather have you discover it as you go along."

A long, ripe moment followed that declaration.

"She'll tell you the details," Erin said. "And by the way, I pay top rates."

"So now you're bribing me. Is this what we've come to?" I gave her a small head-shake. "Something's going on here. This isn't just some yahoo case that dropped on your head. It's more than that."

She stonewalled me across the table.

"Isn't it?" I said.

"She was my best friend in college. In fact, we go back to childhood."

"*And . . . ?*"

"We haven't seen each other in years . . ."

"*Because . . . ?*"

"That's irrelevant."

"No, Counselor, what that is, is bad-lawyer bafflegab. Tommyrot, bushwa, caca, bunkum, and a cheap oil change. Not to mention piffle and baloney."

She stared.

"Old oil sludge," I said. "Remember those ads? Dirty sludge, gummy rings, sticky valves, blackie carbon. And a bad Roadrunner burrito."

She laughed. "Are you all through?"

"Hell no I'm not through. Help me out just a little here. Make at least some sorry stab at giving me a straight answer."

"Marshall was the first great love of my life. Is that straight enough for you?"

"Ah," I said, mildly crushed. My pain was slightly mitigated by the word *first*.

"He can't compare to you," she said. "Never could've, never would've, though I had no way of knowing that back then. Remember two years ago just after we met? I told you then I had known another guy long ago who collected books. I guess I've always been attracted to book people. I couldn't imagine I'd wind up with Tarzan of the Bookmen, swinging from one bookstore to another on vines attached to telephone poles."

"It was written in the stars."

"I'm not complaining. But that was then, this is now. He was my first real love and she was my best friend. More than that. She was closer than a sister to me, we marched to the same heartbeat. I would have trusted either of them with my life. And they had an affair behind my back."

I said "Ah" again and I squeezed her hand. "Jesus, why would *any*body do that to you?"

She shrugged. "It was a long time ago."

"And people do things," I ventured.

"Not things like that."

"So how'd you find out about it? He break down and tell you?"

"She did. Her conscience was killing her and she had to make it right between us."

I took another guess. "So when did you find it in your heart to forgive her?"

"You're assuming facts not in evidence, Janeway." She looked at me across the table, and out of that superserious moment came the steely voice I knew so well. "I'll never forgive her."

"Then why . . ."

"Why doesn't matter. Look, will you do this for me or not?"

I really didn't need to think about it. The answer would have been the same with or without the particulars. All I needed to know was that it was important to her.

"Sure," I said.

2

I left my bookstore in the hands of Millie, my gal Friday, and by dawn the next morning I was well out on the road to Fairplay. I heard reports of scattered snow in the mountains as I headed west, but they didn't bother me much. People who worry about scattered snow are afraid of everything.

I figured I'd stop at the Fairplay Griddle to eat, gas up, and take a leak: one short pit stop and straight through from there. Paradise is in a tiny, out-of-the-way county, in the mountains just west of the Continental Divide. This is almost as remote as a traveler can safely go without backpacks and mules. You don't just stumble into Paradise: you go there only with a purpose. There are two or three small, unincorporated towns and then, at the end of the one paved road, Paradise, the county seat. A dirt road does go south from there, which I had heard was a helluva spectacular ride. In a Jeep, a truck, or with lots of moxie in a car, you can eventually hook up with U.S. Highway

160, the main east-west route across southern Colorado. But you must go over some of the state's most rugged mountains and it's closed in the winter anyway. Practically speaking, the road to Paradise is also the only way out, a hundred-mile round-trip from anywhere.

It was nearly a six-hour drive from Denver, giving me time to brood over my life with Erin and the questions she had raised about my life in books. "The problem is you, sweetheart," she had said on another occasion. "You're letting yourself become too static in your book world. But I'll make you a deal: I promise I'll be happy if you will."

She had sensed my drift toward boredom long before I put it into words. "It's not the books," I told her then, "it's what money and greed are doing to them. The books are still what they always were, some of them are wonderful, exciting, spectacular, and on the good days I believe I could do this forever. But soon all the best ones will be in the hands of Whoopi Goldberg and a few rich men, who will pay too much because they can. They'll drive the market upward till they chase out everybody else."

I cocked my head back and forth and

said, "I don't know if I want to do that."

I had seen this coming. The book trade was then just beginning to peek into the computer world; what has since become an indispensable part of the business was getting itself timidly into gear, and I knew almost chapter and verse how it would turn out. I am certainly no clairvoyant: sometimes, in fact, I can be incredibly dense, but that day I saw the demise of the open bookshop. I saw the downturn at book fairs. Wiser heads scoffed — the trade had always weathered storms, they said — but I feared that soon we'd be in a time when all anyone would need to reach the higher levels of the book world was enough money. Erin had brought money into my business, but my commitment continued to lag. I told her about it one night and she had understood it at once. I said, "When you take the best parts of any business away from the masses and hand it over to the rich, you can't be too surprised when it starts dying on the inside." There had been a time, just a year or two earlier, when this had all seemed so exciting. The thought of dealing in books worth $50,000, of flying off to book fairs here and abroad, had been thrilling as hell. The trade offered unlimited opportunity for growth, so I thought, but one night in a dream I saw where it would end. "I don't think I want to do that," I told her again.

The next day I made some bold predictions.

In a few years much of the romance would disappear from the book trade forever.

The burgeoning Internet, as it would later be called, would bring in sweeping change. There would be incredible ease, instant knowledge available to everyone: even those who have no idea how to use it would become "experts." Books would become just another word for money, and that would bring out the hucksters and fast-buck artists.

No bookseller would own anything outright in this brave new book world. One incredibly expensive book would have half a dozen dealers in partnership, with the money divvied six ways or more when it sold. "I might as well be selling cars," I said.

Strangely, I still loved the nickel-and-dime stuff. But that would change as well as bookstores closed and people became more cautious about what they were willing to sell. The ability to buy huge libraries would diminish and then disappear. Moving to a higher level would mean bigger headaches. The computer would tell us where all the great books were, and the thrill of the hunt would quickly diminish.

That's when Erin first floated her PI idea. "You know what you need to do?" she said. "You need to find the bad people of the book world and put them in jail."

I laughed at the thought. A detective agency specializing in book fraud? There was no way anyone could take such a thing seriously. But then fate took a hand. *The Boston Globe* had covered my first major acquisition, a mysteriously signed copy of the most famous work by Richard Francis Burton, and that story had been sent everywhere in an AP rewrite. Luck, pure luck. But it had led me to two book shysters in Texas, and another case had sent me to Florida. The trade press had taken note and suddenly in the world of rare books I had a name. I didn't need to hang out a shingle, didn't run even one advertisement. Today more than ever, books are money. When the inevitable disputes arose, people came to me, and now I was more inclined to listen. When some unwashed schlemiel called from afar and said, "Are you the book cop?" I said yes and resisted the urge to laugh in his face. Yeah, I was the book cop. As far as I knew, no one else could make that claim.

My original plan with Erin had been a fifty-fifty partnership. Almost forty days after the Burton affair she had called and we had had a hot, sweaty tumble, our first, on the cot in the back room of my bookstore. We laughed and shared a postcoital pizza on the front counter. Everything seemed poised for a great new beginning, but even that first night Erin could sense my growing discontent. "You need to get out more," she said. "I get the feeling that the book business is not treating you as well as it once did." I leaned down and kissed her hand and said, "Hey, I'm fine, the book business is great," but that didn't count because she didn't believe it. "I think under the circumstances," she mused a few weeks later, "we'd better put our active partnership on hold." She still wanted in: she anted thirty thousand to make that point and said there was more where that came from. For now she'd be a silent partner and go back to practicing law to keep off the streets.

She joined a new law firm on Seventeenth Street, a dream job she said, if she had to have a job. "It dropped in my lap all of a sudden, it gives me everything I always thought I wanted. What's really great is how much *they* wanted *me*." Why wouldn't they be enthused, I asked: she had been a brilliant student in law school and a tireless workhorse at Waterford, Brownwell; she had worked on two big water rights cases as part of a team and had won three murder cases on her own. She had built a splendid reputation for herself, there had never been any doubt of her ability to get back into law on the fast track whenever and if ever she wanted, so why wouldn't they jump at the chance to hire her?

We went out to lunch that week. She took me to a fine lawyers' hangout not far from her new office downtown. I shoehorned myself into a jacket and tie and we walked up the street together, chitchatting our way along. The waiter remembered her well from her days at Waterford. "Ms. D'Angelo, how nice to see you again . . . yes, I have your table ready," he said, and we were ushered past the gathering crowd to what looked like the best table in the place. It was set up far away from everything, in a dark world of its own, framed by indoor trees with our own private Ansel Adams nightscape on the wall between us. "So tell me," she said, "was I right or wrong to take this job?"

"I don't know, Erin. How does it feel?"

"I'm a hired gun again. But listen and believe this: I am totally at your beck and call. Say the secret word and I shall give notice that same day and join you in whatever comes of your book world."

"God, what power I have over you."

"Yep. You could join the Antiquarian Booksellers Association and travel to real book fairs everywhere. I'd go along, of course, as your apprentice and eager sex slave."

"I like the sound of that. Especially the last part."

"I would reply with sarcasm, except I remember who raped whom that night."

"I think we were concurrent rapes, as you legal types like to say. We each had a simultaneous leap at the other."

"I had half my clothes off by the time you got the front door open."

"Really? I never noticed. Which half did you leave on the street?"

"Panties in the gutter, bra tossed over the fireplug. Stockings, shoes, and other accessories strewn down the sidewalk."

"*That's* why I never noticed. You blended right into the habitat."

"And now here we are."

Impulsively she kissed my hand.

"Nothing is forever," she said. "I don't know where I'll be in two years, or five, but somehow I don't think I'll be practicing law. Right now it's my strength, it's what I know. And I'm making good money at it."

"Then it's good."

"For now it'll do."

Snow began to fall just before I reached Fairplay. The Griddle was a typical country place, full of smoke and packed with locals talking about winter, politics, and the hunting season. I lingered over coffee and the *Rocky Mountain News* I had brought from Denver. Outside, through a dingy storefront, I could see the snow beginning to stick, and a swirl of it danced across the road like a white dust devil and disappeared into nothing. I watched the gaunt old faces hunched over their ham and eggs and I wondered what it would be like to live here. I thought about Erin and the young woman, still faceless, who awaited my arrival in Paradise.

I left the paper unread and headed on south. The snow thickened, but I got past Poncha Springs, over Monarch Pass and the Continental Divide, and the worst seemed to be behind me. The snow stopped and I came into one of those spectacular midmorning sun-showers that made me glad I live in Colorado, and beyond that was nothing but blue skies and sunshine. A good omen, I thought, knowing better. In this business, in matters of life and death, there are no good omens.

Highway 50 took me straight into Gunnison. It was still only half past ten, and Paradise was due south. I got out of the car and walked the streets till I found a drugstore. If the Marshall case had made the Denver papers, I hadn't seen it, but I imagined to the local weekly press it was a much bigger deal. I stopped at the newspaper office and looked back two issues. On the front page, just below the fold, were two pictures of Laura Marshall, and suddenly the lady without a face had one. The headline said WOMAN CHARGED IN HUSBAND'S MURDER. In the first picture she looked like any other felony suspect: grim, lonely, guilty as hell. She was in handcuffs, being led by some gruff-looking lawman through a rainstorm into what was probably the county jail. Her hair streamed down across her face and her eyes were the only memorable features. The arresting officer was identified as sheriff's deputy Lennie Walsh. I wrote that down in my notebook, and I also noted the tiny agate name of the photographer under the cutline. *Photo by Hugh Gilstrap.*

The second picture was a posed head shot, obviously taken under more favorable conditions. Again I was drawn to her eyes. Just a bunch of dots on newsprint, but as I pulled back from it, a woman appeared. She smiled slightly, looking warm and innocent. In fact, she looked a little like Erin. At some point Erin herself had said that. They were the same age, they grew up together, they might have been sisters. I sat over coffee in the first café I found and read the story twice. It was more headline than substance: a few paragraphs below and around the bold type did tell me somewhat more than I already knew, mainly because what I knew was almost nothing.

This was the story. On Monday three weeks ago, Robert Charles Marshall, thirty-three, of Paradise, had been shot dead in his home. His wife, Laura, thirty-two, had called the sheriff's office and reported his death. The sheriff's deputy, after investigating at the home and interviewing the widow, had concluded that enough evidence existed to charge Mrs. Marshall with murder. There was nothing in the paper about the evidence — no indication whether Mrs. Marshall had said something incriminating or had been Mirandized or when — but newspapers don't usually have information like that. It did say that the Marshalls' three children were now in the care of the victim's parents, who had arrived in Paradise at the end of the week. Marshall and his wife had lived in the area for eight years, moving there from Denver, where they had met. They had been somewhat reclusive and apparently had few friends. The suspect had been arraigned and the preliminary hearing had been scheduled Friday — today — at 1:30 p.m. before District Judge Harold Adamson.

I looked at the clock on the wall: it was 10:43.

I got in my car and headed south. Ninety minutes later I arrived in Paradise.

3

It was a sleepy-looking town, one main street and half a dozen side streets. An old, imposing brick building could be seen from the highway: it squatted on a street a block over and I guessed it was the hall of justice, probably a combination of courthouse, county offices, and, in a connected wing, the county jail. The barred windows were dead giveaways and the two cop cars parked outside were additional clues. I pulled into the lot between them and sat there for a minute thinking. While I sat, the deputy came out and got in his car, giving me the evil eye. I recognized him as the same guy who had booked Laura Marshall. He sat there staring, and a moment later he got out of his car and came around to my window. I ran it down a crack, enough to talk to him, and he leaned over.

"Can I help you with something?"

"I don't know, maybe. I was just about to come inside and ask how I could find the lawyer representing Laura Marshall."

"What's your interest in that?"

"Her attorney called Denver about retaining another lawyer."

He didn't like that. Hotshot city-slicker mouthpiece, I read in his face.

"You the lawyer?"

"I work for her."

"Doing what?"

At that point I opened the door, forcing him to step back against his own passenger door. I got out and we looked at each other. He was lean and lanky, about half a head shorter than I was and thirty pounds lighter. I warned myself not to pop off or start anything dumb, but cops like him bring out the absolute worst in me.

"I asked what you've got to do with this case," he repeated.

Answer the man's question, Janeway, my inner voice warned. *Be civil.* But the same voice asked, *Why, oh why, do I attract these pricks like a magnet?*

"I was sent by Ms. Erin D'Angelo, Denver attorney, to investigate the circumstances of Mr. Marshall's demise," I said. Most civil: almost cordial.

"I thought that was my job."

"C'mon, Deputy, it's cold out here."

"What's that supposed to mean?"

"Just that I'm freezing my ass off. If you want to jack me around, let's do it inside.

Either that or I'll break out my heavy coat from the trunk and we can build us a campfire and send out for Chinese food."

"Funny guy. You musta done stand-up comedy somewhere. What's your name?"

"Janeway. Onstage I was known as the Merry Mulligan."

"You saying you're a cop?"

"I used to be."

This didn't impress him. It never does wow a real cop.

"So, what'd you do, direct Denver traffic?"

"Yeah. I directed a few badasses right onto death row."

He still didn't look as if he was buying it. "You got a license to investigate?"

"Nooo . . . I wasn't aware I needed one."

He didn't like my singsong, wiseass tone. He said, "Maybe you'd better get aware," and I said, "Well, I sure will do that, Mr. Deputy Walsh."

He looked surprised that I knew his name. While basking in this advantage, I said, "And I'd appreciate it if you could show me the statute that requires me to have a license to ask questions in Colorado."

We sized each other up again. I said, "Look, I really didn't come down here to cause trouble. All I want to do is to see

41

Mrs. Marshall and her lawyer for a few minutes."

"Well, you can't," he said smugly. "They're meeting upstairs now, so I guess you'll have to wait till after her hearing."

"Thank you, Mr. Walsh, sir," I said, and I got back in my car.

I drove out of the lot and two minutes later Walsh eased in behind me and turned on his flashing red lights. I pulled over and again he came to my window. I cracked the window and he leaned over and looked at me.

"May I see your driver's license, sir?"

This was said deadpan, as if we had never seen each other before that moment. I fished out my wallet and took the license out of its plastic sleeve. Walsh walked away and got in his car. In my mirror I could see him talking on his radio. This went on for some time, longer than it had to: then he broke out his clipboard and began writing. A ticket . . . the son of a bitch was giving me a ticket for something, I couldn't imagine what. I simmered while he wrote out the equivalent of the Magna Carta on his clipboard. I may have fallen asleep waiting, but eventually he got out and ambled back to me.

"Sir, the reason I stopped you was your failure to observe the four-way stop sign at the intersection you just went through."

"I did stop, Officer."

"Well, sir, that may have seemed like a stop to you, but out here the word *stop* means you come to a complete stop and look both ways before proceeding across the intersection. This is a family community and schoolchildren use that crossing all the time. I don't want to see stops like that in my town."

He tore off the ticket and passed it through the window. "Have a nice day, sir."

I knew better than to argue with a cop like that. I had done my arguing in the parking lot and this was what it got me. I was on his turf — argue now and failure to stop could easily become careless or even reckless driving, with no witnesses to take my side of it. I had two choices, neither of them happy: shut up and pay my fine, take my three-point violation and lump it, or protest the tactics of Deputy Walsh in some local kangaroo court where the judge might be no better than the law enforcement. A bigger question had suddenly become Walsh's connection to Laura Marshall. That's when he'd first gotten his back up, when I had mentioned her name. He pulled around me and drove off and I sat there for another long moment, thinking about it.

4

At one-fifteen sharp I arrived at the county courtroom. I knew, because of the remoteness of the county, that District Judge Harold Adamson probably didn't live here, and in fact his judicial district might sprawl across half a dozen counties. In some of the smallest counties, the county court judge might not even be a lawyer: he could be an ex-cop, a highway patrolman, a businessman, or any respected member of the community. Not surprisingly, the DA had filed this case directly in the district court and Adamson had had jurisdiction from the start. The sheriff would be a county officer based in Paradise. Lennie Walsh, the deputy, might live here or in one of the smaller towns and would be a roving badge, patrolling wherever he was needed or saw fit. These were the characters as the hearing began.

The room was crowded for a workday: lots of interest was being shown in the plight of a good-looking young woman charged with killing her husband. They probably got just one murder case each century down here, and a sexy one like this had filled the seats early. I sat near the door, best seat I could get, surrounded by gawkers and the endlessly curious. At one-thirty a door opened to the far right of the bench and Deputy Walsh escorted Laura Marshall into the courtroom. She wore the plain orange jailhouse garb and kept her eyes straight ahead as she came in. Her hands were uncuffed, as if at some point someone had decided that she was not a high risk to grab the deputy's gun and start blazing away. I thought she looked good under the circumstances. Walsh looked like Walsh — see Janeway's *Prick by Any Other Name* rule. They were met at the defendant's table by an old man with white hair who was well decked-out in a three-piece suit, and Walsh turned Mrs. Marshall over to him. At the opposite table two attorneypeople were locked in earnest conversation. One was a young woman whose looks rivaled the accused's — a surprise to find someone such as she in a small county like this — and the other was a man in his midforties. A shark, I guessed from the look of him.

Almost before I had registered these impressions, the door behind the bench opened and the judge came in. He was on the upper end of the age scale, a stern-looking geezer with a beak like a hawk. His bailiff did the *Hear ye* honors, announcing that District Judge Harold Adamson was presiding, and we all sat down.

"*The People versus Laura Marshall,*" the judge announced. "The parties will enter their appearances for the record. Mr. McNamara?"

The old man rose at the defense table. "Parley S. McNamara for the defendant, Laura Marshall, who is also present. I would also state for the record that my client has contacted another attorney, and —"

"What are you talking about? Are you the lawyer for the defendant or not?"

"I am her attorney, sir, but —"

"But nothing. If you want to bring in someone else at a later time, file a motion and I'll consider it. But as of now, you are her lawyer. Is that clear?"

"As the court knows, criminal law is not my specialty."

"Then why did the defendant engage you? We do have one or two attorneys in this district who have some experience in criminal law."

"Mrs. Marshall wanted someone she knows —"

"Never mind that, you still haven't answered my first question. Do you understand that as of this moment, and until you are relieved by me, you are the attorney of record for Mrs. Marshall?"

"Yes, Your Honor."

"Mrs. Marshall, under the circumstances I must ask you the same question. Do you understand what we just said?"

She looked up at the judge and nodded.

"Speak up for the record, Mrs. Marshall. That man over there is a court reporter: he can't record gestures or nods of the head. You have to answer so he can hear you. Now, do you understand that Mr. McNamara is your attorney until he's relieved, and I don't care whether criminal law is his specialty. He has been a lawyer in this county for many years and I know him to be highly competent. I will not tolerate unnecessary delays in the speedy dispatch of this case. Have I made myself clear?"

The sound of her name had brought the defendant's head up, and she said something so softly the reporter had to ask her to repeat it.

"Mrs. Marshall," the judge said with exaggerated patience, "do you understand what we've just said here?"

"Yes."

"Good. Mr. McNamara, your appearance is noted. For the people?"

The two lawyers stood at the other table.

"Leonard Gill, district attorney, Your Honor."

"Ann Bailey, assistant district attorney, if it please the court."

"Then let's get started."

The judge read the information, and said that the defendant had been advised of her rights and had requested a preliminary hearing. He said the people had the burden of proving that the crime of first-degree murder had been committed and there was probable cause to believe that the defendant had committed it. Gill took his seat and the judge said, "Are you ready to proceed, Miss Bailey?"

"Yes, Your Honor."

"Then call your first witness."

She moved out to the lectern. "Deputy Lennie Walsh."

Walsh testified that on Monday at 3:09 p.m. he had been dispatched to the Marshall home on a code red, a reported shooting.

"When you arrived at the house, what did you find?"

"The front door was open."

"You mean wide open?"

"Yes, ma'am. And it was raining, which made it —"

"Just tell us what you saw, please."

"I went to the door and banged on it."

"You didn't cross the threshold?"

"No, not then. I knocked loudly and called inside."

"Did you identify yourself at that time?"

"Oh, yes. I yelled my name and said I was from the sheriff's office."

"Then what happened?"

"Nothing for a minute. I yelled again and rapped on the door with the butt of my gun —"

"You had your gun out?"

"Well, yeah. I didn't know what was in there."

"Then what happened?"

"Nothing. I had a real bad feeling about it, so I went into the hall. In the front room I could see somebody slumped over the table. I came closer and I saw that it was Mrs. Marshall."

"The defendant."

"Yes."

"What was her appearance then?"

"She was dazed, like she didn't —"

"How did she *look*, Deputy?"

"She was all bloody. I mean, she had blood everywhere. Her dress was torn, just drenched in blood."

"Did she say anything?"

"Yes, ma'am. She said, 'I shot Bobby.' "

"Just like that."

"Yes, ma'am, just like that."

"Then what?"

"I came on into the room and saw the victim on the floor."

"Did you then advise the defendant?"

"I didn't have time. All this happened in, like, twenty seconds. What she said she just looked up and said."

McNamara stirred in his chair. "Your Honor . . ."

The judge furrowed his brow and said, "All right, this isn't the trial, let's hear it."

"She said, 'Bobby's dead, I shot Bobby.' Then she leaned over and fainted."

A look of skepticism spread over Miss Bailey's face. "I see. She fainted. And what did you do?"

"Went over and examined the victim."

"Describe his condition, please."

"He didn't have any condition. Had his face blown half away and another one in the area of the heart. I checked his pulse, and found none."

"What did you do then?"

"I found the weapon and bagged it."

McNamara rose from his chair. "We don't know what weapon he found."

"He found *a* weapon, then," Miss Bailey said.

"Now the prosecutor is giving testimony," McNamara said.

"What kind of weapon was it and where did you find it?" Miss Bailey said.

"A .38 revolver, on the floor by the table."

"Your Honor," McNamara said. "May I please get a word in edgewise?"

"Slow down, Miss Bailey," the judge said.

"Sorry, Your Honor." She looked at McNamara. "You have an objection, Counselor?"

"I could give you a whole laundry list of objections. You assume facts not in evidence, his answer is vague and unclear, we don't know what gun he found, whose it might have been or how it got there —"

"Sustained, sustained," the judge said impatiently. "Let's try to get things in their proper sequence."

Miss Bailey nodded crisply. "So you found *a* gun on the floor, correct?"

"Yes, ma'am. That's when I tried to advise Mrs. Marshall of her rights but she was still pretty much out of it. I tried several times. Then I went outside and called the coroner. I secured the scene as best I could, got Mrs. Marshall up, and put her under arrest."

For a moment it seemed there might be more. The two prosecutors looked at each other and Gill shook his head. "Your witness," Miss Bailey said.

McNamara rose slowly and came across the room.

"Deputy Walsh. When you went into the house, did you take any photographs?"

"No, sir."

"Isn't that standard procedure? Don't you have a camera in your car?"

"Sure, most of the time. It got broke last month."

"Well, is that the only camera in the entire Sheriff's Department?"

"There's one in the sheriff's car."

"So you've been without a camera now for a whole month."

"Three weeks is closer to it. I've been meaning to get it fixed, or put in for a new one."

"Do you still have that camera, Deputy Walsh?"

"It's at home."

"How'd it get broken?"

"I knocked it out of the car one night. It fell on the pavement and got smashed."

Miss Bailey rose from her chair. "What difference does that make now?"

"If he'd had it, we'd have more than his

52

word about the scene."

"But he didn't have it. We do, however, have some excellent pictures, which you can see when we call the coroner."

"Not exactly the same, though, is it?" McNamara said. He turned again to the witness. "Did you conduct any gunshot-residue tests on Mrs. Marshall's hands?"

Walsh looked away for just an instant. Then he looked back at McNamara and said, "Sure I did."

"Where were these tests conducted?"

"Down at the jail."

"And what did you do with them?"

"Sent 'em over to Montrose, along with her dress and the gun."

"Montrose meaning the CBI lab in that town, correct?"

"That's right."

"And that's where they conducted the gunshot-residue tests. Were you told the results of those tests?"

Walsh looked at Miss Bailey, who said nothing.

"Deputy?"

"I was told they were inconclusive."

"Inconclusive. Meaning it couldn't be shown that Mrs. Marshall had fired a gun."

"She had washed her hands. She had blood all over them and she scrubbed 'em almost red at the kitchen sink."

"Were you there when she did this? You seem to know a lot about what she did."

"I asked her. You know, how her hands —"

"When did you ask her that?"

"This was after. After I read her her rights."

"So she had been almost incoherent, and then suddenly she upped and described in detail how she had scrubbed the blood off her hands. Is that what you're saying?"

"I didn't say in detail. She told me she'd washed her hands. I could see from the condition of 'em —"

"That's fine, Deputy." McNamara came around the table and leaned over it, spreading his hands on the edge. "What was Mrs. Marshall's condition when you first saw her?"

"Well, like I said, she was almost incoherent, in shock . . ."

"Which would be understandable, wouldn't it, under the circumstances? How about her clothes? Was she wet? Dry?"

"Her dress was damp, as if —"

"Don't guess what she was doing, please, just tell what you saw."

"I'd say damp."

"But you don't know for sure."

"Well, if you'd let me finish my answer

". . . I didn't exactly take her temperature, I had a dead man on the floor, but she looked to be in some kind of deep sweat."

"Or had been outside. You've already testified about the weather, that it was raining, right?"

"Yes, sir."

"Where were Mrs. Marshall's children when all this happened?"

"When I got there they were asleep in one of the bedrooms."

"They had slept right on through this, is that what you're saying?"

"They were taking a nap when I arrived, that's all I know."

"Did you question them at all about what had happened?"

"No, sir. The oldest one, you know, he can't talk. And the other two . . . I didn't want to disturb them, they're so young. At that point I had Mrs. Marshall's statement that she had shot her husband, so why upset the kids?"

"What did you do with them?"

"Got 'em back to town and called Social Services. Standard procedure. They have a family in Paradise who took 'em in till they made other arrangements."

"Which were what?"

"My understanding is that the grandparents came out a few days later to take care of them."

"The deceased's parents."

"Yes. They've rented a place out on Waters Road."

McNamara cleared his throat and asked his next question almost reluctantly, I thought. "When did you call the coroner, Deputy?"

"As soon as I had secured the scene and made sure there was no further danger."

"Which was approximately how long after you got to the house?"

"No more than a few minutes. Ten minutes at the outside."

"Where'd you make this call?"

"On my car radio."

"You didn't use the phone in the house?"

"No way. I didn't want to touch things in there."

"And the coroner's office has a radio that's monitored constantly, is that right?"

"I can't say about that."

"Did you ever get through to him?"

"No, sir."

It turned out that the county had never had a full-time coroner — a local undertaker named Lew Tatters had served in that capacity for forty years — and aside from the occasional auto accident and a few deaths by natural causes, he had had little to do. He had arrived about three hours later, Walsh said, had taken photographs and examined the body. McNamara looked over at an old man sitting behind the prosecution table and I thought I saw a look of regret pass between them. They knew each other well, that's how I read it; they might even be old fishing buddies, and now McNamara had to put his friend in a hot seat.

"Isn't the coroner supposed to be on call around the clock?"

"Yes, sir. Somebody's supposed to know where he is."

"But nobody did."

"His wife said she could find him."

"But that took a while."

"About three hours, like I said."

"You don't know exactly?"

"Not exactly, no. I didn't make a note of when he came."

"And what did you do with the defendant all that time?"

"Took her down to the jail."

"You left the scene unattended and took her down to the jail."

"Sometimes you gotta make a judgment call. I didn't want to leave the house but she looked like she might be going into shock."

"So you secured the house . . ."

"Ran tape around the doors and locked it up."

"With Mrs. Marshall's key."

"That's right. Listen, I know better than to leave the house. But sometimes —"

"You gotta make a judgment call," McNamara said dryly.

They looked at each other for a long ten seconds. "That's all for now," McNamara said.

This was followed by technical testimony. The coroner was called and McNamara asked him a few soft questions. He had gone on an errand for his wife, who had been feeling ill, but it had taken the drugstore longer than expected to fill her prescription. Then he had met some old pals and they had visited for a few minutes . . . not long, but by the time he did arrive at the house there was no way he could pinpoint a time of death. He had no rectal thermometer and no means of measuring the victim's liver temperature. Lividity was present and rigor mortis had begun. The body had cooled and was no longer warm to the touch. "Could you have been longer than three hours?"

McNamara asked, and the undertaker allowed that he might have been as much as an hour more than that.

The DA had had the body shipped to Montrose for autopsy. There, a forensic pathologist had chopped it to pieces and now offered his opinion on the time of death, probably between 1 and 3 p.m. But this was a guess, he said, subject to a wide margin of error. The coroner fidgeted — he should have done more. A CBI agent, who had examined a .38 revolver and the bullets, gave testimony on that, on Mrs. Marshall's dress, and the fingerprints on the gun. The prints belonged to the defendant and the blood to the victim. The gun was established as the victim's. Lots of detail, little to challenge. At the end of it, the judge said there was probable cause to believe that a murder had been committed and that the defendant had done it. "The defendant is remanded to the custody of the sheriff, and the arraignment will be next Thursday at one-thirty." McNamara said, "Your Honor, I'm gonna move for bail, and I'd like to have that hearing at the arraignment if possible." The judge nodded inconclusively, got up, and walked out. I watched the deputy lead Laura Marshall out through the side door, and I sat there till the crowd thinned out.

At a pay phone outside the courthouse I called Erin's office in Denver. She was in court and unavailable till tomorrow. I called her home phone and left a message on her machine, a succinct report of what had happened. I stood in the cold for a moment, thinking it over. Deputy Walsh came out of the sheriff's office, lit up a smoke, and stared at me across the lot. I took a deep breath and headed his way.

5

He blew a smoke ring as I approached. I walked past him, close enough to reach out and knock him on his ass. This, in a masterpiece of restraint, I did not do. His smoke swirled around us. I pushed my way through it, went into the office, and worked my way around an old man sweeping the floor. He looked like Walter Brennan in his later years, with a gap-toothed face and a name, FREEMAN, sewn across the pocket of his coveralls. Across the way a woman in her sixties sat at a desk, writing in what looked like a ledger. She gave me a pleasant smile, the first decent thing that had happened since I'd arrived in this one-horse town.

"Yes, sir, what can I do for you?"

"I'd like to see Laura Marshall and her lawyer, please."

"Are you connected with her case?"

"Not yet. I represent the Denver attorney she has asked for advice."

She got on an intercom and talked to a Sheriff Gains. A moment later a stocky, gray man of about fifty years came out from a back office. He didn't look friendly or unfriendly. He did look formidable, far more a presence than his underling, who was still outside, smoking.

"You want to see Laura?"

"Yes, sir."

"She's up in the conference room with her lawyer right now."

"If you would tell them I'm here, I'd like to see them both."

He took my name and disappeared up a circular flight of stairs. At the same moment Deputy Walsh came in, reeking of smoke and wearing his attitude like a battering ram. I looked at him and gave him a smile, not a friendly one, and he said, "What the hell're you looking at, cowboy?" I saw the receptionist frown, but Walsh didn't seem to care what she thought. By then he had pushed one button too many and I said, "I don't know what I'm looking at, Deputy. Based on our short mutual experience, I'd guess a crummy little pissant with a badge."

He came straight up, as if I'd just shoved a hot steel poker up his ass. I looked at the lady and apologized for the tone of my voice, but to Walsh I said, "Just so you know, Lennie, that cute little business with the ticket has been recorded and sent off to

Denver with a copy of the ticket and my notes. I'll pay my fine and give you that one, just to show my goodwill and stuff. But if you try anything like that again, I'll have a team of state investigators all over this office. By the time they get through with you, you'll be lucky if the sheriff lets you pick up his lunch at the Main Street café."

"Oh, you're *really* asking for it."

"Yes, I am," I agreed earnestly.

There was a bump at that moment from the top of the stairs. "Come on up," the sheriff called. Deputy Walsh moved to escort me but I turned to him and said, "I think I can find the top of the staircase."

"Don't tell me how to do my job."

"Somebody needs to."

Before he could react to that, I said, "I'll tell you one more time, Walsh, stay away from me." He stood his ground and the woman at the desk saw and heard it all.

I went up alone.

Upstairs, the sheriff led me along a corridor, past what I figured was the jail, and down to an oblong conference room at the end. He opened the door and backed away diplomatically, leaving the three of us alone. "Take whatever time you need," he said. "Press the buzzer near the door when you're through."

63

The door locked behind him.

The room was airy and white. Laura Marshall was sitting at the end of the table. McNamara had been in the chair to her immediate left, and now he stood as I came across the room and we shook hands. He looked to be around seventy but his hand was firm and strong. He introduced me to Mrs. Marshall and I shook her hand, which felt fragile and cool in mine. They motioned me to the chair on Laura's right and the two of them sat expectantly, waiting for me to speak. I said, "Erin sent me," an unnecessary opening since they both knew who had sent me, but I hoped it would get the ice broken. Instead, Laura shivered, covered her face, and wept quietly into her hands.

McNamara looked at me and shrugged. His look said, *Maybe somebody could tell me what's going on,* but I returned his shrug and left it to Mrs. Marshall to tell us. She had now turned away from us, facing the barred window. We could see she was still crying, and it took a while for her to get her control back.

"Laura?" the old man said. "Are you okay now?"

She nodded, but she didn't look okay. Tears welled up again; she said, "I'm sorry," and turned away.

"It's okay," I said. "I've got plenty of time."

I gave the lawyer a questioning look and he nodded. "The sheriff's all right with it. Like he said, he'll let us have whatever we need. He's a decent guy."

"His deputy sure is a piece of work," I said, and McNamara rolled his eyes.

After a while Mrs. Marshall got herself together. I didn't know how long that might last, so I plunged right in. "I guess we need to know what happened. Where you were when it happened. Your version of that Monday's events."

"Just a minute there," McNamara said. "I don't want her answering that question yet."

I said, "Why not?" but I knew just enough law to be dangerous and I could see why not. He didn't want me to know too much, not yet: he didn't want to be limited in what defenses he might mount on her behalf. As an officer of the court, he couldn't use any defense that he knew to be based on false or misleading information. Sometimes it's better not to know. "Let's just leave it at that for now," he said.

But suddenly it was a moot point. Laura reached over and touched the old man's

65

hand. He shook his head as if he had just read her mind but couldn't stop her. "I shot him," she said. She looked at the floor. "I shot Bobby."

She took a deep breath, as if she was relieved at getting it said.

"I did it," she said, stronger now. "I killed him."

6

McNamara said, "Oh, Jesus," got up, walked away from the table, and stood looking down into the yard. Laura and I sat quietly, each waiting for the other to say something. "I got the gun out of his room and I waited for him to come home," she said after a long time. "When he did, I shot him."

"Why'd you do it?"

McNamara turned away from the window with *objection* written all over his face. He settled instead for a slight head-shake, then he turned back again.

"Mrs. Marshall?"

She blinked as if she had lost her train of thought.

"Why?" I asked again.

"Does it matter?"

"It sure can."

"I'm just . . . I don't know . . . if I have any defense."

"You're not in the best position to know that. As I think your lawyer will tell you."

A long moment passed. I said, "Why'd

you ask your lawyer to call Erin?" and she teared up again.

"Oh, God," she said to the wall. "I must've been out of my mind."

"Well, at least you may have a defense there."

"Not when I shot Bobby. I was very clearheaded then. I'm talking about later, when I asked Mr. McNamara to call Erin."

McNamara turned growling from the window. "Laura, for God's sake, you're making this worse every time you open your mouth."

She didn't seem to hear him. "I guess I just wanted to see her again."

Another stretch of time danced away.

"Did she tell you?" she asked. "About us?"

"Some. She's not exactly a fountain of information about it."

"No, I don't imagine she is."

"Neither are you, so far."

McNamara moved around the table, into her line of vision. "Laura, have you heard anything I've been telling you? Did you understand it when I explained what the defenses to murder are, and what limitations are put on each? Are you deliberately trying to put a noose around your own neck?"

She shook her head. "Of course not."

But then she said, "I just don't think it matters much."

McNamara bristled. "What are we gonna do with her, Mr. Janeway? You see how she is?"

"Mrs. Marshall," I said softly, "you really should listen to your lawyer."

"What does that mean?" she said. "Are you walking out?"

"No," I said. "Just don't tell me anything yet that might get pried out of me and used against you on the witness stand. Erin is not your lawyer, I'm not sure this is privileged information."

"I want you to stay."

"In that case maybe I should leave," McNamara said.

She and I said, "Don't," at the same time.

"Stay," I said. "At least long enough to tell her what her risks are."

"What good will that do if she doesn't listen to my advice?"

But Laura said, "Please," and he sat in his chair and watched us.

"Mrs. Marshall, why do you want Erin to represent you?"

"I want to see her again."

McNamara leaned over the table and

made an imploring gesture. "Laura, you can't pick your lawyer for something like this on the basis of a childhood friendship! Mr. Janeway, please! Get her to use her head."

"He's right," I said to Laura.

To both of them I said, "Erin is a very good lawyer. You'd be in good hands. But at this point I'm not even sure she'll do this. I'm not sure she can, legally."

"What's that about?" McNamara said.

"There'd be a conflict of interest. Ms. D'Angelo was once involved with the deceased." I gave McNamara a knowing look, hoping he would pick it up.

"Before we were married, Bobby and I had an affair," Laura said. "He had been Erin's . . . but that's private business. Surely a judge can't dictate who will represent me."

"Mr. Janeway is right," McNamara said. "It's a potential conflict of interest."

"Is that some insurmountable thing?"

"You may have to sign a waiver saying you understand it and want her anyway."

"Then I will. I've got to talk to her. I've got to tell her . . ."

"Tell her what, Mrs. Marshall?" I said.

"How sorry I am."

"I'll tell her that."

"You can't possibly, there's too much between us."

"Then I'll tell her that."

"And what then? Will she come?"

I shrugged. "I have no idea what that lady will do from one day to the next."

"I still love her."

We talked about her childhood with Erin. They had lived as next-door neighbors when they were very young kids; they had always been such great friends. "We were so different, and yet there was a kinship between us that I've never known with anyone else. We never had a cross word, not once that I can remember."

A few minutes later, Laura said, "Does she ever talk about me? Those old days?"

"She hasn't yet, not to me."

"So where are we now in the scheme of things?" McNamara said.

"I'd like to go up and see the house," I said. "Erin wants me to look at your books, assuming the sheriff is finished up there."

"Sheriff's been done at least ten days," McNamara said. "I'd better tell him you're going, though, and you'd better have someone with you. I'll go along if you want."

"That's very generous, Mr. McNamara. I'd appreciate it."

We pressed the buzzer and a moment later the sheriff came and let us out. Across the street I made another call to Erin and was surprised to find her in the office. "Our judge is entertaining some motions," she said. "We may go back this afternoon, we may not. What's happening out there?"

I gave her a report. At the end of it, she said, "Not much doubt she did this?"

"She's not denying it. And the evidence looks pretty strong."

"Well, then . . ."

"Well then what?"

"Come on home."

"Erin . . ."

"Yes? Is something wrong?"

"She wants to see you."

"What for?"

"That's between you and her. As far as her case goes, it seems pretty open-and-shut. There may be extenuating circumstances and I think what she mainly needs is advice on how to plead. The old man who's handling her seems to be pretty competent. He's cautious damn near to a fault."

"Sounds like she's well represented."

"I don't know . . ."

"What don't you know?" There was a

72

pause, then she said, "Come on home."

"I'd like to stay another day. I haven't even seen her books yet."

I listened to the phone static between us. Abruptly Erin said, "They're calling us back, I've got to go. Tell her I'll send her some names of lawyers in her neck of the woods."

I said nothing for a moment. Erin said, "Don't waste any more time, Cliff. You said it yourself, the books probably don't matter. Look, I've gotta go."

She hung up and I stood there looking out toward Main Street. Deputy Walsh came out and lit a cigarette and we stared at each other like two old gunfighters in a bad cowboy flick. It would be so easy to pack it in: take my fee, which I knew Erin would make generous, and forget about Laura Marshall and her tragedy. For the moment it would also be damned near impossible.

7

Deputy Walsh met us in the parking lot. "Sheriff says you're going up to the house," he said. "He wants me to take you up."

"I don't think you need to do that," McNamara said. "House is back with us now. We'll find our own way up."

"He'd rather have me go with you."

Parley looked at me. "No way," I said.

"You really are trying to piss me off, aren't you, cowboy?"

"Trying my damnedest, Red Ryder."

"Sheriff Gains said I should *take* you up."

By then I had had more than enough of Sheriff's Deputy Lennie Walsh. "But that was you and this is me," I said. "The sheriff doesn't tell me when to take a leak, either."

He stood there, seething malice.

"Look at it this way," I said. "If you watch carefully as I pull out of the lot, maybe you can catch me obeying some traffic laws. Then you could give me a ticket for safe driving."

McNamara made a sound that might have been a laugh, maybe only a cough, and I said, "Goddammit, Walsh, I thought the defense had a right to some privacy. Do you really want to make an issue out of this? Where the hell's the sheriff?"

"He went over to Gunnison to see a friend."

"Well, we're going up alone."

Walsh flipped his cigarette into the gutter and managed to flip me off in the same smooth movement. But he got in his car and drove away to the west.

"You boys are off to a great start with each other," McNamara noted wryly.

"Sometimes it happens that way. I do tend to meet more than my share of the world's real sons of bitches."

"Wonder why that is."

"Maybe because they tend to get my back up. I've found that it's best to draw a line with tyrants and let them know right away that there are certain flavors of crap I will not eat."

"I'll bet you've got some kinda blood pressure."

"It tends to stay around one-thirty over eighty-five. How's yours?"

"Mine would be two-fifty over one-twenty if I wasn't on pills." He grunted.

"So much for accommodating the world's cheeriest assholes."

The sky had darkened and the mountains were faint outlines in the swirling gray mist. "Looks like it's gettin' mean up there," McNamara said, smoothly changing the subject. Within three minutes we went through a light snow shower into a heavy, wet autumn blizzard. About five miles beyond the town limit the road forked. McNamara motioned me to the right, and almost at once we clattered onto a snow-pocked dirt surface and began to climb. I put the car into four-wheel drive. The dirt road disappeared and fresh snow swirled down from the dark skies. It came in flurries, then in gusts that shook the car. "Looks like Lennie's goin' up anyway," McNamara said. Ahead, the deputy's car swirled through the snow and a stream of smoke poured from his cracked-open window. I could see his head bobbing fiercely from side to side. "He seems to be carrying on quite a conversation with himself," I said.

McNamara nodded. "Watch out for that one, Mr. Janeway. I've known him since he was a kid and he's never been any good."

"Why does it not surprise me to hear that?"

"I don't know if he'd actually do anything, but he talks a bad show. Struts around flaunting his authority under the guise of protecting the community. Never known him to resort to any brutality, but I don't imagine he'd be the first lawman to shave a point here and there. Just watch your flank, that's all I'm telling you. I'm not one to say he's crooked, but he's always been mean as hell."

"He's crooked too," I said, and I told the old man about my run-in at the stop sign. At the end of the story McNamara was no longer accommodating: he was damned mad.

"That sorry-ass son of a bitch." A moment later he said, "I'll take your case gratis if you want to hang around and bring it to the judge."

"What kind of chance would I have?"

"Hard to say. You'd be in county court, and the county court judge out here is just an old highway patrolman. But he's got a good sense of right and wrong, and he knows Lennie and his ways. I think you'd have a chance."

"What kind of bird is the district court judge?"

He rolled his eyes.

"Oh," I said.

"Yeah. He just got appointed this year. He lives up in Gunnison and has a summer home in Paradise. Used to be a pretty good lawyer, coulda been a real good one, but that's just my opinion. He represented a couple of corporations, one or two banks in Gunnison and Montrose, and I hear did a good job. Worked his way up in the Colorado Bar Association, served on commissions and ethics committees and was real diligent. Then we had a sudden vacancy, the governor picked him, and the appointment went straight to his head. He likes to pontificate from the bench, loves to lecture defendants and their attorneys. He'd be okay, in other words, if he didn't think he was God. He's got a rude awakening coming when he's got to stand for election with the voters."

"So he's eccentric and he's got an ego. Is he fair?"

"He's a political animal is what he is. Out here that means pretty solidly pro-prosecution: a conservative law-and-order type with a short attention span and an impatient streak as wide as the Colorado River. He wears a gun in the courtroom, underneath that black robe."

"You're kidding."

He laughed. "I never kid about the law,

son. Well, hardly ever. Sometimes it gets so strange you just can't help it."

"Now I'm tempted to hang around, just to see him in action."

"You should do that. And while you're here, give Lennie a run through the county court. It wouldn't be any piece of cake, but you know you need to take Lennie to court over that. You can't let that stand."

"Yeah, but in real life I haven't got days to waste on it, only to lose anyway."

"That's what bastards like Lennie Walsh count on."

He was quiet for another minute but I knew it was still grating on him and I liked him for that. "If you don't mind," he said, "I think I'll walk down the street after we get back tonight and talk to people in the stores on that corner. They all know me. I think there's at least a fair chance somebody saw it happen. We'd have him by the balls then."

"You're a good man, Mr. McNamara."

"Call me Parley. And I'll call you what?"

"Cliff'll be fine."

Snow swirled down from the mountaintop and the road ahead looked increasingly forbidding, dark and socked in. It peaked, dipped, and wound upward again. I couldn't see the bottom of the valley now: it was all fog with occasional dark spots. Suddenly I saw Walsh's car ahead of us, moving fast and half-obliterated in a swirl of white powder. "Wonder what that silly bastard is up to now," Parley said.

"Letting us know who the boss is."

"He must be really haulin' ass up there. If it was us driving like that, he'd give us a ticket."

"Maybe we should make a citizen's arrest."

The old man laughed. "I'm game if you are."

Walsh was now out of sight. I asked how much farther and McNamara said four or five miles. Casually I said, "So what can you tell me about Mrs. Marshall and her late husband?"

"I hope you mean just background. I don't want to get into the specifics of this case yet."

"Background's fine. We can hash over the other stuff if and when we find ourselves working the same side of the street."

"Just for background, then, Laura's a good woman. I always thought so, even if nobody else did."

"Are you saying nobody else did?"

"She didn't suck up to the local yokels. That won't ever get you on lists as the most popular gal in this town."

I was formulating another question when he said, "Sinclair Lewis had it right, and not just about Minnesota, either. Little towns like this are the same everywhere. Friendly people who take real deep offense if all that coziness isn't returned in full, right away."

"And Laura didn't?"

"She's just a private lady. Didn't have time for committees and clubs, coffee-klatching and endless bullshit. She had three kids to raise and a house to run. I think she's got a right to her own life without being expected to do things."

"What about her kids?"

"She and Bob had two: they adopted one, years ago when it seemed she might not be able to have any, then surprised themselves and had two of their own."

"What about Marshall?"

"What do you want to know?"

"What kind of guy was he?"

"He was all right."

I waited but the elaboration didn't come. "All right how?" I finally asked. "You mean he walked in good health, he made no obvious enemies, or he was a jolly good fellow?"

"All of the above, as far as I know. Take

81

that right up there."

I turned in to a narrow, rutted road and bumped my way up a slope toward a wooded crest. Again McNamara had lapsed into silence.

"I really am asking just for background, Parley," I said. "I've got maybe another day at the most to formulate a recommendation and then get out of here. In fact, Erin told me to come on home. I'm not even supposed to be here now."

"Tell me about Erin. What kinda lawyer is she?"

"She practiced in a big Denver firm for several years. Worked on corporate matters and on a big Wyoming water rights case. She's a supercompetent generalist. Was on a fast track to make partner by her midthirties but got restless and quit. She's thirty-two now."

"You say she's a generalist. She ever handle criminal cases?"

"Quite a few, actually. Mostly pro bono."

"Those are the ones you've either got your heart into or not. They show me what kind of lawyer you are."

"She wasn't assigned to do 'em, I'll tell you that. She did a lot more than the company wanted her to do, and she won a helluva lot more than she lost. She's a good trial lawyer, and I'm not just saying that because I like her. If Laura Marshall were my sister, I don't think I could find her anyone better."

"She'd have one strike against her before she even gets her coat off. The judge won't ever say so out loud, but he doesn't like women attorneys."

"Well, the prosecution has one too, so at least they'd start out evenly handicapped."

"Yeah, but he knows that one. Watched her grow up. And she is the prosecutor."

Suddenly I saw the house through the trees. It perched on a hilltop facing a sweeping mountain range and overlooking a valley. It was visible for just a few seconds, then swallowed by the snowstorm, then visible, then gone again. "We're gettin' there," McNamara said. "You see any sign of Lennie's car?"

"Not yet."

We made a sharp turn and started up a long last incline, coming between two pine trees into the front yard. "Where the hell's Lennie?" McNamara said softly, almost to himself. There was no car anywhere in sight, and no tracks in the fresh snow. "You see anyplace he could've pulled over?"

"Maybe he ran off the road somewhere. He was going way too fast."

"We'da seen him, though, if he'da cracked up. I don't see how we wouldn't see him, wherever he went off."

I pulled up in front of the house and we got out. From the front porch a picture-postcard vista of snow peaks stretched across the full horizon and around to the side. "This must've cost the Marshalls plenty," I said. "How much land they got up here?"

"Oh, a hundred acres easy. Enough to keep the bastards at bay, so there won't be any Holiday Inns going up right under their faces."

"Must've cost 'em," I said again.

"Actually, Marshall's grandfather bought this tract back in 1930. You could get land up here for a song then. If you think this is remote now, think how it was then. He picked up the whole thing for next to nothing. They started building this house a few years later. It started as a cabin — that's the main part of it — and later they added more rooms. That's what gives it its rambling look. Different generations added to it."

I walked out to the edge of the porch. "Wow," I said, breathing in the cold air.

"I don't think Laura and Bobby are rich by any means, so don't assume that. I think it's been a struggle the last few years just to keep up the taxes on this place. But that's life in America. Just because you've got something fine like this, that don't mean the bastards'll let you keep it."

We stood there together, listening to the wind whipping across the hill.

"Now where the hell has that silly sumbitch gone?" He jingled a small key ring in his hand.

I figured Lennie was just being Lennie, screwing with our heads. I stood at the top of the steps looking out across the meadow. From there I could see the weather moving in, rolling across the opposite range. I could see the road disappearing as it came, and the trees being consumed along the lower rim, almost at eye level with where we were standing. And suddenly I saw something move.

"There he is."

McNamara squinted, but Lennie, or whatever it had been, had disappeared.

"My eyes ain't what they once were," the old man said.

"He's gone now anyway."

"You sure it was him?"

"Actually, no."

McNamara said, "I'm gettin' damned tired of this," and he turned toward the door. At that moment Lennie stepped out of the woods across the way and stood watching us with a rifle in his hands.

It was almost too dark to make him out: in another five minutes I wouldn't have seen him at all. McNamara got the door open and said, "Come on in," but I stayed there watching Lennie watch me. Lennie lifted the rifle to his shoulder but I didn't move. We stood still, a pair of fools playing chicken, until he lowered the gun and stepped back into the trees. What was he trying to prove, that he could kill me? That he could do it from some vast distance and there was nothing I could do to stop it? That he was crazy enough? What does one fool ever prove to another?

"Come on in," McNamara called out again, and I turned away and went into a dark front hall.

"Just so you know," I said, "I saw Lennie across the way. This time there wasn't any doubt about it. He was pointing a rifle at us."

McNamara turned and faced me. "Why in the *hell* would he do that?"

His face was a pale blur and I couldn't read the silence that followed. His voice had been incredulous, as if even Lennie couldn't be that crazy. What would the natural conclusion of such doubt be? . . .

That *I* was the crazy one?

"He *must* be nuts," he said, and I felt better.

He shook his head. "This really makes you wonder, doesn't it?"

He turned and walked ahead of me into the house, putting on lights as he went. The hall stretched straight on back through the house, past another hall that led, I assumed, to the bedrooms. Off to the right was a large room of some kind; to the left, another big room where the tragedy had happened. *The death room,* as the press would probably call it.

McNamara went left and turned on the lights. I came to the door and stood there for a moment looking at the carnage. The carpet had been a light tan — probably lighter than it now seemed, I thought: now the center of it was dominated by an ugly black bloodstain. How many death scenes had I seen like this in my years as a Denver cop? I didn't know what it would tell me this time; maybe nothing, but a cop always had to look, and in that moment I was a cop again. McNamara had gone across the room, stepping gingerly around the blood to stand near an old-style rinky-tink piano. Behind the piano was a pair of French doors, which were curtained with some flimsy lace stuff. I didn't move. McNamara watched me as if he'd seen me work in some past life and knew what to expect. My eyes roved around the room and finally came back to where the old man was.

"Ugly, isn't it?" he said.

"It always is, Parley."

"What're you lookin' for?"

"No idea," I said. "Maybe I'm just hoping the room will speak to me."

"You cops are funny birds."

"Yeah. Some of us are a riot."

Eventually I came into the room, taking care not to touch anything. Yes, it had been three weeks. The sheriff had gone over it and he had had technicians out from the CBI, but to me it was a new scene. I could now see for myself what Parley had just told me: that this house, this cabin, had been built in pieces, with God knew how many add-ons over time, and this main room had probably been here for the full sixty years. There was nothing new-looking anywhere in sight. Straight across the room was a rustic rock fireplace. To the left of that, a glassed-in porch that in good weather would overlook the mountain range. But now darkness had spread beyond the glass, and with the lights on it seemed even darker, as if night had been upon us for hours.

"So what's it tell you?" Parley asked.

"Nothing yet." I shrugged: I really didn't expect much. "It's cold."

My eyes roved back to the left. There, near the fireplace, was a couch and a small circle of chairs with a coffee table in the center. Two floor lamps were placed behind the chairs, making it a cozy little reading circle when the fire was lit. In fact, a small stack of books was on the table and instinctively I moved across the room to see what they were. I looked down at *The Quality of Courage*, a recent book with Mickey Mantle's byline.

"Was Marshall a baseball fan?"

He shrugged. "I really didn't know him that well."

I bent over and touched the book by the edge. "Can I borrow your gloves for a minute?"

"You think they'll fit you?"

"You got big hands, Parley. They'll be good enough."

I pulled the right glove on. It was snug, not quite tight.

"What's the deal?" Parley said. "Sheriff said they were finished in here."

"Maybe, but I don't see any residue on these books."

89

"You mean fingerprint dust?"

I nodded. "Just call it an old cop's habit. I don't like to touch things where somebody's been killed."

I picked off the Mantle book, holding it by the corners, and laid it flat on the table beside the others. Under it was a novel, *The Ballad of Cat Ballou*, and under that a thing called *How to Be a Bandleader*, by Paul Whiteman. Under that was *The Speeches of Adlai Stevenson*, and at the bottom was a cheap tattered paperback, *Gabby Hayes' Treasure Chest of Tall Tales*.

McNamara seemed to sense my surprise. "Something wrong?"

"I don't know. This is just the strangest damned group of books I ever saw. Way too weird for anybody to be reading them."

"Then why are they here?"

"Exactly."

I looked at them again.

"Are they worth anything?" Parley asked.

"Not so you'd know it. The *Cat Ballou*'s got a little sex appeal because of the film, but I don't think it's ever gonna be this century's answer to *War and Peace*." I couldn't help laughing. Singsong, I said, "Adlai *Steven*son and *Gabby Hayes?*"

"It does kinda blow your mind, doesn't it?"

"Best laugh I've had all day."

But then my eyes wandered back to the bloodstain, and that was no laughing matter. We stood transfixed for another moment. A hundred thoughts ran through my head, none of them worth a damn on the face of it. I walked across to the piano, turned, and said, "I'm missing something somewhere."

"Maybe you're trying too hard to make sense out of something that's just . . . you know, happenstance."

"Maybe."

A moment passed.

"It's not happenstance, Parley. Happenstance would be five disparate books, maybe an eclectic mix of fiction and non. But what does this little collection tell you? I mean, Paul *Whiteman*? A history of the Whiteman band maybe, but a book on how to be a bandleader? Were either of the Marshalls fans of band music?"

"You'll have to ask her."

I touched the Mantle, opened the cover. "It's signed."

"What do you mean signed? Who signed it?"

"Mantle."

"So what does that do for it?"

"Makes it ten times the value is all. It's

probably a hundred dollars signed. Maybe a bit more now, I don't know, they keep going up. I haven't had one in a while."

"Still, not exactly a motive for murder."

"No."

But I had a hunch now. I opened the Whiteman. It was signed in Whiteman's distinctive hand. The Gabby Hayes — signed, an uncommon signature from any perspective. I had never even seen one and I guessed it might be as high as two hundred.

"Look at this," I said. "The *Cat Ballou* is signed by Nat King Cole and Lee Marvin from the film. I'll be damned."

I opened the Stevenson. On the half title was a tiny signature, a hand I knew very well.

"John Steinbeck," I said.

"What about Stevenson?"

I shook my head. "Stevenson doesn't matter: his signature's common as dirt and just about as cheap. Steinbeck's name on wallpaper's worth three hundred."

"I don't understand. Why would John Steinbeck sign that?"

"Maybe he gave it to somebody. He admired Stevenson and he wrote the foreword to the paperback of this book."

I looked around the room with a new

eye. "Well, damn, Parley, I think we've found something here."

"I'm not sure what. Maybe you should look in the library across the hall."

It was one of those moments, wasn't it? Even before we went there I had a hunch what I'd find: a wall of books, and as I began taking them gingerly off the shelf and opening them, the hunch grew into a certainty. They were all signed, either by their authors or by well-known figures associated with their stories. Leonard Bernstein. Alfred Hitchcock. Wernher von Braun. Duke Ellington. Al Capp. John Wayne.

And on and on.

"Man, Parley, these are worth some money."

"How much money?"

"I don't know. There's gotta be a thousand books here. If all of them are signed, even if the average is only — hell, I don't know, say two hundred — what've you got?"

"Two hundred grand."

"And that's probably wholesale. John Wayne didn't sign many of his books. He's four hundred by himself."

At that moment we heard a bump outside.

"Sounds like Lennie's come home to roost," Parley said.

But when I went to the door, no one was there.

I walked out onto the porch. The night was full, the grounds dark as pitch. I went out to the steps and shouted at the mountains. "Hey, Lennie! You out here?"

He was there. I could feel the slimy bastard all around me.

Suddenly nervous, Parley said, "Come on inside."

"Listen, you prick," I said to the darkness. "If you ever point a gun at me again, I'll take it away from you and shove it and that badge up your ass. You got that?"

I stood there feeling naked. I felt vulnerable and alone, damn foolish, a silly cock framed like a bull's-eye in the door light, but unwilling to move.

"Come on in here," Parley said from somewhere far behind me. "Come on, Janeway, you're giving me the creeps."

Inside, I heard him take a deep breath. "What do you want to do now?"

I thought about it. "I don't know. This changes everything."

"Does it?"

"Sure it does." I thought about what might be done and how to proceed. "We've got to talk to Mrs. Marshall about these books."

"Surely she knows what they are."

"You'd think so, but if they were valuable, wouldn't she say that? This wouldn't be the first time somebody died and left a spouse in the dark."

He didn't seem convinced. I said, "Well, look at it this way. She's sure not handling it like it means anything to her. I've got a feeling she hasn't got a clue what her books might be worth."

I glanced back into the room. "Other than that, let's keep it quiet for now. These books are unprotected in a vacant house, far from anywhere. A book thief could clear this room in an hour, so nobody needs to know but her. That includes the sheriff and Lennie, no aspersions on either of those fine gents. Let 'em think these are just what they look like, a bunch of cheap books."

I looked it all over again. "I wouldn't mind spending a day in here, just to go through it and see what she has. I could give her a loose appraisal if she wants it."

"You can ask her in the morning."

I could see he wanted to leave. Outside, the snow was piling up, but damn, I hated to leave those books like that.

"C'mon, Cliff, it's gettin' cold in here. We can't do anything else tonight."

"One more thing. Just give me a few more minutes."

I walked through the room making notes in my notebook. I wrote down where things were and put in my impressions. I jotted down some titles and where they were on the shelves. It wasn't much, just enough that, maybe, I'd know if someone had come in and disturbed them.

We were halfway back to town when suddenly Lennie pulled in behind us. He followed us on in as if he had been there all along, dropping off as we passed the sheriff's parking lot.

8

McNamara was a widower who had lived in the county thirty years. "I eat down to the Paradise Café ever since Martha died," he said. "We never had any children, so that's where I do my socializing, such as it is. You feel like grabbing some supper over there?"

"Sure."

We sat in a corner booth and I learned that his wife had died two years ago. They had been together almost fifty years. I could sense some of his loss when he mentioned her, and maybe I could imagine the rest of it.

"I try to keep busy," he said. "Sometimes I go a little stir-crazy, but most of the time I find enough work to do."

Actually, he said, there wasn't much legal work in a small county like this. "The house keeps me busy. I work in Martha's garden and putz around. Funny, I never gave a damn about the garden till she was gone, and then it became more important than I'd have believed to keep those green sprouts coming. I feel good watching it bloom in the spring, kinda like she's still here. But there's no gardening this time of the year and now I miss it. I do keep my shingle hung out. If a legal dispute does come up, I usually get it. I'll travel if the case calls for that . . . over to Hinsdale County, up to Gunnison. That's rare, but I keep busy."

He broke some bread. "For a while I thought of moving to Chicago. I was there on a visit to my sister when I met Martha. Christmas, 1939. Now my sister's long gone too. When Martha died, I thought maybe I'd move back there, but in the end what the hell would I do? I'm too old to get a job, even doing legal research, and I think the big city would be worse than living out here in the sticks. At least I know this kind of solitude: the other I can only imagine, but what I imagine is pretty excruciating."

He laughed. "Hey, don't get the wrong idea. I don't feel sorry for myself. I've had a pretty good run at life. Where you staying tonight?"

"Hadn't thought about it." I looked outside at the snowstorm. "I'd better start thinking right after we eat. I'd hate to have to sleep in my car."

"Don't worry. There are only two places,

the Paradise Hotel and a motel back out on the highway, but neither one of 'em ever fills up. I wouldn't wish those places on my worst enemy. The old sheriff used to sometimes let people sleep in the jail. I'd rather sleep there than in either of those fleabags."

The waitress, a buxomy gal named Velma, poured some coffee and flirted with Parley. He watched her ass as she walked away and we smiled foxily at each other. You never get too old to look.

I paid our tab. "Put your money away, I'm on an expense account."

Outside, he huddled into his coat. "You could stay with me if you want to," he said almost shyly. "The room's warm and private, it's free, and the roof don't leak."

"Well, that's generous of you. I wouldn't want to put you out."

"Ah, hell, you'd be doin' me a favor. I'd like the sound of a voice in the house."

"In that case you're on."

"Now let's walk up the street and see if anybody saw your little run-in with Lennie this morning."

His house was at the south edge of town, on a one-acre tract with trees and light underbrush and a clearing in the back that was probably the garden. The house had been built in the twenties and was still solid. "I don't have much to do to it," he said. "I paint it every five years or so and I had it inspected in 1980, but it's solid as Gibraltar. I expect to be here for the duration, however long that is."

Inside it was spotless, with the kind of spit-and-polish attention that made me stop at the door and take off my shoes. He's keeping it that way for her, I thought. He said, "Don't worry about it," but I removed the shoes anyway. He fired up a big fireplace and I got the tour. "This place has always been too big," he said. "Martha wanted it that way, in case her brothers came to visit. They did a few times, but now they're gone too."

We walked back through a hallway and he turned on the lights as he went. "My only complaint about it these days is that it gets so god-awful dark in here. I never noticed that before, but now it can be depressing. So if you see a dark corner, feel free to turn on a light. Back here are the bedrooms."

There were three rooms with beds. "You can have your pick," he said. "My room is clear over on the other side of the house, so you can bump around, sing in the shower — you won't bother me a bit. We don't get TV down here. The signals just won't come in over these mountains, so I hope you brought a good book to read."

I stashed my stuff in one of the bedrooms and joined him in the front room for a nightcap. We talked about my case against Lennie if I chose to bring one. Only two of the stores on that corner had still been open, but Parley had collected three names. "I'll talk to the others tomorrow."

At Jenkins' Hardware the proprietor had not only seen it but had discussed it with a customer, who was also willing to talk. Lennie's tactics were well-known in the county. "I think we've got a chance not only to get it dismissed but also to cause Lennie some general embarrassment," Parley said. "That's got to be worth doing."

"You're sure taking a lot of trouble with this."

"It's what I do. You can't let an asshole make a mockery of the law."

"No," I said.

"Does that mean you'll fight it?"

"Hey, how could I not fight it after all your hard work?"

"That's the ticket, boy, no pun intended.

If the judge won't listen, I'll appeal the son of a bitch, I don't care if it is just a traffic dispute." He laughed suddenly. "I'll get my friend Griff Edwards to do a piece on justice in Paradise for the *Paradise Mountaineer.* Embarrass the sons of bitches, that's language they understand."

We talked about Mrs. Marshall. I asked how long he had known her and he said, "Just about as long as she's been here. Eight years or so. But long don't mean well. She and Marshall kept to themselves."

"Didn't you tell me you knew her better than him?"

"When she first came here, she got talked into being on an old-town preservation committee. That's how she met Martha and that's how I met her. We had dinner once, the four of us, and whenever they went out of town, I'd drive up there and keep an eye on their place. That's about the extent of it."

"Did they always have a big library like that?"

"If they did, they had it hidden. I guess the first time I saw those books was three or four years ago. And it's grown some since then."

"Did either of 'em ever tell you what it

was, where they got it?"

"No, but I didn't ask. Lots of people have books."

"You mean you just said, wow, what a lot of books?"

"Something stupid like that. It was just a wall of books to me."

"Did you get any feeling for how they were getting along back in the beginning?"

I didn't think he'd answer that, but he said, "Laura never struck me as a happy woman. I always liked her, but she was . . . private . . . if you know what I mean."

"Secretive?"

"Don't read your own stuff into my words, son. *Private* means *private:* not that she had anything to hide, just stuff she'd rather keep to herself that wasn't anybody else's business anyway."

He poured himself another shot, gestured to me, and I shook my head.

"Right from the start I sensed some tragedy in her life," he said. "That wouldn't have anything to do with your friend the lawyer over in Denver, would it?"

"Could be."

I sipped my brandy. "I'll be talking to Erin in the morning. I'll see if she'll tell us about it."

"Just tell her I'm a curious old bastard. Got nothing to do anymore but poke around in other people's business."

"Yeah, Parley, I'll be sure and tell her that."

The big question was still there between us. At some point I asked it.

"So what do you think happened?"

"I don't know that, do I? I don't know much more than what you heard her say this afternoon. I told her a dozen times not to say anything . . ."

"Well, now that she has . . ."

He shrugged. "Could be any number of things. Maybe Marshall was a womanizer and she got tired of it. Maybe he abused her and she got tired of that. We know it wasn't for any big life insurance claim. The policies they had wouldn't amount to a hill of beans. So far she hasn't shown much willingness to talk about the two of them. I don't know if these things happened, but I will tell you that Laura never struck me as a woman who'd put up with much bullshit. That's why one day she walked out on the preservation committee, right between the crumpets and the tea. Too much bullshit, too many pissy little kingmakers more interested in having their way than getting things done. That seems to be the way of all committees, from the UN all the way out here to West Jesus, Colorado."

He coughed and leaned forward, warming his hands. "There's another theory, I guess, but so far it's just my own intuition." He grinned like an old fox. "Would you like to hear it?"

"Sure I would."

"I don't think she killed him at all."

9

"Then who did?" Erin said.

"He doesn't know, or isn't telling," I said. "So far it's just a feeling he's got."

I listened to the telephone noise while she mulled it over almost three hundred miles away. I was standing at a downtown Paradise pay phone, basking in the great Colorado autumn morning. The snow had stopped during the night, the sun had cast the valley in a brilliant glow, and all along the street I could hear the scrape of steel on pavement as people dug out and got ready for a new day.

It was Saturday and I had called Erin at home. She listened intently: there was no talk now of come on home or pack it in. I heard her sip her coffee and sniff. Her voice was thick, as if she was getting a cold.

"He doesn't know who did it," she said at last. "He doesn't know who *might* have done it, or why, or why *she* might be covering up for someone. He doesn't know *her* all that well either. This is just some gut feeling he's got."

This was not said sarcastically or to diminish anything the old man believed. It was just Erin, in her lawyer voice, putting some facts in order.

"Anything else?"

"I asked the same questions you just did," I told her.

"And he had no reason at all for his hunch."

"Nothing he was willing to put to words, let alone take into court."

"Where were the kids when all this went on?"

"In their bedroom, asleep, way over on the other side of the house."

"And the sounds of gunshots didn't wake them?"

"She says not."

"You believe that?"

"I'm just telling you what she told McNamara."

"A .38 makes a lot of noise," Erin said.

"Tell me about it." I touched my shoulder, where I had once been shot by one. "I guess it's possible. There are three big rooms and a hall between the kids' rooms and the front room where Marshall was shot. Maybe, if all the doors were closed."

"I don't suppose you've seen any of the reports yet."

"Not yet. Parley's got the CBI reports and other evidence the DA has."

"What'd the CBI say, did he tell you that?"

"He's not ready to tell us that; not till we know we're either in or out. He did say it was two days before the CBI got out there."

"Jesus! What was that all about?"

"They weren't called right away. A lot of the physical evidence — the bullets, the blood, some fibers, some hair — was collected by the Sheriff's Department and sent over to the lab in Montrose. Parley was pretty disgusted."

"He should be." I knew what she would ask next and she asked it. "How do you read him?"

"He's a solid old guy, sharp under all that folksy stuff. I wouldn't blow him off."

"But you haven't really questioned her yet?"

"Just what I told you about yesterday."

"No idea what the books might mean, if anything?"

"Not yet."

A moment passed. I thought it could go either way. She was making a decision now, and maybe then I'd have my own decision to make. "You said he was into books. Even way back when you knew him."

"Yeah, he was," she said. "I told you about that, remember? . . . That night we met in your bookstore two years ago, I told you my first boyfriend was a book freak like you. But I guess, given the way it all turned out, I didn't know what he was into." She sniffed. "Any reason to think the books might be part of it?"

"Nothing I can put my finger on. They might be a motive for something."

I looked up and saw Lennie Walsh drive past. He turned in to the parking lot at the hall of justice and sat in his car, smoking and talking to himself.

"Go over and see her," Erin said. "This time don't pull any punches. Ask her about the books and see if McNamara will confront her on this confession she's so eager to give him. Make an issue of it. Tell her if she lies, or evades your questions, you're out of there."

"I guess I can do some form of that."

"However you do it, let's get a straight story from her and see where we are."

"One more thing. McNamara wants to know what happened between you two."

"What for?"

"He says he's a nosy old bastard who likes to pry."

"Ha. He asks good questions. That's one

I would've asked as well."

She thought about it, then said, "Go ahead and tell him they had an affair behind my back. See what he thinks of my conflict of interest."

Again I was shown into the conference room on the second floor. "You'll have to wait for Parley," said old Freeman, the custodian. "He's down talking to the sheriff about another matter and he doesn't want your lady questioned until he can be here."

It was a half-hour wait. When Parley came in, he said, "They don't want to dismiss your ticket outright. I could have Christ and twenty-six disciples lined up to testify and he'd still want to take Lennie's side of it. They're all down there now hashing it over. Secretly I think the sheriff is pretty damned mad about it. Like I told you, this is not the first time Lennie's done this kinda thing."

Another fifteen minutes passed before Mrs. Marshall was brought in. I couldn't tell from the sheriff's expression how the wind was blowing, but he didn't look happy. He escorted Laura to the same chair and left us there.

I watched Parley, waiting for his lead.

"Laura, we need to talk turkey, you and me."

"Can Mr. Janeway stay?"

"It might be just as well, for right now, if it was just the two of us."

"But he needs to be here," she insisted. "So he can tell Erin what was said."

He looked at me, clearly annoyed. "Dammit, Janeway, is this woman of yours gonna come down here or not?"

"She'll come," Laura said, surprising us both. "I know she'll come."

"I talked to her this morning," I said. "She has not accepted your case, Mrs. Marshall, she certainly can't be considered your attorney at this point. And for what it's worth, I think she'd agree with the advice Parley is giving you."

"This is not a question I'd normally ask," Parley said. "Now I think you've got to tell me what really happened the day Bobby was killed."

"I did tell you."

"So far you've only said that you shot him."

She nodded warily. "What else is there?"

"Was there something remotely like a reason? How'd your dress get torn?"

"It was a private matter between us."

Parley rolled his eyes back and closed them.

"That won't make any difference

111

anyway," she said. "What happened is what's important, not why it happened."

"Is that what you think? Well, missy, where's your law degree?"

I saw two things in her face: a flash of anger and an immediate look of regret. "I'm sorry," she said. "I know I'm making it harder for you."

"It can't get too much harder than impossible. You'd better come to realize a few things, and right now's not a minute too soon. You're in a bad spot."

"I know that. I know it. What would happen if I just plead guilty and throw myself on the mercy of the court?"

"You could do that. Without any mitigating circumstances, and based on what I know of this judge here, you might get out in time to see your great-grandchildren graduate from college. That's *if* you get out at all, and *if* he doesn't fit you for a hot seat at Cañon City."

"They won't execute me."

"Probably not. This state doesn't have any stomach for its own death penalty statute. The point is, they *could;* that old man downstairs could put you on death row, where you might sit for years before some other old man commuted it to life. Or he could give you life without possibility of parole right out of the gate. Do you know how difficult it can be to even get something like that reconsidered, let alone overturned? Whatever your reason is for not talking about it now, that'll look pale as the years pass. You can trust me on this, Laura, if you don't believe anything else I tell you: the day will come when you'll wish to God you had listened to good advice when you heard it. Then it'll be too late. The very best you can expect to do is twenty years of damned hard time. That's what I want you to think about."

"What do you think I've been doing? If there was anything I could tell you . . ."

"You can start by telling me why you shot him. And don't keep saying it's a private matter. When you shoot somebody dead, there's nothing private about it anymore."

"What difference does it make if you can't use it anyway?"

"Is that what you're saying? There may be mitigating circumstances but you won't let me use them even if I know what they are. Is that what you're telling me?"

"I didn't say there were mitigating circumstances, you did. That's different from the reason why, isn't it?"

"Don't do this to yourself, Laura. Don't

play games with your lawyer."

"I just can't get into it," she said, and the room passed into a long, deadly silence.

"Let's try it once more," Parley said. "Look in my face here, not at the floor. I'm your lawyer. That means you can talk to me and nothing you say will ever get out of this room without your permission. If you've got second thoughts about having another party present, Mr. Janeway will leave us in private. This will stay between us. But you've got to tell me what happened."

"I just can't get into it. How many times have I got to say that?"

"Goddammit, you are into it, you're up to your pretty neck into it. Don't look down, look at me and tell me who you're protecting."

"No one. *No* one! Why would you even ask that? I told you I did it."

"I don't believe you. I think you're protecting somebody. Who could that be, Laura? Was it one of the kids?"

Her eyes opened wide. "Don't say that! Don't even *think* that!"

She looked at me and said, "I want another lawyer."

She looked at Parley. "Why won't you do what I want? It's my life, isn't it?"

"Did Bobby abuse you in some way?"

"No!"

"Did he abuse the kids?"

"*No!* Stop this! Stop it, I want another lawyer."

"Well, that's certainly your right. But any lawyer worth a damn will ask these same questions. This stuff won't just go away, Laura. And the truth has a way of getting out, no matter what you want."

"I've told you the truth."

"Yeah, well, I don't think so. You're lying right now, I can see it in your face. And I can't think of anybody you'd lie for except the kids."

She shook her head.

"Was it Jerry?"

The room turned suddenly hot. Her face was flushed.

"Was it Jerry, Laura? Did Jerry shoot Bobby?"

"You must be mad. He's a child. For God's sake, he's only eleven years old!"

"How old do you have to be to pick up a gun?"

"I'm not listening to this. I want to see Erin."

"Well, I'll do my best to get her here. Maybe she can talk sense to you."

He looked to me, I thought for support.

I said, "He's right, Mrs. Marshall. Erin would ask exactly the same questions."

"If Jerry did this, you've got to tell me," Parley said.

"Stop saying that!"

"As I was *about* to say, he's a minor. That would make it an entirely different ball game with its own set of rules. With a kid that young, they look at treatment rather than punishment. If the circumstances —"

"Mr. McNamara," she said icily, "I think I'm going to ask you to leave."

"I might as well leave, for all the good I'm doing you. If you come to your senses, you call me."

He pressed the buzzer and stood near the door. I pushed back my chair. But suddenly Mrs. Marshall reached over to me and said, "Can you stay?"

"You'd better ask your lawyer. Parley?"

"What have we got to lose? Talk some sense to her. Get her to listen."

The sheriff arrived. Parley said, "Mr. Janeway will remain for a while and talk to Mrs. Marshall as Ms. D'Angelo's representative. Attorney privilege still applies."

"Sure, I guess so," the sheriff said. "On that other matter, I've got a deal for you."

"No deals. I want that citation dismissed. No fine, no points: I want it taken clear off his record."

"Let's go downstairs and talk it over."

"Talk your damn heads off. I'm goin' out and get us some more witnesses."

The door closed. I could hear them arguing their way down the hall. The room became quiet as Laura and I waited for the other to speak. She looked to be on the verge of tears again. I smiled at her, half in sadness, half in hope.

"I looked at your books," I said.

"More junk I'll have to get rid of."

"Don't do that. Not yet."

"Are you telling me they're worth something?"

"They're worth something."

"Bobby always said they were. I never believed him, even though he spent enough money on them. I thought he was just justifying his habit."

"I could make you a rough appraisal if you want one."

She looked as if she wanted to laugh but couldn't. "What good will money do me now?"

"You'll have legal expenses to cover."

"Of course. Of course, what can I be thinking of?"

"I think you could get some real money for those books."

Her eyes opened wide as the first realization came over her. "How much money? Are you saying I could pay my legal expenses with them?"

"Maybe."

"What's so special? They look like ordinary books to me."

"May I ask where they came from?"

"Bobby started buying them way back when we were young. I never paid much attention. We had more money then."

"And you never discussed what they were or what he planned to do with them?"

She shook her head. "He was full of secrets. Even when we were kids, he was like that. Erin thought she knew him but she didn't. She had no idea. God, don't tell her I said that."

"There's no question he owned them?"

"What do you think, he stole them?"

"It's just a question, Mrs. Marshall. You're going to need some money."

"I guess I am."

"And you need to make sure nobody's got any kind of a claim on your books."

"I don't even know where he'd have kept records of that stuff."

"Let's make an effort to find out."

"What if there's nothing?"

"Cross that bridge when you come to it.

You've got possession. A third party would need his own proof to show ownership."

"This all seems so trivial now."

"It's not trivial. You're gonna need a lawyer. For what it's worth, I think Parley's a pretty good man."

"I'm sure he is. I know he's trying to do what he thinks is best for me."

"I take it Jerry is your son?"

"Oh, please, don't you start."

"I'm just trying to get it straight."

"There's nothing to get straight. Jerry had nothing to do with this."

"Hey, that's cool. If that's how it was, that's how it was."

Then, after a long, quiet moment: "You say the boy is eleven?"

She stared at me.

"The reason I ask is it's bound to come up again. What McNamara's thinking, others will think. I understand how you'd want to protect him, but it would be smart not to be so touchy about it."

"Wouldn't you be touchy if someone accused your son of murder?"

"I'm sure I would. But when you fly off the handle, that doesn't protect him, it has exactly the opposite effect. When you get defensive, people naturally think you're covering up for somebody. Who would that be but one of your kids? If he didn't do it, just say so, but say it calmly, as if the question itself is too ridiculous to worry about."

"Do you even have any children, Mr. Janeway?"

"No, but I can imagine how fiercely I'd want to protect them. The trouble is, you're going about it the wrong way. If Jerry didn't do this, just say so."

"I thought that's what I was doing."

"You were getting pretty shrill. Try turning down the volume and say it."

"The volume won't matter now. Parley will never believe me."

"If Jerry really didn't do it, you'll have to convince him. My advice would be to tell him the truth. Whatever that is, just get it said."

I let that settle on her. At some point I said into the quiet, "Erin is not leaning toward taking your case. You should know that before you chase a good lawyer away. There's too much old baggage between you, she'd need a waiver, and even then she doesn't think it's a good idea."

"I'll give her a waiver, I said I would. I'll sign anything."

"You're not listening, Mrs. Marshall."

"Please. Call me Laura."

"You're not listening, Laura. You haven't seen her in years. You've got some notion of her from when you were kids together. Maybe there's still some of that left in her, I don't know, but she's been on her own a long time now. Even if she did come, she'll ask the same questions, and I'll tell you right now, you can't stonewall her."

"You don't know how we were. You have no idea."

"That makes no difference now. If she does come to see you, it may be because of how you were, but I can promise you she won't stay for that reason. That was a long time ago and a lot of stuff has happened. She might just want to put something to rest between you."

"She won't do that."

We sat quietly for a full minute. At last she said, "What are you thinking?"

"Right now, just wondering how the hell I can reach you."

"I've *heard* what you're saying."

"I don't think so. Listen, this is what Erin told me to say to you. If you lie, if you stonewall or evade, I'm out of here."

Her eyes filled with tears. "She still hates me."

"Laura. Listen to me. That doesn't matter. It doesn't matter. Nothing matters

121

right now but getting your story straight. If one of your kids . . ."

She shook her head. "Don't say that. Don't say it anymore."

"Laura, listen —"

"I can't let this happen. I can't."

"Just listen for a minute —"

"I can't. I won't."

"Did your son shoot your husband?"

"*No!*" she whispered.

"The only way Erin might come is if you tell me the truth."

"I am."

More time passed. At some point I said, "I was a cop for a long time, did you know that? I was a pretty good cop. I had good juice. That means I knew nine times out of ten when I was being lied to."

"I'm not lying."

"Laura, you are one of the worst liars I've ever seen. Don't take offense, that's actually a virtue. Some people can't lie. I've seen a hundred of 'em try over the years and I imagine old Parley has seen a hundred more. And Erin is better than we are at sniffing out a lie. If you think she'll ride over here and buy into this, think again. The only possible way to get to her is to stop the lies."

"I know that. That's what I'm doing."

I shook my head.

"I am," she said. "I *am*."

"If that's your final word on it, that'll have to be what I'll tell her." I pushed back my chair. "I'm sorry I couldn't be more help."

I was halfway to the door when she said my name: "Mr. Janeway . . ."

"Yes."

"You can't just walk away like this." Her voice cracked. "Please, I need you."

"I know you do."

"Will you help me?"

"I can't if you don't let me."

"I'm afraid. Oh, God, I'm scared."

"I know you are."

"Not for myself," she said, and I knew then we were finally at the truth. "Not for me."

Suddenly she said, "Will you stay?"

"I'll do what I can do. But you've got to talk to me."

"I will, I promise. I trust you."

"That's a good start."

Again I sat in the chair across from her. Tears streamed down her face. She took a deep breath and trembled. "You can't tell anyone I said this. Only Erin."

"Okay."

"You can't tell *anyone* else. Not even Parley."

"I won't, without your okay."

"He'll want to use it. That's why you can't tell him."

The moment stretched till I thought it would break. When she spoke again, she whispered so softly I had to lip-read her.

"Jerry shot him.

"Jerry shot him," she said again.

"My God," she said. "Oh, God, I still can't believe it.

"Jerry shot Bobby," she said in her disbelief.

She shook her head. "Remember what you said. What you promised. No matter what happens, you can't tell anyone."

Then she broke down and wept uncontrollably on the table.

10

"Are you okay now?"

"I think so."

"Good. Maybe you can start putting things back together."

"Why? What for?"

"For your kids."

"Of course . . . of course. What am I thinking? It's amazing how you have to keep reminding me of what ought to be obvious."

"You're not thinking straight, that's all it is. I've seen it happen before."

"Not like this, you haven't. I betrayed my dearest friend. How could I have done that? She was the only friend who ever mattered to me, and she mattered more than anything. But I betrayed her and my life has never been the same again. I haven't been thinking straight for ten years."

"For what it's worth, I hope she does come."

"But you know she won't. I can see it in your face."

"I don't know that at all. She's not one to play games. If it had been out of the question for her to come, she never would've sent me over here."

"I guess that makes sense. Oh, God, how I want it to. Can I . . ."

"What?"

"Can I tell you what happened between Erin and me?"

"I don't know if —"

"Please, I want to. It was my fault, right from the beginning. No matter how much Bobby pressured me, there's no excuse for what I did. That night we drank too much and got way too silly, but that's no excuse. As long as I could see and hear, as long as I had a coherent thought running through my head, I was responsible. Now there's nothing I can say except I am so, so sorry. Whatever they do to me here, I need to say that to her. Erin and Bobby were so much in love; you'd have to have seen them together: if ever there were soul mates, they were, and I destroyed them. I've thought about her every day, every hour: I see her face everywhere. I've never stopped loving her. But Bobby and me, that one night we got drunk and did it. When you've betrayed someone you love, the hurt never goes away, it defines you. The betrayal becomes what you are, a fair-weather friend who couldn't keep her pants on when she had to."

"Sounds like you've paid for it."

"Oh, yeah. Oh, yeah, oh my God, yes. It'll never end."

"Never's a long time, Laura."

"Tell me about it."

"Maybe after ten years it's time to cut yourself some slack."

"That'll never happen. What I did has consumed me. I know it's unreal, it must sound sick the way I dwell on it. I just can't shake it, and it only gets worse with time. I feel guiltier now than I did right after it happened all those years ago."

"Did Bobby know?"

"What, how miserable I am? Oh, yeah, he lived with me for years, how could he not know? Bobby gave up on me long ago."

"Maybe he shouldn't have. He had to at least share the responsibility for what happened."

"I can't look at it that way. I don't know how to, I just don't know how. All I know is, Bobby and I were never any good together. How could we be? Erin was always there between us. I could feel her walking beside me, she was on the porch where we sat after supper: she was even in our bed.

The bed was the worst. I got so frigid Bobby couldn't come near me. We haven't touched each other in four years. That's about when he began seeing other women. You can't blame him, can you?"

"I'm trying to retire from the blame business. That includes you, by the way."

"Thank you. You're a kind man, Mr. Janeway. Are you and Erin lovers? . . . Never mind, that's none of my business. Sorry, I just found myself wishing, you know? She should be with someone like you."

"Mrs. Marshall —"

"Laura."

"Laura . . . do you want to tell me what happened the day your husband was shot?"

"It won't matter. You can't use it."

"Let's take it one step at a time. Right now I'd just like to understand it."

"I'll tell you, then. I've got to tell someone or go crazy."

"Take your time."

"No, I need to get this said now or I'll never say it. Bobby and I were never happy, we never had a moment's peace. I told you why but I know you can't understand it. It was all me, I've been consumed by guilt."

"Then why'd you marry the guy?"

"That was the reason. To try to make the guilt go away. Have the marriage justify the affair, if that makes any sense. But does that really matter now?"

"It might. When you go to trial and bring in issues that the average Joe can't identify with, it helps if you can explain them."

"Surely all this won't come up."

"Don't count on that."

"God, what a nightmare. How can I explain such crazy behavior? If I said that one of us had a terrible conscience and the other did it for spite, would you believe that?"

"Is that what you're saying?"

"I told you it would sound crazy. Jesus, are real lawyers going to be this hard?"

"They can be a lot worse than this. If they can make you look like a fool, they will. You don't want to help them do that."

"I *was* a fool. This sounds like a stupid soap opera. No one will believe it."

"Millions of people watch soap operas and believe them. Just tell the truth and don't worry about melodrama."

"When Bobby said we should get married, it just seemed right. Erin was finished with both of us, we couldn't hurt her any more. Did I love him? I must have, right?

Why else could I betray my friend? Marrying Bobby was a way of proving to Erin that what we had done was more than trivial. If it could only be dismissed as a cheap fling, what did that say about us? Does that make sense?"

"If that's your reason, sure. What about his?"

"He said he loved me. He'd been falling in love with me for a year."

"And out of love with Erin?"

"He said he loved us both."

"Do you believe that?"

"How would I know? I never gave him a chance. I think he tried, but I couldn't."

"So what happened?"

"Bobby thought if we had a child it would help, and we did try in those first few years, but no child came. We moved out here and adopted Jerry. He had emotional problems, he was nearly four years old when we got him, and he couldn't talk. He wasn't what they called highly adoptable; he had been horribly abused by his birth parents, that's why getting him was so easy. Jerry has always had problems, he still can't talk, can't or won't. Except with me. He talks to me."

"Has anyone else ever heard him speak?"

"He doesn't talk in words, it comes out in

looks between us, in things he does. It's a very simple level of communication. But I know what he wants, don't ask me how, I just know, and he knows what I expect of him. It's all in the eyes. His eyes are like Erin's were as a child: brown with those flecks of green around the edges. I loved him to death the first time I laid eyes on him. We were like the walking wounded together."

"What did his parents do to him?"

"Do I have to go through that? At one point to stop him from crying his mother put him naked in a cold basement and left him there without food or water for two days . . . stuff like that."

"I get the idea. I assume you had him tested, to see —"

"Oh, sure. There didn't seem to be any real reason why he couldn't speak, but he never has. He's never said a word since we got him, but he's aware of everything around him. If I say, 'Bring in some wood, Jerry,' he'll go right out and get it. I never have to belabor anything, his hearing's extremely sharp. The psychologist ran an intelligence test on him."

"And that showed what?"

"There seemed to be no reason why he couldn't speak. But he won't."

"So he was nearly four when you got

him. And then you had two of your own."

"The twins, Little Bob and Susan. What a surprise that was. It must've happened the last time Bobby ever touched me. One of the last times, and we get kids from it."

"How old are they now?"

"Five."

"There's no real reason to ask, but I take it they were both normal."

"Oh, sure. I was the one who wasn't what you'd call normal."

"What does that mean?"

"I can't tell you that. You'll think I'm a monster."

"Let me guess. Your own blood children drove you two farther apart."

"It was Erin again. I know this sounds sick, but they seemed like her children to me. They were the kids she should have had with Bobby. I tried to love them. I did love them. I do, I swear I do. And I've been a good mother. But it was Jerry who had touched my heart, who had nothing to do with Erin or Bobby or me. If there was any light in my life at all then, it came from Jerry."

"You loved him. Don't beat yourself up, I can see how that could happen."

"I loved him more than my own blood children. People will think I'm sick if that comes out. I can't help it: he was my baby, my poor wounded child. The night we brought him home, I swore to Bobby I'd never let anything hurt him again."

"So what happened the day of the shooting?"

"I had gone out for a walk. I was on my way back when I heard a shot from the house. I ran across the field and up onto the porch. Bobby was lying in the front room. Even before I saw him I had this terrible feeling: I could smell the gunpowder, and something else . . . something foul. I knew it was a death smell. I went into the room and there Bobby was. Jerry had the gun in his hand . . ."

"What time was this?"

"I don't know. Suddenly I can't remember times. Middle of the afternoon?"

"What did you do?"

"You mean right then?"

"Yes. That first moment, what did you do?"

"Took the gun away from him and just hugged him."

"Then what?"

"Had him take a bath. Burned his clothes."

"Where did this take place?"

"In the back-room fireplace. Then I

opened the window back there. I didn't want the smell of it all over the house when the police arrived."

I made a note. "Then what?"

"Sent him back to the bedroom: told him I wanted him to lie down till I came for him again. Then I handled the gun and got blood on my dress. Ripped it up some. Then I called the sheriff."

"So right from the start you were thinking —"

"— that I would confess, yes, of course, that I had to protect Jerry no matter what."

"It hadn't surprised you, then, that Jerry had shot your husband?"

"Of course it shocked me."

"But that's different."

"Yes. I was shocked, not surprised."

"Why not?"

"Jerry knew."

"Knew what?"

"What went on with Bobby and me."

"Did Bobby abuse you?"

"Not physically. Never."

"Did he ever touch Jerry?"

"He knew better. I'd have killed him for real if he had."

"But there was no love lost between them."

"Jerry never liked Bobby."

"You know that for a fact?"

"Oh, yeah. That child seemed to know everything. He knew how unhappy I was and Bobby was the reason."

"Did you ever tell him that in so many words?"

"That's hardly the kind of thing you tell a child. I would never tell him anything that would undercut Bobby in his eyes."

"But . . ."

"Jerry knew. He just did, I know he did. We talked about it, Bobby and me, how we had made such a mess of things, and sometimes I think Jerry overheard us. There are places in that house where a child can hide and hear everything. I'm telling you, Jerry knew. At night when Bobby would come home with some whore's perfume on his clothes, I'd sleep alone on the couch in the front room. And I'd wake up and Jerry would be there, asleep with his head on my lap, holding my hand."

"So Jerry had a good reason to hate Bobby, is that what you're saying?"

"I don't know what you'd consider a good reason. He killed him, didn't he?"

"I don't know who killed him."

"But I told you —"

"You didn't see him do it, did you?"

"But no one else was there."

"No one you saw."

"What are you saying?"

"How long did it take you to get to the house, after you heard the shot?"

"I was out at the edge of the meadow. Still, not much more than a few minutes."

"Did Bobby have any enemies?"

"Oh, Janeway! What are you thinking?"

"Same thing you're thinking, Mrs. Marshall. Let's go over it again."

11

Erin flew into Paradise International late that afternoon on a single-engine private flight from the Jefferson County Airport. It had taken her less than half an hour to make the arrangements. She had used this pilot on cases for Waterford, Brownwell, when other days were waning and her schedule was tight, when she needed to get to places like Laramie or Rock Springs or Albuquerque and had no time for long car trips. This was a ninety-minute hop over the hills from the Denver suburbs.

Paradise International was a bit of local sarcasm, the name painted on a board and tacked to a tree. It was a long dirt runway nestled in a valley about five miles from town, with two tin hangars, a radio room, and a rustic coffee shop. I waited just inside the coffee shop, my eyes scanning the sky to the east. Erin had said they'd get here by five, and at four-thirty the valley was already in deep shadow. Whatever daylight was left was high above us, wasted on the tops of the mountains.

"Can this guy land in the dark?"

"If he's more than a half-assed pilot he can," said the old fellow on duty. "We'll give him some lights to help bring him down."

He flipped a switch and the airstrip was defined by two long strings of what looked like Christmas lights. "There ye go. Just like the Macy's parade."

A moment later the plane made radio contact. "Your bird's about twenty miles east of here," the old man said. "Be on the ground before you can hawk up a good spit."

I walked nervously into the coming night. I am always nervous when someone I care about is flying, especially over unpredictable mountain air currents in a glorified egg crate with one little engine, a single heartbeat from disaster. But ten minutes later the plane broke over the hills and glided under the sunset into the purple valley. I watched it bump along the runway and come to a stop a hundred yards away.

Erin had dressed for weather: corduroy pants and a flannel shirt, scarf, boots and a heavy coat, a furry Russian-style pillbox hat and gloves. The pilot was a young stud named Todd Williams, who wore a leather cap and let his matching coat flop open in the wind. Erin made the introductions: we shook hands and Todd said he'd take care of his plane and join us in town. "We'll be at the jail for a while," I said. "After that you'll find us in the café on the main drag. You can't miss any of it unless you miss the whole damn town."

In the car I said, "You're looking good."

"I'm getting a cold," she said. "And frankly, my attitude sucks."

She didn't have much time: "I'm supposed to be working on my case this weekend. If I go into court unprepared on Monday, I'm in deep soup. I've got to be back before noon tomorrow."

"Are you nervous?"

"What have I got to be nervous about, she's the one in jail." She cut her eyes at me from the far corner of the car. "Yeah, I am. Did you tell her I was coming?"

"Haven't seen her since this morning. Wouldn't have told her anyway."

"Good. That first few seconds may tell us something." She flipped through some notes. "I want somebody to go up to that house and examine the back-room fireplace."

"I can do that."

"I'd rather have two of you together when you do that."

I had left word with Sheriff Gains that we'd be coming over to the jail sometime before dinner, but the only car on the lot was the deputy's. "Looks like you're about to meet the town charmer. Might as well get it over with."

We walked into the jail. Lennie Walsh was sitting behind the desk, smoking.

"Deputy Walsh," I said. "This is Ms. Erin D'Angelo. We'd like to see Mrs. Marshall for a few minutes."

"Visiting hours are posted on the door."

"That doesn't usually apply to a prisoner and his attorney."

"It does if I'm on duty. It's my call."

"I cleared this with the sheriff this afternoon."

"He didn't say nothin' to me about it."

"So what does that mean? Do we have to wait for him to get back?"

"Be a long wait. He went up to Gunnison, won't come back till Monday noon."

"So what do we do?"

"Come back Monday."

Erin pulled up a chair and leaned across the desk. "Deputy Walsh."

She offered her hand. He looked at it for so much time before finally taking it that I wanted to reach over and knock him off the chair.

"Help me out here, please. I've come here at great expense to see Mrs. Marshall."

"Shoulda called first."

"Maybe so but there wasn't time. I'm involved in another case in Denver, I'm supposed to be working on it even now. This is the only possible chance I'll have to speak with her for at least two more weeks."

"I appreciate how busy and important you are, Ms. . . . what's your name?"

"D'Angelo."

"Whatever. Like I was saying, I appreciate all that. At the same time, you can't expect us to drop everything when you walk in unannounced like this."

"Am I missing something here? Would it work a vast inconvenience on this department to let me see my client, please, for just a few minutes?"

"No inconvenience at all. Monday at ten."

"Deputy . . ."

He smiled pleasantly. "Yes, ma'am?"

"We're getting nowhere," she said to me. "Does your friend McNamara have a home number where the judge can be reached?"

"What are you callin' the judge for?" Lennie said. "You wanna piss that old man off, you just call him at home."

She ignored him. "Let's go."

We got up and started for the door.

"I don't know what you think the judge is gonna do," Lennie said.

She stopped at the door and turned. "I'll tell you what he'd better do. If he doesn't get you off your dead ass *right now*, I will delay this trial until next March and have good cause to do it. This is inexcusable. We'll be back in an hour. Deputy whatever."

"That was fun," I said.

"As long as it's my biscuits he's got on the fire, not yours."

"He's had mine."

I told her about my ongoing shitfight with Lennie Walsh.

"God, where do you find these guys? You run afoul of the worst creeps even in the middle of nowhere. You must run ads in the paper looking for them."

"Yeah, but then I find guys like you, and Parley, to pull me out of hot water."

"I like old McNamara better all the time," she said. "Haven't even met him yet and he reminds me of one or two old lawyers I know."

The waitress came. I told her we were waiting for a couple of people and she went away. Todd Williams, the first of our people, arrived a few minutes later. He was a flamboyant, young, blond hot dog but I liked him. He flopped next to Erin and draped his leather cap on her chair.

"Plane's all secured and here we are. I've been in some dead places with you, Miss Erin, but this one's unreal. What the hell are we supposed to *do* here tonight?"

"Speak for yourself. I've got to work."

"There's not even any TV in this place."

"There's a pool hall up the street," I said.

"Where do the ladies hang out?"

"I haven't found that out yet. The only one I've seen is our client, and she's in jail."

"Maybe we should go ahead and order," Erin said. "McNamara can catch up to us. I don't want to let too much grass grow under my feet, give that idiot at the jail any more excuses."

"You actually intend to call the judge?"

"If I have to. But I'm betting the deputy lets us in without a squawk when we go back." She smiled and clutched her purse. "Five'll get you ten."

"Not me," I said.

"Todd?"

"I don't even know what we're talking about."

I told him while Erin was signaling the waitress. "I'd never bet against this woman," Todd said while Erin was ordering. "You boys would make lousy lawyers," she said between instructions to the waitress. "You bluff too easy." She asked for a bottle of wine, paused when the waitress wondered if she wanted the big bottle or small, and said she'd come over and look at what was available in a minute. "I wonder how big the big bottle is," she said, and the woman told her she could bring half a gallon if we were superthirsty. Erin suppressed a laugh. "You bluff too easily," she said again, looking at me. "I can always bluff Williams out, but I expected more of you, Janeway." To the waitress she said, "Thank you, I'll come look. Put all this on one bill, please."

The waitress went away. "I'll bet it's Gallo," Erin said softly. "Any takers?"

She went away to look.

"She sure is hyper tonight," Todd said. "She tries to seem easy but I could tell the minute I picked her up, she's really uptight about something. This must be a tough case."

Erin came back and flopped. "I took the Gallo," she said. "Don't ask what the other choice was."

"I ate in here last night," I said. "They run a truck up to the window and pump the stuff into fifty-gallon drums."

Parley arrived as the waitress brought our wine: a nice bottle of French merlot, five years old. She uncorked it and poured a thimbleful for Erin to taste. "Lovely, thank you," Erin said, and she smiled at me brilliantly. "You never know, Janeway, you never know. That's five dollars you could've won from me tonight and we haven't even seen the deputy again."

Four glasses killed the bottle. I made the introductions and offered a toast to friendship.

Erin and Parley talked; Todd and I listened. The old man gave her his assessment of the case based on what he knew. "Some new things have come to light," she told him. "I can't go into them until we talk to the client, which I hope will be within the hour. I'll see her again tomorrow morning, and we'll decide at that time if I'm going to represent her. If I'm not, she needs to get someone right away. Cliff tells me he likes what you've done to this point."

"I'll take it if there's nobody else. I'm no criminal lawyer and I've told her that. I'd probably do as well as the public defender, but I'm not way up on her list of favorite people just now."

"What's that about?"

"I think Jerry did it and had the temerity to say so. She flew off the handle when I said that."

"That was then, this is now. But we can't talk about that yet, Janeway's tied our hands till we get her okay. Listen, if I do take this case, would you be willing to help?"

"Yeah, sure. I guess so."

"There's going to be lots of stuff that I can't be here for. It'd be great to have somebody here in town who knows the people and the turf."

"Kind of a second chair, you might say, huh?"

"Yeah, but you'd actually be doing most of the real work till I can get clear. We'll talk every day on the phone. Bill your time at your regular rate and send the bills to me. Once we get the client to understand what our defense is going to be, whatever that is, I think she'll be easier to get along with."

Supper came and we ate it. The wine was the high spot.

"We'll have to get us a place to stay," Erin said.

"You can all stay with me," Parley said.

"Best hotel in town," I said.

"That's good," Erin said nervously. "That's good."

She paid the bill. "Guess we'd better get on over to the jailhouse and see if anything's changed. In case it hasn't, do you have a number where I can reach the judge?"

"Oh, yeah. Wish I could be there when you call him."

Lennie was sitting at the same table, reading an old copy of *Startling Detective*.

"Didn't get any call from the judge," he said.

"I haven't talked to him yet. Do I have to?"

He grinned maliciously. "Naw, go on up. I was yanking your chain. If you hadn't flown off the handle and got all pissy on me, you'd be up there talking to her now."

"Thank you."

"You know the way, don't you, cowboy?"

"Come on," I said to Erin.

"Might take a while for me to get her up there," Lennie said. "Prisoners are eatin' supper now."

Upstairs, we sat in the conference room and waited. An hour passed.

"He's really rubbing it in, isn't he?" Erin said.

"Goddamn little tinhorn asshole."

She laughed. "Why don't you tell me what you really think of him?"

"Little tinhorn turkey-jerk South-Succotash pisswater asshole."

"That's very good. Don't hold back your best stuff on my account."

I filled the air with invective, one long impossible sentence, and we both laughed.

"Prisoners," I said derisively. "If he's got more than one prisoner, I'll be amazed."

"Keep a record of all this," she said. "Write down everything that's happened since you first laid eyes on him. Did he actually point a gun at you?"

"You think I made that up? But I was the only one who saw him. Even Parley found it hard to believe."

"Write it all down anyway, dates and times, everything. He sounds really unstable, but maybe we'll want to give him some grief down the road."

Footsteps came along the corridor. Erin took a deep, shivery breath, her last concession to nerves, and put on her steel face. Lennie held the door open and let Laura come into the room.

She stopped in shock and put her hands over her cheeks. Tears began at once.

Lennie spoke but his voice seemed far away. "So how long's this gonna take?"

"Go away, Deputy," Erin said.

"Hey, I got my own supper to eat sometime tonight."

"Then go away and eat it. I'll try to be brief right now, but I'll want to see her again tomorrow morning."

He grunted and closed the door. Erin waited, listening to his footsteps as he went down the hall. She and Laura looked at each other.

"Don't do that, please," Erin said. "Don't cry."

"I can't help it."

"We don't have time for old tears."

"I'm sorry."

"Sit down here."

Laura sat trembling near her, fighting the tears. "I knew you'd come. I knew it. I've dreamed of this." She broke down and sobbed into her hands.

Erin looked at me and her eyes were a thousand years old. She reached out and touched Laura's back, not an easy thing for her to do, and I winked at her.

"We can't waste time," she said. "You heard what Barney Fife said."

"I'm sorry. God, I'm sorry. I am so sorry for everything."

"Listen to me. Whatever we do here, that old stuff has nothing to do with it."

Of course this was not true: she knew and I knew and probably Laura Marshall knew that the old stuff was the cause of everything, but she went on as if none of us knew, staking out her turf. "I don't want to get into any of that. I'm here to talk about your case, not rake over old times. Can we please be clear on that?"

Laura sniffed and dabbed at her eyes but the flow wouldn't stop.

"I just don't want to talk about it," Erin said.

"Do you hate me?"

"I don't want to talk about it."

"I'm sorry, I'm sorry."

Erin looked at me and said quietly, "Is this place secure? Can we talk?"

"It should be. It would be stupid and very rare for them to bug a witness room." I shrugged. "With a cop like that idiot, who knows?"

"Let's just chat a bit tonight," Erin said.

On a legal pad she jotted a note.

"How've you been?"

"Not so hot," Laura said.

"Are they treating you okay in here?"

"I guess so. I'm going nuts. I've never been in jail before."

Erin wrote something on her pad. Laura said, "Are you going to help me?"

"I'll see if there's anything I can do. But you've got to be straight with us."

"I will, I promise."

"No more evasive stuff."

"I swear."

"That means everything is fair game. You hear what I'm saying? Everything."

"Of course."

"Good."

Erin started to write something, then changed her mind.

"How long were you out on the meadow before you heard the shot?"

"I don't know, maybe fifteen minutes. I wasn't thinking about it."

"Think about it now."

"Fifteen minutes," Laura said. "Twenty at the outside."

"Then you heard the shot."

"And I ran back to the house."

"And you've said that wouldn't have taken more than a few minutes."

She nodded.

"And from then until the deputy arrived, you heard no sounds of anyone or any vehicle coming or leaving."

"I don't know." Laura closed her eyes. "I don't know."

"If you do remember anything like that, tell us at once."

Another half minute passed. Again Erin asked, "Did you see or hear anything that might lead us to believe someone else might have been there?"

Laura looked to be in deep thought.

"This could be important," Erin said. "If you heard anything, either before or after you went into the house, I need to know exactly what you remember."

Laura nodded, her face intense.

"Let's go over a few things again," Erin said. "Why did you tell Mr. Janeway you killed Bobby?"

"I wanted to protect Jerry."

"You thought your son had done it."

"Yes. But now . . ."

"Are you willing to accept it if Jerry did shoot Bobby?"

Laura shook her head and looked away.

"Look at me."

Laura looked up.

"The fact is, we don't know who did it," Erin said.

"That's right. Janeway showed me it might've been someone else."

"But right now we have no other suspects."

"No."

"You see what I'm getting at?"

"I'm not sure."

"We have one version of what happened. Yours. Unless Jerry comes to life and begins talking up a blue streak, yours is the one we're going with."

"But what if that means . . . ?"

"If I take this case, my job is to get you off. That means everything else is up for grabs, everything. If Jerry did it, we'll have to deal with that later."

"Oh, God, Erin . . . oh, Jesus . . ."

"We've got to be clear on this. I will not have my hands tied."

A long moment unrolled. Erin wrote something on her paper.

"Make up your mind," she said.

Laura nodded.

"Be sure."

"Yes."

"Mr. McNamara will be talking to you again in the coming days. I want you to be as straight with him as you will with me. He's to be told everything you remember, as soon as you remember it. If you think of something you'd forgotten about, I want you to call him. Are we clear on that?"

They stared at each other.

"Okay?" Erin said.

Laura looked unhappily at the wall.

"Okay?" Erin said again.

"Okay."

"Okay, then. Don't talk to anybody else. No reporters, no lawyers, especially not that cretin who minds the jail. Talk to nobody but one of us. Can you do that?"

"Yeah, sure."

"Refer anything you're asked to me or McNamara. Try to get some sleep, I'll be back early in the morning."

"So what do you think?" Erin said.

"I like her."

"Yes, she's always been very likable."

"There's a guarded statement if I ever heard one."

I pulled up at Parley's house and we sat there a moment letting the car run and the heater warm us. Erin took a deep breath. "Yeah, it is," she said at last. "I'm trying to figure out what I feel about her after all these years. I may never know."

"There's something about you two," I said. "In some ways you're very much alike; in others —"

"— we could be from different species."

"Yeah. Somehow I can't picture her being you."

"I think when we were kids she was suspicious of my motives. She never seemed to believe I liked her as much as I did; she always had something to prove. She was dirt-poor, her people had nothing: her father literally worked himself to death. When she was a teenager, she took on a full-time job to help them out, going to school the whole time. Man, I admired her spunk. In time I think she knew that and we became good friends, then best friends. If she had any shallowness, it was a certain preoccupation with the rich and famous. Easy for me to say, I was one of the privileged, but I always thought she was too enchanted with stories of wealthy, fabled people. She seems different now. Different and yet I still see flashes of her old ways. In her face. In her eyes."

"Do you still hate her for what happened?"

"I never hated her. I just can't do that. I sure tried to, when the hurt was new and raw: I cursed them both a hundred times a week but I couldn't ever come to hate her. I'm afraid in my youth I bought into the old stereotypes. It was the man's fault. He was much easier to hate. What can you expect from a man, you're all a bunch of randy old goats. But it was different with her. She took my man, but women have lost men forever and lived through it. What he took from me was just as priceless."

"Did he ever try to make it up?"

"Oh, yeah. He called a lot, at first half a dozen times a week. And I did talk to him about it, at least in the beginning. I guess I should say I heard him out. I didn't have much to say, but I thought I owed it to him to hear what he had to say. We had been together for years, we were high school sweethearts, and even before that we were so close. So I felt I should at least listen."

"What did he say?"

"Oh, he tried to blame her. But it takes two to tango, doesn't it? At least she never tried to duck the blame, I've got to give her that. She cried and said how sorry she was, but never once did she say it was his fault."

"Well, I think she's suffered for it."

"Good."

A long moment later, Erin said, "If I did hate her, this would be the perfect opportunity for me to get back at her. Wouldn't it?"

"If you were that mean-hearted. And a good enough lawyer to be just bad enough to lose her case."

"What's your guess about that?"

"You're one of those two things. But only one."

"Thank you, I think."

"I'm not worried about you. You wouldn't do that. I think you already know what you're going to do."

Another moment passed, lost in thought.

"I couldn't even say her name in there. I'll have to get over that."

Suddenly she said, "I've got to get her off, Cliff. I've got to get her off."

12

We sat up past midnight in a three-headed council of war. Erin sent Todd to bed early — "Go read a book," she said, "we have some lawyer stuff to hash out" — and he departed cheerfully for the third bedroom down the hall. Most of our talk until then had been about tomorrow's agenda. "I want to go to the jail as soon as deputy whatever will let me in," Erin said. "I don't think I can count on getting in there much before eight o'clock. And I've got to see that kid before I leave. I know he doesn't speak but I need to spend a few minutes with him anyway."

"What do you want me to do?" Parley said.

"You come with me, if you will. That might make it easier for you to work with her after I've gone. All billable hours now, so keep track."

"Would it be out of line to ask who's paying for this?"

"Nothing's out of line. Until she gets out and decides what to do, I'll pay the bills. Is that a problem?"

"Not for me it isn't."

"Good. I think it'll be best if just the two of us see her tomorrow. You understand that, Cliff . . . just the lawyers and the client this time around?"

"Do I look like I'm getting my feelings hurt?"

"In the afternoon, after I'm gone, Parley can bring you up on what was said."

"I could also put this time to good use. At some point I've got to spend a day with her books. Make a list of what's really there. And we've got to get those books out of that house. I could rent us a U-Haul, go on up there, and spend the day packing 'em up, doing the donkey work while the brain trust does whatever it does down here."

"I don't know. Somehow that strikes me wrong."

"Why, for God's sake? What's the down-side in that?"

"I don't know. At the moment, we're the only ones who know about those books."

"That doesn't necessarily change just because we've moved them."

"It tells the other side something I might not want them to know yet. I don't think we should move them without noticing-in the DA on what we know, and I'd like to at

159

least ask our client about them first. I know you mentioned them to her, but let's see what she says when we get more specific."

"Can I at least have the keys so I can go up and take another look?"

"Can you make an inventory just by looking at the titles on a shelf?"

"I can make a *list*. I can do that much, which is a helluva lot more than we've got right now."

"A list, then. If you need to take something off the shelf, fine, but then put it back where it was."

Parley handed me the keys.

"Erin," I said in my pleading voice, "we are going to feel mighty stupid if anything happens . . ."

"I know . . . I know. Let me think about it, how to proceed. You go on up early tomorrow and make your list, then we'll talk again."

"We could be fairly inconspicuous, if you want to move 'em," Parley said. "Let Cliff inventory and box 'em up and then we go up there after dark and load up the truck."

"And put 'em where?" I said.

"What's wrong with right here? I've got a room that's not being used."

We looked at each other for half a

minute. Then Erin said, "I'm just not comfortable with us going in there at night and stripping the library. I know we *can*, that's not the question: legally the house is back with us, we've got the keys, we can *do* what we want with it. But that kind of thing can come back to haunt us. If you're right about the books and they're worth real money, that becomes a potential motive."

"Against our client," Parley said drily.

"It could cut both ways. This could be a motive for anybody."

"So if this anybody killed Bobby, who and where is he and why hasn't he made some attempt to get the books?"

"That's what we don't know," Erin said. "Maybe he's afraid to go up there now. Maybe he's afraid of a trap."

"You could almost make that feasible, if we had some other name to work with."

"Who else might benefit from the victim's death?"

"Well, I've been all through the DA's file," Parley said. "I've looked at every scrap of evidence they've got, and I don't see anybody there who'd fill that bill. They're going with a fairly simple and straightforward case. The blood was all over her dress, and most damning of all, she confessed. Never mind that she

161

might've had second thoughts about the confession later, she still confessed. Where's Mr. Anybody figure into all that?"

"I don't know. Look, the books have been there three weeks now and nobody's touched them. It's possible that they'll only be in jeopardy if you call attention to them. That's the wonderful thing about books, isn't it? They never look valuable to an unwashed second-story man."

I sighed with exaggerated patience. "Erin, we've got to get them out of there. We might as well take out a STEAL THESE BOOKS ad in the newspaper."

"But what's likely to happen when we do that? More to the point, what happens to the books as evidence in some future action we may take, based on facts we don't yet know?"

"Right now we don't know what the hell's in there. My opinion is based on a ten-minute walk-through. Do you have any idea how unprofessional that is?"

"No, but I'll bet you'll tell us." She smiled sweetly and made a short list of notes, structuring the next day. "I'll bet Parley will tell us his opinion as well."

"Jerry shot Bobby, just like Miss Laura said."

"As theories go, that's not bad. I'm certainly not above using it if we have to, even though it'll make our defendant very unhappy."

Erin shuffled through her pad. "I guess we need to talk about a change of venue."

"I can't see any downside to getting it out of here," Parley said. "This county is way too small, not to mention small-minded."

"But if we move for a change of venue, that would delay the trial. Adamson's almost certain to want to continue it, and I don't think he would grant it anyway. We'd have to appeal the delay, waive our right to a speedy trial, and how will our defendant like being locked up an extra two to four months while all this is going on? She's strung out as it is."

"I sure don't like the idea of trying it here."

"Neither do I, but it may be the lesser of two evils. We need to get things moving, especially if we think they've got a weak case."

"I don't know," Parley said. "I'm glad you're here to make that call."

Erin pondered what we had said. "Look, their case starts with that stupid deputy. I've only had the briefest pleasure of his company but I think he'll be a weak link right out of the gate. From what I've seen so far, the investigation is pathetic."

"The DA thinks it's in the bag."

"Let him think that. I'd like to hold his feet to the fire and see what evidence he's actually got; we may find out he's not as well prepared as he thinks he is. We know they have no written confession. Their investigating officer is a certified wild hare, and he did everything during that first critical hour by himself. I'd like you to file a boilerplate motion to suppress everything he did and found up there. Let's push for an early trial date, hold their feet to the fire before they realize there are all kinds of holes in their case; before they have a chance to prepare."

She studied her notes. "Cliff, it would help if you can find out anything new about our friend Lennie — what his movements were that day, what he did, who he talked to and what was said, where he was when he got the call, whether he took a leak at the scene and where — you know the routine. Make a chart showing all that. Give us anything that shows him as a wild man. And you'll need to interview him as well."

"That'll be fun."

"Parley, you could set up the interview, then take Cliff with you when you go."

"Ambush the bastard."

Again the room went suddenly quiet.

Then Erin said, "I don't know how you work, Parley, but I like to start with my own theory of what really happened. Even if it's early, even though this'll all change as new facts come to light. Puts the onus on us and gives me a focal point to carry into the next day's work."

"So what's your current theory for this one, as if I didn't know."

"The victim was killed by an unknown assailant. The alternate suspect theory. That gives us an excellent place to dig around."

"Some third party did it. Great defense if we can sell it."

"You know how the alternate suspect idea works. I don't have to name names or prove it, but if I can get it planted that Bobby had enemies and that someone else might have been at or near the house that day, they'll have to deal with it." She looked at me. "Let's see if we can find who might have done this, who might have had a reason to shoot Bobby. That would be a fine use of your spare time. And if you actually find such a creature, I will swoon into your arms with delight."

"Now you know why I work so cheap," I said to Parley.

He shook his head. "I don't think we've got diddly-squat along those lines."

"Not yet," Erin said. "But we do need to find out if anyone had a motive and opportunity, and who that might be."

She wrote some notes. "Maybe a jealous husband, someone who lost his shirt in a business deal with Bobby, maybe some real estate venture that went sour." And at last she said, "And the books could be a motive."

"Wow, the books could be a motive," I said. "Why didn't I think of that?"

"Because you're too busy being a wise guy."

"So if the books are a potential motive, we need to find out where Bobby got them," I said. "Who'd he buy them from? Why? Was he buying them to resell? If so, where was his market?"

"Whatever you can find that backs up the alternate suspect theory. If we can do that, we've got something to work with."

"And if we can't," Parley said, "then we're back to Jerry."

"But for today let's believe somebody else was in that room before Jerry came in and picked up the gun."

"Jerry and Laura . . . they're both innocent."

"They're both innocent."

"Lots of luck."

BOOK II
THE PREACHER
AND THE MUTE

13

It was a long/short night: long on worry, short on sleep. I thought about those books almost constantly and I fell asleep sometime after midnight. I awoke three hours later dreaming of a vast library, all signed and inscribed books stretching in neat rows for miles, as far as the eye could see. For another half hour I lay in bed hoping for sleep, which I slowly realized would not return. Eventually I managed to get out of bed without disturbing Erin, dressed, and sat in Parley's big front room. I stared into the black nothing until, driven by some inner demon, I got on my coat and went out.

I didn't know where I was going: at that time of night I'd have to drive at least sixty miles to find even a trace of life. I cruised through the town, hoping for an all-night coffee shop, knowing there could be no such animal on this far-flung planet. Not a light shone anywhere at four o'clock in the morning — not a movement, not a hope, not a living soul.

Understanding comes slowly at that time

of day, but as I drove along the abandoned streets, I recalled the dream of the endlessly inscribed books. I passed the courthouse for the third time, turned around abruptly, and headed out of town. A few minutes later I reached the dirt road heading up into the hills.

I was halfway up the mountain when I finally realized that I was going up to the house. At that early hour I had no plan or reason, beyond what we had discussed the night before. I sure didn't expect the real killers to be hard at work stealing Mrs. Marshall's books at the exact moment when I happened to show up: it was only profound restlessness that drove me on. Friday's snow had melted away, but I remembered the terrain fairly well and my headlights picked out some landmarks that were vaguely familiar. I was pretty sure that just ahead was where Lennie and his car had disappeared into the swirling snow. I slowed to a crawl and alternated my headlights between dims and brights, stopping wherever I saw a nook or a break. Occasionally I got out and walked along the road, staring at nothing across the deep black infinity until I ran out of light and had to pick my way back to the car.

I had driven all the way over the crest

when I found a rocky-looking trail on my left. It meandered precariously down into the void, one of those places that looks bad anytime but just reeks of peril to a stranger on a black morning. Maybe this was it, maybe not: I wasn't about to drive in there in the hope I'd be able to turn around: I'd have to walk down. I found a place where I could hide my car off the road. Then I put on my heavy coat and hood, got out my flashlight, fixed my beam on dim, and started along the trail.

I found a place no more than forty yards down: a wide spot where his car could have been parked and easily turned around. A footpath went on from there, around the gulch and along the face of the hill. Instinctively I knew Lennie had been here. I sensed it, I smelled him as I got closer. I couldn't see a damn thing, only what was straight ahead in the beam of my light and no more than three feet of that. The path was okay: not many rocks or sudden dips to send a silly hiker careening off to break a leg or worse, and I kept at it slowly. In recent years I had made a startling discovery, that when you're going nowhere anyway, there's no real hurry to get there.

And I knew something else. If this was where Lennie had been, he had probably left me a few clues. I moved ahead with my light on the ground, and ten minutes later I saw a small rocky recess, protected from the weather and just big enough for a man to stand in. There was the inevitable pile of cigarette butts, soggy from snow runoff, but a clear enough sign that I had arrived.

Good old reliable Lennie, the son of a bitch.

I stopped and sat on the ground to wait for the new day.

Dawn doesn't even think of cracking in the Colorado mountains before six at that time of year. Six couldn't be too far away, but as I sat and the dawn didn't break, I lost track of the time. Soon I slipped easily into my own personal brand of Zen. The minutes passed . . . it might've been an hour, might've been two weeks, it didn't matter because I wasn't thinking about it now. I had no goal beyond the number ten, staring at the black wall and counting to ten, starting over, doing it again and again with only an empty mind to keep me company. This is how a moment passed, then an eternity, and the dawn finally cracked. November in the Rockies: I was aware of it without ever seeing the crack, which would be somewhere slightly aft and off to port. I didn't turn my head but there was some suggestive thing, just the slightest hint of firmament across the way, though I couldn't really see it yet. I counted to ten and counted again, and at one point I wished I'd known about this Zen tool years ago when I had been a cop on stakeouts.

So that's what this was then, a stakeout. I hadn't thought of it that way until this moment, but, yes, I had come here to watch the house with only a hunch that if nothing had happened by now, something might just be overdue. Slowly the day brightened, gradually I saw the road on the opposite hillside, and suddenly the house took shape in the trees across the gulch. I made a small adjustment and burrowed deeper into the underbrush, drawing my coat up around my face so seeing me would be difficult and maybe impossible from there. I imagined all kinds of evil afoot, I pictured someone standing just inside the Marshall living room scanning my hill with binoculars. But I sat still, staring at the house. I counted to ten a hundred times, I stared and I counted, and in this way the time passed.

At some point I came fully alert and looked around. For the first time I took note of the day. The dawn never did have any real crack to it; the sky was gray and snow was swirling over my head, blowing down the gulch and around the house and over the mountaintop. I thought of all the stakeouts I had done and how Jesus-Christ-boring they had all been. I had been here now five hours — I looked at my watch — but the day was still early and at that point I didn't even allow myself the luxury of feeling like a fool. I counted to ten and cleared my mind.

I counted to ten and the snow piled up on my hood, on my shoulders, and settled in a deepening mound around my ass. Trickles of water ran down from my head and across my cheeks from my eyes.

I counted to ten.

Much later I thought of Erin.

Looked at my watch. It was half past eleven.

She'd be finished interviewing Laura Marshall by now; she and Parley would have seen the mute boy. She had taken the case, I had no doubt, and she'd be getting ready to fly back to Denver. She'd be pretty well pissed: this I knew. Briefly I wished I had written her a note of some kind, but how could I know at four o'clock in the morning that I would lose my mind and disappear? What would I have said? *Don't worry if I lose my mind. Don't fret if I disappear for a while. I'm on the case, love, Janeway.*

Yeah, right. What does "for a while" mean? All day? All week?

How long would this madness continue? How long before I packed it in?

Not yet, came the quick answer. At some point, obviously, but not yet.

I counted to ten and the hours passed.

I had been there more than ten hours. Ten hours of counting to ten. My watch told me so, but it didn't seem to matter. If I left now and something happened to the books, what kind of idiot would that make me? I was becoming a captive to my own mad fears.

Did this mean I was prepared to sit through the night? The snow had fallen throughout the day and I knew I must look like some stupid abominable snowman sitting here alone. Erin would be back in Denver by now. She knew me well enough not to worry, I hoped. She would know I was off somewhere on the case, she'd know I would never do anything to screw it up. But that knowledge might be starting to pale by now.

Oh, yeah, Erin would be pissed.

Too bad for her. She should've taken me more seriously about the books.

I looked at my watch. Four o'clock. I'd had nothing to eat since last night, and only the snow for water. Strangely, it seemed like enough. My hunch was stronger now than it had been this morning, and that's what kept me here. I sucked on a snowball and laughed as that silly bumper sticker DON'T EAT YELLOW SNOW wafted through my head. I made sure to pee downhill so as not to foul up the water supply.

At four-thirty I finally took a break and hiked out to my car. The road was now tightly snowpacked and I made good time to the edge of town. There I stopped at the café, got something to take out, and called Denver from the pay phone while they were cooking it.

Erin wasn't home. I left a message on her machine, told her I was alive and well, apologized, and told her to look for me when she saw me. Then I took my luke-warm sandwich and a bottle of beer and headed back uphill. I had a fresh new commitment and a crazy, growing sense of urgency. I didn't like being away even for half an hour.

How can I describe the twenty-four hours that followed? To say I ate my food, I sat and I waited: these things have no meaning in a surrealistic world of silence and white flutter. The snow fluttered and the darkness fell, and sometime after that I hiked back out to the road and got my bag from the car. From there the hike to the top was arduous: the snow was deep and I didn't want to take a chance on it, even with four-wheel drive, and I didn't want to leave deep furrows showing that a car had been here. So I made the climb, finally reaching the house at nine-thirty by my watch.

I stood on the porch for a time, watching the snow fall, seeing nothing beyond my reach. At some point I let myself in.

I took off my shoes. Followed my light down the hallway to the library. Took a deep breath of relief as my light revealed the tall shelves of books, apparently undisturbed since I had last seen them.

I unrolled my sleeping bag on the floor, got out my notebook, propped my flashlight, and started the long job of making a list. I made it in order, as the books were shelved, and after a while I got into a rhythm. I used my own crude shorthand and things went faster after that. Still, it was after midnight when I finished.

A check of Bobby's office revealed nothing. His desk contained only the insurance policies — life, house, and car.

I walked through the house to the back room, bent down, and looked at the fireplace. The grate looked undisturbed, still full of ash, and I stood there for a full minute looking at it in the soft glow of my light before judgment reared its head and told me to leave it alone.

I was bone-tired now. I put my sleeping bag at the end of the hall and crawled inside it. In less than five minutes I was sound asleep.

The hours blended together: blended, fused, became a single black unit of time.

I don't remember waking up. Sometime before dawn, I rolled my bag by the dim glow of my flashlight, locked the house, and trudged back down the hill.

I don't know why, I just felt better from the vantage point across the gulch. I took up the vigil again, sitting in the trees, counting to ten, staring across the way as the land went gray, then pink, and the sun came out.

The sun . . . what a crazy, happy sight that was. Strangely, it didn't matter after a while. The sun shone bright but at midmorning clouds blew out of the west and made the world gray again. I remember two thoughts from that second day: *This has got to stop* and *Just a little longer.* A little longer and surely I'd be ready to pack it in. Thus did the hours pass: I counted to ten, 10 trillion times I counted, and in the late afternoon a gentle snow-flutter blew down from the mountain.

Again I walked out to the car. Drove into town for my fast-food dinner. Called Erin, got her machine, decided to go back for one last look.

Good thing, too. The two men were there when I got back.

14

They were sitting in a pickup truck. If they had been there awhile, it had been a very little while. They sat in the cab with the motor running — I could see the exhaust even across the gulch — and they appeared to be in earnest conversation at the deserted look of the place. Two guys in a picture of indecision. They hadn't come up here to steal Laura's books: they'd had another purpose and now they were stymied at what they had found. This was all speculation on my part, but moments passed and they still didn't move. What else could have stopped them? Suddenly the horn blew. It echoed across the meadow and down the gulch, and when no one came from the house to greet them, they turned the truck around and got the hell out of there.

I ran now: slipped and slid back along the trail to the road, arriving just in time to get a good look at the truck as it came past. It was a late-model GMC two-seater, green with a black, waterproof tarp covering the open bed, licensed by the state of

Oklahoma. It roared by in a blizzard of snow: I was crouched in a ditch and I cursed when I could read only the last three plate numbers. Five-six-three, I thought, five-six-three. I was still committing it to memory as I got my own car and rolled down the mountain behind them. At the juncture of the main highway, I got lucky: I saw their taillights through the trees just before I blundered upon them.

I eased up to the bend, got out, and walked to the edge of the trees. They were parked at the stop sign facing the main road not twenty yards away. I got the rest of the license plate number and committed it to memory.

They were talking earnestly again about something. More indecision, this time perhaps over which way to go. To the left just a few miles away was the town, a warm bed, and supper: to the right, nothing but seventy-five miles of bad road, high mountain passes, and snow.

They turned right. I got back in my car, pulled up to the stop sign, and sat for a moment watching their taillights recede in the distance.

It was five o'clock: night was quickly coming on and I had lived in Colorado long enough to know better. To dare the remote high country in wintertime with a truck was bad enough. To take the same road alone in a car, even with four-wheel drive, was irresponsible and damned dangerous. There are easier ways to commit suicide.

But I knew I was going. I looked at my gas gauge — three-quarters of a tank — and I gave the books a final wave and headed south.

C'est la vie.

I had gone no more than five miles, just past the so-called airport, when I passed an open road barrier. The sign said ROAD CLOSED NOV 15–APR 15. They should've closed it last week, not next, I thought grimly . . . they might've just saved three lives by doing that. But a fool will always find some way to kill himself, and I thought other optimistic things as the road began to climb. This is when a book thief will choose to show up at the house, I thought. He'll empty out that room in a heartbeat and nobody will see him, nobody will know which way he or the books went, or what it was all about. In the spring, when the highway department clears this road, they'll find Janeway's leathery corpse perfectly preserved like the two-thousand-year-old man, his car half-buried under a snowdrift. This was not funny: there was too good a chance of something just like that happening. Turn around, kid, I thought, the hell with those guys: go back and babysit the books. But then I could see their taillights again, climbing toward some unseen summit, and that drew me on. Those boys hadn't just materialized at the house, and I wanted to know what they knew. I could always turn around if it got bad. So I thought. I could always turn around.

They were maybe a quarter mile ahead, rolling along at a pretty good clip. I was able to make good time as well. The snow had been drifting during the day, but there had been no traffic across the pass to pack it down and my tires got good traction on the gravel. The road was dark and getting darker by the minute: the snow seemed suddenly heavier, at last I had to use my lights, and I knew that far ahead the two guys would be well aware of my presence. I imagined them saying, *Who is that crazy bastard back there?*

Such is life, I thought. *Such is life and death.*

My mind was a jumble of thoughts, none of them good, as I climbed toward the great Continental Divide. In another week this drive would be impossible. This road should already be closed, I thought again. What are the highway people thinking?

There comes a point on such a journey when final thoughts of turning back are cast aside and forgotten. I had reached a summit, and for a while I rode along at the top of the world with swirling mists on either side. The effect was bizarre, almost grotesque in its dark beauty. There was a dense cloud cover and yet a full moon broke through almost continuously, lighting up a road that seemed like a silver ribbon around the universe with spiraling galaxies on either side. I couldn't see the truck at all now, which only increased my paranoia, and ahead was a fearsome-looking storm-thing that almost turned me back even then. That was my point of no return . . . if I went into that cold hell, I was in effect giving myself up for dead anyway, I was going all the way. The snow hit like some kind of battering ram. I felt the car shiver in a fierce crossing wind. Oh, baby, this was nuts. But then the car pushed through it, the moon broke through, and for that moment I could see forever. Again I could see the road running on and on: I could see another mountain range in the far distance, and down the road, at least a mile away, I saw the truck.

I stopped for a moment and sat watching, idling. Something wasn't right.

The truck didn't seem to be moving, that was the strange thing. There was no movement at all to the picture ahead: it was as if the two guys had stopped to talk it over yet again. I knew, having driven these mountain roads for years, that the downslope is the dangerous part. I could feel the ice under my wheels: even at a crawl and with four-wheel drive, if I hit the brakes the car would slip. Suddenly I knew something else. Those guys weren't moving because they had lost control going down. They had run off the road and got stuck. Here they were, miles from anywhere, and unless they had a radio, I was their only hope.

I sat there and the moon went south, the world went dark, and blowing gusts obliterated everything. There was no question now about what to do: I had to go check on those guys, had to roll up and introduce myself and pretend to be a hail-fellow-damned-well-met, just an unwashed slob as crazy as they were, and see if they bought that. I had an uneasy feeling about it, but I no longer had a choice. I got out of the car and opened the trunk, fished around in the far back, and took out my gun. Made the unnecessary checks (it was always loaded, always ready for some ugly job) and put it under the seat, just a long stretch from my left hand.

"Let's go get 'em, Danno," I said out loud.

I took my time getting there. For a few minutes the blizzard was horrendous. I couldn't see more than a foot of road ahead, and I crawled along at the speed of nothing. I took heart in the occasional pockets of clarity, but it was a long time, at least twenty minutes, before I saw the truck's lights again. When I did, the effect was startling: I came across a flat spot and the snow whipped past, just before the ground dipped precariously, deeper into the valley. I stopped at the edge. This is where he lost it, I thought, and at the same instant my vision cleared and the truck was there, not fifty yards away. He had slipped easily off the road — I could see his mistake from the distance: he had taken way too much liberty on the flat, and then when the sudden downgrade began, he had not been ready for it. I started down slowly, and as I did one of the men ran frantically into the roadway, waving his arms. Here we go, I thought.

I rolled down the window and a coarsely bearded face filled it.

"Jesus Christ," he said, almost out of breath. "God bless America, brother, am I glad to see you! Whoever the hell you are, you sure look good to me right now."

"Run off the road, did you?" I said stupidly.

"Yeah. My goddamn brother and his balls of steel. If he doesn't kill us yet with his daredevil bullshit, I'll be one surprised mother."

"That looks like a pretty ugly crack-up from back here. I got a rope, if you'd like to try pulling it out."

"No way, pardner. He wrapped it around a tree while he was at it. We'll have to send a wrecker back after it when we can. Will you give us a lift out of here?"

"Sure. Where you headed?"

"You mean I got a choice?"

I laughed. "Straight ahead seems to be it for the moment."

"Wherever there's warm and something to eat. We know a fellow in Monte Vista."

"I'm going right through there."

He went back to the truck and I sat idling. So far, so good. I didn't know them, they didn't know me. A minute later the other one arrived: a spitting image of the first, except that his beard had a few streaks of gray. "Howdy, stranger," he said. "I guess Willie already told you, we're damned glad you came."

"You guys hop in. With luck, maybe we'll all survive."

"That's fine. If you don't mind, we've got some merchandise we've got to carry with us."

"Sure. Will it fit in the backseat?"

"Oh, yeah, long as the three of us can sit up front."

That was fine with me: I remembered what Jack McCall had done to Wild Bill Hickok and I wasn't partial to having either of them at my back the rest of the way down. I asked if they needed any help and the guy said no, they could get it. In fact, what came out of the truck took them each four loads to carry out of there: eight cardboard boxes a foot deep and about two feet square. I turned on the overhead light and saw the name *Daedalus* printed boldly on the sides of each box. I knew it well: Daedalus Books was one of the better remainder houses of the book trade. I bought remainders myself about twice a year, and I had half a dozen identical boxes in the back room of my store. They were ideal for shipping or for transporting books to book fairs.

I decided not to comment on any of this yet: there would be time enough later, if the situation felt right at some point. The two guys slammed the back doors and got in the front beside me. "You guys must be twins," I said, offering a hand. "Cliff Janeway."

If I had earned any kind of name in the book trade, these boys hadn't heard it. I had been thinking about giving them a phony name: the book world is so small and insular. Sometimes it seems as if everybody knows everybody, but they showed no reaction to my name. This, I thought, was good.

"Wally Keeler," said the reckless one.

"Willie Keeler," said the other, from shotgun.

I didn't recognize their names either. If they were accomplished grafters, I might expect to, again because book people love to talk and word gets around. We shook firmly and I backed out onto the road. "You sure that's everything?"

"Everything we can carry tonight."

I started down. "Man, we've all got to be a little crazy to be out here tonight."

I said this in my self-deprecating, no-offense-intended voice and Willie gave a dry, humorless laugh. "You got that right."

"Don't start, Will," said his brother. "It wasn't just my say-so."

The tone was far from cordial. Willie gave a derisive grunt and the atmosphere in the car was poisoned by sibling discord.

"So what're you doing out here?" said Wally.

"Made a hot date with a waitress over in Alamosa," I said.

Willie laughed. "That must *really* be a hot date."

"It ain't that hot." I looked at them in the reflection of the odometer. "Never woulda started across that pass if I'd known what was ahead of me."

"Good thing for us you did, pal."

"Then it got to a point where it seemed just as easy to keep going as to go back."

"That's all I was saying," Wally said. "Didn't hear any fuss about it till things turned ugly."

"Maybe if you tried staying on the goddamn road, things wouldn't turn ugly. Oh, no, not you. Every fuckin' highway is the goddamn Indianapolis 500."

"Listen, you son of a bitch —"

"Hey, fellas," I said. "You boys wanna

fight, at least wait'll I get us out of here."

"Yeah," Willie said sourly. "Show some manners, asshole."

Nothing more was said for a while, but the air simmered with their anger. We bottomed out in the valley and started up again. I thought about asking them what their business was: nothing too inquisitive, just making-conversation-type conversation, but it didn't feel right yet. Ahead the road looked better: I could see the moon clearly now, and I had high hopes that the worst was behind us. We wound our way upward and upward, and then, at the peak, another mountain range loomed ahead.

"Goddamn brand-new truck," Willie said suddenly.

"I'm not gonna tell you again, Willie —"

"Looks like better weather ahead," I said in my jolly-boys voice.

"Couldn't get much worse."

"Where you boys from?"

Willie said, "Raton," and Wally said, "Tulsa."

"He lives in Tulsa," Willie said quickly. "What about you?"

"Denver."

"What're you doing out here?"

"Just a little R and R."

I let a moment pass, then asked the

question. "How about yourselves?"

"Same answer," Willie said. "We came over to see a fellow we know."

I took another moment, then: "What line of work you boys in?"

This time the pause gave them time enough to concoct some serious fiction. Apparently Willie was not a stupid man: he figured I had seen the Daedalus imprint on the boxes. So I thought in the ten seconds it took him to answer.

"We're book wholesalers," he said.

"You mean like traveling salesmen?"

"Yeah, something like that. We represent a book dealer who sells remainders. We've got a five-state region where we market our stuff."

I knew this was fiction. In fact, remainder-house reps never carried boxes of books: instead they arrived with half a dozen briefcases full of dust jackets. I had spent more than one afternoon sitting across the counter from remainder salesmen, looking at jackets one after another, saying, "Three of these," "Five of these, please," and so on. But to Willie I was polite and ignorant. "That sounds interesting."

"It's all right. What do you do?"

"I play the ponies," I said in a masterpiece of my own spontaneous bullshit.

"You're a gambler?"

"It's not exactly gambling," I said.

"Aw, c'mon. You tellin' me you play the horses for a *living* and it's not gambling?"

"Not in the long run. Not if you're careful and know your business."

"What the hell, then . . . are the races fixed?"

"Not at all. I've just worked out a formula."

"Damn, I could use some of that formula."

"I'm not saying I never lose," I said easily. "When I do lose, I take it big in the shorts. But I win a lot more than I lose, just by knowing when certain horses are miles better than the competition. I play small fields, no more than half a dozen in a race, so a good horse doesn't get screwed in traffic jams. I bet big, and I put it all on the nose."

"You must get no odds at all."

"You never do with a sure thing, but it's better than you'd imagine. I average four-to-five. Eighty cents on the dollar. That's fine if you've put down ten grand to win eight, and you win nine out of ten."

"Jesus Christ," Wally said. "Man, I wouldn't have the balls to do that."

"You've got to know how to pick the right horse, that's for sure. Can't just play every four-to-five shot that steps on the racetrack."

"Deep pockets probably don't hurt either."

"Don't kid yourself; my pockets aren't that deep. I've got a little money in the bank, but there've been times when I came this close to looking for a job. Once I was down to my last grubstake. Then I won fifteen in a row and was back on top again."

"Jesus. How long've you been doing this?"

"Ten years."

"Jesus! You never know who the hell you're gonna meet."

I almost wanted to laugh. This all sounded real because it *was* real. Once I had known a guy who had lived just that way. He had a powerhouse system and he had put two kids through school with it. He had won fifteen in a row many times and once had a fabulous win streak of twenty-three. But then came the day he hit the inevitable skids, lost six big ones, and died in the stretch. The last I heard he was working in a gas station, but I knew enough about his good years to make the story fascinating to a pair of wannabe fast-buck artists.

We talked our way up the pass and

across it: they asked naive questions and I gave them sophisticated answers that sounded legit even to me. It kept them away from each other's throat long enough to get us into relatively flat country, then across that on the swing into Monte Vista.

"Looks like we survived," I said.

"Yeah," Willie said. "We can drop our goods and get home from here. Pal, you sure came along at the right time. Don't know what the hell we'da done without you."

"Happy to oblige," I said.

"We need to get together sometime. We could maybe go racing and you could show us that magic system you've got."

Ahead the lights of Monte Vista stretched across the horizon. It was a small town, no more than four or five thousand people: strange place for a book drop, I thought.

"Turn left up there," Wally said. "That gray building in the middle of the block."

I pulled up in front. "Lemme give you boys a hand with that stuff."

"Oh, we're fine now."

"I could use a stretch about now, if you don't mind."

"Hell, then come on in. The least we can do is give you a cup of coffee."

There were no signs anywhere on the building: just a plain warehouse of some kind. In the front was a small room that looked like an office. A light was shining in the window and another somewhere back in the building itself. Willie climbed a ramp and rang a bell. An outer light came on and a door went up. I saw a man standing there in silhouette. There was my third alternate suspect.

He loomed over the Keeler boys like a giant. Behind him I could see a long row of bookshelves, and beyond that another. Books on the shelves, books on the floor: I had been in a hundred places like that, but those had been bookstores, open for business.

The three of them looked at me down the ramp. "Come on in," one of them said.

15

I climbed up the ramp and met a thin, towering creature. "This is Mr. Kevin Simms," Willie said, and Simms shook my hand warily, limply. He was at least six-ten, a beanpole with a severe look on his face. "What's going on?" he said, and immediately the bickering began again. Willie said, "A. J. fuckin' Foyt here lost the goddamn truck is all," and for most of the next minute Simms had to stand between them to prevent what each tried to sell as true mayhem for the other. They screamed insults and I stood back and watched it all and tried not to laugh. In fact it was no laughing matter. Even before I stepped into that room I had a hunch, it wasn't a good one, and I was already planning my exit strategy in case something went suddenly, desperately wrong. Simms seemed to be the authority here, and above all the screaming I had sensed his distrust. This was more than a look I picked up over the bickering brothers, I was getting powerful vibes even with nothing to back it up. But I had learned long ago to always, always trust my own juice. I was still alive because I had listened to that inner voice at least three times when it counted.

Simms would be the dangerous one. I could feel his suspicion rippling across the gap between us: I could see it in his eyes. If something happened, I would take him down first and fast. I would get him with a sucker punch if I had to: a hard shot under the sternum should take out what wind he had. I didn't figure the brothers as patsies, but I liked my odds against the two of them without the severe-looking giant in the mix. At last Simms shouted, "All right, knock it off!" and the Keelers immediately pushed away from each other and stood apart, seething. "What's the matter with you two?" Simms yelled. "Are you both crazy?"

"It was an accident," Wally sulked. "That's all it was, a goddamn accident, and now he's trying to make out like it was some kinda diabolical thing I did on purpose."

"We can do without the language," Simms said. "I hope I don't need to tell you boys again, I don't like having the Lord's name taken in vain."

"Sorry," Wally said.

"You too, Willie."

"*Me?* What did I say?"

"Just . . ." Simms closed his eyes. "Just . . . *watch your mouth.*"

He opened his eyes wide and they stared straight at me: the coldest, bluest eyes I had ever seen. "So, sir, I take it you came along and pulled these two out of trouble."

"I was coming over the pass and I was able to give them a ride," I said. "I was in the right place at the right time."

"You can say that again," Willie said. "Tell you what, Preacher, if it wasn't for Clint here, we'd still be back in that snowbank."

The blue eyes fastened on me. "Your name is Clint?"

"Cliff."

"Then it's good indeed that you came along . . . Cliff."

He didn't seem much interested in last names and that was fine with me. Willie said, "I told him to come in and have some coffee," and the Preacher said, "That's good. You'll have to make some."

"Y'know what?" I said. "Maybe I should move on down the highway. I'm meeting somebody in Alamosa."

"He's got a hot date," Wally said.

I saw Simms react again with distaste.

"When're you meeting this dish?" Wally said.

"She gets off at eleven."

"Alamosa's just up the road," the Preacher said. "Let us extend you some courtesy: warm yourself, and then you can be on your way."

He rolled down the ramp door and locked it. Not a good sign.

I smiled, Mr. All-Easy America. "You ever play basketball?"

"I never had time for games."

"I guess maybe it's just the name, Kevin. You remind me of Kevin McHale."

"I don't know who Kevin McHale is."

"Great basketball player for the Celtics."

"Preacher probably never heard of the Celtics either," Wally said.

Simms gave him a cold look but Wally said, "Preacher'd blanch if I told him what you do for a living."

Simms looked at me. "And what might that be?"

"He's a gambler," Wally said, enjoying the moment. "An honest-to-gosh hossplayer, Preach."

"Hey, you," Willie said from some distance. "How about remembering that this guy saved your butt back there."

"Well, I am most extremely sorry, sir," Wally said, grinning at me. "I certainly had no intention to offend."

"That'll be the damned day," Willie muttered.

"How's the coffee doing?" Simms asked.

"It's getting there," Willie said.

I looked at Simms and said, "You guys mind if I look around?"

"You interested in books?" Simms said.

"Sure, isn't everybody?" I said, knowing full well how few people really are, how pitifully few ever read anything more than the morning newspaper.

"I do read a lot," I said. "And I've got a small collection of first editions."

"What kind of first editions?"

"Mostly modern stuff. Literature . . . you know, fiction. It's nothing special, just books I liked reading and wanted my own copies. Nice stuff in nice jackets, all since around 1945. With a few exceptions."

"Then do by all means, look."

I moved away from them and wandered along the first row. It was all modern, a mix of fiction and fact but all firsts, very nice, and no remainder marks. "Any of this stuff for sale?" I called.

"Everything's for sale," Simms said.

"No prices on any of it, so I just wondered."

"Make yourself a stack, I'll be reasonable."

I found my first signed one: *The Philosophy*

of Andy Warhol, with his drawing of the Campbell's tomato soup can. I knew some dealers were asking big money for that book, but even signed it was far from uncommon. I had sold it several times for around three bills.

"Just so's we know we're on the same page, what do you want for the Warhol?"

"That's signed, you know, with a drawing. But I'd take two hundred for it."

"Okay." I began to stack up some stuff. "I could be in here all night."

"Take your time," Simms said. "I happen to have all night."

"Unfortunately, I've got to be in Alamosa."

"Yes," he said, the distaste still evident on his face. "I almost forgot."

"Coffee's ready," Willie said.

"Never mind the coffee, we're doing business now." Simms tried smiling to blunt the harsh tone of his voice, but his smile, like the rest of him, was ice-cold. To me he said, "I'd have him bring it back to you, except —"

"— books and coffee don't mix."

"Exactly."

I browsed for another twenty minutes and had what I estimated would be eight hundred retail. "I really do have to go."

"Well, have your coffee while the Preacher tallies you up," Willie said.

I took a cup and shot the breeze with Willie. Simms shuffled through the stack and said, "How about five hundred?"

"That'll work." I fished five bills out of my wallet.

The money disappeared into a thin hand. Wally laughed and said, "The hoss racket must be pretty good, hey, Preach?"

I sipped at my coffee. "You a real preacher?"

"Oh, yes, indeed," he said, and in that moment a kind of fever lit up his eyes and I could see the face of zealots everywhere. In that moment a collage of righteous oppressors swirled through my head and I saw our Preacher in medieval days, sentencing harlots to be stoned. I saw his face behind the judge's bench in the modern Middle East, condemning a woman for showing her face in public. I watched him deny help to a sick child, ordering parents to pray and leaving them with their guilt when help failed to arrive. Somehow the failing was theirs, their son was dead because they weren't good enough, they hadn't prayed hard enough, and the Lord wouldn't hear them. Modern medicine would have saved the child but damned his soul. The Preacher moves on and finds another sick kid and keeps on preaching. Jesus, Muhammad, and Moses, he is everywhere. I saw him on the stage, sending the farmer to death in *The Crucible* for refusing to confess, and he was that preacher's real-life role model, Senator Joe McCarthy, damning by innuendo, wrecking lives and getting away with it by preaching to the fear of a gutless majority. I hated zealots, and in the moment he knew that, he saw me as clearly as I had seen him. We spoke cordially but he knew me well. I was the enemy.

He said, "So how are you with the Lord, stranger?"

"Well, Preacher, I do the best I can. You know how it is."

"I know very well how it is. And it may be that you think you do the best you can, that's what a lot of people think. But deep inside you must know that gambling and women are not the way."

"Then I'll have to try and do better." I looked around and said, "Maybe I'll give it all up and become a bookseller."

"That would depend on whether you have a greater goal and what that is. Books can be a simple means to an end. Whatever I make here, for example, goes directly into the service of the Lord."

I wanted to get away from his Lord and my own inevitable damnation. "I bet you'd sell a lot of stuff here if you'd hang out a sign and open it up."

"Undoubtedly. But then I'd have . . . *people* . . . pawing over it. It doesn't take long for *people* to mess things up. People have no idea what's coming."

I looked around: there were still dark corners crammed with books, places that I hadn't even seen yet. "You've been collecting this stuff quite a while I'll bet," I said. "You must have twenty thousand books in here."

"Oh, at least that."

"I get down this way occasionally. I really would like to spend some time here."

"I'm sure that could be arranged, if I'm here. You'd have to take a chance. Just pull up and ring the bell. Now that we've done business together, I'll let you in."

"Maybe I could call ahead."

"I don't have a telephone," he said.

That seemed to settle it, but at that exact moment a phone rang somewhere. I looked at him and he looked at me. I tried not to react, but there are times when no reaction says more than an outcry. I was dying to say, *Thou shall not lie, Preacher,* but

205

instead I picked up my books and sidled toward the door. He moved across the room, surprisingly quick for a big man. I shouldn't have been so surprised: Kevin McHale was pretty quick, too.

He was standing in my way at the ramp door, and in that half moment I wasn't at all certain how it would go. I was right on the verge of throwing that punch but I waited. I looked down at the lock and said, "Well, Preacher, it's been real."

He had about two seconds to get out of my way. He may have sensed that, because he moved aside and flipped open the lock, bent down, and pulled up the door.

"Have a good time in Alamosa," he said, but his tone said the opposite. His tone said, *Get syphilis, go blind, and die in agony, whoremonger.*

"Night, boys," I said to the Keelers.

I hurried down the ramp, got in the car, and backed out into the street.

16

I drove around the block and parked; got out, drew my heavy coat tight, and pulled the hood over my head. I walked back to the corner and stood in the shadows watching the book warehouse. I'd give a thousand dollars to be in there now, I thought: an invisible man or a mouse in the corner. I'd give a hundred if the Preacher had provoked me just a little more. I wished to hell I could've thrown that punch. But that was crazy.

Time passed. Was this going to be another marathon stakeout? I didn't think Zen would help me much this time: I needed to be awake and alert now till something happened. I had slept only a few hours last night, and I knew that soon I'd begin paying a stiff price for that. At the moment I seemed to be okay: I was still in the grip of a heavy blood rush, drawn on by the excitement that always comes with sudden discovery, and I was in no immediate danger of falling asleep on my feet. I might be good through the night, if I had to be.

But within minutes I felt the most crushing fatigue. When that comes on, it comes so damned quickly . . . one minute you're fine, the next you feel your blood beginning to thicken and you're dead on your feet. I toyed with the idea of getting closer. I needed any kind of movement: if I could wiggle under that ramp, better yet crawl under the floor of that room, I might be able to hear something. At least that would keep me going.

I struggled against it for ten minutes and felt myself losing the battle. That relentless light from the office window was having a mesmerizing effect.

Gotta move. Can't stay here. Gotta move now.

I crossed the street and walked boldly up to the ramp. Nothing was going on anywhere. No sound from inside, not even a muffled voice beyond that rolling tin door. I knew I couldn't stand there long . . . one or all of them might come out anytime now, but the crawl space under the warehouse looked so cold and dark that I hated the thought of going there.

I heard a bump and that opened my eyes wide.

A footstep: not inside, but somewhere much more immediate. The sound of a boot on gravel and a smoke being lit.

Now a voice. "That goddamn Preacher better stop talkin' to me like that."

Wally. Apparently they had come out through a door on the other side of the building and were standing just a few feet away. Willie said, "Yeah? What're you gonna do about it?"

"Maybe I'm gonna quit this shit."

"Do I look like I'm stoppin' you? You wanna quit, quit. Soon as we get the truck out and see what the insurance will fix for us, you can go wherever the hell you want."

"You can have the fuckin' truck."

"Big deal. Don't do me no favors, okay?"

"Man, this's bullshit."

"Then quit. You see anybody out here stoppin' you?"

"Nobody anywhere's about to stop *me* if I want to quit. The money ain't that good, and it's a pain in the ass when you gotta watch what you say around the sumbitch *all* the fuckin' time."

"Then fuckin' quit and for Christ's sake stop talkin' about it."

"If I do quit, it'll be my own choice, and I'll do it in my own good time."

"You ain't gonna do a goddamn thing. Just gonna talk, just like always. Talk-talk-talk-talk-talk."

"You're gonna push me one time too many, Willie."

"Talk-talk-taaaaaalk," Willie said in a croaky parrot voice.

"Listen, you son of a bitch —"

"Let's just shut the hell up about it, that's all."

They stood smoking for a while.

"Where the hell is that Preacher?" Wally said.

"He's on the phone," Willie said with exaggerated patience. "Didn't he just tell you he was gettin' on the goddamn telephone?"

"What's he gonna be, on the telephone all damn night? It's colder than a witch's tit out here."

"You'll be warm enough when you get to California."

"You gonna stay here and take care of the truck?"

"Somebody's got to. You'd just fuck that up too."

"Willie, I've really had enough of you and your bullshit."

Willie yawned loudly as the lights went out and a door slammed. I eased down below the ramp level and the Preacher's gaunt silhouette came around the corner. The three of them crossed the street and got into a car. I waited till they were half a block away, then I ran back for my own car. As I pulled onto the highway, I could see them stopped two blocks away at a red light. Easy to follow in a small town, as long as I stayed back far enough and they didn't see my car. But in the next block I had to run a red when they were on the verge of disappearing around a corner.

I had a flashing vision of Lennie Walsh hiding in the weeds with his ticket pad.

I hoped they weren't going straight on to California now.

I felt new waves of weariness and I knew I'd never make it.

They drove out to the edge of town and turned into a long dirt driveway that led back to a house surrounded by trees. I parked and waited till I could see some lights: then I walked back through the underbrush, keeping low as I approached the house and taking it slow as I went. I reached the edge of the trees. I could see them going back and forth between the house and a garage off to one side. I stood still, hiding myself behind a big ponderosa, and at some point they finished whatever they'd been doing in the house and moved out to the garage. A long open space was between my tree and the house, a gap where I'd be a sitting duck if anyone walked out through that half-opened door. I took it anyway: walked across as if I'd been born there and flattened against the dark outer wall. I eased down to the edge, peeped around, and froze.

I was looking down the length of a Ford station wagon, a dozen years old and sporting current Oklahoma plates. Around and beyond it were several dozen bookshelves, all packed with books, most draped with sheets of plastic, I assumed to protect against blowing wind and snow when the door was up. The station wagon had been backed into the garage, the tailgate was up, and the three of them were loading boxes into it: Daedalus boxes, I could see through the windshield and across the front seat. They were being stacked three across, four down and three high, making a solid block, unlikely to shift even on a long ride. Thirty-six boxes, ideal for shipping: I did the math. Four stacks of octavo-sized books could fit in each box: ten books per stack . . . fourteen hundred books, give or take a dozen or two.

"Here's your big list," Preacher said, handing a sheet of paper to one of the Keeler boys. "Study it tonight."

"What time do you want to leave?"

"If we can get out of here by seven, we can be in Salt Lake City tomorrow night. That'll give us plenty of time to work the bookstores the next day."

"Salt Lake's always pretty good," Wally said.

"That's because nobody else thinks it is," Preacher said. "People don't know what to look for."

"Maybe *we're* gettin' better too," Wally said. "Don't you think we're getting better, Preach? Bet you never thought us yokels would ever learn this stuff."

"Don't brag on yourself too much. Vanity is a sin in the eyes of the Lord."

"I'm goin' to bed," Willie said.

Wally laughed. "You gettin' up in the morning to see us off?"

"Not if I can help it. I'm sayin' adios right now. Don't shake me unless the world's ending."

"Don't speak too lightly of that," Preacher said.

He reached up and slammed the tailgate shut. Wally began turning out the lights and I moved away, back into the darkness.

I could still hear them when they came out. Preacher was telling Willie to call him once they had some idea about the damages to the truck. "We'll be in the Motel 6 in Salt Lake. After that I can't say. We'll probably go south across Nevada. You know I don't like to stay in Las Vegas."

"No books there anyway."

"You can catch us in Burbank at the Motel 6, but probably not before next Thursday or Friday, just before the fair sets up."

They walked in the shadows across the yard. "I think this is gonna be a good year," Preacher said. "Good all around. We got some nice things that ought to move fast at the prices I put on 'em. Next year maybe we'll go back East."

They went inside. I waited till the lights went out, then I backtracked out to the highway, picked up my car, and checked into a motel.

I took a shower and called Erin. She answered on the first ring.

"By God, it's good to hear your voice," I said.

"Well, listen to this. Should I be relieved, angry, or something in between?"

"I was hoping for overjoyed. Maybe even sexually aroused?"

"I've never been interested in phone sex. Mildly overjoyed might be the best I can do on such short notice."

"How the hell can anybody be *mildly* overjoyed?"

"I have superb control of my emotions. Where are you?"

"Motel in Monte Vista. I may be going to California."

I told her what had happened. I talked for ten minutes.

"Wow. I should pay more attention when you talk to me, shouldn't I?"

"Yes, you should. That's why you sent me out here, or so I thought."

"And now you want to go to California."

"I'm on the fence about it. It may be a colossal waste of time and money. But on the other hand . . ."

"You don't want to lose them."

A long silence spread out between us.

"I think you should go to California," she said. "Aside from having fun at the book fair, you can do a little work to shore up our alternate suspect theory."

"Have we really got a chance with that?"

"Colorado isn't very clear on it. But if you can find enough evidence to raise a reasonable doubt, that someone else may have killed Bobby, we'd have a real chance to raise it. Those books could be the key. We're moving them out of the house tomorrow."

"Good. Who's moving them?"

"A fellow from town will do the lifting and toting. Parley will be there to watch, along with somebody from the DA's office."

There was a pause, then she said, "We thought about it, talked it over, and there seemed to be more reasons to notice the DA in now than there were not to tell them. If these books do become evidence, which looks increasingly likely with your discoveries, we can't spring their significance on them at the last minute, as much as I'd like to. I'd like to have Parley examine that fireplace ash while the DA's there, but there's a possible downside to that. I don't want them finding something we didn't expect. Laura still seems determined to protect Jerry no matter what, and it would be nice if she didn't incriminate herself any more than she has in her effort to do that."

"So we need to know first if there's a chance of anything else in there."

"Yep. This is actually a good test of her story. But let's talk to her again and make sure before we do something we can't undo. If she waffles, we do nothing with the grate, we keep it to ourselves and leave whatever's there alone."

"Are you okay with that?"

"Sure. My first duty is to defend my client."

"Good. I'll stick with the books for now. Where are they being stored?"

"There's a room they use for an evidence locker just off the sheriff's office. Parley's going to examine each book for signatures and anything else he thinks you might find interesting."

"He seems pretty diligent."

"I think he's great. A good old country lawyer. I can trust him to do things right the first time."

"Unlike some people you know."

I asked about strategy and she said, "As of this moment, paint Bobby as a shadow man who knew strange people and was into things his wife didn't know about. But we've got a lot of work to do there. We'll need to know a lot more about him."

I listened to the telephone noise. At some point she said, "He must've changed a lot since I knew him. I remember him as a happy-go-lucky kid, always laughing, always so open about everything. He wore his feelings on his sleeve."

More time passed. "I'm lining up some good expert witnesses," she said. "I'm getting a psychologist to come talk to our client. We've got to bring him in from Chicago, but he's really superb in the fields of coercion and mental stress. I'm hoping he'll help us construct a good case for why our client lied."

I noticed she still couldn't say her client's name.

She had seen all of the DA's evidence. "I've got copies of the deputy's report, the autopsy, the fingerprints and ballistics from the CBI. If necessary we'll get our own experts to go over it and put our spin on it. We'll see how it goes. They're putting a lot of stock into her confession. And there's no question she handled the gun."

"And the gunshot residue is inconclusive."

"She admits she washed her hands, scrubbed 'em red, in fact, trying to get the blood off. If we can get her confession suppressed, I'll feel a lot better."

"How'd your second interview go?"

"It was okay. Easier somehow than the first. I stayed cool and so did she, for the most part. She cried once; other than that, she was almost like any other client. Of course we both knew better. I explained what we're going to do and how, all subject to change. And I interviewed her at some length about what happened that morning."

"Any surprises?"

"We'll have to comb through it all and talk to her again. I'm having my notes typed up this morning and I'll send a copy to McNamara. You can see the report when he gets it."

"Did you see Jerry while you were in Paradise?"

"Only for a moment. As you can imagine, Bobby's parents are not real eager to help our case. They used 'going to church' as an excuse."

"How did they wind up with the kids?"

"They came out and offered, and that's what Social Services decided."

"And Laura has no say at all in it."

"She's not in a real good position, Cliff. They tend to look at what's right for the kids, not what the defendant wants. And they'd always rather place children with family."

"So what's gonna happen to Jerry?"

"That's not clear yet. His mother was schooling him at home. Old Mrs. Marshall used to be a teacher, long ago, so they may just leave him there till the trial's over. None of this is set in stone. Social Services still has it under advisement. There's a lawyer in the county who's been assigned as guardian ad litem — protector of the children. My guess is they'll leave them there till we all see how the wind blows."

"You've been busy."

Softly she said, "Yeah. And it's never too early to begin preparing for the possibility that we'll lose."

"Did the old folks remember you?"

"Oh, sure. I think they blame me for letting Bobby get charmed away from me. Because I wasn't forgiving enough, somehow I caused his eventual death."

"There's logic for you."

"I'd like you to try talking to Jerry, if you ever stop wandering in the wilderness."

"Why me?"

"Because, in addition to being good with thugs and killers, you're pretty good with kids, kittens, and other furry creatures."

"I'm good with women too," I said, and I heard her cough.

"The old Marshalls," I said. "What kind of people are they?"

"I always thought she was a really sweet woman. He's a bit cold, but you can't have everything. So what are you going to do now? You'll have a fine time trying to follow those guys across nine hundred miles of open country, if that's what you have in mind. They've seen your car, you know."

"I don't need to follow them. I know where they're going."

17

I got almost eight hours sleep and was back on the road by nine. I wasn't about to go over that pass again, even in daylight. The weather forecast was for slippery conditions at the top of the world, with gale-force winds and blowing snow. Instead I went up 285, connected with 50, and stayed with the main highways on the longer, saner loop back through Gunnison and on south to Paradise. I had ten days until the Burbank Book Fair opened in north L.A. It was a two-hour flight from Denver. I could put the time to good use and catch up with my book suspects later. I still had no idea what I'd learn from them; this was nothing more than a grand hunch. But if all else failed, I could buy something great at the fair. I could schmooze with old pals and write off the whole trip as a booking expense. There are worse ways to spend one's time and money.

I arrived in Paradise in the early afternoon and went looking for Parley. I checked at his house and the café, then went on up to the Marshall place. At the top of the hill I saw his car among several others: Lennie Walsh's police cruiser, two black sedans, and a medium-sized, closed-bed truck with a ramp that extended onto the front porch. I pulled into the yard, got out, and started across the yard. Suddenly the judge was standing in the doorway in a plain black business suit, a matching hat, and a red tie, a picture of authority even without his robe. I was astounded to see him there.

"So who're you?"

"I'm with Mr. McNamara, Judge."

"Let me guess. You would be Janeway, the one that started all this goddamn trouble."

"That could be one way of looking at it. I'll be glad to apologize if that makes any difference."

"Don't get smart with me, son. Where'd you get to know so much?"

"I'm a book dealer."

"And I'm Whistler's great-grandfather. Where've you been all day?"

"I had to go down to Alamosa."

"What for?"

"Personal business."

"What personal business would you have in Alamosa?"

"Well, Judge, I can't exactly talk about it.

That's what makes it personal."

He bristled. "If it had anything to do with this case, I've got news for you, it ain't personal. Are you a lawyer?"

"No, sir, I'm not."

"Then how about getting the hell out of here? We've been doing just fine without you, and you can see McNamara later on in town."

"I'd rather stay, if it's all the same to you."

"If it was all the same to me, I wouldn't have said get lost just now, would I?"

I put on my appeaser's face. "Judge, may I please make a point?"

"Let me make one first. How'd you like to spend the night in jail?"

Suddenly Lennie appeared in the doorway, his timing too perfect for coincidence. He stood smiling malignantly behind the judge, just out of the old man's sight.

"I came up to assist Mr. McNamara," I said. "That's really all I'm doing."

"What makes you think Mr. McNamara needs your help?"

"Because I know books. And he doesn't."

"This boy thinks a lot of himself, Judge," Lennie said. "He's a real piss-ripper."

"Where the hell did you come from, Deputy? Don't you know better than to walk up behind me like that?"

"Heard your voices. Sounded like you might need me for one thing or another."

"I need you for anything, I'll call you. Goddammit, make yourself useful. Go tell Miss Bailey this Janeway fellow's finally out here."

"Yessir."

A moment later the young prosecutor came out. She was sharp-looking in her own dark suit with amusement showing around the corners of her mouth. "Well, if it isn't the elusive Mr. Janeway," she said. "Ann Bailey."

We shook hands. "Okay if I take him in, Your Honor?"

Inside, I spoke to her in a whisper. "What the hell's the judge doing up here?"

She took a moment to answer. "Maybe he's just unorthodox."

"How does he think he can preside over a case if he gets involved in it?"

"That would be his problem. And maybe yours."

"Maybe yours in the long run."

"We'll see. I guess His Honor felt an irresistible impulse." She took a deep breath. "This is a very big deal you dumped on us, Mr. Janeway."

"Makes you want to rush right back to town and dismiss the charges, doesn't it?"

"Yeah, right. I was thinking more along the lines of, it gives her a great motive we didn't even know about."

"I see. She killed him for his books, is that what we're thinking now?"

"People have been killed for less than that. How solid are your notions of the values of these things?"

"I didn't know I had given out any solid values."

"They might be quite valuable: Wasn't that how McNamara put it?"

"I don't know, I wasn't there when he said it. Anything could be quite valuable."

"You're cute, aren't you? Nimble too. Have you ever done any fencing?"

"You mean for real?"

"Sure, for real. It's a great sport."

"I'll take your word for that. I usually confine myself to verbal jousts."

"I was on a fencing team in college. We even got to the national finals. I bet I could stick you just full of holes."

We had reached the door to the book room. She stopped and turned: she must've been looking straight up at me but I couldn't see her face in the darkness. "I am told you were a Denver cop," she said.

"A long time ago, in a galaxy far, far away."

"You are much too modest, Mr. Janeway. You're not that old and it wasn't that long ago. You left some deep tracks when you stomped out of the department."

"Easy to find, if all you care about are the newspaper accounts."

"So shoot me at sunrise. I did have a colleague in Denver dig them out and fax them to me. But I always knew you'd have your own version of it, which I would be only too delighted to hear. I might even buy you a cup of coffee for the privilege."

"By the way," I said, rather obviously changing the subject, "what's the judge really doing up here?"

"Whatever I said, it would just be an opinion, and just between us girls."

"I'm all ears."

"He's bored, he's got a gap in his schedule, maybe he just finds the idea of all these valuable books in a house on a remote mountaintop fascinating. As we all do, Janeway, as we all do. But, hey, I agree with you. You could move to have him recuse himself from the case, you'd certainly have grounds. If you wanted to go that route."

"I don't make those decisions."

"Whatever you do, please remember: nothing I've said here is to be repeated."

I heard Parley's voice from the other room. Miss Bailey said, "Don't do anything without telling us first. Don't pick up anything, don't move stuff around — you know the routine. I know you were in here the other day, but it's different now. We're treating this room like a whole fresh crime scene. Got it?"

"Yes, ma'am."

"Then let's go in."

The room indeed looked different today. They had set strobe lights along the perimeter and the scene was harsh-looking, the ceiling garishly white. The bookshelves still looked full of books: on second look I could see that the top shelf had partially been cleared, but at that rate we'd all be here till next Easter.

Parley came over and said, "Am I glad to see you. We're gettin' nowhere fast." Another man was kneeling near the fireplace, looking at something. "Leonard Gill, the DA," Parley said in a whisper. "He's going over everything with a fine-tooth comb. He's trying to establish some kind of rough value for these things, and none of us has a clue. So far he's only allowed two boxes of books to be loaded in the truck. Maybe you can speed things up."

"I don't think so. Let 'em get their own

expert, if that's how the wind's going to blow. I didn't come up here to make their case for them."

"God, we'll be here all week."

"He'll get tired after a while."

"You don't know this boy. Come on, I'll introduce you."

We approached the fireplace. The DA was looking at a book. I craned my neck and saw the distinct handwriting on the title page: *Martin Luther King*.

"Hey, Leonard," Parley said. "This is Cliff Janeway."

His handshake was abrupt, like everything else about him. On balance, I knew I was going to like dealing with Miss Bailey a lot better.

"This book worth any money?" he said as if the world owed him a living.

"Maybe."

"What does that mean?"

"It means maybe it is, maybe it isn't. This is some circus you've got going here."

"I thought you were supposed to help us move things along."

"What do you want from me, a signed affidavit? This isn't an exact science; you don't just prop up a signature and put an ironclad price on it. That's not how it works."

"Then how does it work?"

"It takes research. It takes time. You can't do it here."

"Then where can you do it?"

"If I were doing it, I'd have to bring a ton of reference books out from Denver."

"Then let's get 'em out here."

I laughed; couldn't help myself. "Mr. Gill, I don't work for you. Whatever values I might eventually put on these books is between me, Mr. McNamara, Ms. D'Angelo, and our client."

This snapped him back to reality. "I'm going to have to hire somebody, is that what you're saying?"

"I would think so, yes."

"Under the circumstances, then, maybe you should leave. You're doing nothing but cluttering up the process."

"And what'll you do after I'm gone? Assign some whimsical values based on your own vast knowledge?"

"What exactly are you saying?"

"It's you who's wasting the time. You can be up here for a month of Sundays and you won't have any better idea than you've got right now. Our idea was simply to get the books secured. Get 'em inventoried, get 'em down to the evidence locker, and get a lock on that door. Worry later about what you've got. And by the way, you shouldn't stack books in the box edges-up like that, they'll get cocked."

"Which means what?"

"The spines will get bent out of shape. To put it in basic terms, you're damaging the hell out of Mrs. Marshall's books. I'd advise you to lay 'em flat instead."

He motioned to Miss Bailey and they moved away for a confab. Parley and I walked discreetly out into the hall and talked in low voices.

"Has everything you've seen been signed?"

"So far."

"Jesus Christ," I said. "Martin Luther King."

"Is that worth some money?"

"Hell, *yes.*" I laughed. "Try fifteen hundred and you won't be too far off on the high end. But it's a tricky signature. King is like Kennedy, other people signed for him and left no way for an untrained eye to tell the difference. Secretaries got very good at signing his name."

"Why would he let 'em do that?"

"Because people like King were pestered to death by autograph hounds and book collectors. They allowed their secretaries to sign without worrying about the havoc they might be causing. Evelyn Lincoln signed for Kennedy all the time. Somebody from the campaign brings in a book, it disappears into a back room and comes out signed. Compare it to a facsimile and most times it takes an expert to know the difference."

"Man, that doesn't seem right somehow."

"It isn't right, but it happened anyway. Depended on the nature of the guy in office. Lyndon Johnson signed almost nothing himself; unless it was shoved right under his face, it's all secretarial and autopen stuff. But anything with Harry Truman's name on it is probably real."

I told him about the burning of Jerry's clothes in the back-room grate. "Erin wants to keep that quiet for now." He nodded and we waited some more. In a while Miss Bailey came out and said, "Look, we're willing to cooperate if you will. Let's get the books out of here. Make a list and if you're willing to give us a copy, maybe we can do this reasonably quickly."

Parley looked at me.

"Sure, we'll share the list," I said.

Ten minutes later we were moving books off the shelves as fast as I could check them off against what I had written in my notebook. The money began adding up in my head, a ballpark figure, to be sure. There'd be some surprises, there always are. But at least now the books were safe. At least now I'd have a starting point.

18

I got my first disturbing look at Jerry late that afternoon. The victim's parents had rented a house near the edge of town, not far from where Parley lived. They had taken what they could get on short notice, and the house had no telephone as yet, so Parley said it would be a drop-in-and-take-your-chances affair. I walked over: two blocks up the main road from Parley's place, then right on a dirt road for another half mile. Parley had given me a verbal road map and I knew the house when I came to it. It was well back from the road at the bottom of a hill near the creek, barely visible through the woods.

Jerry was sitting alone in the front yard, watching keenly from a swing as I stopped on the road: a typical kid with a mop of dark hair, wearing corduroy pants and a sweater. Even from that distance I could see awareness in his face, as if somehow he sensed who I was and why I was there. I knew this was impossible but the feeling wouldn't shake. I came into the yard and said, "Hi, Jerry," but I knew better than to approach him before going to the house and announcing my presence. I said, "Is your grandma home?" but if he comprehended, he gave no sign of it. I came up through the trees and moved past him, up the path to the front door.

A woman in her sixties came out as I knocked. "I hope you're not selling anything."

"Erin sent me. My name's Cliff Janeway and I'd like to talk to your grandson for a few minutes."

"What for? He can't talk."

"Yes, ma'am, I'm aware of that. But we thought it might be helpful . . ."

"Helpful to who? She killed my son. Why should we help her?"

"It's not a question of why, Mrs. Marshall. We just want to know what really happened."

"Isn't that fairly obvious?"

"What's obvious isn't always what's true. That's why we have courts, to sift what people think happened from what really did happen."

This could go either way, I thought. I watched her agonize over it for half a minute. "We don't think she did it," I said at last.

"Lawyers always say that. I heard this was cut-and-dried."

234

"Prosecutors like to say that. And newspapers always make it seem that way."

"Well," she said as if momentarily confused, "if she didn't do it . . ."

Her eyes wandered out to the yard, where Jerry hadn't moved, and I saw a slow-creeping awareness come over her.

"My God, are you suggesting —"

"No," I said quickly. "That's not even a hint of what I'm saying."

"Well, if it wasn't her, who else could it be?"

"That's what I'm trying to find out."

She shook her head. I had an urge to tell her that there had been time for a third party to be in that room and her son may have known some shady characters. But I couldn't say that at this point.

"Look, Mrs. Marshall, I know this is difficult. I don't want to make it harder than it already is. I'm hoping you'll understand the difficulty on our side. We just want to find out what happened."

Her eyes narrowed. "You're going to make out like the boy did it."

"Don't do that, Mrs. Marshall. That's not fair to anybody at this point."

"Then what am I supposed to think?"

"Nothing, yet. Just let the facts come out."

"I understood she was going to plead guilty . . ."

"I don't know who could've told you that, but it's just not true."

"She was going to plead guilty. Then you lawyers came, and —"

I felt the interview getting away from me, spinning out of control before it got started. "None of that is true," I said in a slightly pleading voice. "Look, I know you wouldn't want to send her to prison if she's innocent. Even if there are hard feelings, nobody would do that."

I let that settle on her for a minute. Then she said, "What do you think this child can tell you? . . . This little boy who can't even speak his mother's name?"

"I don't know."

She thought about it. "Am I required to allow this?"

"Not at this moment."

"What happens if I say no?"

"I could ask for a court order. They'd probably want to videotape it and do it in the courthouse. They might have some psychologist brought in from Denver to ask the questions. I'd rather not do that now, unless it's necessary."

She thought about that and took her time.

"If I did let you talk to him, I'd have to be there."

"Absolutely."

"I'd want to know what questions you're going to ask him."

"That depends on him, I don't have anything written out. Maybe I'd just want to say hello for now."

"I don't know what good you think that'll do."

"I don't know either. Maybe none."

"If you upset him, if you start asking questions I don't like —"

"I'll leave. I promise."

Again she wavered. She was curious now but suddenly a little afraid as well. I could see the fear in her eyes as she stared out at Jerry on the swing. She turned and looked up at me and I could almost read the fear in her face — *What if he's right? What if that kid murdered Bobby, and if he did do that, what's to stop him from killing us all in our sleep?* I wished I could reverse the clock and take back everything that might have put that idea in her head. I wanted to go back a few hours and rethink the wisdom of coming out here in the first place, but there was no going back: there never is.

"Come on," she said abruptly, and I followed her out into the yard. Jerry sat up

237

straighter at our approach, like a bird watching an animal it has never seen before. His eyes never left my face: he seemed wary, not afraid, and as we came closer, I noticed a splash of freckles across both cheeks and his nose. He looked like a kid I might have known in my own childhood.

"Jerry," Mrs. Marshall said. "This is Mr. Janeway. He just wants to say hello."

I sat on the ground across from him and looked into his blue eyes. "Hi, Jerry," I said. He looked so familiar to me: it was almost spooky, till suddenly I realized that his face was the spitting image of Alfalfa from the old *Our Gang* comedy shorts.

"You look like one of the Little Rascals," I said. "Anybody ever tell you that?"

I asked if he had ever seen those comedies on TV.

"They don't have TV here," Mrs. Marshall said. "Just as well, judging from what's on it."

"It doesn't matter," I said. "For what it's worth, you look like Alfalfa. He was a great movie star, long before I was born."

I said, "He's the one I always liked as a kid."

I reached out my hand. "It's good to know you."

"Shake the gentleman's hand, Jerry," Mrs. Marshall said.

Reluctantly Jerry put his hand in mine and I squeezed it and held it for a moment. There was something about this kid: even if he couldn't show his feelings, I could almost sense the hurt in him. I felt him tremble and I thought, *Oh, kid, if there's any way I can take some of that pain on my shoulders, let me have it, I'll take it all if you'll just give it to me.* "Don't be afraid," I said. "I'd like to be your friend."

I reached out to touch his shoulder but he drew back sharply. "It's okay," I said.

I was about to say I was a friend of his mother's when Mrs. Marshall said, "I told you. Didn't I tell you you couldn't talk to him?"

"His arm seems to be hurt," I said.

"It's fine."

But I had a hunch, as strong as any I could remember. Before she could object, I had touched his shoulder and peeled down the sweater, revealing an ugly bruise.

"How'd he get that?"

"He fell off the swing. It's fine, it's nothing to worry about, leave him alone. You had no right to touch him."

I backed quickly away. "Can I ask him about what happened that day?"

"I don't think that's wise."

"Only if he saw it. If that bothers him, I'll leave."

"It makes no sense. Why ask the question when you know he can't answer you?"

"If I just asked him . . . what happened to his dad."

"You're going to upset him."

"Jerry," I said.

"I think you should leave now," Mrs. Marshall said.

"Okay." I was good and goddamned frustrated, but a deal is a deal.

"It's been good meeting you, Jerry."

Suddenly he grabbed my hand and held me tight. Mrs. Marshall said, "Jerry, you stop that," but I looked back at her and told her it was okay. "It is *not* okay," she said. "How do you expect us to teach him any manners if you come behind me and say that's okay?" I offered a sad little apology but I was looking at Jerry when I said it. His mouth opened and I had the crazy thought that he was about to speak, and that once he did, all the mysteries of his universe would roll out in a deep, bassy voice. But Mrs. Marshall said, "I think that's enough," and I got up slowly and followed her back to the house, giving Jerry a wink over my shoulder. At the door I turned and waved to him.

Inside, Mrs. Marshall fidgeted nervously. "What did that prove?"

I just looked at her, which made her more fidgety.

"You had no right to touch him. You shouldn't have done that."

"I'm sorry it upset you," I said. But I didn't apologize for touching him.

"What'll happen now?" she said.

"That'll be up to Erin. I'm sure she'd like to keep him out of it but I don't know if that'll be possible."

"Did he really see what happened?"

"He might have."

"Oh, God. God, what a thing," she said, and her voice was thick. "Do you actually think he could've done this himself?"

"No," I said, as earnestly as I could. "Nobody thinks that, Mrs. Marshall, I promise you."

In fact, I didn't know what to think. All I could go by was my gut.

I looked around at the sparse furnishings. She said, "We had to move in here on a moment's notice. Good thing we're retired."

"What about the other two kids?"

"My husband has them. They went downtown for some ice cream." She looked at the clock. "They'll be back any minute."

She sensed an unasked question and said, "Jerry certainly would've been welcome to go with them, if that's what you're thinking, but he didn't seem to care. I'm sure they'll bring him back some."

I nodded a *That's good* motion and again she looked around uneasily.

"Mrs. Marshall, may I ask you a few more questions?"

She looked wary but she didn't say no so I pushed ahead.

"Has Jerry shown any unusual behavior since he's been with you?"

"What do you mean? I haven't been around him long enough to know what's usual. All his behavior is unusual, wouldn't you say?"

"Nightmares. Does he ever scream in the night?"

"If that child has ever uttered a sound, nobody I know has heard it."

"What about nightmares? You can have those even if you don't scream."

She didn't answer for a minute, long enough to be an answer in itself. "Sure, he's been troubled," she finally said. "God help him, who wouldn't be?"

"How can you tell?"

"I'll wake up and find him standing beside my bed. Just standing there trembling." She looked worried, as if suddenly the thought frightened her.

"Does he do this every night?"

"I've only had him for two weeks. But, yes, so far he's not had a night when he's slept all the way through."

"What do you do when you find him like that?"

"Put him back to bed. What else is there?"

"Does he ever resist that?"

"Just that first night."

"What did he do then?"

"Struggled a little. Got away from me and ran outside."

"Where outside?"

"Back to the shed, that ramshackle old thing behind the house."

"Was he trying to hide?"

"Who knows what's in that child's head? Whatever's troubling him, I couldn't leave him there in the middle of the night."

We looked at each other.

"Well, could I?"

"No," I said. "Of course you couldn't."

"Don't be judgmental, please don't do that. We're really doing the best we can here. We're trying to help, but this isn't the greatest situation in the world, either."

I wasn't aware I had looked judgmental and said so. "I'm sure it isn't easy for you, Mrs. Marshall."

I thought hard about my next question before I asked it: I didn't want to scare her more than I already had, but it had to be asked.

"Have there been any signs of anybody around the house?"

"What signs? You mean like a prowler?"

"No, I didn't mean that. Never mind, it's a silly thought."

But it wasn't a silly thought and, yes, it had frightened her. Something had certainly scared Jerry. Maybe it was just a nightmare after all: God knew the kid was entitled to a bad dream if he had seen something.

"What is it you're trying to find out? What do you want from us?"

Perhaps I hadn't known until that moment, but hearing the question hurled at me in that tense voice, suddenly I did know. *I want to know he's safe,* I thought, but could not quite bring myself to say. I didn't like that bruise on his shoulder and I didn't like the old woman's evasive eyes. To call his safety into question would disrupt them all, maybe for no good reason.

But the fact remained: if Jerry hadn't killed Marshall, somebody else had. I looked across the road at the gathering dusk, at the trees now deep in gloom. Somebody, I thought: maybe someone he saw, maybe someone who saw him.

19

I walked back to town and ate in the Main Street café. I didn't want to go back to Parley's; didn't want to talk to anybody about what I had seen or what its significance might be; most of all I didn't want to be talked out of what I knew I was about to do. After a mediocre meal I walked out to the edge of town where I had seen a bar called the Red Horse Tavern. I went in, blended with the dark, and sat in a corner nursing a beer.

Two hours later there I was again, hiking back on the road to the grandparents' house. My feet made soft crunching noises in the frozen snow and I felt the stinging air around my eyes and nose. I had just a trace of a low moon lighting my way around a thin, circular cloud that hung in my face like a halo. This wasn't much help: the tall hills on both sides blotted out most of the deeper countryside and I could only see the road, and nothing past the ditch, for thirty yards ahead. Beyond that it was all hope-and-grope, a shadow world broken by the dim and very occasional light of a cabin off in the trees. In the woods away from the road the night was as black as I had ever seen it, murk that couldn't be penetrated without a light.

I had bought a penlight at the five-and-dime and this I clutched in my fist as I walked, keeping my hands in my pockets and letting the moon show me the way for as long as it would. I could think of a thousand places I'd rather be than out here tonight, but I had a hunch and I couldn't shake it. I psyched myself up for another long watch.

I trudged over a rise, vaguely remembering the terrain from my trek up here a few hours before. The night was bleak and a wind whistled down through the pines, chilling even through my heavy coat. I started down the long incline to the arroyo at the bottom where the creek ran through. The air wasn't yet cold enough to freeze the creek over, and I could hear the trickle about sixty yards away, so much louder here in the pitch-dark night than it had been in the daytime. I remembered a small bridge where the creek curled around from the foot of the mountain and darted across the road. Beyond that, far back in the trees, was the house. I still couldn't see the place: it was fairly early yet, nine o'clock would be a good guess, but there were no lights anywhere.

I crossed the bridge and a few minutes later reached the driveway, a long, looping dirt road where I could finally see a faint light from the front room. It flickered through the trees. No *Tonight Show* back there. No TV to lull them into some nightly catatonic state of mind. I had a feeling that the old Marshalls would be going stir-crazy after less than two weeks of it. I stood on the road, lost in the shadows of the trees around me, and I stared at the light from the cabin and wondered what to do next.

I did nothing for a while. At some point I stepped into the drive and groped my way along it. The sound of the creek got louder as the house emerged in a tiny ring of light. I could see a partial outline of the porch, only from the front door to the living room window, but it was hard to get better bearings in the deep mountain night. How close did I dare go, what would I say if someone popped up and demanded answers, what was I looking for anyway? — these were questions that defied easy answers. I stood there for at least another ten minutes and nothing got any clearer.

The answer I wanted was inside the house, not out here.

I didn't trust the Marshalls with that kid's welfare.

There it was: I didn't trust them. I had only that bruise to hang this on, a strange place, I thought, for a bruise to be, from a fall off the swing.

As if anything is ever that plain and that simple in this life. I hadn't yet met the old man but there was something about the old woman, some kind of fear of her own. For the moment that was plain and simple enough, and that's why I was out here tonight.

Oh, God, Erin: Am I about to screw your case beyond redemption? I hoped not, but I remembered Jerry's Alfalfa face and I couldn't just walk away from him.

I was now no more than twenty yards from the front porch. The house was deadly quiet. Nothing moved except that rushing stream somewhere beyond the shed in the backyard. I felt desolate. It boggled my mind that anyone would consign three children to this after what had just happened to their father. Those kids needed music and light and whatever good cheer there might be in the world. But this was what they got from a system that never had enough time, never enough people.

I stood just outside the tiny circle of light cast by the living room lamp. I stood there for another twenty minutes. Didn't move at all until I saw a shadow pass across the front room window.

It was the grandfather. He had turned and was now standing with a drink in his hand staring out at the yard. I dropped back a step and saw him look over his shoulder and say something. He took a deep hit from his drink, emptying the glass, then he poured another. I could see the Seagram's label clearly in the lamplight, and he was taking it straight-up from a tall highball glass, enough to put him on the short list for a liver transplant if he wasn't there already.

I stood in the dark and watched him drink.

I stood in the dark.

After a while he moved across the room. There was a narrow side window and I eased over that way, one step at a time. The light was dimmer there, probably all of it coming from the one lamp near the front of the room. Here we go, I thought.

Here we go.

I walked boldly across the lighted space and slipped around the edge. Flattened myself against the dark wall, as I'd done at the Preacher's place, and felt my way along until I could take a quick look inside.

The two of them sat facing each other. He was slumped on the sofa, a big man with slate gray hair and mean eyes. Okay, now I had seen him. Now I could be fair about it and say I had seen the bastard and I didn't like him. Good objective judgment. I didn't like his ass. I had the uneasy feeling that either of them would gladly sell Laura Marshall down the river, guilty or not.

She was in a chair staring beyond him at the wall: a picture of two people going mad, just as I had imagined it. She said something but I couldn't make out what. He took another swig of whiskey and that was his response. She said something else or perhaps again and his head snapped up. He yelled, "Shut up, goddammit, shut up!" His booming voice carried easily through the wall. The kids would sleep well through that, I thought. He leaned forward with his elbows on his knees, his head down and the drink in his hands, and what he said then was inaudible, but when he looked up, I could fry an egg in the hate on his face.

There's trouble in Paradise, I thought.

These were not happy campers.

Not happy with the kids. Not happy with each other or themselves.

Then why are they here?

Why face three months in hell if it wasn't for the love of the children?

I backtracked into the woods, away from the light, and stood watching. I stood there thinking. Brooding.

I circled the house, carefully getting the lay of the land. A back porch opened from the kitchen, and I could see through the screen, on through the room into a short hallway. I saw the light from the front reflecting off a stove and a refrigerator, and on either side were the two bedrooms. One for the old folks, one for all three kids. I moved away from the porch and looked into a window, pale with the distant light. Again the door was open and there was enough light from the front to make out a few objects. I saw what was probably a dresser with a mirror and a small table and a double bed, empty. This was where the old people slept. I didn't dare look in the other window: I had a vision of Jerry lying in that room, staring at the glass, ready to be scared out of his wits if a face suddenly popped up.

At least I knew where things were. I circled the house and stood in the dark.

Time passed and the light from the window was hypnotic.

Eventually it went out and I stood trapped by the night, sealed in a drippy world of uncertain blindness.

This was infinitely more depressing than the stakeout on the ridge. Then I knew that dawn could not be far off: now I had no faith that the sun would ever come up again. Now I couldn't see the house, I couldn't use my light. I couldn't see the trees or even a hint of anything out there in the black. I knew from my police days how these stakeouts could weigh down the spirit. Too many nights just sitting and watching got to everybody eventually. Even in the old days, with a partner to talk to, with food and light and the steady chatter of the police radio, the negative effects tended to accumulate. Too much of it made reality slip away. But I stood leaning against a tree, hanging in there, struggling to count to ten but seldom making it past four.

I don't know when the shock came — it was well after midnight, maybe much later. Suddenly a light went on in the kids' room. I must have been asleep on my feet. I felt it first — sight came later, like an exploding galaxy — and I jerked back, lost my balance, and fell facedown on the rocky earth. I rolled over and the vision of that yellow-white window hit me again. My heart leaped into fast-forward and I felt my hands, slick with blood. I felt a stinging pain where I had tried to break my fall and had hit the rocks. I rolled over and got to my feet, pressed my hands against my pants, and held them there just as Jerry appeared in the window. With a jerky, frantic look he pushed up the sash and stuck his hand through the crack, flailing at the cold air. I heard a child's voice from inside the house: "Gramma, Jerry's being bad again!" Jerry leaped back from the window. Almost immediately the door flew open and he came running out wearing only his pajamas. He rushed across the yard and into the trees toward the road.

A minute later the woman appeared on the porch, dressed in a nightie with a coat thrown over her shoulders. In another minute the man loomed up beside her. "I am getting *god*damn tired of this shit!" he bellowed at the darkness.

He screamed at the night: "*Jerry!* Goddammit, you get back in here!"

"Ralph," the old woman said.

"Don't Ralph me." He came to the edge of the porch. "Boy, you better knock this off! If I've gotta come find you again, it'll be too damn bad!" He waited a moment, then yelled, "*Jerry!* I'm not kiddin', you get your ass back in here, *right now!*"

Nothing happened: no sounds above the constant noise of the creek, no movement in the woods where Jerry had disappeared.

"That goddamn little fucker!" the old man said. "I oughta leave him out there."

"You can't do that," the woman said. "Jesus, Ralph, he'll freeze to death."

"Let him freeze, the little bastard. I didn't sign on here to put up with this."

"Ralph, stop this and go find that boy before something awful happens to him."

"I'll find him, all right."

"Don't you hit him again."

"Don't you hit him again," he mimicked.

Ralph disappeared into the house and a minute later he came out fully dressed. He charged off the wrong way into the woods, yelling and kicking at the undergrowth.

Gradually his voice began to fade as he went back toward the creek.

I headed down the other way, toward the road. A path cut through the trees and at the end of it I found the kid shivering and huddled in the ditch. I reached out my hand to him and he cringed.

"Hey, Jerry. You don't want to stay down there, kid." I opened my coat and held out my hand to him. "Come on up here. Come get warm."

I shined the little light in my own face. "I met you this afternoon, remember? Come here, I won't hurt you."

I got down on my knees and handed him the light.

"You musta been having a bad dream, son."

Yeah, a dream called life.

I knew he was cold, I could hear his teeth chattering, but I didn't try to rush him. I sat on the ground and let him touch my hand, and after a while he did crawl into my lap and I pulled the coat tight and held him against me till he stopped shivering. I could feel his heartbeat, his breath against my neck, both hands clutching my shirt.

"It's okay, kid." I touched his head. "It's okay now."

This was something to say and it filled the moment. But in real life I had no idea what was okay, and in that moment I couldn't imagine what to do next.

Follow your heart, Janeway. That's what got you here.

My heart was full of anger.

I didn't know what Ralph's problem was and didn't care. Right now, at this moment, I only wanted to kick him a new asshole.

Do that and explain it to the judge.

Ralph had custody and I had only a bad attitude, which grew worse every minute.

But in the heat of that moment I didn't care about the judge or the old man's custody. I sat on the edge of the ditch and Ralph's voice got louder as his search widened. In the same time my own choices winnowed downward from almost nothing.

I could take the kid home with me, the riskiest and craziest thing to do.

I could give him up, which I hated.

I could confront the old man here in the dark woods.

Intimidate the bastard. I was good at that, I knew how it was done. It had failed to work once, with a brutal thug who finally had to be convinced the hard way.

I heard footsteps. He was coming now, tearing through the underbrush. "Jerry," I said into my coat. "You've got to go back."

His fists tightened on my shirt and his head burrowed under my chin. Something about this kid, something other than the obvious, touched me deep, but here and now I couldn't find a handle for it.

"I'm sorry, kid."

I couldn't elaborate: I was out of time. The old man loomed up not twenty yards away, a shadow talking furiously to himself. "I'll kill that little bastard," he said.

I felt my own fury rise up to meet him.

"I'll kill him," he said, and in the same heartbeat I got up close, right in his face. "How'd you like to try that with somebody your own size?"

He cried out, spun away, dropped his light.

I kicked it out of his reach and he fell trying to get it.

For God's sake don't touch him, I thought.

I didn't need to, he scared easy enough. I could taste this old man's fear and I liked the taste of it. Killer-soft, with snakelike malice, I said, "How'd you like to try that with me, Ralph?"

I had truly scared the hell out of him. He wheezed, hyperventilating, and finally managed to croak, "Who the f-f . . ."

I covered Jerry's ears and said, "I am your worst fuckin' nightmare, old man."

I heard him struggling to his feet.

"Who're . . . y-y . . . who'r . . ."

"You touch this kid again and you'll find out who I am."

"How'd . . . d'you know . . . m-m-n . . . ame?"

"I know everything about you, Ralph. I know how you like to beat up little kids."

"That's a-g-g-od-amn-l . . . lie."

I let the moment pass in ominous silence.

"I didn-n't mean that. Some-omebody's t-t-ellin' you lies, tha's all . . . I . . . meant."

"You must think I'm playing around with you, grandpa. Is that what you think?"

"No . . . G-g-od, n-o . . ."

"Because if it is, you are making a monster mistake."

He tried to speak but his voice quaked and he couldn't get it out.

"Have you been listening to me at all, old man?"

He tried a single watery word but sucked air in through his nose and lost it.

"Was that a yes, Ralph?"

"Y . . . y . . ."

"That's good. Maybe you just don't realize how soft the human body is. Maybe that's your problem. You don't know how easy a body can be broken or torn up. How easy an arm can be pulled out of its socket, or a skull fractured . . ."

"Oh Christ . . . oh Christ . . . please J-es-s . . . on't do that . . ."

"I'm not talking about me, Ralph, I'm

259

talking about you. You push a kid around, you can mess him up bad."

"I nev . . . n-n-n, uh, n-never hurt him . . . he just gets wild . . . n . . . eeds d-d-dis-pline."

"Maybe you're the one who needs the discipline."

I felt him cringe back into the dark, a typical coward. "Please . . . don't do that . . . p-p-lease don't . . ."

A moment passed. In the distance I could hear the old woman calling Ralph's name. Ralph tried to say *please* again but couldn't quite get it out.

"That's much better. *Please* is a good, kind word. You should use it more often."

I picked up his light and tried to give it to him, but it fell short and I left it there. I wanted to brush off his coat for effect but didn't.

Don't touch the old fucker, I thought. *Not even a finger. Don't touch him at all.*

"Your grandson is cold, Ralph. Take him inside and warm him up. Give him some hot chocolate. And do yourself a helluva big favor. Remember what I said."

The night has a thousand eyes and I told him that.

"You so much as touch him again and I'll know."

I uncovered Jerry's ears and let the quiet night surround us all.

"I'll know, Ralph," I said.

I am in deep shit, I thought. But if anything had felt right in a long time, that had.

I turned away and left Jerry in the woods with his so-called grandfather.

20

A judge is the ruler of his kingdom. He sits on his throne and makes decisions that affect people profoundly and change their lives. If he's a good judge, his decisions are not only good law, they are made with conscience and rooted in humility. If he's not a good judge, he comes to his throne steeped in arrogance and concerned mainly with his own ego. If he's a bad judge, he combines the arrogance and the ego with bellicose intolerance, and, in the worst cases, ignorance.

Sometimes he may go too far and get overturned. Occasionally he is reprimanded or removed from the bench, but all too often he's left alone and his bad decisions stand for years, maybe decades, till the principals die or just don't care anymore. The law has many soft spots where there is no black-and-white and the judge's discretion is broad. A capital offense in one kingdom has far fewer dire consequences a few miles away, in the land across the river where laws are different. This is not a job for ego, yet the job nurtures and in fact demands it. The job cries out for wisdom and compassion and anger, and half a dozen other qualities that are incompatible or almost impossible to find beating in a single heart. In the country of the law the one-eyed judge is king. Contempt of court is a potent weapon and it too is a sword with a wide blade. The judge can be lenient, understanding, or an absolute tyrant. Mess with the judge and you can go to jail.

I had met all kinds of judges in my police career: I remembered bleeding-heart liberals who wore their politics into the courtroom and mean-spirited old bastards who suffered no slight, real or imagined, to their dignity. I had known a judge who had ruthlessly punished defendants because of a dislike for their attorneys, and another who was a notorious woman-hater, finding any flimsy excuse to let vicious rapists back on the street. A lot of judges hold a cop's balls to the fire: such are the times we live in. One judge I knew had the memory of an elephant, had been quick to form a bias and quicker yet to take offense. He had wielded his power heavily and had been known to remind attorneys years later of small incidents he had found offensive. Most judges I had met were at least okay; a few had been superb, and one on the lowest end of the spectrum was a moron who had barely eked out a passing grade on his fourth try at the bar exam. Amazingly, he survived on his suburban-Denver-county court bench for almost twenty years and finally died there.

The Honorable Harold Adamson seemed to possess at least some of the bad traits. I knew he was eccentric: I couldn't think of any other judge in all my days on the fringes of Denver law who'd have gone up to the scene of a case he'd be hearing. The judge wouldn't want to get that close; judges just didn't do that. Still, Parley considered his knowledge of law sound, his understanding of due process at least okay. It was his ego that got in the way, overruling knowledge and dismissing due process when it suited him. Since his appointment to the bench a year ago, he had become like a new cock in a barnyard, and that night I had a hunch I was about to fall directly into his crosshairs.

In the best of all worlds old Marshall would have accepted the heartfelt advice I had left with him and would suddenly have become endowed with infinite kindness and the spirit of grandfatherly love. He had seemed thoroughly frightened, but I knew that, like the judge, I had stepped over a line and my own comeuppance was a phone call away. I opened my eyes in the morning as a car door slammed, and when I went to the window, Lennie was standing in the front yard smoking. He finished his weed, tossed the butt in the snow, and headed up the walk to the front door. I met him there.

"Mr. Janeway?" His official voice: the ticket-writer, as if we had never met.

I stared at him and he said, "Wonder if I might have a word with you."

I stared some more. This wasn't my house, it wasn't my place to invite him in.

"We had a complaint last night from a Mr. Ralph Marshall. Are you familiar with that gentleman?"

"I know who he is."

"I thought maybe you would. Apparently some skulker came out to his house in the middle of the night, threatened and terrorized himself, his wife, and the children who have been put under his care. You wouldn't know anything about that, would you, sir?"

"Did he say I did?"

"What Mr. Marshall said or did not say is between himself and our office. Right now, would it be too much trouble for you to answer my question? *Now,* sir. It's really a simple question. Did you threaten Mr. Marshall last night?"

"Mr. Marshall wrenched his grandson's arm damn near out of its socket. I told him not to do that anymore."

"You didn't knock him to the ground?"

"I never touched him."

"That's not what he says. And he's got scrapes and bruises all over his face. Any idea how those would've gotten there?"

"Mr. Marshall was drunk. He fell in the dark woods."

"So you say. Doesn't sound like you're denying it was you out in the woods."

Behind me I heard Parley come into the hall. "What's goin' on here?"

"It's nothing," I said. "The deputy wants to ask me a few questions."

"About what?"

Lennie handed me a piece of paper. I recognized the look of it.

"This is a summons ordering you to appear later this morning at a hearing in Judge Adamson's court."

"Hold on, what's this about?" Parley said. "We haven't had notice of any hearing."

"It's a summons to appear at a hearing on a temporary restraining order against your client."

Parley laughed. "You call this notice? What the hell's going on here?"

"Look, I came out here to serve him and now he's been served."

Lennie turned and walked away.

Parley stared at me. "Jesus H. Christ."

"All I did was talk to him, Parley."

"Well, goddammit, that's enough. Tell me exactly what happened."

We sat at the kitchen table and I told him.

"God almighty," he said. "Haven't you got any sense at all?"

"Apparently not. I didn't have a lot of time to think about it."

"Christ in a hot-air balloon."

"Look," I said, "I want you to stay away from this. For the sake of your client, consider me resigned from your case, as of six o'clock last night."

"So now what, you're gonna be your own lawyer? You really are losing your marbles, kid."

"Yeah, I know. What can I say, I screwed up. I want to stay away from your case as much as possible from here on out. Don't bail me out, don't put in any appearances. If you want to do something, call Social Services and get that kid out of there."

"You're outta your goddamn mind.

Erin's gonna love this."

A few hours later I met the judge in his arena.

The courtroom was empty, except for the judge, the deputy, and a reporter. The hearing was announced and the judge peered down from on high.

"Well, you're just like Charlie Chaplin, aren't you? You seem to pop up when I least expect you, and when I do expect you, you're not there. Would you explain to me, please, what the hell you were doing out at the Marshalls' last night?"

"I went to see the kid. I had visited with him that afternoon and I was concerned for his safety."

"What about his safety?"

"He's being abused by his grandfather."

"What does that mean? You don't mean to insinuate he's . . ." He made an obscene gesture with his hands.

"Not that kind of abuse."

"What, then?"

"He beats the kid."

"Is that all? Listen, a little birching never hurt a kid yet, and from what I've heard, that one's a handful."

"He can't *speak*, Your Honor, and I'm not talking about a little birching. I'm talking about a *beating,* Judge, a beating bad enough to leave his whole shoulder black."

"In case you hadn't heard, Mr. Janeway, there's a system in this state. Social Services is in charge of the kids. There's a guardian ad litem who's been appointed —"

"I know all that, Your Honor . . ."

"Then why didn't you report all this to the guardian?"

"There wasn't time."

"So you thought you could ride in there and rescue this kid yourself. Is that about what happened?"

The hell with it: I launched into the tale. I told him about my interview with the grandmother and my growing sense that something was wrong. Call it an old cop's instinct: call it a feeling, a hunch. I told him about the bruise on Jerry's shoulder and how I had found it. I told him about the grandfather and how he had chased the kid through the woods, threatening him with more violence. "That's a toxic old man the kid's been put with, Judge; he's already been slapped around at least once and would have been again if I hadn't been there. The old man drinks like a fish and talks like a drunken sailor. Maybe he loves the hell out of his real, blood grandchildren and hates this one, I don't know. Last night Jerry ran away and hid freezing in a ditch, wearing nothing but a pair of pajamas, while the old man thrashed drunkenly through the bushes, cursing and threatening to kill him. I'm afraid for his safety, and if somebody doesn't take him out of there, whatever happens to him is on all your heads, all of you, I don't care who's got jurisdiction or who wants to pass the buck to some other department. I'm going to make it a personal cause to see that everybody in the state of Colorado knows about it."

Stunned silence. For long seconds the judge stared as if he couldn't believe what he'd just heard. Then he leaned over his bench and said, "You *dare* come in here and talk to me like that. My courtroom is not a soapbox. You must want to go to jail, fella."

"Lock me up, I don't give a damn, but somebody's got to do something for that boy. This is a kid who may have witnessed the bloody murder of the only father he knew, and now the *system*'s got him sentenced to a dark house that's no better than some prison camp, with an alcoholic who seems to resent the hell out of him,

270

and I can't get you to care. If that kid doesn't get help soon, he may go off his rocker for good, so put me in jail if that's your only answer."

"Is this your doing, Mr. McNamara? Is this how you're going to try this case?"

I turned and saw Parley sitting behind me. "Well, Judge —"

"Don't blame McNamara for what I say. This has nothing to do with his case."

The judge rapped his gavel. "You're in contempt of court. Five-hundred-dollar fine."

"I won't pay it."

The judge laughed. "You are a piece of work, aren't you? You waltz in here and expect who? — me, I guess — to take those children away from their grandparents, who have relocated from Denver, gone to a helluva lot of trouble, and you expect me to do this on your say-so."

"In the first place, they are not the grandparents of the older boy. They came out here to take care of their dead son's blood children. There's no reason to assume that they care at all about —"

"You're wasting my time. What the hell is wrong with you?"

"I must be stupid, I guess. With all due respect, sir, one of us seems to be."

"Why, you arrogant young snot. How'd you like to double that fine?"

"Judge, at this point I don't care."

"Then go ahead, sit in jail and think about it. On Friday I'm leaving to hear a case next week in another county. If you haven't had a drastic change of attitude by then, you can sit there for three weeks till I get back again."

He shuffled through some notes on his bench. He looked up and said, "Jail this bastard."

"Yes, *sir.*" Lennie approached the bench and said, "Put out your hands, cowboy."

Behind me, Parley said, "Your *Honor,* I don't think the handcuffs are necessary."

"I don't tell the deputy how to handle his prisoners. You break the law, you might just get humiliated."

Out in the yard, Lennie gave me a shove. I crossed the lot in shackles and people watched from the sidewalk.

"Step lively, dickhead," Lennie said. "Your ass belongs to me now."

"You belong in a circus, Lennie," I said.

21

I was almost a model prisoner. The sheriff asked what had happened and the deputy told him he had brought me in for contempt, trespassing, menacing, and half a dozen other possible charges. The sheriff nodded and said, "Thank you, sir. It always helps to know why we have people in our hotel here. Did he give you any idea how long you're to be a guest of our county?" I told him it seemed to be open-ended, probably till I had a change of heart. The sheriff said, "Any idea when that might be?" and I said, "Sometime between tomorrow morning and whenever hell freezes over." The two of us laughed while Lennie stood apart and found it all unhappily unamusing. The sheriff said, "Goddammit, Lennie, get them handcuffs off this man," and I was taken, uncuffed, back to the cellblock, which consisted of half a dozen cells and one big barred room, the bull pen.

Three of the cells were occupied: two Indians and a mean-looking white guy, all of them, I later learned, being held for drunk-

and-disorderly. I was put across from the bull pen, away from the others, where we could all look across and see each other. There's not much privacy in jail. The cell consisted of a four-by-eight barred room with a bed and a toilet. I figured the doors were opened during the middle of the day and the men were allowed to stretch themselves in the relative expanse of the bull pen. I sat on my cot and stared at the wall.

Parley came in within the hour. We met upstairs in the conference room.

"Janeway, did I have a mental lapse in there or did you really call the judge a moron?"

"I called him stupid. There's a difference. A moron can't help what he does. A stupid man can, but does it anyway. That's what makes him stupid."

"Look, I'm trying to get you out of here, but unless you crawl up there and kiss his ass in open court, it's gonna take some serious finagling. At least I think you got his attention about the kid."

"Then my living has not been in vain. What's happening?"

"We called the guardian ad litem, who's having the kids picked up today. He's going to talk to them away from the grandparents. Even if Jerry can't talk, the little ones might know what happened to him."

"That's a start. If that doesn't work, I may have another ace up my sleeve."

He closed his eyes. "Dare I ask?"

"There's a fellow I know at *The Denver Post*. I did him a few favors when I was a cop. He specializes in tearjerkers and knows how to write 'em. I think he'd love this story. Former Denver cop jailed by Podunk County judge, who won't give kids an even break. I think he'd walk all the way out here for that. I'd be disappointed if it didn't make page one, under the fold. Streamed across the top if I get lucky. Read by everybody in the state and re-written for every local newscast."

"You really are crazy."

"Tell the judge you're trying to talk me out of going to my very good friends in the Denver press. Tell him I'm a wild hair, hard to control."

"I think he already knows that."

I looked at him across the table. "A tyrant can survive for years in his own dark world, Parley, but he can't live long in the sunshine. And I think this one knows that."

I pondered the mess I had created and it still felt right. "You need to call Erin."

"Already did. Caught her at home and

gave her a full account."

"And what was the word from she-who-must-be-obeyed, the prisoner asked in fear and trembling."

"She sighed mightily. I think you actually might've done her proud, which only goes to show she's as crazy as you are. She did tell me to bail you out."

"No way, Parley. Not yet."

The morning dragged by. I sat in the cell and marked time, a room away from where Laura Marshall also sat marking time. I stared at the wall and counted to ten.

At noon, more or less, the sheriff came in and let the two Indians out. "You boys behave yourselves or next time you're goin' to court."

He stopped at my cell. "How you doin'?"

"Lovely."

"I gotta be gone till tomorrow. You and Lennie try to be good to each other."

"If he comes near me, I'll rip his heart out."

He leaned close, looking for some sign I was kidding.

"Sheriff, I think you're a decent man. But Lennie would rape his own mother and then tell her what a lousy lay she is. Tell him to stay away from me."

"Freeman's gone till Friday. Lennie'll have to bring you your food."

"If he brings me anything, he'll wear it out of here."

Lennie came in at three o'clock. I could see he had been told something because he did a cell check or a head count, proving he could count to two, without ever coming near my side of the jail. He opened the other prisoner's cell door and said, "Okay, Brady, get the hell out of here. Sheriff's orders. If it was up to me, you'd sit here for another week." I heard them shuffling down the hall together.

The jail was on the east side of the building, so darkness came fast and early. I sat and stewed, alone. By five the whole cellblock was in deep shadow. I assumed there was a light somewhere, which Lennie had apparently decided I could do without, and in fact I was just as happy without it. Now I could lie back on my cot and pass the hours in my vacuum, dreaming of happier times and better places. Occasionally thoughts darker and more worldly forced their way into my space, but I met them all knowing that, hell, tomorrow was another day.

I fell asleep. When I opened my eyes, the

darkness was everywhere, the silence deaf-
ening, and I knew someone was standing
out in the cellblock.

Guess who.

I couldn't hear him, couldn't see him,
but I knew he was there.

"Hi, Lennie," I said. "You come in here
to play mind games?"

Nothing moved.

"I like mind games," I said. "It's hard
matching wits with a half-wit, but I'll see if
I can crawl down in the slime, somewhere
near your level."

There in that darkness, seconds were
eternal. The clock ticked in my head.

"You are laughable," I said. "You are all
the Keystone Kops rolled into one sad
little twisted man. A sorry, strutting, self-
important fool."

I told him other things between tickings
of the clock and he never fired back.

"You're a goofball. Everybody here
knows it.

"You are beneath contempt," I said.

"You drag that noble word *asshole* down
to new depths. Next to you an asshole is an
icon. You are the apex of assholery,
Lennie. You even understand what I'm
saying?"

Under all that bluster, I had him figured

for a coward. I told him so and dared him to prove me wrong.

"I know you're ignorant," I said. "That's a given. You make lousy decisions and then hide behind your badge, and that's the worst kind of cop.

"You couldn't find your ass with both hands and the Hubble telescope.

"You're a cockroach, Lennie.

"A maggot.

"Whichever's worse, that's you."

This went on for a while: me talking to the darkness; him out there listening.

Listening . . .

. . . till suddenly, at some point, I knew he had slithered away.

22

The next face I saw was the sheriff's. I could see the morning sun on the trees through the jailhouse window and I sat up on the bed, amazed I had slept so well. The outer door clanged open and he unlocked my cell. "Get up, Janeway, your lawyer's here."

We walked up the steps together. "What'd you say to Lennie last night?"

"Me? I never saw the guy after it got dark."

"He's actin' funny, like he doesn't want to come near you. I thought you two might've had some words."

"Damn, I thought we were getting along just fine."

"You hungry yet?"

"Yeah, actually."

"I'll bring you some grub, if there's time."

Parley was waiting, as usual, in the conference room. As soon as the sheriff left us, he said, "You ready to get out of here?"

"What have I got to do?"

He told me. At six-thirty this morning,

the judge had called him at home. After a visit late yesterday afternoon with the guardian ad litem and a Social Services caseworker, the kids had been taken to Denver and were in safe hands. The grandparents had already left town and the grandfather had suddenly declined to press charges. "You can walk out of this if you'll just apologize and eat some crow," Parley said. "I think he's motivated to dispose of it."

"And the kids are okay?"

"Yep. I talked to the social worker myself, just before they left. They won't be coming back here again. So what do you say?"

"Sure, I'll apologize."

"Make it good. If we don't get this done this morning, you may sit in here till sometime next month. He's willing to see you at eight-thirty."

"Then by all means."

"I'll come for you in an hour. And Cliff, please, be contrite. This isn't according to Hoyle and it'll be hard for you to choke down, but he wants it on the record, in open court. You okay with that?"

"Sure. I'll eat everything he puts on my plate."

Lennie was nowhere in sight in the jail. I

had a pretty good breakfast, the sheriff released me in the care of my attorney, and we walked together across the parking lot to the courthouse entrance. The judge was already on his bench. The only people in the courtroom at that hour were Himself, his reporter, Parley, and me.

"The prisoner will face the bar," he said.

I stood before him and the lecture began. I had shown crass indifference to Himself personally, to his position, to the Court and the Law. I had been insulting, degrading, disrespectful, contemptuous, and foul. I deserved to be jailed and to sit there for however long it took until I realized the error of my ways. But he had bigger fish to fry. "Have you had enough time yet to reflect upon what you said?"

"Yes, Your Honor."

He shook his head. Not good enough. "Do you *beg* the Court's forgiveness?"

"Yes, I do. Yes, sir, Your Honor."

"Do you realize how out of line you were in both your choice of words and in the tone of your voice?"

"Yes, Your Honor."

"Then *say so!*"

"I was wrong. I know that now. I was disrespectful and insulting, I got swept up in the moment and said things that never should have been said. For any insult I may have given the Court or Your Honor personally, I am truly, deeply sorry, and I humbly beg the Court's pardon."

He looked down as if he didn't believe a word of it. But he had run out of groveling exercises to put me through, and all that remained was his decision.

"Fine reduced to one hundred dollars," he said. "Get the hell out of here."

23

It was now midmorning, the arraignment was just three hours away, and Parley and I had a short telephone conference call with Erin to plot strategy and deal with the likelihoods of the day. At the arraignment, Laura would enter her plea and would request bail. This was a formality: the judge wasn't about to grant it, and Erin had chosen to push for the earliest trial date she could get. Now she was convinced that the prosecution would be going to trial with a weak case. "I don't think they know how weak it actually is, and I don't want to give them time to find out. We don't want our client to sit in jail any longer than she has to."

First, she said, there should be no more talk of the books to anyone. "They may bring out their own book expert from somewhere, but that'll be costly. If it doesn't seem to be an issue to us whether they're valuable or not, maybe they won't. Unless we can tie those three book guys to Bobby, and put them in the area on that day, the books only cloud the case. At some point, probably after Cliff gets back from Burbank, we'll have to make that call, maybe list them as witnesses, and get them subpoenaed."

After the arraignment, Parley would file our motion to suppress evidence. This would be based on our contention that the deputy had acted unlawfully from the beginning; that Laura's verbal confession was illegally obtained, and evidence from the house had been improperly seized. "I smell blood," Erin said.

Parley and I went upstairs and sat in the conference room waiting for our client to go over some last-minute details before arraignment. The sheriff brought Laura into the room and left us, and we talked through the lunch hour. Laura listened intently to Parley's account of my adventure with the in-laws and the judge, and now the room was quiet except for the periodic hissing of the radiator. She was suddenly giddy over the kids and there was a feeling of hope on her side of the table. Parley's next words brought her down to earth. "It won't be enough to show that there was this two- or three-minute gap from the time you heard the shot to when you got up the meadow to the house and found Bobby dead on the floor. Even if we accept the theory that Jerry might've done it —"

"*I* don't accept that."

"You did readily enough, before Janeway talked to you."

"Please," she said, looking away from him. "Let's not start this again."

Her roving eyes stopped on me. "Listen to the man, Mrs. Marshall," I said. "That was the deal, remember."

"He still thinks it was Jerry."

"I think it's a strong possibility," Parley said. "I haven't seen any facts to counter that theory."

"There could've been somebody there."

"Sure, it coulda been the Godfather or the ghost of Alferd E. Packer, but it's up to you now to tell me who it was."

"I don't know." She shook her head. "I don't know."

"So you want us to build a defense based on the premise that some unknown party, neither you nor Jerry, did this. Even allowing for the fifteen minutes you were walking, that's not much time for a third party to have been there and shot Bobby and got away before you could see him."

"But it could have happened."

"Anything's possible, but right now we've got nothing to hang that on. I may have asked you this before, but tell me again. Did Bobby associate with any unsavory people?"

"Well, sure, there were some women . . ."

"Any specific women you can think of? I'm not talking about hookers, Laura, I mean women of the town, people who might be the cause of a jealous rage by a third party."

"I can't think of any."

"Did he gamble?"

"Not that I know."

"Did he owe any big debts?"

"I don't think so. In recent years, I haven't known much about his business."

"Did he have any enemies?"

She shrugged.

"Can you think of anybody else who might want to harm Bobby, or any reason that someone unknown might want to?"

"No," she said softly.

"Nobody?"

"No."

"Then it's back to you and Jerry."

A silence settled over the room.

"We know he didn't kill himself," Parley said. "Either of those shots would have been instantly lethal, so he couldn't likely have fired the second one, could he?"

"I'm not helping you much."

"No, and you didn't help yourself when

you had Jerry bathe and then burned his clothes."

"I told you why I did that."

"Why doesn't matter. What does matter is that any evidence from the shooting that was on his hands or in his clothes may be long gone now."

"I was stupid. It never occurred to me that I was destroying evidence which might've proved his innocence."

"Or the other way around. And if you did prove his innocence, where does that leave you?"

"As the only suspect," she said.

Almost a minute passed while we sat and Parley drummed his fingers on the table. "I've got to tell you something, miss," he said. "Your friend Erin might have a few ideas, but if she does, she's more than just a good attorney, she's a damn genius. As it stands now, you have only one defense."

"Jerry did it," she said glumly.

"No, you *thought* Jerry did it. That was your first reaction, that explains everything. People will *understand* that, Laura, it gives you at least a fighting chance, so that's got to be your defense. You thought what anybody would think under the circumstances, and you reacted and did what any mother would do. You tell 'em exactly what happened, tell the truth, then describe what you thought and what you did. You came up the hill and into the house, and there was Jerry with the gun in his hand."

"For Christ's sake, I *can't* say that."

"You'd better say it and forget about Christ, say it for your own sake."

She watched him drum his fingers. "What if I said . . ."

"What? What if you said what?"

"Can't I say I thought someone else might have been there?"

"No, you can't, because you *didn't* think that. You never gave that a thought till much later, it never crossed your mind in that room on that day. You've already told both your attorneys and Janeway here what you were thinking, and we can't put on testimony that we know to be false. Now do you understand what I've been trying to tell you from the first day? How what you say to us limits what we can do?"

He leaned over and engaged her with his eyes. "Get used to this fact, Laura. We can't defend both of you. It's impossible."

"What would happen to Jerry? If I did tell what happened, what would they do to him?"

"Nothing compared with what they'd do to you."

"Could I be involved . . . have a say . . . in what kind of treatment he gets?"

"I'm not the one to ask about that. My only job here is to help Erin get you acquitted. I'm not a social worker or a child psychologist. I'm not Jerry's lawyer, I'm your lawyer, and my job is to defend you in court."

"Damn, I just hate this."

"I know you do. But think what happens if you go to prison. What happens to Jerry then? Whatever that is, you won't have a damn thing to say about it, ever. By the time you get out, he'll be a middle-aged man and you'll be lucky if he even remembers you. You've got at least a decent chance to beat this, Laura, and that's my honest opinion. Get this legal crap behind you. Stop fighting us at every turn. Let us do our jobs."

They hemmed and hawed some more, but this was the story she would take into court. She was not a stupid woman and she saw that now.

Parley pushed back his chair. "Cliff?"

"Yeah, I've got a few questions . . . if that's okay."

I didn't have any notes: all the time they had been talking I had silently been ticking off questions on my fingers, my own crude way of putting things in order. "Mrs. Marshall," I said, "where were the guns kept?"

"Bobby kept two rifles and the shotgun in a cabinet behind his desk. The handgun in a holster over his chair."

"None of them under lock and key?"

"No. They were much too easy to get at."

"Did anyone know about the handgun?"

"Other than me, sure, all the kids have seen it at one time or another. I told Bobby I didn't like having it in the house. I hate guns. We used to fight about it . . . when we still cared enough to fight. When we moved into separate bedrooms, I just gave up. What he had in his room was his own business."

"Then you never went in there at all."

"Well, you know . . . there were occasions. Bobby wasn't a neat man, and there were times when things just had to be picked up. I couldn't stand to live like that."

"So you went in the room, what? Once a week?"

"Less than that. He left the door open when he wasn't there, and when I could see green mold growing across his desk . . . maybe I shouldn't exaggerate, but he was so annoying. When it got too bad, I went in and straightened it up."

"Did you ever see his gun when you went in the room?"

"You couldn't really miss it. It was always in that holster."

"In plain view?"

"As you got close to the desk, you couldn't miss it. You couldn't see it from the door, or out in the hall."

"He never took the gun with him when he went out?"

"He had another one in his truck."

"But this gun in the bedroom might've been seen by anybody who came calling."

"Sure, if anybody ever did. We didn't entertain or have casual callers."

"Have you ever heard Bobby say anything about a man called Preacher? Tall, skinny guy, his real name's Kevin Simms."

"I never knew his name. But, yeah, now that you mention it, someone like that did come up to see him occasionally."

"What about?"

"I have no idea."

"What about two brothers named Willie and Wally Keeler? They may just be grunts. Muscles with beards."

"I never saw those two guys," Laura said. "I know the tall one, or some very tall man, came up to the house a few times to see Bobby."

"When was this?"

"Oh, gosh, I don't know. Quite a while

back. Maybe as much as a year ago."

"And you never found out even in a general way what it was about?"

"Never cared, never gave it another thought till you asked me just now."

"Did he either leave or pick up anything while he was there?"

She shook her head. "I don't know."

"Did you hear anything that was said? Anything at all?"

She shook her head. "I just wasn't interested. I'm sorry, I'm no help at all. God, I feel so stupid. Is this important?"

"We don't know what it is yet, Mrs. Marshall."

"I wish you'd call me Laura."

"When he came up there — how long did he stay?"

"Less than an hour. They went into Bobby's room and talked, then he left."

"And Bobby never mentioned it, what they might've been talking about?"

"Like I said, we weren't sharing much by then."

"That's fine. Just a few more questions."

She was on edge now, as if she had failed some crucial test and dreaded the next one. I told her it was okay, she had done well, but she looked doubtful.

"When you burned Jerry's clothes, had

you been using the fireplace that day?"

"No, none of the fireplaces. I had the furnace on to warm the house."

"So you lit the fire only to burn Jerry's things."

"That's right."

"What exactly did you put in the fire?"

"Oh, gosh. His shirt was drenched with blood, and his pants. I think that's all."

"Underwear?"

"I didn't see any blood there, so I put those things through the wash."

"What about his shoes?"

"They seemed fine."

"Are those the shoes he's wearing now?"

"They were his everyday shoes. I suppose he's still wearing them."

"What about the fire? How long did you let it burn?"

"I poured coal oil all over his things, then doused and lit 'em again when the fire died down. I didn't want to leave any trace."

"And that's when you called the sheriff."

"When the fire was pretty well done and I had aired the place out."

"You opened the windows?"

"Yes, just long enough to get the smell of kerosene out of there."

"And that would be the last time that

fireplace has been touched or looked at."

"Yes, but I'm sure there couldn't be anything left."

"And there'd be nothing else in there that could hurt your case."

"No, how could there be?"

"Be very sure of that. The DA will probably have to be in on the discovery if we find anything. So if there's anything else in that grate . . ."

There was nothing, she said again.

After the arraignment we called Erin from Parley's house. Now we had a trial date: it would start in the last week of January. "Okay," Erin said, "let's go look in the fireplace tomorrow. And she'd better be telling us the truth."

The next morning Parley and I went up to the house and checked the grate in the back room. Parley stood back while I prodded gently among the ashes. "There's something," he said, and I held it up with the poker: a significant piece of plaid shirt that had separated and dropped behind the grate. It had been hidden for weeks under the ash and had been thoroughly soaked, presumably in the victim's blood. We also found a photograph of Jerry wearing that shirt, framed on the mantel in the front room. It had been taken last June and still had the photo lab markings on it, including the date.

I called Erin from the telephone in the house and told her what was there.

"Are you sure there's nothing else in that grate?"

"I can't be absolutely sure without sifting through it and disturbing everything."

"Don't do that. Give me your best guess."

"If there's anything there, we can't see it."

"Don't move anything. Leave the shirt fragment right where you found it, then call the DA and have them come up and get it."

24

I arrived home with a week to spare before Burbank. I spent a day on a grand tour of my own turf. I hit every bookstore in Denver: I talked to people and no one had ever sold the Preacher a book or seen him in action. That night I took Erin out to eat and caught her up on everything that had happened. She had won her trial and was heading into another next week. After that she had a clear schedule and had already given notice that she would be out of town for a while. Her best estimate for joining us full-time was early December.

I caught up on business — researching and pricing books, returning overdue phone calls, paying bills, giving my employee some time off. On Monday I went out to Social Services to see what I could learn about the kids. I finally spoke to a woman in her fifties who knew about the case. She had a fairly complete report, including my own role in getting the kids away from the Marshalls. The nameplate on her desk said Rosemary Brenner.

"I can't tell you much of anything you don't already know," she said. "The two young ones are in foster care here. They are in a good home and are doing well. The older boy is also here in Denver."

"That sounds like they've been separated."

"For the moment. Maybe you can tell me a few things about him."

"I can't imagine but I'll try."

"Do you know anything about his birth parents?"

"Not much. They didn't do him any favors in life."

"I'm aware of the abuse. Right now I'm more interested in his ancestry."

"Why does that matter? Do you think he's retarded?"

"I didn't say that."

"No, but with a question like that, it figures."

We each waited for the other to say something. She said, "We really haven't had him very long yet. It's hard to tell at such an early stage what he might be."

"I can ask Laura, but I'm going out of town. I won't be seeing her again till next week."

"I'm interested in who the parents were, where they went, who their parents might have been. Maybe I can find out on my own if I know the agency that handled the adoption."

She smiled like someone who knows something and wants to say it, but can't because of rules and procedures. I said, "You probably know this. That kid may be a witness to the murder of his adoptive dad over in Paradise."

"That's what I understand. And if that's true, it only adds to his problems. But I really can't tell you anything else at this point."

"Not even whether he's retarded."

Again the enigmatic smile, this time with a slight headshake. "From what we've seen so far, Mr. Janeway, that boy is far from retarded."

She took note of my surprise and said, "That's really all I can tell you now."

"Will he ever be able to talk?"

"Can't say yet."

"Can I check back with you?"

"Call me next week if you want to. We'll see where we are then."

25

The Burbank Book Fair was held twice a year in the Burbank Airport Hilton Hotel. Erin and I had done this fair ourselves a year ago, setting up our booth in the far corner of the sprawling room. That had been our year of discovery, traveling to book fairs and sales, sampling the life, meeting the people. A book fair resembles a book sale only in that books are sold at both; in other ways they are as different as a fine uptown bookshop is from a Goodwill store. At the vast Planned Parenthood sale in Des Moines, bookscouts begin gathering before dawn. They will wait all day, some bringing lunches and lounge chairs, decks of cards, dominoes, even miniature TV sets, to ward off boredom. They will travel hundreds of miles and wait more than eight hours just to get a thirty-second jump over the serious competition when the doors open. In that thirty seconds a good scout, if he's also lucky, can slurp up ten serious first editions at fifty cents each, stash them under a table, and toss his jacket over the pile, his eyes warning predators of split lips, severed arms, and death, while he scouts the tables again. When the doors open, it can resemble the Oklahoma land rush.

A book fair is a different animal. There's not much land-rush mentality here: everybody knows these books will all be priced more or less at retail. No $500 treasures will be lingering in some $2 pile of dreck: there are no $2 books anywhere on the book fair floor. Twenty dollars is about the lowest price, even for dreck. Occasionally there's a legitimate $500 title priced at $300, and if it hasn't already been sold to a dealer before the sale, chances are it'll still be there by the time the second or third wave of customers gets around to it. If the cheapskate customer comes back on Saturday and the book's still there — a chancier prospect — the dealer may be motivated to give a slight additional discount, and on Sunday, if the book has somehow slipped through all these cracks, the motivation may go up another notch. The cheapskate customer might not even have to ask: just fondling it lovingly might bring a comment, "I can do better than that if you need it." A bookman who has not had a good fair may be willing to deal on Sunday, to help cover his overhead, for the costs of doing a book fair only begin with booth fees that seem to go up every year. For a major fair put on by the Antiquarian Booksellers Association of America the fee can be $4,000, and even for a smaller fair like Burbank it can run a grand. There is also transportation for the dealer and his help if he brings someone; there is airfare, often from one distant planet to another; there are lodgings and meals and, finally, the rental of glass cases for items held truly dear, for the oddly precious or the true sweetheart that, the dealer will be happy to tell you, is rarer than a chicken's lips. And the books are supposed to pay for it all, on markups that are often just double their cost, and sometimes, for expensive items, quite a bit less.

I didn't remember the Preacher from my earlier trip here and there wasn't much chance I'd have missed him, even in a hall with more than two hundred booths. A man like that stands out like a white buffalo, as Marshal Dillon once said, and I had visited every booth and talked to every dealer before the gates opened to the public. This is a large part of the book fair culture. People schmooze, they go out to dinner in crowds, they drink and talk. Dealers come to buy books as much as sell them, and I have known bookmen who happily break even on the fair circuit year after year and come for the buying opportunities. It is something of an open secret in the book trade: the most important hours of a book fair weekend are those before the fair opens to the unwashed public at four o'clock on Friday.

One incident last year had burned itself into my memory. I had set up my booth at 8 a.m., as soon as the committee got the tables up and the tablecloths spread. The public may think it gets first dibs on books being displayed by dealers from all parts of the nation, but in fact by the time the gate opens, those books have voraciously been picked over by the other dealers for six or eight hours. From the moment the boxes are opened and the books come out on the tables, there is wheeling and dealing all across the floor.

I had drifted into a booth that day, where the dealer had just unloaded his boxes from the truck. Nothing had been put on display yet: just a sign propped against the table announcing the fellow as a specialist in modern first editions. As he opened his stash, a small crowd gathered. The first book out was a pristine copy of *Laura*, the 1943 mystery novel that had become such a memorable movie the following year. Gene Tierney, Dana Andrews, Clifton Webb, and Vincent Price had lit up the screens for those wartime crowds, making the single name of the title a household word and giving the author, Vera Caspary, a brief day in the sun. As a mystery it wasn't a bad story, but its real story as a collectible book has been phenomenal. Two factors made the literary quality of the novel almost incidental. It had a reputation as a great film of its time, and the book was impossible to find, anywhere, at any price.

It was a book so scarce that no one in the crowd had ever seen one. No one in a roomful of fairly sophisticated book people had any idea what its value might be or what the demand was. There had been no recent pricing history, unheard of for such a modern book, and as I looked down at the pulpy jacket, I thought how unusual that was, for a major American house like Houghton Mifflin to have issued this and nothing was ever seen of it anywhere. They must've printed all of ten copies, I thought then. The book as I remember it was far from pretty: the jacket showed just the simple face of the heroine, who has allegedly been murdered as the story starts, painted against a bland background. I didn't know it then, but a few dealers with contacts to rich collectors had been searching for that book for years, keeping its name a deep secret in the hope that one would pop out of the woodwork.

I remember the stir that went around that circle as the book made its sudden appearance: not quite a sigh, certainly no more to give it away than the eyes of a cunning gambler might reveal in a high-stakes card game. It was a feeling I got, some invisible, inaudible chemistry that had spread from one man to the next. "What do you want for *Laura*?" said the man to my left. The dealer opened the cover and the boards creaked, it was so fresh. Tucked in was a review slip, sweetening the deal for whoever bought it. "How much for *Laura*?" the guy asked again, but it was clear by then that the dealer had heard him, he just didn't know what to put on it. "Six hundred," he finally said, and in a heartbeat the guy said, "I'll take it," and began writing his check. Six other guys stood by, suffering for their good manners.

The fellow picked up his book and walked out of the booth. A small trickle of dealers followed him and I went along for the ride. "What're you gonna sell that for?"

someone asked, and the man turned and faced the little circle of colleagues. He pondered it a moment, said, "Fifteen," and the second dealer wrote a check in the middle of the aisle, using a friend's back for a desk. A smaller group followed him into the next aisle, where again the book changed hands, this time for three grand. It traveled back the other way now, halfway across the hall, before the question was asked again. "Six thousand net to you, soldier," the man said, and it sold again, for the fourth time, without ever reaching the booth that would finally handle it. I think of that book when sleep is elusive and the parade of books begins in my head. I am a bookman. When the hour is late, I count books, not sheep, and I learned something that day.

Another thing I had learned: Los Angeles had not been a regular pit stop for the Preacher and his boys. I had spent all day Thursday and Friday morning drifting across the vast LA bookscape in my rental car, and no one I met knew anything about a lanky bookseller and his two bellicose sidekicks. I had a hunch the Preacher was new, not only to Burbank but to Colorado and the West as well. His facility in Monte

Vista had a temporary look to it, despite the thousands of books he had stored there.

I got out to the gate at three-thirty, half an hour before the doors opened. A line had already formed and was growing. Wherever there are books, there are early birds, but this was a much quieter bunch than I had seen in Des Moines. The line was sprinkled with lawyer types, doctors, stockbrokers: collectors looking for a perfect copy of a long-cherished book had a good chance to find it at a book fair. "On these three days," one of the fair organizers was fond of saying, "this is the best bookstore in America."

The doors opened at four sharp and I wandered up the aisle nearest the west wall, pausing to chat with people I knew and pick up a few things along the way. I bought a nice second-state Richard Burton for three grand net and a couple of early Steinbecks. I wavered on a Jim Cain and finally passed because of a slight problem with the jacket; then I found the same title, *Mildred Pierce*, in a booth not twenty yards away, a perfect copy that ended up costing me almost twice as much but made my good day better. I love to buy books I love, and I am in no hurry to sell them.

I talked to some people I knew from Santa Barbara and during a lull I described the Preacher and asked if they had seen such a man. "Yeah, he's over in the middle row, about halfway back," my friend Jim Pepper said. "A really weird guy but he's got some interesting stuff."

There were five long rows of booths, at least forty book and autograph dealers in each row. I knew it could take all night to work my way across that floor, but I wasn't in any hurry: the Preacher was here for the duration. In fact, there were moments when I almost forgot him as I strolled along chatting. But not many moments and not very long.

I was tempted by a nice mixed-state *Huckleberry Finn*. I should buy this and sit on it, I thought. In five years it'll double, and go up from there. But I passed.

I bought a lovely *In Cold Blood*, signed by Capote: not too common signed, thus slightly pricey in the here and now. I bought it for my futures shelf.

Enough, I thought. I left my stash under Pepper's table and moseyed over to the middle of the floor. It was well after six when I saw the Preacher looming above the crowd. I had no idea where this was going, but I had not made the trip only to view him from afar and turn away. I zigzagged my way across the aisle and back, looking in one booth after another, a picture I hoped of book-browsing nonchalance. Now I could see Wally Keeler in the corner of their booth, showing someone a book. I came closer, and some unseen force, maybe the same kind of thing in the gambler's steady eyes or the bookseller's bluff, drew the Preacher slightly, momentarily away from his customer.

He looked straight at me.

There were no nods between us: almost immediately he looked past me, as if he had missed the connection, as if I wouldn't know better. I turned in to a booth two down from his and browsed the merchandise. The books all blurred now: my mind had shifted into its cop mode, and my juice was flowing like sixty. In the end there was no way to plan this. As that great philosopher Doris Day would say, what will be will be.

I walked into their booth.

"Hi, guys."

I didn't expect sudden warmth to break out from the Preacher: the man had none to give, but Wally's unfriendly face immediately told me something: *They know who I am.* It had been a stupid mistake, giving them my name. The Preacher turned away from his customer and a faint smile crossed his face. "What are you doing here, gambler?" he said. I went along with the charade, seeing how far it would go. "Came out for the racing season," I said, lying affably. "How's the fair treating you?" He nodded and said it was early yet, things were just getting started. "Buying much?" I said casually, and I didn't need to wait for the answer that never came. These boys had come to sell books, not to buy them. I made a point of looking at Wally. "How you doing, Wally?" I said easily. "Where's your brother, still back in Colorado, trying to get that truck out of the hills?" He muttered something and turned away, and I thought, *Oh, yeah, they have learned a lot about my big stupid ass since I saw them last.*

I looked over their books: a mix of things with some common stuff out front and the high spots on a shelf that had been set up at the back of the table. Some of their books were signed, some weren't. I picked up every one and looked them over, and the night waned while I stood in their booth. The hell with them, my cat was out of the bag now.

It was nearing eight when the real hostility began to show. The crowd had thinned in this part of the hall, and I could sense their rapt attention to whatever I was doing. I could feel their annoyance, especially Wally's. An old gentleman came into the booth and engaged the Preacher in conversation about a signed Robert Frost. While they were talking, Wally eased into the back of the booth and said in a low voice, "What the fuck do you want, Janeway? What the hell are you doing here?"

"I'm looking at books, Wally, what's it look like?"

"Yeah, well, why don't you do it somewhere else?"

"I like it here. You guys are so friendly and stuff. I like friendly people."

"Lemme tell you something, pal. Don't fuck with us."

I smiled. "Wally, I've fucked with guys who could tear your head off."

He moved away and fiddled with some books in the opposite corner. I eased out closer to the Preacher and without being too obvious, I hoped, listened to his conversation with the Frost collector. It was a common, cheap book, *In the Clearing*, with a black state jacket with white lettering, issued in the last year of Frost's life. I heard the collector say, "The jacket's pretty rough on that," and the Preacher said, "I'm not selling it as a pristine copy, friend. You know the signature's worth the seventy-five I've got on it, and if you want it pretty, you can find a jacket for that book anywhere." The Preacher wasn't motivated to deal and the collector cluck-clucked and moved away. I watched over the top of a book as the Preacher reshelved it and turned his attention to someone at the front of the booth who seemed to be more serious. I moseyed over under Wally's watchful eyes and picked the Frost off the shelf. Then something happened that changed the course of everything. Wally came across and reached for the book. "That's not for sale."

I had no intention of buying it, but now I drew the book protectively back under my arm. "It's on an open shelf, it's gotta be for sale," I said.

He took a step closer. "Maybe it's not for sale to *you*."

I got my back up and reached for my checkbook.

"I don't think you hear so goddamned good, Janeway."

"You don't think, period. What are you, some bush leaguer? That's a good way to get bounced out of here, not to mention blackballed at any legitimate book fair that hears about it. You really wanna push this? I've got a good grapevine and I can spread news fast."

Suddenly the Preacher loomed over us. "What's going on here?"

"Your caveman doesn't want to sell me this book. It's marked seventy-five, here's my check for it."

He looked disdainfully at the book and said, "Why would you want that?"

"Maybe 'cause I've got a jacket, maybe 'cause I'm crazy. But I'm a customer who's just written you a check after standing in your booth for an hour. Now the question is, are you going to sell me this book or do I really have to get annoyed over a stupid thing like this?"

The Preacher gave Wally one of his seriously frigid looks. "For gosh sakes, Wally, don't you know better than that? Of course we'll sell him the book."

He took my check, bagged and sealed the book for clearance through security, and deposited it in my hands. "Enjoy it," he said coldly.

Then suddenly he made a mighty effort to warm up. He smiled and said, "Wally's just annoyed, that's all. It's probably because you didn't tell us the truth back in

Colorado. He'll get over it. We don't want any hard feelings."

"Hey, that's cool, Preacher, I don't hold grudges."

"That was quite a story you fed us back there. I don't know why you thought it was necessary, but people do things for all kinds of reasons. If we gave you any grief, let me apologize for both of us."

"No need at all, we got it resolved, everybody's happy."

Wally didn't look happy, and his unhappiness doubled when the Preacher said, "Will you be here till closing? Let us buy you a late dinner and make up for any annoyance we might have put you through."

I wouldn't eat with these snakes for my pick of his books, but I didn't come twelve hundred miles to play it safe. I clapped Wally on the shoulder and said, "That's real decent of you boys. You don't have to do that, but if you insist, I'll be back."

I drifted over to Pepper's booth. He was curious, as usual.

"So'd you buy anything from that tall guy?"

"I'll show you if you don't bug me about it."

We opened the bag and he looked at the

Frost. "Not much margin in this."

"I know, I know. You're bugging me about it."

"So what's the story?"

"His factotum got my dander up. Tried not to sell it to me before I even told them I wanted to buy it."

"Now why would he do that?"

"Good question."

He looked at it carefully now. "The signature doesn't look right."

I looked at it over his shoulder. I had seen Frost's signature many times, not nearly as often as Pepper had, but it looked okay to me.

"There's something wrong with it," he said more definitively. "You gonna leave it here for a while?"

"I can leave it all night if you want to read it."

"Yeah, right. I was thinking more along the lines of, I take it to an autograph dealer I know over in Row Four. He can tell us right away if there's a problem with it."

"I'd appreciate that, Jim."

I drifted across the floor again. It was now well after eight and I still had most of two rows that I hadn't yet seen. But I worked them quickly, my mind no longer on books but on something far more serious. At ten minutes to nine I circled the room and returned to Pepper's booth.

"We think it's a fake," he said. "It's a very good fake, but I'd take it back to him before we close up tonight and get that check back."

"You hang on to it for me. I'll see you tomorrow, and thanks."

He dropped the book in the bag, resealed it with his own sticker, and I drifted back toward the middle aisle again. I knew I'd have to watch my flank now. I was going unarmed into a hostile meeting, however friendly they might want it to seem at the moment; the odds were two to one, and there was a dead man in Colorado. At least I went knowing these things. I hadn't just fallen off the Kiowa County Bookmobile.

26

They were rolling a cloth covering over their books when I arrived. Wally had brightened his act, no doubt on orders from his boss: he gave me his signature grin, one of those crap-eaters that only his mother could have loved. "Hey, Cliff," he said, "no hard feelings, huh?" I said no, hell no, we were fine, and he went into his charm mode, as charming as lung cancer. "I'm glad the Preach talked you into coming with us. Sometimes I forget my manners when I've got a hard-on for somebody else. I'm still pissed at Willie over the truck, that's all it is."

He yakked it up and I asked politely about the truck. Willie was trying to get it towed into Alamosa, where the repair shop told him the tariff could amount to seven grand. "Might as well take the bastard out and shoot it," he said, and I avoided saying the obvious, that he was the one who'd been driving that night.

The Preacher was busy with a last-minute customer, who surprised him and bought a $250 book. I could see it was signed and I eased closer to see what it might be. Wally kept talking, his voice droning like that of some perp trying to draw attention away from what really goes on, but I just nodded dumbly and kept moving slowly to the front. I saw a name, Larry McMurtry, and recognized the graphics: the guy was buying a copy of *The Desert Rose*, a common book unless signed, and this one had the impatient, almost-unreadable scrawl that McMurtry's signature was becoming. The Preacher bagged the book and sealed it. Behind me Wally chuckled, a halfhearted guffaw that telegraphs deep annoyance under false camaraderie. "I swear to God, Janeway," he said, still forcing the silly laugh, "goddamned if you aren't the world's nosiest bastard."

The Preacher looked back at me as he finished his deal, the guy walked away, and we three headed for the gates. "So what're you in the mood for?" the Preacher asked affably. "There's a good Moroccan restaurant I know of, but it's off the beaten trail and a bit of a drive."

"Sounds great," I said.

"You can ride in front with me. Plenty of room for those long legs of yours."

This time I wouldn't even consider getting in a car with Wally at my back. I said, "I'll follow you," but he tried to insist. "I'll bring you back," he said, but I told him no, I wanted to go straight to my hotel after dinner. There was an awkward pause: we all stood indecisively in the parking lot as Pepper walked out with a couple of bookpals and came past, giving us no more than a brief glance. He moved on without saying a word.

"I'll follow you," I said again, with no room for argument in my voice.

"Let's go then," the Preacher said under that snaky smile.

My simmering suspicion came to a boil as we drove. Twice he stopped and reversed his direction as if he had lost his way. I bet myself a dollar that there was no Moroccan restaurant: *none that he knows about*, I thought. We were now in a grim part of town, dark and close, not at all typical of any part of Los Angeles I had ever seen. We had been driving almost haphazardly for twenty minutes when he pulled to the sidewalk and stopped. I could see in the glare of an oncoming car that they were talking earnestly. The car passed us and the block fell again into deep blackness, with only a dim and distant streetlight revealing the outlines of their heads through the glass.

They started off again but the same thing happened, down into some dim ghetto where the likelihood of any good restaurant diminished with each block. He stopped again and I pulled up behind him, wishing I had my gun.

He opened his door, got out, and came back to me. I rolled down my window and he leaned way over and looked in. "We seem to be lost. I've only been there once, thought I could find it again."

"Do you remember the name of this place?"

He shook his head. "I'd know it if I saw it again, but I have no idea where we're at now. I think we'll have to find someplace else."

"Well, I'm not particular, let's grope around. I don't know the town any better than you do, but I'll take what comes."

He got back in the car but didn't move for another moment. They were still talking up a storm, and I'd bet myself another dollar it wasn't about the neighborhood, restaurants, or the kind of food we'd eat. We headed off to the west, and eventually we hit something that looked like it might lead to a main drag. The Preacher turned south and I stayed close on his tail. In one place he almost lost me — a traffic light that he took speeding up on a late yellow. Two cars were approaching the intersection on the crossing street and I had to stop. By then the Preacher was almost a block ahead.

I went across on the red but now I had a new hunch, that whatever he had planned for me, he was losing his nerve. Too much indecision, too much talk: his backbone's starting to ooze a little, I thought, maybe his taste for what had seemed good to him at a distance didn't look so good now. Maybe Mr. Kevin Simms would be just as happy to shake me and write it off with an apology tomorrow.

I closed the gap between us and we came to a wide boulevard with lights and motels and gas stations. He went past a couple of restaurants and I flashed my lights in his mirror. "Time to eat, boys," I said to the back of their car. "Let's do something or get off the pot." He turned around the block and came through the neighborhood again, stopping at the place with the deep, dark parking lot.

He pulled into the shadows at the far corner of the lot and I parked beside him.

"This wasn't what I had in mind," he said when we stepped out.

I'll bet it wasn't.

But they were stuck with me now. The Preacher said, "Well, let's make the best of it," and we started around the building to the front entrance. Inside, the place was about what I expected — a hash house, with an ancient cashier who doubled as the hostess and two harried-looking waitresses. The cashier said, "Be with you in a minute," but she couldn't seem to unlock the cash drawer and she didn't seem to care. Meanwhile, people were standing in a growing line to pay their checks, we stood at a sign that said PLEASE WAIT TO BE SEATED, and I could see that the Preacher was getting impatient.

The old cashier had called one of the waitresses over and was getting detailed advice for working the till, repeating everything that was said to her and still not comprehending. "Say, can we ever get some help here?" the Preacher said loudly, and the people waiting in line stared at him darkly. At last the other waitress came and seated us. She was young, was having a bad night, looked strung out and near tears. The Preacher's opening salvo, "I hope the food in this place is better than the service," brought the tears closer. "I am very sorry, sir," she said softly. "Please, what can I get for you?" She had her order pad out and her pencil poised, and he stared at her in that cold way he had and said, "Would it be too much to ask for some napkins and place settings, a few of the niceties of civilization? What is this,

322

your first night on this job?"

"I'm sorry, I'm sorry." She turned away and he shouted after her, loud enough for the cook to hear, "This table is dirty too."

By then I was getting damned tired of the Preacher. I said, "You really shouldn't do that, you know."

"Do what, demand just a modicum of decent service?"

"Abuse the waitress. You should never abuse a waitress, Preacher, that's not in sync with the Golden Rule. Imagine if she were your daughter."

Before he could reply, I said, "How old do you think she is, seventeen? Maybe she's not very good but this is probably her first job, so let's cut her some slack."

I pushed his buttons again. "And maybe you can tell me before things truly go to hell why we're really here."

"What on earth is that supposed to mean?"

"It means, what do you guys really want from me? Why bring me way out here when there's obviously no Moroccan restaurant closer than Rick's Café in Casablanca? Why the hail-fellow routine all of a sudden until now, when your real colors begin to come through? I'm really curious about that, Preacher, why the pretense of a night on the town when the fact is you don't like me any more than I like you?"

The waitress returned with the table settings and a steaming towel to wash off the tabletop. "I'm sorry," she whispered again. "I'm very sorry."

"Don't worry about it," I said. "We're probably not going to stay, but that's not your fault."

She left us and the Preacher said, "I was right about you the first time I saw you."

"You probably were."

"A troublemaker. I knew it then and I can see it now."

"Yeah, but I was right about you too."

"And what might that bold assessment have been?"

"Not a preacher at all, just a crooked two-bit book shyster who'd better hope there really isn't any God."

"Man, you better watch your mouth," Wally seethed.

"Oh, yeah, I wouldn't want to get *you* mad at me. Jesus, I quake at the thought."

"I'll make you quake, pal. You wanna step outside?"

I laughed and said, "No," still laughing.

"I didn't think so. C'mon, Preacher, let's get out of here. I told you this guy was bad news."

"Oh, Wally, I'm much worse news than you know. I'll tell you what bad news I am, I am wise to your book scam. I know the Frost I bought had a fake signature, probably that McMurtry as well, and I can't help wondering how many more fakes you're selling as the real thing."

The Preacher paled. "I have no idea what you're talking about."

"Then try this. How well did you know Bobby Marshall? Well enough to kill him, maybe? Did you boys have a falling-out over the money?"

"You're crazy. You really are a crazy man. I don't know any Bobby Marshall. If there's something wrong with that book, bring it by in the morning and I'll give you your money back, no questions asked. *No* questions asked."

"I might do that. Maybe I'll have a few questions for you while I'm there."

"Never mind your questions, you bring that book back. In fact I insist on it."

"You can't insist on anything, Preacher, it's my book now. That means I can keep it, give it to the cops for evidence, or run it through a paper shredder."

"Evidence of what? What cops are you talking about?"

"Keep on playing that role. I'll call

ahead to Cañon City and tell 'em to have their tailor make a set of jailhouse threads, extra tall."

They got up and left, slamming their way through the door.

I sat there, and in a while the waitress came timidly by. I apologized for my companions and said, "On second thought, miss, I think I will eat. I've just been working up an appetite."

The food was actually worse than the service, but I had survived the East Colfax Roadrunner and I still believed I could eat anything. I left the waitress a sawbuck, the second-best thing about this lousy night. That look on the Preacher's face had been the best. That had been worth the trip.

I walked casually across the blacker-than-hell parking lot, aware of a growing unease that might have nothing to do with the Preacher or his lowlife sidekick. I was thinking about the case now, about dead Bobby Marshall and his guns, his loner ways and his books. As much as I wanted it to make sense, it didn't.

I had to go almost to the wall before I could see my car. The Preacher's car was gone, but I remained on full alert. I scanned the area and made my approach slowly, looking first to starboard, then to port, whistling softly, jingling my keys in my pocket. I didn't expect any real trouble now but I was ready for it. That was Wally's bad luck when he leaped out of the shadows and came at me with a pipe wrench in his hand.

His first swing grazed my shoulder as I ducked under it. His second grazed nothing but air. He never got off the third swing.

I belly-punched him hard and he flopped on the ground with a pathetic whooshing sound, a sorry grunt, and a little cry of pure misery. I heard the wrench hit the pavement.

"Hi, Wally," I said. "I think you dropped your wallet."

He managed to croak out three words. I thought they were "Oh, you asshole," but I couldn't be sure. He wavered for a moment on the cheeks of his ass, listed sideways, and toppled on his back. He looked up briefly at the terrible swirling universe, then he rolled over and tried to suck up all the gravel in the parking lot.

I got in my car and picked my way back to Burbank.

27

I was out at the book fair again in the morning. I wanted to touch their books, see what was signed, what was not, and just be a continuing irritant. I wanted to stare up the Preacher's nose and see if he'd tell me something new. Sometimes it happens that way: a jolt like I had given him last night takes time to work through the brain and get a guy talking. Even if he lies, you learn something.

By the time I went through admissions and got out to the middle of the hall, it was nine-fifteen. His booth was empty, his books were gone, his tablecloth rumpled and thrown on the floor.

It was the talk of the fair. When a dealer signs on at a book fair, he commits himself for the entire weekend, but sometime in the hour before the doors had opened, the Preacher and Wally had come in, and in fifteen minutes they had dismantled their booth and hustled themselves out to the back ramp. There had been a strenuous argument with the fair organizers. The Preacher had offered no excuse, not even a hint of a family emergency: "The only thing he said was, 'I've got to go, get out of my way,'" said the dealer directly across the aisle. "In the end, what can you do about it? They're his books, it's a free country, all you can do is tell him to go to hell if he ever tries to sign up for a fair around here again."

I sat in the makeshift cafeteria and drank some serious coffee. By now they're in San Bernardino heading east, I thought. They'd be in Monte Vista for at least a day, clearing out that facility. They wouldn't move those books in fifteen minutes.

I called United Airlines and got on a noonday flight to Denver. Picked up my books, said adios to everybody, and headed for the gates.

28

I knew it would take them thirteen hours for the return trip to Colorado: that's if they drove straight through, spelling each other at the wheel. They'd be there sometime late tonight, not in any great shape to move twenty thousand books, but well motivated. There'd be three of them by then, but even at that it seemed like an all-day job.

They couldn't do anything about the road time: it takes as long as it takes to drive nine hundred miles. Figure half a day to get a rental truck and move the books if they were true supermen: the only way it could be done, even in that time, was to hire some help. Assume that. Assume they would get home bushed after thirteen hours on the road and start loading immediately. Figure they'd be out of there before noon tomorrow.

Meanwhile, my flight would touch down in Denver a little before four o'clock. Just about the time Wally and the Preacher would be streaking across Arizona, I'd be in the air. When they reached Four Corners, I'd be heading down I-25. I had time, unless they called ahead and had Willie start breaking down the warehouse now . . . which of course they would do.

I called Erin from a phone booth. Got her machine.

I tried her again from my hotel.

Tried her again at the airport and got lucky. I explained things fast, with my flight being announced in the background.

"I can get you down there," she said. "There's an airfield in Alamosa: you could use Todd and we could have a rental car waiting for you. The question is, what are you going to do when you get there? Leaving a book fair early isn't against any law I've ever heard of. You can't have them arrested, you have no proof of anything, so what are you going to do about it?"

"What I always do. Grope, hope, wander in the wilderness, play it by ear."

29

"There she is," Todd said, nodding toward a string of lights in the distance. "We'll be on the ground in a few minutes. Then what?"

"Then I get in my rental car and drive to Monte Vista and you get to go home."

He banked low over the hills and started his approach into Alamosa. We had said nothing about my purpose on the trip down, and now I read more into his question than the usual small talk. "I don't know," he said at last. "What if I ride along with you instead? Just to keep you company."

"It's only twenty miles, Todd."

"Twenty miles on the ground can be a long, lonely trip."

"This sounds like a put-up job," I said. "Erin's handiwork is hard to miss."

"It's nothing she said. I just got a feeling."

"Uh-huh. So what didn't she say?"

"Just that there's a warehouse full of books that might be evidence in this case you're working on for her. Might be some bad apples guarding it."

He talked to someone on the ground and eased the plane into a landing pattern.

"It's just a thought," he said.

"Did she tell you there's a remote chance it might get ugly?"

"I can handle ugly."

"There's also a question of the law. We don't know yet whether the guys who get arrested, if anybody does, will be them or us."

"I guess that's why we've got us a good lawyer."

We bumped twice on the landing strip and he taxied us in.

Twenty minutes later we were in a rental car heading west on U.S. 160. It was just after seven-thirty: by my best guess, Wally and the Preacher were out on the same highway, somewhere in Colorado, heading our way through Cortez and Durango.

We got into Monte Vista a little before eight. It was a cold, clear night and the streets were almost empty. I drove past the Preacher's house first, only because it was on the way. It was locked and dark. We moved on across town, easing into the narrow lane where the warehouse was. "There he is," I said. "Looks like he's all by himself."

Willie had the door up and had pulled a

large U-Haul truck up to the ramp. I could see him working feverishly around the edges of the truck, loading boxes as fast as he could carry them. From that limited vantage point, I could also see one long row of bookshelves and part of a crossing shelf, both empty. Todd said, "If he's been working like that all day, he won't have much fight left in him." I said, "Let's hope," but just in case I got my gun out of the backseat. Todd stared at it as I gave it a check and snapped the holster on my belt.

"Why don't you sit here and be the lookout?" I said.

"Are you trying to insult me?"

I reached over and squeezed his shoulder. "Yeah, I was; glad you didn't take it personally. What I really want you to do is hang back in the dark and don't let him know you're there till we see how the wind blows."

"I'm not a bad guy in a fight, you know."

"If it comes to that. The idea here is *not* to fight unless we absolutely have to. If these books do turn out to be evidence, the last thing we want is to taint it with some gestapo tactic."

I flicked off the interior lights and we got out. "Easy with that door," I said, and we pushed them almost shut and left them that way, making no noise. I walked as quietly as I could along the graveled path, and I could see Todd's shadow moving forward across the driveway. To the left of the ramp was a small steel stairway, and I took the steps carefully, two at a time, coming only to the edge of the door.

I could hear him now, rummaging somewhere in the back. From there I could look into the room and see how much work he had done. He had to be well motivated to rent the truck, box those books, clear out this room and the shelves well into the back, all alone. The Preacher must have called him early, maybe before they even went to the hall and broke down their booth. If I had put some fear in all of them, that's what I wanted, that's what I hoped.

I heard him grunt: a tired man struggling with the endless parade of boxes. He came into the room and we stared at each other for the smallest time, a second maybe, before he dropped the box of books on his foot.

"Willie," I said softly. "Looks like you've been at this awhile. You need some help?"

He sat on the floor beside the box, which had split open on two corners and was spilling books on the floor.

"You shouldn't be doing this alone," I

said. "You'll get a hernia."

I still hadn't crossed his threshold yet. "Really, I'd be happy to help if you need it. Just say the word."

Just say hi, you son of a bitch, and invite me in.

"Who the hell *are* you?"

I told him my name, knowing full well that's not what he meant. I had my coat pushed back so he could see the gun on my belt, not much of it but enough. All legal, all kosher: I had a proper, legal permit for my nonthreatening gun.

"May I come in, Willie?"

"Yeah, sure," he said numbly, and I stepped into the light.

"Looks like you guys are clearing out fast. What's the deal?"

He still looked stunned, as if I had just hit him between the eyes with a two-by-four. "Who are you?" he said again.

"I hate to say this, but I'm the guy who's about to send your big ugly ass to jail."

"You gotta be kidding."

"Do I look like I'm kidding? And by the way, in case you've got any crazy ideas, do I look like I'm stupid enough to come here alone?" I called out through the crack, "How's it look out there?" and Todd, giving it both balls and a bucket of octane, said, "Everything's fine, boss."

"So where are we in the scheme of things, Willie? The Preacher and that idiot brother of yours will be here in a couple of hours. Question is, where will you be?"

"I don't understand."

"Come on, Willie, don't play stupid. Maybe you're just trying to buy some time, but your choices at this point are pretty well limited. You can stay there on the floor and we can all wait for those boys to arrive. You can keep loading your books. You can decide to cooperate. I guess you could start a fight, but that would be disappointing and unfortunate. If you get my drift."

He shook his head, like a man still in some kind of shock.

"How much more have you got to do back there?"

"Oh, Jesus," he said. His look said, *Oh, God, tons.*

"I think it's only fair to tell you," I said: "you can load them, but don't count on leaving here with them."

"Then what's the point?"

"Exactly."

He leaned forward and massaged his foot, still trying to buy time.

"Willie?"

"I'll wait for the Preacher."

"That's fine. You can all go together when you go."

"Go where?"

"I think you know where."

He got up slowly. I moved a step closer.

"No sudden moves," I said. "If you've decided to wait, you can sit in that chair against the wall. That would be my advice."

"What if I don't take your advice? What if I just walk on out of here?"

"That would be your choice. The wrong one, I think."

"But you're not gonna stop me, are you?"

He was beginning to get the drift of things now. He knew I had no authority except force, which as things now stood would be illegal.

"What if I get in that truck and just drive off?"

"I'm afraid I will have to stop you then."

"But not if I walk off."

"We'll have to see about that."

He started to move toward the door. I was standing in his way and I could see the fear on his face and in his eyes. He took another step. One more and he'd be in my face.

He took the step.

I moved aside.

He walked out the door.

I came out on the ramp and saw him hobbling down the steps.

"You're making a mistake," I said.

He flipped me off and kept going, past the truck and on down the road.

"Follow him," I told Todd. "Keep well back, try not to let him see you. When you find out where he's going, come on back here and let me know."

I sat in my rental car and watched the warehouse. An hour passed.

So far, so good, I hoped. I hadn't touched anything. Hadn't searched, seized, stormed the gates, roughed up anybody; hadn't really threatened except that one warning about stopping him if he tried to take the truck. I didn't know how a court might interpret that if it ever came out; maybe I hadn't done anything wrong, but I wished now I hadn't said it. At least I had left us with a fighting chance, but so far it was a moot point. We still had no case against them for anything.

I saw Todd come into the road. He opened the door and got in beside me.

"He went to the bus station. He's there now: looks like he's waiting for a bus out of town."

"Okay. Take the car and drive out to a

phone booth. Call Erin and tell her what's going on. Tell her the warehouse is wide open, the truck's sitting here full of books, the Preacher might pull up in another hour or two and I'd be interested in her advice."

I was painfully aware how thin my legal situation was. *Christ, we've got nothing on these guys,* I thought again, but I said, "Tell Erin I tried not to compromise things too much."

I stood off in a small grove of trees. This time Todd was gone ten minutes.

"She says hang loose and call her yourself when you can. If they take off, get their plate numbers so we can find them if she wants to subpoena them down the road. And don't do anything she wouldn't do."

Yeah, like I'm supposed to know what that is.

"She says she trusts you."

I fought back a laugh. "Damnedest thing I ever saw. Hard to tell which side of the street I'm working on. It almost seems like I'm making their case for them."

He had brought some coffee. I took one of the two steaming cups, said, "Bless you, my son," and tried to lighten the moment.

Ten o'clock came and went. The truck filled my vision, blocking the interior lights like some solar eclipse where only the glow around the edges is visible. At ten-thirty I stirred restlessly. "Time they were getting here."

Almost in the same breath I saw the Preacher's station wagon turn in to the road. *Uncanny,* I thought. *Maybe it's a sign, maybe a harbinger. But of what?*

We slumped below the dashboard. They had pulled up beside the U-Haul and now got wearily out of the wagon. I had my window cracked; I heard the Preacher say, "Something's wrong." They stood in indecision; then the Preacher walked warily around the U-Haul and looked inside. "He left the keys in it."

He went to the little iron staircase and I heard him call Willie's name. "Something's not right here," he said.

For a moment I thought they might make some kind of run for it — jump in the wagon and leave it all here. But he overcame his fear and went up the steps to the ramp.

"Willie?" he called softly.

Wally was still standing at the bottom of the steps. But he climbed to the ramp as the Preacher disappeared inside.

"I'm going in," I said.

"Let's go, then."

"Same as before. You be the backup out here."

I got up the steps to the door and Todd stood in the shadows at the front of the truck. I heard the Preacher say, "Let's get the truck and get out of here."

"What about the rest of the stuff?"

"Leave it."

"God, Preach, there's five thousand books left back there."

"You want to go to jail over five thousand cheap books? Now come on, let's get these lights off and get the place locked up."

I stepped up to the doorway. They were standing just across the room, about fifteen feet away. The Preacher's eyes narrowed to slits as he saw me.

"I knew it would be you," he said. "I knew it the minute I got out of the wagon."

"You're a smart man, Preacher."

"Not smart enough, apparently."

We looked at each other. Wally stood limply and stared at nothing. The Preacher said, "You're trespassing. I could have you arrested."

"Willie invited me in."

"Willie doesn't pay the rent here. He has no authority."

"Hey, you weren't here, Willie's your authorized agent."

"We could argue that all night. Where has Willie gone?"

342

"I really think he's leaving town, Preacher. Last time I saw him he was walking down to the bus station."

The moment ripened. "So what happens now?" he said.

"I guess we wait for those cops you were about to call."

"I don't think so."

I could see his attitude changing by the moment. From fear he had become antagonistic. I had nothing on him and he was beginning to know it: If I had any proof of anything, where were the cops? A slimy smile now spread across his face. "You're not gonna do a thing, are you?"

"We'll see."

"Wally, get in the car and go get your brother."

"Listen, Preach —"

"Will you just shut up for once in your life and do as you're told? This guy's got nothing on us, nothing. If he tries to stop us, I'll sue his socks off. Go get Willie."

Wally came toward me. "Move, Janeway."

"Or what?"

"Or I'll move you."

"You tried that in California, fatso."

He kept coming and I backed out onto the ramp. I eased down the iron staircase

343

and around the truck, till I could see Todd standing at the driver's door. How easy to grab the keys: easy and so illegal. But I was out of options.

"I'm not gonna tell you again, Janeway, get out of here. If we go at it again, it'll have a different ending this time."

I moved out of his way and he grinned. "That's better," he said, easing stealthily around the truck toward the station wagon. He looked like he was about to hyperventilate with fear. I could've nailed him then: he was a sucker for a punch of almost any kind, but I let him go past to the station wagon and watched him drive away. When I looked up the ramp, the Preacher was in shadow, but I sensed that a deeper change had come over him. "Go ahead, stand out there all night," he said. "You've got nothing on anybody." He backed into the warehouse and left me out in the dark.

30

We sat in the car, watching the building from a grove of trees down the road. Wally returned with Willie in half an hour. Willie looked pretty despondent. He stood outside for a moment, then trudged up the ramp and disappeared inside. We sat in the car, in plain sight for anyone who looked our way. Wally hadn't bothered to look but the Preacher knew we were still here: he had come to the door once and given us a long, hard look down the length of the rutted dirt road in the light of the distant streetlamps.

"What's he gonna do?" Todd said at one point.

"He's gonna finish loading those books and then they'll all drive away."

"You gonna stop him?"

I laughed drily. What did I know? The Preacher had visited the murder victim at least a few times during the past year. Nothing illegal in that. They had talked in the victim's home, and that, for all we knew, had been the extent of their dealings with each other. The only witness who could place them together at all was the dead man's wife, who wasn't paying attention and barely remembered the Preacher visiting.

Of course they might have met any number of times in town, in Chicago, Rio, or in Cape Town. Perhaps they were hatching the second coming of Hitler, or maybe they were old pals from way back, who were just catching up with each other.

So what did I know? Nothing. What did I think? I figured Marshall and the Preacher were involved in a book scam together. The Preacher had scouted the books and Marshall was able to get them signed. What mattered was that they be cheap books, easily found for a few bucks in junk shops and bookstores. The Preacher made up a list, a roster of authors to look for. He and his boys traveled and found the books and Marshall got them signed — by a bunch of people who were dead by then.

Pretty good work if you can do it.

These books were by or about people whose signatures were worth something on the face of it. Personalities, not just your average Joe–schmuck writer types. At some point the Preacher or his boys would come back and pick up the signed books from

Marshall's mountaintop. They'd leave him some more, take away the old ones, and peddle them. So they were involved on both ends of it and Marshall was the man in the middle, who talked to God and had John Wayne's name appear by some kind of immaculate inscription on his book. *Presto!* A $30 book becomes $400, and the signature was good enough that nobody questioned it when it was offered for sale.

That's what I thought. I should've thought it earlier.

Too much goes down on faith in the book trade, I thought.

We go by experience. If something looks good and we've got no reason to doubt it, we buy it. Then we sell it, and it passes — perhaps forever — into the vast book world.

Except for extremely valuable signatures, this is how it's always been.

Maybe that'll have to change now.

This still didn't begin to solve Laura Marshall's problem. I kept remembering something the Preacher had said to Wally in that moment just before they had seen me standing on the ramp — *You want to go to jail over five thousand cheap books?* Nobody but a grafter talks like that. So the

Preacher and the Keelers were grafters, I knew that much, but how did that tie in to Bobby Marshall's murder? Wally and Willie had gone up to see Marshall on the mountain that day, bringing him a new load of books. They didn't know he had been killed. *They didn't know.*

Jerry did it. I kept coming back to that thought. The real motivation had nothing to do with the Preacher or his books. As much as I wanted to make a murder case against these birds, I couldn't.

They rested on the loading dock. For a time they seemed to be sleeping.

"They're rubbing our noses in it," Todd said.

"And they're just plain tired."

They started at it again around three o'clock. I could see Wally and the Preacher working around the edges of the truck, and every so often the Preacher would stop and peer down the road. Once he came out and sat on the ramp, taking another obvious break with his legs dangling off the edge.

"He's undecided," I said. "We all are."

Todd took a deep breath. I said, "They're afraid to finish. Scared we'll follow them right on across the country."

At six o'clock Wally left on a breakfast run, returning thirty minutes later with three cold-looking McDonald's bags. I looked at Todd sadly and shrugged. "This won't get any easier. It may be a huge waste of time."

"But you don't want to leave yet."

"No, but you can. I'll get back to Denver okay on my own."

"I'm in no hurry. Just making conversation."

We sat, and Wally, on one of his smoke breaks, gave us a look that even Todd, half-asleep on the seat beside me, picked up. "They're laughing at us," he said. "Cocky bastards."

That's when I gave voice to a notion that had begun stirring around in my head. "How'd you like to sit here and watch while I go over to the house and see what I can find there."

He sat up and opened his eyes wide. "I hope you don't mean what I think you mean."

"Just a look around is all I'm thinking."

"Outside the house or inside?"

I said nothing and felt him squirm on the seat beside me. "Jesus Christ, Janeway, you're not gonna burglarize their house?"

I wished he hadn't said that. All I could do now to keep him from being an accomplice was deny it.

"I'm not burglarizing anything, Todd. Whatever I do, we'll find that out when I get there. All you've got to do is sit here and watch."

"That's all. Just sit here and watch."

"That's all. If it starts to look like they're wrapping things up here, you might drive over to the house and blow the horn. If you feel like it."

"Just blow the horn."

"Three times. Just drive past and give it three quick blasts. Then you drive on back here and park in this same place. If I don't come in ten minutes, you take off and go back to Alamosa. You turn in the car, get in your airplane, and haul ass for Denver."

A long, sober moment passed. I drew him a crude map from here to there.

"Naturally, you don't have to do any of this," I said.

I saw his backbone stiffen. "Hey, don't worry about me, I'll be there."

I got out and took a small leather tool pouch from my suitcase in the trunk. I hadn't used it in years, but it was like my gun and my credit card: *Don't leave home without it.* It slipped easily into my coat pocket. I waved cheerfully at Todd through the glass and started up the road.

31

It was a ten-minute walk to the Preacher's house. I made it in eight. My heart quickened as I walked into the long dirt road and saw the grove of trees looming ahead. This would hardly be the first time I had stepped over the line, and the risk always came with a rush. I knew how quickly and badly it could all go wrong. In the old days I worried only about covering my ass and dismissed the ethical argument too easily. Occasionally I had debated it with my lawyer friend Moses, who passionately believed that the end never justifies the means. "Once you step outside the law," Mose said, "your whole cause sinks right down to the perp's level. Even if you think you're right, the end can't justify the means." The trouble with that notion, I said to him then, is that it worries too much about rules and not enough about protecting one terrified, flesh-and-blood victim. Look, the system's never going to be perfect anyway, I said loftily, so why not bend it a little if you can put away a true badass who might otherwise slide and could still do great damage? "If you really believe that, why don't you just go out and shoot him?" Mose said. I grinned wickedly but he wasn't worried, he knew what my limits were. I had a strong unwritten code. In it was everything I knew in my heart about right and wrong. Moses knew I wouldn't abuse a suspect. I'd never lie under oath. I wouldn't trump up a case or manufacture evidence. I might open a locked door, but to purists like Moses even that went too far. He wanted the game played according to Hoyle, but Hoyle never had to work three months on a case only to see it disappear because some judge was having a bad-hair day or an essential witness had been intimidated. Hoyle had no idea how much real evil there is in the world: he didn't even know how many rotten lawyers there are, eager to earn a dirty fee by putting some baby-killer back on the street. "Listen to yourself, Cliff," Moses said. "Can you imagine what would happen if every cop went by the law of the streets? Just do whatever you want, as long as *you* think your cause is right. Jesus Christ, we'd have absolute chaos." I couldn't speak for other cops: all I could do was counter chaos and Christ with my own logic, earned in the heat of battle. Rules can't cover every situation, I said: sooner or later some decent soul gets the shaft. There are times when the *only* way to get a very bad guy is to play by his rules.

The rush came stronger and faster than I remembered it. This situation was different from anything I had done in the old days. I wasn't just a wild-hair cop, putting nobody but myself at risk. Today I represented Laura Marshall, and what I did might have serious consequences for her case. I probably wouldn't be able to use anything I found except for my own information, but sometimes that's enough. A fact discovered illegitimately can lead to a bigger fact, which might suggest a more legitimate path to its so-called discovery. What's the bigger risk, ignorance or jimmying a door? This was what I told myself as I walked up through the trees. In another few hours, whatever was in that house would be gone, maybe forever: maybe burned, maybe shredded, maybe trashed. The Preacher would be gone, the Keeler boys, gone. For all their sudden nonchalance, they were about to disappear, and they might be hell to find again.

I knew how it was to justify an act. But I had a weird feeling this time. I had the creeps but I pushed ahead anyway.

Slowly the garage emerged through the

trees, then the house. The place looked as bleak and uninhabited as it would soon be. I took a pair of rubber gloves from my inside coat pocket, ripped open the package, and stuffed the wrapper back in the same pocket. Stepped up to the door. Knocked loudly and stood back.

Nothing.

I looked around at the trees. Peered down the road as far as I could see. Took out my picks and in less than a minute I was inside.

I closed the door. Locked it. Crossed the room. Opened the window, just a crack. Enough, I hoped, that I might hear a horn blow from the road.

I looked in the living room.

Back in the bedroom.

No books, just a pair of unmade beds and a TV set. This would be where the Keeler boys slept.

On the other side, the Preacher's room. No books here either.

I eased into the room. The Preacher's bed, also unmade. But less disorder here.

A bathroom, off to my right. The door open, with sunlight shining in through a window, giving the bedroom a dusty kind of haze: I could see dust swimming in the air, as if something had just disturbed it.

I looked into the bathroom, which was musty and basic. Washbasin, toilet, shower stall in the corner. Dark over there . . . dingy . . . the shower curtain scummy, not even a hint of what I assumed was its former opaqueness.

Mold everywhere. These boys were slobs.

Across the bedroom, a filing cabinet. Locked. A wooden cabinet with a tough old-style lock.

It took a while but I got it open.

Files.

Dozens of folders in each drawer. I would never have time to go through it all.

Sift . . . skim . . . separate the wheat from the chaff.

Each of the files was labeled with a small, circular tab.

Names of people I didn't know.

Names of companies. Subjects . . .

Publicity . . .

Sermon topics . . .

Clippings . . .

World catastrophe . . .

Day of Reckoning . . .

More of the same in the second drawer.

Miracles . . .

Events . . .

Biblical prophesy . . .

And on and on.

The third drawer looked more promising. A dozen fat files.

Books . . .
Keeler . . .
Marshall . . .
Personal . . .

I began there, in his personal file. Touched its top pages almost timidly, then leafed quickly through it, and out of the mass of paper the real man emerged.

His name wasn't Kevin Simms, for starters. He was Earl Chaplin of Jonesboro, Arkansas, thirty-six years old last November.

And he wasn't a preacher, except in the most unsavory sense. He had a certificate from some biblical diploma mill and apparently aspired to do his work on television, where he could fleece a flock more effectively and rake in money with both hands. He was the kind of preacher who makes real ministers cringe.

He had an address in Oklahoma, where he intended to establish the roots of his so-called ministry. I took out my notebook and wrote it down.

There was something else about Earl Chaplin. He was a racist.

I leafed through papers from the John Birch Society and the Ku Klux Klan. He had been a kleagle in Alabama, but had resigned five years ago. I could guess why, and it had nothing to do with any sudden change of heart. The kind of ministry he envisioned didn't thrive on a pulpit of open racism, but he still got letters from Klansmen around the country, with references to mud people, sheenys, and right-handed Jesus-lovers.

God was alive, he loved money, and he was all-white. I had only been in the Preacher's house a few minutes and I had already learned these valuable lessons.

He was a compulsive file-keeper. He kept everything, including his grade-school report cards. He had been a mediocre student, a misfit. Notes from a fourth-grade teacher to a parent or guardian: *Earl needs to apply himself. He can do much better.*

Why would he keep this kind of stuff? The only answer is no answer at all. There's no accounting for people and what they do.

Quickly now I took down everything I could get about him: all his vitals, everywhere he'd been, everywhere he'd lived, every church where he had held a membership. I had his address in Alabama, his car registration, affiliations, blood type. I had his army deferment. They don't take giants.

From the Keeler file I took down an address in Oklahoma. The brothers had been nickel-and-dime booksellers for years and had known Kevin Simms since his Earl Chaplin days in Arkansas.

Quickly I skimmed some of the Preacher's personal letters. He railed against Democrats and thought even Republicans were communists. What this country needs is some backbone, he wrote. We needed to invade Cuba for real, not pussyfoot around like Kennedy had done. The old John Birch line, with a few worldwide twists. Get Castro, then take care of the Middle East: Iraq, Iran, and Syria. Knock off those three mongrels, cock our guns, and dare any turban-topped gook nation to look at us crosswise.

Time to move on. I had enough stats to find him wherever he tried to hide.

I looked in the *Marshall* file and one thing was immediately clear. He had known Bobby Marshall for several years and they had had a much deeper relationship than Laura knew. There were typewritten, signed letters from 1986, referring to meetings in Denver and on the East Coast. They had gone bookhunting together in New York, sometime last year from the look of it, and the books they talked about were exactly the kind that had recently come into question. Cheap books, common, easy to find, but books that would take a sharp rise in value if signed: nothing too splashy, nothing that might get noticed. Literature if the author was reclusive, thus scarce. But mostly sports figures, film stars, personalities.

The letters were formal throughout: *Dear Mr. Marshall . . . Dear Mr. Simms.* Marshall had signed his full name, *Robert Charles Marshall,* in light blue ink, fountain pen not ballpoint, and the Preacher had typed his phony initials, *KS,* at the end of his. Marshall's letters were all originals on his letterhead; the Preacher's were carbon or Xerox copies with no signatures.

They were strictly business. A relationship powered by money.

I went through the whole file. This took far more time than I wanted it to.

At some point I looked up, gripped again by that creepy feeling I had brought into the house. Nothing specific: no noises inside or out, not even a chirping bird or a scurrying squirrel outside the window. It was the wrong season for chirping birds, but I was spooked anyway.

I walked to the window and looked down the drive. It looked like some still-life painting. Not even a breeze to flutter the dead leaves.

I watched and I waited. I had enough now, I could button it up, lock everything back the way it had been, and get the hell out. But I couldn't pull myself away.

The thing that bothered me as I dipped back into the file was that the deal between Bobby and the Preacher had no beginning. The earliest letter just appeared, as if their acquaintance had begun in a vacuum, telling nothing of any prior contact. It spoke of a meeting they would have in Gunnison, but there was no indication that they had had others before it. The letter dealt with books as if each knew perfectly well what the other was talking about, yet there had been no foundation to indicate that this was so. One day they might have been strangers, the next day they were partners in crime. Why? Where had this begun? Whose idea had it been? None of those questions, or any of a dozen others I might ask, had even a hint of an answer.

I am bringing some books out next month, the Preacher wrote at one point.

Don't come out to the house, Bobby had written. *I will meet you in Gunnison.*

A time and a date was mentioned.

I want to keep our transactions strictly be-

tween us, Marshall wrote. And yet the Keeler boys had come driving up to the house, bold as brass, three weeks after the murder. What did that mean? Had they changed their plans by telephone? I looked at more letters but could find no evidence that they had ever spoken on the phone.

Four large book exchanges were discussed in the letters I saw. These spanned two years, and Marshall, in an early letter, insisted that no record be kept of the money that changed hands. But the Preacher had cheated: he was a compulsive record-keeper and a born-again cheat, so he had these crude notes tucked away, chicken scratches on common loose-leaf paper. He had paid Marshall $15,000, cash in a suitcase, for delivery of five hundred books. No mention was made whether this was a full or partial payment. I did the arithmetic and guessed it had been paid in full. Five hundred times two hundred was a hundred grand. The books had probably cost an average of $10 — $5,000 for basic seed money — still an $80,000 profit. My best guess was that $200 each would be a very low retail average. And they'd want to keep it low retail to move 'em fast.

Suddenly I saw how I would do it if I

were running this scam. I would pay Marshall as little as possible and blow the books out as cheaply as I could. If I went to a book fair with John Wayne's book signed, I'd have a reasonable chance to sell it for four bills. Price it at half that and it would fly out the door. I would want to move them fast without selling much to other dealers. No matter how good the forgeries were, there would be talk if too many turned up at once, so I wouldn't put these out at all before the gates opened. I'd wait until the unwashed public got in, then I'd slip them onto my table two or three or half a dozen at a time. Maybe I'd also have a far-flung little network of dealers I could sell to around the country, dealers who didn't do book fairs and wouldn't think twice about buying a signed book that looked real. As long as I didn't get too greedy in any one place, I'd be fine. Spread the stuff around, let it get absorbed into the vast wasteland, and if the signatures were good enough, they'd never be questioned by anyone. Once they were out there, strewn across the country like manure in a garden, who would know where they had come from? Who would ever see them again?

Many would disappear for years, till the

collector died and his widow liquidated his estate. Then they would pass, again largely unnoticed, into some other collector's hands. If they had been good enough to pass muster once, why not again?

A forger is like any other con man: he counts on the greed of his customer. The buyer wants it to be real, and if it quacks like a duck and waddles like a duck and has webbed feet and a duck face, well, damn, it's probably a duck. If the price is way down near wholesale, why wouldn't he buy it? Why wouldn't the next generation of collectors buy it as well?

Provenance? Forget it, we weren't talking about Hemingways or signed Salingers here. Who asks at this level?

The more I read the more I believed that the Preacher was following my own game plan almost to the letter. Five hundred books sounds like a bunch, but I could sell these like hotcakes.

Marshall was a good forger. None of the signatures I had seen looked in any way suspicious. The Robert Frost I had bought looked real enough to fool me, until a question arose and I looked closer. Even then a specialist had to tell us for sure. It was a damned good fake.

Either Marshall himself had been that

good or he'd had access to a good forger.

I stood at the file, trying to imagine who that might be.

I was still standing there when the horn blew.

32

Everything I did in the next few minutes was driven by instinct. First I lifted one of Marshall's letters, a one-pager that did nothing but confirm a meeting. I folded it carefully along the original folds and slipped it into my pocket.

Insignificant . . . small enough, I hoped, that they wouldn't miss it.

Almost in the same motion I pushed the file back into the cabinet. I slammed the drawer shut and shoved in the long steel rod that was supposed to lock it.

The lock wouldn't catch.

I shoved it again and banged it with my palm. Finally had to leave it that way.

I faced the open window. I heard a bump.

Another bump, closer now. I was out of time.

I heard the squeak of a loose board on the porch and a soft breath from the breathless room next door. Footsteps came in through the kitchen. There was a pause, then the unmistakable ratcheting noise of a shell being jacked into the chamber of a gun.

"I knew it." The Preacher's voice had a

soft, steely edge that I hadn't heard from him before. "He's been in here."

Wally grunted. "Everything looks the same to me."

"How would you know?"

"I got eyes, Preacher. Maybe I'm not as dumb as you think I am."

The footsteps came closer. I flattened myself against the wall.

"I think you're just lettin' him spook you," Wally said.

"A lot you know. Every time I turn around, he's there. I can't even take a leak without running into that guy in the same stall."

"You got him on the brain is all."

"Don't tell me what I've got. Go look back in your room. I'll stand here where I can see both doors."

I heard Wally move down the short hallway. They'd be in here next. I stepped back into the bathroom and eased my way around the toilet.

The floor creaked under my foot.

"What was that?"

"Jesus, Preacher, it's just me. That guy's gonna give you a nervous breakdown."

I stepped into the shower stall and carefully, noiselessly, pulled the scummy curtain tight. A moment later I heard Wally say, "Well, he ain't back there."

"Never mind the sarcasm. You go look around outside. I'll check in my room and we can bring over the truck and load this stuff up and get out of here. The sooner we clear this town, the better I'll feel."

I heard his footsteps coming close. In the distance a door closed as Wally went out. The Preacher started across the bedroom and stopped. I heard the filing cabinet open and close.

"Wally! Get in here! He's been here! He's broken into my filing cabinet."

"Maybe you just left it that way."

"Shut up, Jesus, shut up. Just get out there and find him. I need to look through these files and see if anything's missing."

"You think he might still be out there?"

"How do I know where he is, he's like some phantom, he turns up everywhere."

"Look, Preacher —"

"Just shut up and get him."

"Yeah? What am I supposed to do if I do see him?"

The Preacher said something in a low voice. Wally said, "Yeah, right," but he clumped out anyway. I heard him a minute later, walking through the weeds outside the bathroom window. In the other room the Preacher had begun talking to himself.

"God *damn* it."

A moment later, barely audible: "Oh, that fucking bastard."

I heard the rustle of papers, a quick shuffle through the mound of files. This went on for some time, until Wally came in again.

"Anything missing?"

"Doesn't seem to be."

"There you go, then."

"There you go *what?* For God's sake, just go! Go *find* him!"

I heard him slam the cabinet drawer.

Footsteps, coming my way. Very close now . . . he was in the bathroom, a few feet away. The toilet seat banged up. The Preacher broke wind loudly as he peed.

He stood back, breathing hard. I could see his shape in the light coming in from the window. I thought he had turned and was facing the shower but couldn't be sure. I put my hand on my gun and waited. I heard him breathe. I lifted my gun to my side.

Suddenly his shadow filled the shower curtain like the image of that old-woman figure in *Psycho.* He jerked it back, we stood looking at each other with guns ready, and in that second all the worst consequences of my breaking and entering were there in my face. This was why I had been spooked, that half-formed hunch that I would not help Laura but would ruin her case. He could have shot me then and been legally justified: he had the law on his side and if I shot him, I'd be up the creek. I thought he must know that. If I thought anything in that wild, crazy instant, that would probably be it, but who can tell whether instinct in the heat of a moment is the same as thought?

He must know that. He knows it, but he's no killer.

He can't kill me. It takes a certain kind of man to do that and he's no killer.

He didn't move for what seemed like a long time. In fact it was all part of the same few seconds. The sun coming through the window broke over his shoulder and fell on my face. I felt his eyes burning out of the shadows. Neither of us spoke: there was no outrage or fear or anything else. But what I did then may have saved one or both of us. I grinned at him . . . and I winked.

I heard a little cry come up from his throat. He shook his head and closed his eyes as if he could blink me away, then he took a step back and lost his balance. He almost fell, almost lost the gun as he grabbed frantically for something to hold. The gun went off and blew a hole in the roof. He kept flailing and finally grabbed the shower curtain and it ripped halfway off its rod, then the whole rod came loose and he fell back against the sink, tangled in the scummy plastic. I heard him cry out as he struggled like a live fish in Saran Wrap. "Ah!" he yelled. "Ah! . . . Ah!" . . . and he rolled over and fell again, this time through the open doorway and flat on his back in the middle of the bedroom. He scrambled up and crawled out into the hall. I couldn't see him now but I could hear him, running through the house and out onto the porch.

I heard the car start as I went cautiously into the bedroom. His tires sent gravel flying into the air, and from the doorway I saw Wally, running along the road, yelling for him to stop.

I looked back just once. The filing cabinet was still wide open with the files in plain sight, and in that last crazy instant I was tempted to go at them again. Common sense said, *What are you, out of your mind?* I had pushed luck far past its limit, and Prudence, that cautious old whore, wanted me to get the hell gone. I hustled out the back way and across the yard, around the garage, and into the trees, on through the thick underbrush in the general direction of town. The day felt suddenly warm in the wake of my near disaster, and again I thought, *Damn, I've gotta change my ways,* even as I knew I probably wouldn't. If I had ever listened to Prudence, I wouldn't be here now, shooting my own case full of holes. I'd still be a career cop. Laura Marshall would sink or swim without my help. I wouldn't have become a bookseller or made these discoveries, wouldn't have met Erin in the first place.

I turned back up toward the warehouse. It never crossed my mind that Todd might be gone: it was the kind of day when no one does what he's supposed to and nothing quite happens according to Hoyle. I got in the car beside him and he drove us away without a word. It was clear enough what had happened here: the Preacher had come roaring up and he and Willie had taken the truck and vanished in about two minutes. I didn't need a crazy man's Baedeker to figure that out, and Todd didn't want to talk about it. We drove past the open ramp door and I glanced into the room. I could see books scattered across the floor, out onto the loading dock, and down the ramp. A few had fallen into the tall grass across the yard and their pages billowed at us in the wind. I had a sudden hollow feeling and a strong premonition that I would never see the Preacher again.

So is this where it ends? Does it just fizzle away with disappearing perps and me with no good answers?

This was the damnedest case. We had a crazy judge and a crazier deputy, at least two hundred grand of worthless books, and none of our suspects or their motives made any sense at all. I thought of Lennie and the Preacher, linked only by their arrogance and in the similar ways I had backed them down, and I wanted to laugh.

We passed Wally, trudging along and muttering under his breath. He glared at us as we sped by but I looked straight ahead as if he didn't exist. An hour later we were in the air, banking north-northeast toward Denver. It was a quiet ride, almost stilted. Todd asked me no questions and I told him no lies. He was a smart guy, Todd, and he understood that the less he knew the better. Better for himself, better for Laura Marshall's prospects, better for Erin, and most of all for me. I had nothing to say to any of them. Soon enough I'd reflect on what it all might mean, but for the moment I was happy just to be alive. Moses had been right, and one day over a deep highball I would tell him so. But I wouldn't take any pride in my sudden enlightenment or how I got that way.

BOOK III
CHRISTMAS IN PARADISE

33

Erin made plans to move over to Paradise in early December and we prepared for the hearing on our motion to suppress. Now I was wary of my involvement in the case and warier yet of telling Erin why. I would have to, of course, but not now and not by telephone. She sounded unusually optimistic as November winnowed down: "Apparently Lennie never heard of the Constitution," she said. "Their investigation sucks. All their evidence is tainted." I thought of my own potentially tainted evidence, if we should ever get that preacher on the stand as an alternate suspect. "The DA has no idea how badly his witness may have screwed things up," she said. *And you, sweetheart, have no idea how I have screwed up,* I thought. In my mind, Lennie and I faced each other in a titanic battle of morons. *Gunfight at the Dipshit Corral.*

I tried to redeem myself in legitimate work. The books were in limbo in the sheriff's evidence room and I had spent three days examining them. I was certainly no handwriting expert, but I was reasonably certain that the majority and perhaps all were forgeries. Too many seemed signed with the same kind of pen, the same ballpoint ink. Erin was thinking of hiring an outside handwriting expert and was still mulling it over as December approached.

She considered the usual battalion of expert witnesses, who would testify if needed about things they hadn't seen based on textbook science and likelihoods and their own professional experience. I have never quite trusted professional witnesses: I understand the need for them in this day and age, but in the end they are hired guns lined up to discredit the same witnesses for the other side. An expert is impressive as hell until suddenly the opposite truth comes out. They are trained to know things, yet we have seen even the best of them make mistakes. I remembered the handwriting experts with impeccable credentials who got hoodwinked by that ingenious murderous forger, Mark Hofmann. The experts knew everything about paper and inks, they knew all the tricks, while Hofmann was nothing but a self-taught madman. And he fooled them.

Our witnesses would talk about everything from the condition of the house to the condition of our defendant's mind. Our psychologist, an expert on coercion and mental stress, had interviewed Laura twice and could buttress her story of why she had initially lied. He was a solid guy Erin had used before, a young dynamo who had testified in dozens of cases and presented an unshakable demeanor, she said, in court. In Denver, Erin had spent a lot of time with Jerry and his guardian ad litem, trying to communicate with the kid and figure out what he might have seen, whether he could somehow give testimony in writing and what this testimony might reveal. She had found an expert on juvenile witnesses, but at this point none of us knew what Jerry had actually seen or done, or what we might want him to testify to. He was a risky wild card at best, and Laura was still trying to insist that he be left out of it.

At the end of this parade Erin had her book expert, me. The DA had contacted his own rare-book authority, a dealer named Roger Lester, who had recently moved to Denver from New York. Lester had opened a shop downtown, on Seventeenth Street, and had taken out one of those splashy quarter-page phone-book ads, putting my own modest one-inch ad to shame. *International book searches,* it said. I didn't do that. *Expert appraisals,* it offered. I did do that, at least well enough to know that one man's expert is another man's idiot. *Highest prices paid for good books,* it blared. Yeah, well, people could say whatever they wanted in the yellow pages, and in fact Lester might be very good. I fought back my drift toward reverse snobbery and prepared to like the guy.

He would arrive in Paradise the second week in December to do his appraisal for the state. "They still don't know that our own assessment of the books has changed," I told Erin on the telephone. "They have no idea yet that any of them are forgeries, and unless he figures that out on his own, they're going to assign the values as if they're real." I sensed Erin's amusement and read between the lines. Gill was going on the old sucker's assumption that one out-of-town expert was worth ten local guys, and Lester after all was from New *York!* — Jesus, he must know *lots* of good stuff. Let him come, I thought. Let him make his appraisal and we'd see then how good he was.

All these witnesses and more, at $100 per hour and up, travel time extra. The DA would try to show that our experts were simple mercenaries, bought and paid for.

After that I was crushingly restless in the little town. I had begun a search for the Preacher and the Keeler boys, in case something turned up suddenly that focused new attention their way. I had called the president of the ABAA as well as the officers of several regional booksellers groups from Texas to Minnesota; I had described the Preacher and what kind of scam he had tried to pull in Colorado. If everybody called just five book friends and had them look for new booksellers in their towns that fit the description, maybe we'd hear something, maybe we wouldn't. In the case of the ABAA alone, the night had more than eight hundred eyes, and the Preacher would be an easy man to spot.

I bird-dogged Lennie's movements the day of the murder, but all he had done was play checkers with Freeman until the call came in at 3:09. I had still not interviewed the photographer who had taken that first-day picture of Laura being booked. His mother had had a heart attack somewhere in Florida and he had gone out of town.

I left a note on his door and checked it every day.

But there was a feeling as winter settled in that the town was deader than Bobby Marshall's moldering carcass; that whatever might have been here was long gone. Paradise was a spent force, a crime scene sucked dry. If the Preacher had been a compulsive record-keeper, Bobby had been his polar opposite. "Bobby burned everything," Laura told us. "He was secretive, I told you that, he didn't want old letters around to tell people what he had done in life." The Preacher had left no visible tracks in Paradise, I could find no one who remembered him, and this in itself was troubling. If he had passed any time here with Bobby, even if their meetings had been few and far between, someone should have seen him. People in small towns talk and they notice and remember a stranger, especially one as unusual as the Preacher. But in the days I spent talking to people, I picked up nothing.

The one line in the Preacher's files that troubled me more as time went on might in fact have been meaningless. *We'll meet downtown*, Marshall had written, but now I had to figure that this might not mean in Paradise at all, it might mean Gunnison or Denver. I drove over to Gunnison to poke around, ask about the Preacher and show pictures of Bobby Marshall. It was a futile, frustrating morning. I went on to Alamosa and Monte Vista; I checked the garages and found no evidence that the truck had been towed in or repaired. I checked the Preacher's house and found it empty with a FOR RENT sign up in the yard. I wasn't surprised, but again I knew I couldn't have stopped him. There was no criminal charge outstanding against this man, Parley said: "All we've got is your suspicion."

Erin took this news calmly, as if she had expected it. Never discussed in those critical days was what I knew and how I had come to know it. That's the trouble with burglary as an investigative tool: you can't testify without being willing to say where your facts come from, and an attorney can't put on testimony that she knows to be false. I could imagine what she might've heard from Todd, but I didn't ask that either and she didn't say. "I've got some things to tell you when you get here," I said.

We were all touching base daily by telephone. I gave her full reports on what I was doing, but it amounted to little more than wheel-spinning. Again I spoke with everyone I saw — on the streets, in the bars, in the stores — and all I picked up was what I already knew. Laura and Bobby Marshall had been rich topics of gossip for years. Occasionally they had been seen in the town, but always apart. She shopped alone and he drank and schmoozed occasionally with locals at the High Country Tavern. After her early stint on the town preservation committee, Laura had kept to herself, a trait that always encourages talk in a small town. Bobby had been more outgoing, which had become their saving grace as a couple. He bought drinks and laughed; he told good stories. But none of his drinking acquaintances was more than that: none could remotely be elevated to the status of pal, and no one knew any reasons why anyone would kill Bobby.

"I've been thinking about how we'll work together if it does go to trial," Erin told Parley one night. "I'd like you to carry the brunt of this case. I'll be the second chair, at least as far as the world can see."

"Uh-huh. And the reason for that would be . . . ?"

"Obvious. My relationship with the defendant and the appearance here that I'm a carpetbagger. The judge knows you. And there's a third reason. I think you're a real solid lawyer."

"You'll still be calling the shots, I hope."

"We'll call 'em together."

On December 3, Hugh Gilstrap, the newspaper photographer, returned to town and left a message. My hunch about him suddenly grew stronger: again I sensed a fellow who had been in a position to know something and was maybe just waiting out there to be asked. I made arrangements to see him late that morning.

34

He lived alone in a small house about five miles from town, a slate-gray man in his fifties who liked to fish and shoot pictures. We sat over a pot of the blackest coffee I ever had, straddling our chairs at the potbellied stove in his rustic front room.

"I don't actually work for the paper," he said. "I might freelance if something comes up that strikes my fancy. That's pretty rare in a quiet county like this. They pay almost nothing but it keeps my hand in, you might say."

He was putting together a collection of artsy and idyllic high-country photographs, he hoped for a book. He had moved to Paradise ten years ago after a stint at *The Denver Post*. "That was a real photographer's newspaper in those days," he said, pouring coffee. "Best in the country back then, bar none. Every day the entire back page was given over to us photogs, the whole page was nothing but pictures, with maybe one little graph of text. We always resented the hell out of every word they made us use. If a picture was good enough, it ought to explain itself. That was my philosophy as a photojournalist. It's what we all pushed for — two or three pictures and no words on that great big page."

His mother had died. "Best thing all around. She was pushing ninety and had already had a stroke, a year or so ago. But I had to stay with her, you know what I'm saying?"

"Sure I do."

"That's why I've been gone so long," he said by way of apology.

We sat and talked about mothers, the weather, the high country, and the nightmare that Florida was becoming. I didn't push him. I had a hunch and I had learned in my police career to let guys like him get at things in their own way.

"Too many people today, that's what's happening to Florida," he said. "They're getting at us here too; the goddamn Texans are already pouring in here like a bunch of crazy people."

In a hopeful tone of voice, I said, "Maybe we won't be around to see it," and he smiled and said, "Maybe, but it's happening faster than you can believe."

I knew we were getting along when he

asked if I wanted some lunch. I said sure, if he'd let me buy him a beer in town sometime. "I remember you, you know," he said. "You worked a downtown homicide I covered for the *Post* years ago. I can't remember the guy's name now, some skid row nobody, but I remember you. You were damned helpful and I got a picture page out of it."

Good, I thought: another strike against the no-good-deed-goes-unpunished rule.

"A great page," he said. "Dark and moody, in one of those dingy old upper Larimer Street hotels. Just the body, sprawled out on the floor in that big empty room, wearing nothing but a pair of dungarees."

"His name was Jason," I said, remembering. "That's what he went by. Nobody knew his real name. They kept him on ice for a month and finally buried him in an unmarked potter's field grave."

"Yeah, I covered that too."

It was almost two o'clock when he said, "I take it you want to know about Lennie and what happened that day." I nodded and he said, "In case you hadn't noticed, Lennie Walsh is a nickel-plated asshole. Just imagine the most screwed-up possibility in any situation and that's what

Lennie'll do. That's the short version."

The long version was more interesting. There had been nothing on the police radio that day: "There's usually nothing out here anyway, but sometimes I leave it on back in the shop . . . turn it up loud so I'll hear it if anything does happen and play soft classical music on the phonograph. I get the itch, you know, to be out there again. Late that afternoon I went out to the grocery store, just for a few minutes, but that doesn't matter, I got a radio in my car. So I just happened to be in the right place when Lennie drove by like a bat out of hell. I knew right away that something unusual had happened. Whatever it was, he didn't want it out on the radio for anybody to hear. He came by real close and I could see he had a prisoner in the backseat. A woman. I put it together pretty quick; it was Ms. Marshall."

"You knew her?"

"Oh, yeah, I worked with her on the preservation committee a few years back. We both got disgusted and quit about the same time. Who's got time for all that bullshit?"

"So your opinion of her was . . ."

"A real straight shooter. She says what she thinks and I like that."

"So what happened then?"

"I followed them on back to the jail. By the time we got there the rain was really pouring down. This was just before the season turned. Still, we don't get many rains like that, it tends to be snow. But it rained like hell for at least twenty minutes and they sat there for a while in the car. The windows were all fogged over and Lennie seemed pretty damned engrossed in whatever he was saying to her."

"No idea what that might've been?"

"That's how he is."

"That's his notion of technique," I said.

He nodded. "All these years of struttin' around and he's finally got himself a real case. Nobody even remembers when they last had a killing here. So this is a big deal."

He sipped coffee. "So I got out of my own car and draped two cameras around my neck. I don't think either one of 'em saw me. I know he didn't, 'cause when he pulled her out of the car —"

"She was cuffed then, right?"

"Yeah, he had her hands cuffed in front of her and another set of cuffs holding her tight against the door. He had to fumble around for the keys to get her loose from the door handle, and all that time both of 'em getting wet as hell in this freezing rain. I shot 'em three or four times through the lens, him groping around for the keys and her standing there looking like the world had just ended."

"But he didn't see you then . . ."

"No, he had his attention on her, and she looked to be in real bad shock. Even when he came my way, he didn't see me. He had an arm over her shoulder with a good grip on her like he was afraid she'd crumple and fall over. The wind was blowing, made him pull his hat way down and walk like this. He was surprised as hell when he walked her up to the door, looked up, and my flash went off in his face."

I savored the moment vicariously. He could tell and he laughed thinking about it.

"Then you shot more than the one they printed."

"Oh, hell, yes, shot 'em half a dozen times with each camera. I got a good one of him yanking her out of the car by her hair."

"Jesus Christ, you're kidding."

"Not so you can tell it. He was pretty damn rough with her, like he'd been frustrated questioning her."

"Did you give that one to the paper?"

"Yeah, but I knew when I did it they'd never use it. They don't want to make local law enforcement look bad . . . as if Lennie doesn't do that all by himself."

"And you've still got these pictures?"

"What kinda photog would I be if I didn't have? Lemme tell you something, Janeway, you always shoot way more than you'll ever use. Then you pick the two or three best ones and send them in. The paper will still print the weakest one every time."

"I guess management's the same all over. It doesn't matter whether you're a photographer or a cop or a junior vice president at General Motors. So what happened when your camera went off in his face?"

"Well, he got belligerent: got his ass right up on his shoulders like he always does. One thing you can say for Lennie, he finds so many ways to be consistently ignorant. So he comes at me like this . . . like he's gonna rip my camera off my neck. Just leaves his prisoner standing there in the cold rain and says, 'Gimme that goddamn thing, you son of a bitch.' "

I laughed out loud and he joined me in undisguised mirth.

"What a flaming ignorant hemorrhoid he is. So I just said, 'Touch my camera and

I'll sue you and this county clear into the next century.' He blinked and stood there, musta been all of half a minute, and this whole time Ms. Marshall, who could still barely stand up, was left shivering there in the rain."

I covered my face in near helpless laughter. "Jesus, what a jackoff."

"Oh, yeah. Oh, yeah! Like the silly sumbitch never heard of freedom of the press or the rights of prisoners — he thinks that dumb badge of his gives him license to be the county's official Nazi storm trooper or something. Didn't she tell you about this?"

I shook my head.

"I shot her three or four times over Lennie's shoulder while he was standing there trying to decide what he could do about it. But that's nothing — what happens next is just ungoddamn real. He takes her in and books her. They go into the back office, but I had come on in the front. Hell, I ain't about to let a turkey turd like Lennie Walsh push me around, and this was a public building so screw him. I could see him through the glass, talking, probably reading her her rights, I thought then. She looks just stunned, like she's got no clue what's happening to her or why. Then

Lennie glances up and sees me standing out in the office watching them, and it's like he don't have a clue whether to come throw me out or cut me some real wide space. Suddenly Laura sits up and says something and it hits him like a slap. He spins around and says something back at her but I can't see what it is. Whatever she said, it really knocks him for a loop. Suddenly he gets the old man down, the old jailer, and they haul her upstairs to that little holding cell off the bull pen. He comes out into the office and I say to him, 'What're you bookin' her for?' He starts to brush on past me and I repeat the question. 'What's the charge, Lennie?' I say. But all he says is, 'Get away from me. Get away if you know what's good for you.'

"Out he goes, into the lot. I'm right behind him, and as he gets into his car, I say to him, 'Are you puttin' that woman in jail in those wet clothes? Because if you do and if she catches pneumonia, I'm here to tell you, I'm a witness to how she was treated.' He slams the door and yells at the top of his lungs, 'Get away from me, goddammit!' and I've got to backpedal fast to get out of the way when he rips out of there. He heads back out of town, it looks like up to her place again. Back I go into the jail. The office is pretty well deserted by then, but I make enough of a fuss to bring old Freeman down. 'What's he holding her for?' I ask, but the old man knows nothing, or if he does, he's not telling. 'Where's the sheriff?' I ask. Well, the sheriff's gone to Gunnison of course, he's a good enough guy but he's always off in Gunnison chasing nooky, he's got some widow woman there he goes to see every chance he gets. 'Listen, Freeman,' I say. 'Ain't that woman got any warm clothes?' I can see by the old man's face what the answer is, he don't even know, so off I go, downtown to the old five-and-dime down on the main street. I get her a robe and a blanket and I beat it on back to the jailhouse.

"I've got to bully that silly Freeman to take me up to her, and all he can say all the way up the stairs and the whole time I'm talking to her is, 'Jesus, Hugh, Lennie ain't gonna like this.' So we get up there and I look at her and she still seems stunned: at first she don't seem to know who I am, she's just sitting on the cot shivering. Then she says my name, just, 'Hullo, Mr. Gilstrap,' and by God my heart goes out to her. So I hand her the robe through the bars and then the blanket and I tell her to get those wet clothes off. When I see that she comprehends what I'm saying, Freeman and I leave her alone to change. Five minutes later I go back in there and she's sittin' in her robe, wrapped in the blanket, still cold and shivering but at least not wet. So I bully some more blankets out of Freeman and we hand 'em to her through the bars. Then Freeman says, 'Dammit, Hugh, you really got to leave now.'

" 'In a pig's eye,' I tell him. 'This woman is entitled to counsel and I'm gonna see that she gets it.' So I look at Laura through the bars and I say, 'What did they book you for?' Then she says, right in front of me, Freeman, God, and everybody, 'Bobby's dead. I shot Bobby.' "

He shrugged and looked dire. "I know that's not what you want to hear."

"No," I said. At least it's consistent, I thought.

I looked at Gilstrap and he had a wide grin on his face, and in that moment I knew my hunch was still alive and kicking. "So you wanna hear what happened next?" he said.

"Sure I do."

"I talked to her through the bars for a minute. 'If I were you,' I said to her, 'I wouldn't say another thing till I see a lawyer first.' She says, 'I don't have a lawyer,' and I offered to call old McNamara for her. That's how he got into the case."

"Didn't Parley ever ask you about any of this?"

"Why should he? We just talked briefly on the phone that first day. I told him Mrs. Marshall had been booked and had asked for him. I figured she'd tell him. Then I went out of town and I've been gone ever since."

A long moment passed, but I knew there was more, I knew it the way a cop sometimes knows these things, and in the few seconds before he spoke again my own common sense told me what it was. I didn't dare believe it till he sank back in his chair and spoke. "I was about to leave when she said, 'Where are my children?' "

I took in a sudden deep breath. "Oh, man."

"Yeah. 'Where are my kids?' And I had to tell her I didn't know, and she got real upset. I told her not to worry, I was sure they were okay. But even then I knew."

"Lennie left them up there."

He laughed. "That stupid bastard. He's so anxious to clear the case solo he forgets about the kids. Seals up the crime scene with them still inside it, gets all the way down here and never gives the kids a thought till she asks where they are."

"Oh, *man*," I said again.

"Yeah. Naturally I can't prove any of that last part. But what else do you think could've happened?"

"I think we'll find out. Will you testify to what you just told me?"

"The facts of it, sure. That's my civic duty."

"We'll need your pictures too. A contact sheet would be nice for now."

He thought about it for a moment and said, "It won't surprise you to know that I've already been called by the DA."

I wasn't surprised: I would have been surprised if he hadn't.

"I don't think they'll be real anxious for me to be a witness." He laughed again. "Lennie's gonna shit a screaming green worm when he finds out you talked to me."

"Yeah, he is." I looked at him and tried not to laugh. "Hugh, that's the least of what he'll shit."

35

"I don't remember any of that," Laura said.

"What exactly *do* you remember after the deputy arrived?"

She shook her head.

"It's just that your memory is so clear and specific until then," Parley said.

"Yes, it is."

"So what happened to you?"

"I don't know, I must've fainted."

"Had you ever done that before?"

"Never. God, I've never fainted in my life. I don't believe in women who faint."

"Then what —"

I put a hand on his knee. Laura had closed her eyes, as if she might faint here in the jail. But suddenly she said, "You're right, everything was crystal clear up to that point. As long as I was moving, as long as I had a purpose, I was fine. I didn't look at Bobby at all, I just did what I had to do. It was afterward, when I had called the sheriff's office, that's when I remember looking over at Bobby on the floor. What an awful sight, just . . . it was just, Jesus, horrible. He had no face. The whole back of his head . . ."

"Take your time, hon," Parley said.

"I remember I had to hold on to something to keep my balance, even sitting down. I was sitting at the table and it was like this wave of nausea and — what's the word? — dizziness, vertigo, whatever you call it, came over me. I put my head down on the table and closed my eyes. I do remember that."

"Where were the kids all this time?"

"I had sent them to their bedroom at the far side of the house. I told Jerry not to let them out, and not to come out himself, until I came back for them."

"Did they know what had happened?"

"Jerry certainly did. I tried to keep it from the little ones."

"So you laid your head down on the table. What's the next thing you remember?"

"Being in jail."

"You don't remember the deputy arriving?"

"No. I think I had left the front door unlocked and I guess he just came on in."

"You don't remember him knocking or calling out?"

"No."

"You don't remember anything about what the deputy might've said to you, or what he might've done while he was there?"

She shook her head and shrugged.

"Nothing of the ride down?"

"I remember his smoke," she said suddenly. "Oh, God, I'll never forget that. It was stifling in that car, and he smoked till I thought I was gonna throw up."

"But you didn't?"

"Didn't what?"

"Puke in his car."

She shook her head. "I don't know."

"And that's all you remember?"

She nodded yes. Then she said, "I remember a voice, I guess it was his."

"Do you remember what it said?"

"He called Jerry a . . . he called Jerry a *retard*."

"I thought he didn't see Jerry."

"I don't know. Must've been later, in the jail, when I asked where my kids were."

"You remember anything else he might've said?"

"No. Just the voice in all that smoke."

"Okay. So you were in jail, then what?"

"It was cold. I was wet and it was very cold. I thought all this must be a dream. But I remember someone giving me some blankets and a bathrobe."

"Do you remember who it was?"

"Mr. Gilstrap," she said after a moment. "He's a photographer. You remember, we were all on a committee together a few years ago."

Parley made some notes. Again with that suddenness, Laura said, "I remember . . ."

"What?"

"I don't even know if this is real."

"Tell me anyway."

"It feels like a dream. But I remember a voice saying, 'You might as well sign a confession right now, honey, it'll go easier on you if you do.' "

Again she closed her eyes. " 'You might as well tell old dad all about it.' I seem to remember somebody saying that. 'C'mon, sweetie pie, write it down for daddy.' "

"But you don't remember who it was."

"I couldn't say for sure. Couldn't tell whether he was my friend or my enemy. He was a sweet-talker one minute, angry the next." She shook her head. "Does any of this matter now?"

"Yeah, it matters." Parley made some notes. "What did the deputy finally have to say about your kids?"

"He came in later and said they were fine. Said I could see them, in fact. I had a few minutes with them right here in this room."

"You say he came in later. How much later?"

"I have no idea. But it wasn't right away. I don't know. My whole sense of time that day was shot."

"When you saw the kids, did you ask them where they'd been?"

"No. I was too anxious to calm them down for anything like that. I knew I must look a fright and I wanted them to know I was okay."

He looked at me. "Janeway?"

I leaned over toward Laura. "Do you know anything about Jerry's birth parents?"

"No, nothing. Why is that important now?"

"I promised the caseworker I'd ask. No idea who they were?"

"No."

"Do you have the name of the adoption agency?"

"Somewhere, I think. I haven't looked at any of those records in years."

"What about the books? Did you ever hear any talk that maybe they weren't real?"

She looked puzzled at that and I said, "Like maybe the signatures were fakes?"

"No, I would have told you that. I didn't even know they were signed." She watched Parley gather his notes. "Does this mean they're worthless?"

"It sure would knock 'em for a loop," I said. "Without those signatures most of them are just used books."

"Let's not worry about that yet," Parley said. "Right now you just worry about remembering what happened. If you think of anything else, you call me pronto. Don't tell anybody else what we were talking about. Nobody, Laura. Not a word."

Out in the parking lot, he said, "It really doesn't matter about the books anymore, does it? If we get our motion to suppress, they won't have a case. A lot depends on the only other witnesses in that house that day — the kids — and what if anything we can get from 'em."

We called Erin that night. She was remarkably calm about the developments of the day. The news was good but we hadn't won yet. On her end her juvenile expert had interviewed the children several times. "It looks more and more like the little ones didn't see anything. And so far we've had no luck with Jerry, who may have seen everything."

I could almost hear her thinking. "Cliff," she said. "You were going to call that social worker back about Jerry."

"I had good vibes from her. Like she had something to tell me but couldn't."

"So call her. If she'll see you, come on back to Denver."

36

I met Rosemary Brenner for the second time the next afternoon, at the main office of Denver Social Services. She was eating lunch at her desk: an apple and a banana.

"How's Jerry doing?" I said.

"Surprisingly well. Have you found out anything for me?"

"Laura doesn't know anything about his parents. What's happening on your end?"

"Quite a bit, actually. We've had a number of meetings since I saw you, and your name has come up several times. It may surprise you to hear this, you've tried so hard to put people off, but it seems you do still have one or two advocates in this town. I've even heard it mentioned in passing that you've got a certain code of honor."

"Don't let that get around. It almost sounds like a certain strain of clap."

She smiled and dropped her banana peel into the trash can. "I'm only saying I like what I've seen of you and I do tend to trust you. But you must know we have rules and procedures, and people who forget that soon find themselves standing in unemployment lines. I'm not quite ready to retire from here in disgrace."

"I hear you."

"I would like nothing better than to have this charge against Mrs. Marshall resolved, however it goes. But if you want me to help you, I need to know that this kid's life won't be turned into some circus."

"At the same time —"

"He's a possible witness in your homicide case. I know."

"Some of this is going to be out of our control, Rosemary. We'll all do the best we can do, but surely it's in that kid's best interest for us to clear this case."

"I think we'd all agree with that. And there have been new developments. I was told I could show some of them to you, if you ask." She smiled foxily. "Are you asking?"

"Sure."

"We have an unusual situation here, something I've never encountered in all the years I've been doing this. On the one hand we have the interests of justice; on the other, the welfare of this child. That in itself isn't an unheard-of conflict, it's the way the pieces of it fit together this time that's unusual. The interests of the child may be vitally linked to the outcome of your case, but we don't yet know how, or what that outcome ought to be, at this point in time."

"We think she's innocent."

"I'm sure you do. If you're right, winning your case becomes urgent for both sides. Ideally, then, we'd like both sides to be served. But the child's interests have to be my top priority."

"I understand that."

"Let's make sure you do before we go any further. If I can get your word of honor that you'll try not to make a spectacle of this, I'll show you something that may enlighten you. At this point it's my call."

I felt the warning bells in my head. "I don't know what you're asking me to do."

She liked that: I hadn't just leaped at her with a rash promise, and I could see the approval on her face. She said, "Don't run right out and leak this to the press. It's all going to come out anyway, we know that. But I'm hoping maybe you can help us understand it better before that happens."

"I won't give anything to the press. But what could I possibly —"

"Think about it a minute. We're still discovering things. It changes almost daily, sometimes by the hour."

A moment passed. She said, "I'd do this if I were you."

"Then I will."

She leaned slightly over her desk and said, "Are you familiar with the term *savant?*"

"You mean like in idiot savant?"

She made a face. "That's an old expression, Janeway, well out of favor today. I would have hoped you'd know better."

"Oh, Rosemary, I have *deep* pockets of ignorance. But I'm always open to enlightenment."

She smiled. "Today we call them autistic savants."

"Is that what Jerry is?"

I saw her hand tremble. "He may be far more than that."

She leaned over the desk and said, "Did you see the movie *Rain Man?*"

"Sure. Great film."

"Remember how the Dustin Hoffman character was?"

I remembered Hoffman talking incessantly, often to himself: how he could cite endless sports statistics and instantly do unbelievable square roots in his head, but could barely function in what we think of as a normal world. "That's one example of an autistic savant," she said. "There aren't many of them in the world, and within that small group there are smaller groups, some so brilliant in their one field that they leave what we think of as normal minds in the dust. A mathematical savant may need help tying his shoelaces, but he can tell you in a second what day Christmas fell on in the year 1432. A musical savant can hear a classical piece one time and play it perfectly. Some of them have hundreds of scores in their heads and can do them flawlessly even years later. Just mention a name and out it comes."

She opened her desk and took out what looked like a small, detailed pencil sketch. "Recognize that?"

"Sure. It's the room where Marshall was killed." I held it up to the light. "This isn't a police sketch."

"No," she said, and again I felt the chills, the hair rising on my neck.

She took out another. "Ever seen that?"

"It's Marshall's study. That's his desk in the foreground, and behind the desk is the cabinet for his guns. There's the shotgun, leaning against the wall."

"How about this?"

"The library across the hall from the room where the murder happened. Look at those *books,* the definitions are incredible.

You can actually read some of the spines. If you know the books, you can picture the jackets from the little piece that's visible here."

"Take a closer look."

She handed me a large magnifying glass and I went straight to the books. What the glass revealed was nothing less than a photograph would show. This was better than a photo: it had detail beyond clarity, far past the ability of a camera except in perfect, extraordinary light with the best equipment and a master photographer. In the sketch the drapes were open: you couldn't see them, but a stream of sunlight poured in, hitting the floor in front of the bookcases and lighting up the corners of the room. My eyes went back to the books. The titles had been filled in with the steadiest hand, his pencils razor-sharp, his eye missing nothing even in recall. I saw a title, *America, Why I Love Her.* "That's the John Wayne book," I said, and Rosemary leaned over to look. "Look at this," I said, "he's even got a hint of the publisher's name at the bottom." I touched it with my finger, careful not to smudge the delicate pencil markings as I pointed out the name, Simon & Schuster, at the bottom of the spine. "We wondered about that," Rosemary said, "whether he got that kind of detail correct. But where would it have come from except from what he actually saw? I wouldn't imagine he has any idea what a Simon & Schuster is."

"I held this book in my hands," I said. "It's now in the sheriff's evidence room. This copy has a chip on the bottom edge of the jacket and he's even put that in." I went on down the bookshelf and it was almost as if I had stepped back into that house.

"He put in pieces of publishers' names on many of them," Rosemary said. "Harper & Row, Random House, Doubleday, on and on."

"Yeah," I said, "and all of them are right."

I ventured an opinion. "It must've taken him days just to do this one."

"Most of these sketches took less than an hour. The library took half a day."

I didn't know what to say, an extremely rare occurrence.

She rustled through some papers. "Here's one that's different."

Everything about it was shadowy, misty as in a dream: the room, the furniture, and even the brightly sunlit porch were indistinct. I could see a figure outside on the porch, but nothing, not even the sex of the subject, could be told. He, she, or it stood about five feet from the window, apparently trying to look in, but I couldn't be sure of that, either.

Rosemary said, "What do you make of that?"

"I don't know."

"No idea who that might be?"

"No."

"He was almost in a trancelike state when he made this. Later, when we tried to talk to him about it, he got upset."

"Upset how?"

"Cringed on the floor. I don't have to tell you, we didn't show that to him again."

A moment later she said, "I was wondering if this could be his way of getting at whatever happened."

"I don't know. If you're thinking it's a literal interpretation, a few things don't work. The sunlight, for example. It rained the day Marshall was killed."

She handed me another sheet: the same scene only darker. This time the porch was so shrouded that the figure was all but invisible, less than a shadow, present only by suggestion in the slightest human-sized darkening of the background. I stared at the two pictures. "What are the little pencil numbers at the top corner?"

"That's ours. That's how we kept track of what order they came out."

"He did it in sunlight first."

"Yes, in about twenty minutes. I wasn't there, but I hear he was totally absorbed. Finished it, then ripped it off the pad and threw it down on the floor and started the dark one immediately."

"You didn't show him the dark one?"

"God no, not after the first reaction we had."

"How'd you learn he could do this?"

"He was sitting quietly in the counselor's office and there was a magazine on the table. On the back cover was one of those *Draw Me* ads for an art school correspondence class. Suddenly he reached over and took up a yellow pad and drew the model. Then he put in the headline, in almost perfect block type, then he started on the text. We got him a sketchpad and some pencils, then an easel, then a *lot* of pencils and somebody to keep them sharp. He's been doing it nonstop ever since."

"Have you talked to the DA about this?"

"Not yet. We'll have to, of course."

"Of course," I said.

"A young woman from the district attorney's office made a few attempts to talk to him. We haven't seen much of her lately."

I looked at number 54 in the upper corner. "I take it you've got more of these."

"Dozens."

"Could I see them?"

"They aren't all here, but sure, at some point. Here's another one." She opened her drawer and handed me another sheet, numbered 85.

"That would be the twins," I said. "Little Bob and Susan. Damn, their faces are so real."

"Notice the loving looks he was able to put on them. You can almost see the affection he has for them. And I understand *that's* highly unusual. You don't often get feelings like this . . . usually it's just what he saw."

The twins were sitting in a room that I hadn't seen: probably their bedroom at the house. Behind them were two bunk-style beds, and on the wall a picture, a mountain scene that Jerry had also rendered in detail, a picture within a picture. Beside it was a calendar with its days marked off and a clock showing that it was one o'clock in the afternoon. Light could be seen shining in from some window off to the left.

"He did another one like that," she said.

I stared at the second picture. "It's not exactly alike."

"The clock's different. It seems to be later the same afternoon. The twins are gone and the light's not as good."

"And the picture's been moved on the wall."

"A little, yes. A foot or so to the right. Maybe he's correcting something. That might be the whole reason for the second picture. He drew some of you."

"Really?"

"Several, actually. In all of them you're in a wooded place at night. Maybe you'll see those at some point. For now —"

"I know where they came from and I know what I look like."

"He seems to like you. Like the twins."

"I helped him out of a little problem he was having."

I knew she wouldn't be satisfied with that, so I told her what had happened in the woods that night. I told her about my subsequent run-in with the judge and my night in the Paradise hoosegow, and this was followed by a moment of near total silence. Slowly the sounds of life returned: someone talking in the hall, the ticking of the clock on her wall. We made eye contact again and something had changed between us.

"Did Jerry put words to any of these?"

"He can't write," she said. "Here, I've got a couple more to show you. Do you recognize this man? He looks like a cop."

"Lennie Walsh. He was the arresting officer. A real bastard."

"Only part of the scene is shown . . . just that slash down the middle of the page. What do you make of that?"

Lennie stood in the death room, radiating anger. He had a notepad in his hand and his mouth was open.

"He looks like he's screaming at somebody," she said.

"Laura, no doubt."

"Is he allowed to talk to her like this?"

"Depends, I guess. He shouldn't, if he is."

"He looks like an ugly man. I don't mean necessarily in the physical sense."

"I know how you mean it, and you're right." I looked up at her. "This guy's a caveman, Rosemary. He shouldn't be allowed to talk to anybody."

"I wonder why there's only that little slice of picture. Just on this one."

"The kid was probably seeing them through a crack in the door. Didn't want them to see him." I looked up at her and smiled. "But I think you knew that."

"I imagine I could've figured it out."

I went through all the pictures slowly, trying to burn them into my mind. A full minute later she said, in that same too obvious voice, "So I take it this is important."

"Oh, please." I held my hand over my heart.

A big piece of another minute passed. "Please," I said again.

"I've got one more to show you."

She had saved the best for last. When she showed it to me, I felt light-headed, almost faint at the implications. Again we were in the murder room. In the seconds after I had looked at it, I looked again and saw all the little things that didn't matter. I could see on through the front porch to the fierce rain falling on the meadow. I could see, half-lost in that mist, the fence where Laura had been standing when she heard the shot. I could see a hint of the hill across the way, where I had staked out the place and watched the Keeler boys drive up to the front door. None of this mattered as I looked again at what the picture really showed: the broken police tape that Lennie, that incomparable moron, had used to seal the room as a crime scene. I could only read part of it clearly but I knew what it said, I knew the words POLICE LINE DO NOT CROSS by heart: I could see that image almost any night in my dreams. This one had been partly crushed and tossed over the table.

There was blood on the wall, bloody little handprints, fingerprints on the tape, smears everywhere. None of this had been mentioned in the evidence.

Be still my raging heart. First the stupid bastard had left the kids inside, then he had gone back up there and washed off the walls in an effort to hide what the kids had done. He had committed a crime and a second fatal error trying to cover up the first.

Rosemary smiled sadly. "Just be careful, Janeway. Let's do this right."

37

Erin and I finally talked about the case after supper. She listened in stony silence as I told her about my adventure with the Preacher, my burglary of his house, and what I had found there. Gradually her eyes narrowed to slits, she suffered through the account to the sorry end of it, and then, in a masterpiece of brevity, said, "Okay, let's move on." This was fine with me: she knew now and if she didn't want to beat it to death with too much talk, I figured there was a reason for that. She was much more upbeat about my conversation with Rosemary Brenner. The savant discovery was exciting but it had a troubling edge to it. Why had Laura failed to tell us about this? Could she possibly not have known? "I think it's reasonable that she never associated it with Bobby's murder," I said. "She didn't know Jerry's abilities would suddenly become important." Still, Erin said, now we had to ask her these things. The hearing on our motion to suppress was two days away. "I'm going over tomorrow anyway, so I can do that." She had to tie up some loose ends here in the morning and she should be in Paradise sometime after noon. "I think I'm going on ahead," I said. "I want to look at the house again."

If she suspected anything, she didn't ask. I hadn't told her about the picture in the kids' room. If the picture had in fact been moved, there was probably a reason, and I didn't want to make that discovery openly on my own. I didn't want it to come from me at all. We went to bed at eleven; I got three hours of restless sleep and was on the road in the dark early morning. I turned in to Paradise just as the sun was breaking over the mountains. Parley was already up when I arrived at his house. "Just in time for some flapjacks and eggs."

We sat at his table, eating a breakfast guaranteed to shorten any life span.

"I take it Erin called you," I said.

He nodded and offered more pancakes, which I waved off with an appreciative gesture. "So where are we in the scheme of things?" he said. "Do I want to ask you what really happened between you and that preacher man?"

"Probably not." A strained moment passed. "I think I should stay out of the court's way as much as possible from here on out. Not be an obvious part of the team, so to speak. Just between you and me, though, I'd sure like to go back up to the house before the world finds out about Jerry."

"That's no problem. The DA turned the house back over to us. I've got the keys."

He noticed my surprise. "Mainly what they cared about was getting those books out. The house had already been gone over, hadn't it?"

"That's what I understand," I said. "Miss Bailey did say they were treating it as a whole new crime scene."

"I guess Gill overruled her on that. Probably figured there wasn't much to be gained by doing it all over again, not after Lennie'd been plowing ass-first through it. And they didn't know what we know. If you still want to go up, leave those dishes and let's go do it."

Twenty minutes later we came up the rise to the meadow. It looked different, peaceful now in the warm sunlight. We stood on the porch for a moment, gazing over the distant mountain range; then Parley unlocked the door and the dark interior pulled us in where death was still part of the air. I stared down at the black bloodstain.

"What is it you're lookin' for?"

"Just looking. Can I wander a bit?"

"Sure. Long as you don't mind me wandering with you."

I wandered into the library, where long rows of empty shelves now faced the two doors. "Not much to see here anymore," Parley said.

I went on back into a dark hall. I could feel his scrutiny and hear his footsteps just a couple of feet behind my own. At the end of the hallway was a closed door. I got down on my knees and looked at the doorknob.

"Is it possible to have some light in here?"

He turned on a dim hall light. "That's not much, I'm afraid."

"I think there's something here. You got a flashlight in the car?"

"In the glove compartment."

"I'll come with," I said before he could ask.

We retrieved the light together; then, again in the hallway, I lay on my back and lit up the bottom of the doorknob.

"There is something here," I said. "It's black now, but I think it's old blood."

He lay down on the floor beside me.

"Don't touch it, Parley. I think it may be a fingerprint."

"Damned small one if it is." He shook his old head.

"Can I open this door? I'll be careful."

The door opened into the kids' room. I rolled to my feet and gave Parley a hand, and he got up with a grunt. The room looked exactly as Jerry had pictured it: the calendar frozen on that day, the clock still going, the picture there on the wall where, perhaps, someone had moved it. I walked through the room looking at the walls. I looked out the window.

"You see something out there?"

"I don't know, I thought I did."

He went to the window and just that quickly I touched the edge of the picture and tilted it slightly off-center.

"Nothing out there. You sure get jumpy when you come up here, Janeway. Must be something about the thin air."

I laughed politely and waited for him to notice the picture, even though I had no way of knowing what if anything might be there. Parley looked up.

He sees it, I thought. But he turned away and said, "You finished in here?"

"I don't know yet. Let's look some more."

Goddammit, Parley, look at the friggin' picture!

422

He stared out the window, his mind obviously in neutral. To him the case was in good shape and I was spinning my wheels. Annoyed, I said, "It takes you a while to wake up in the morning, doesn't it?"

He looked at me curiously. "Why, am I missing something?"

"Hell, how would we know, you're in such a helluva hurry to get out of here."

"There can't be much left to it after that mob's been through here, can it?"

"I wouldn't say that. Didn't we just find a print on the door?"

"That could be an old Popsicle smear for all you know. What do you want to do, toss the place again?"

"As a matter of fact, yeah. I sure would like to give it more than just a casual once-over. Look, we know Lennie locked the kids in the house. We've already found what may be blood or Popsicle residue on the doorknob. Whatever it is, you should be excited about it, not walking around in some stupefied state."

A flash of anger spread across his face, replaced by embarrassment. "Okay, so it takes me a while to get goin' in the morning. What do you want me to do?"

"You look on one side of the room, I'll look on the other."

"What'm I looking for, more blood?"

"Hell, anything. Look under the bunk beds with the flashlight. Let's be careful, so we don't contaminate it any more than it already has been."

"Hey, I'm awake now, you don't need to belabor the obvious. What're you gonna be doing while I'm crawling around over here?"

"I'll look in the closet and around the dressers."

I tried to forget him then: just let him be, I thought; let him find it in his own way and in his own time. But as time passed I found my patience wearing thin. *What the hell are you* doing *over there?* I wanted to shout. *Does something have to rise up and bite you between the legs before you —*

Then he said, "Cliff," and I knew by his tone that whatever was there, he had found it. I leaned out of the closet. He had the picture off the wall and was holding it by its corners. On the wall was a full black palm print with four partial fingers.

38

By midafternoon the house was again crowded with people. Erin and Parley had agreed that the DA would have to be informed, *noticed-in* in legal jargon, and people began arriving just after one o'clock. For the third time there was a full-court press by the prosecution with cameras and lights and people coming in and out. Erin came in at two. Ann Bailey arrived a moment later, looking furious. She and Erin nodded crisply to each other. Meanwhile we began building our record of what we had found there. "We'll need our own photographer," Parley said, but the only one in town was Hugh Gilstrap, who would also be our witness. "I don't think that'll hurt his credibility," Erin said. "Let's hire him if he'll come up, deal with him like any other professional, and keep our distance otherwise." Then she stood back and watched the circus, saying nothing in that first hour while the lab man shot his photos of the wall.

Gilstrap arrived and duplicated the scene for us, and in the late afternoon we conferred with Miss Bailey.

"We'll want to send this palm-print over to the CBI in Montrose," she said.

"We'd have no objection to that," Erin said.

"It does mean we'll have to cut this piece of wall out. I don't think we could lift that print off without destroying it."

"Ann, it's pretty clear that one of the kids made that mark," Parley said.

"Yeah, well, let's find out for sure this time."

"You'll at least agree that it's not Laura's print."

"I'm not agreeing to anything at this point."

"Ann," Parley said patiently. "You've gotta know —"

"What, that our deputy screwed up? Even if that's so, that's all we know at the moment. You want me to what, dismiss this case on the basis of that?"

"This case is bullshit."

"Is it? Do I have to remind you that she confessed? She confessed, Mr. McNamara. The first words out of her mouth to your own witness were 'I shot Bobby.' She said it at least twice after that, and we have witnesses."

"This isn't getting us anywhere," Erin said. "We'll see what happens at the hearing tomorrow."

"We'll see," Miss Bailey said. She sounded confident but Erin met her eyes and put on that enigmatic face and Miss Bailey looked away. Was that my imagination or was it the real crack in the wall of ice she showed to the world? She had to be seriously worried about Lennie at this point. What she might not know was how worried she ought to be and why. She spoke to Parley. "Can we agree on taking out that piece of wall? Or does that have to go through an act of God like everything else in this case?"

Erin nodded and Parley said, "The defendant gives you her blessing to desecrate her house."

"Then let's get it done. I *had* a dinner date tonight."

A technician came in with a drill and a small saw. "Take that whole square, everything the picture was hiding," Miss Bailey said, and five minutes later the piece of wall was free and bagged. "I want the doorknob too," Miss Bailey said, and it was carefully removed from the door and bagged.

Gilstrap shot pictures of the whole process. Miss Bailey said, "We're going to seal the house again, I'll need your keys, please," and Parley turned them over.

They wrapped up their work in the early evening. Miss Bailey stayed until the end and Erin stood off to the side and watched her. Again the house was locked and sealed with crime tape and we all moved outside to the cars.

"Tomorrow, then," Miss Bailey said.

Erin nodded. "See you then."

That night we had a two-hour meeting with our defendant in the jail. Laura's defense, simple and old as time, would be that she hadn't done it. If she had confessed to anyone, she had done it under stress, out of fear for her eldest son.

This was it, then: the murder of Robert Charles Marshall had been the work of some unknown party, for reasons unknown and perhaps ever unknowable. This fit somewhat with the shadowy figure Bobby had become, and the burden of proving otherwise would belong to the state. In death no one could pin him down: there were no files in his cabinet, no letters from the Preacher or anyone else. "He burned a lot of stuff," Laura said. "He was always burning stuff in the yard. As he got older, he seemed to be slipping deeper into paranoia. He had become obsessed with his privacy."

Erin took lengthy notes. She couldn't

imagine Bobby that way, she said: he had always been so outgoing when they were young. "He was like a different person then," Laura agreed. "You can't imagine how he'd changed. I lived with him for years, and there were times at the end when I barely knew him."

She had thought seriously of divorce, especially in the last three years. "But then I considered the children and I couldn't do it. The little ones loved Bobby."

"He was good to his own children?" Erin asked.

"Oh, yeah. He loved them and they loved him. I have *no* doubt of that. And he tried with Jerry too, I'm not saying he didn't try. In his own way Bobby was a good man and he sure didn't deserve what happened to him."

"How did he try? What did he do?"

"Oh, he'd take Jerry for walks . . . not real often, but sometimes they'd walk down the road and Bobby would try to talk to him. Then when they came back, he'd take Jerry into his room and they'd . . ."

"What? What did they do?"

"Talk. I don't know, they'd be in there for maybe an hour. I couldn't make out his words but I could hear Bobby talking through the door."

"Not angry, though."

"No, I'd have gone in and stopped that. Bobby's voice was always very soft."

"Did he sound like he might be trying to teach Jerry something?"

She almost laughed at that. "God, no! Bobby was no teacher, that's for sure."

"I don't mean teach like in schooling."

"Then I guess I don't understand you."

"Persuasion," Erin said. "Like maybe he was trying to persuade Jerry to do something."

"If he was, he never got anywhere. Jerry just didn't like Bobby, I told you that."

Laura watched Erin writing in the long silence that followed.

"Did you ever suspect that Bobby had any improper relations with Jerry?"

Laura's eyes opened wide. "My God, what are you suggesting?"

"I'm just asking questions. What are you thinking?"

"But you can't mean anything like that. Jesus, Erin, you knew Bobby, you know he'd never do anything like that to a child."

"As it turned out, I didn't know Bobby at all, did I?"

Laura stared at the wall. "I've told you before, you've got a right to be angry with both of us. But you can't believe that."

"Look," Erin said, "let me put it in very straight terms, okay? Did Bobby ever abuse Jerry, any of your kids, sexually?"

"That's offensive."

"That's what I get paid for," Erin said. She smiled slightly, perhaps at the fact that she wasn't getting paid yet for anything. "I get paid to ask offensive questions."

Laura took a long time to answer; too long, I thought. At last she gave us a slight headshake.

"Did Bobby ever molest Jerry?" Erin asked.

"Of course not."

"Pardon me for lingering on this, but you don't deny it with any real conviction."

"What do you want me to do, scream?"

"Damn it, I want you to tell the truth."

"No," Laura said. "No, no, no."

"No what? No, he didn't, or no, you won't tell me the truth?"

"He didn't. Of course he didn't." But then, into the silence, Laura said, "What are you going to do? What are you thinking?"

"I'm asking you a question. Which you are doing your best to avoid."

"What if I said . . ."

Erin arched her eyebrow.

"I never actually saw anything, but once

or twice I wondered. That's all." Her face was flushed as she stared at Erin. "That's *all!* There's nothing else to say! It's just something you think in an odd moment. Surely this won't come out."

"Not tomorrow. But if it goes to trial, we'll have to see what's there."

"It would give me a great motive for shooting Bobby."

Erin said nothing, but I saw awareness light up Laura's face. It was also a sudden new motive for Jerry.

"You have any questions, Cliff?" Erin said.

"Yeah, I do. I want to ask a few more things about Jerry."

"Oh, Christ, will this never end?"

"It's just that he seems to have an amazing talent."

The silence stretched and became awkward.

"Laura?"

"What do you want me to say?"

I shrugged. "Just a reaction would be a start. Some kind of acknowledgment that we're on the same page."

"He's an artist," Laura said at last. "Jerry is a great natural artist."

Clearly annoyed now, Erin said, "You never told us about that before."

"You never asked me. Is it important?"

Parley gave a little laugh and looked away.

"Is this important?" Laura asked again. "What's it got to do with what happened?"

"You've *got* to stop making those judgments," Parley said. "If I can only do one thing on this earth, I would like to get you to stop playing lawyer. Do you think you could possibly do that?"

"What don't you understand about what I did? I didn't want him to be involved in any of this, is that so hard to understand? I didn't want everybody probing him like he's some kind of guinea pig, like you're doing right now . . . upsetting him with all this terrible stuff. Anyway, how is it important?"

"Jerry's been drawing almost nonstop all week," I said. "Scenes of the crime. Pictures of that day — "

"Jesus Christ, this is *exactly* what I was afraid of! It's not enough that he had to go through it, now you're all going to drive him crazy worrying about it."

"Nobody's asked him to draw anything. From what I understand it was a spontaneous thing."

"What difference does it make how it started? Now they've got him started, it doesn't matter how, and they're going to keep after him till they break him down. Jesus, hasn't he had enough trouble in his life?"

She looked at Erin. "I knew I shouldn't have tried to fight this, I knew Jerry would be dragged into it, and now here he is; he should be drawing pictures of the mountains and the streams, and instead they've got him reliving all this terrible stuff."

The room went suddenly quiet. Then Erin said in her hard voice, "Get used to it. Jerry's a material witness in a murder case. The questions are just getting started."

Laura shook her head. "I should never have agreed to this."

"Agreed to what?"

"Any of this. You knew from the start I didn't want to do this."

"Then tell me, please, what *do* you want to do?"

"What I should've done all along."

"You'll have to say it."

They looked at each other.

"Well?"

"I've got to change what I . . ."

Erin gave a dry little laugh. "Change what? Your plea?"

"If I have to, yes."

"Then you can do it without me." Erin

began gathering her papers.

Laura, with a sudden look of alarm, said, "Where are you going?"

"Where do you think I'm going? I do have one or two other things to do in my life."

"You're angry. I could always tell when you were angry. Still can."

"It doesn't matter what I am. I told you before, I haven't got time for this."

"Wait a minute —"

"What for? So I can watch you throw yourself to the wolves? I don't think so."

Laura looked at Parley. "Can she do this? Can she just walk out on me?"

"I can do whatever I want," Erin said. "I'm not your attorney of record. He is."

"Wait a minute. Please, Erin, *please!* You've got to understand something."

"No, *you* understand. What is your case? Did you kill your husband or not?"

They looked at each other.

"Did you?"

Laura shook her head.

"Then that's how you'll plead. Not guilty. Not maybe not guilty with footnotes for unanticipated contingencies. You will not even think of offering yourself as a sacrifice for Jerry or anybody else. No extenuating circumstances, no waffling. You are not guilty. Once and for all, can we at least be clear on that?"

"All right, yes . . . yes, okay . . . okay."

"Get that apology out of your voice. You aren't maybe not guilty, you will not plead guilty if suspicion falls on someone else, you are flat-out not guilty. That's what we go with, wherever it leads."

"You don't understand. You can't understand."

"Here we go again. Please listen carefully. I don't *care* why you think you've got to lie. I can't care about stuff like that. The only thing I need to understand or care about is what this case is, not why you want to cloud it up with other issues. You're going to kill yourself with that argument." Erin pulled her chair closer. "Do you want me to help you or not?"

"You know I do."

"Then stop worrying about Jerry and get your own story straight. Let's go over it again . . . what you'll say if we go to trial and how you'll say it."

Because much of the doubt we would cast over the state's case had to come from Laura herself, she would have to testify at the trial. Parley was clearly nervous about this. He still considered her too unpredictable, too easily shaken when the inevitable questions about Jerry arose, but Jerry was in it now and nothing could be done about that. The ashes from the back-room fireplace were part of the evidence. The sheriff had bagged and taken the entire grate, and he had noted a charred smear of blood on it, and traces of blood scattered throughout the ashes. The shirt fragment looked identical to Jerry's shirt, just as Laura had said. "I think we have a reasonable doubt," Erin said. "But Laura can't escape it, it's coming in, what she did with Jerry's clothes is not going away. Now we've got to make them understand why."

I knew Erin considered Jerry one of our strong suits. She liked our chances but she retreated from optimism if we tried too hard to agree with her. "They're pushing a weak case, and that's always a reason to worry. Like they've got something we don't know about." She considered Gill easily capable of pushing it for political reasons. This was the county's first murder case in forty years, and he didn't want to back away and he sure didn't want to lose it.

It was late when we left the jail. The town was dark and the café about to close, but Parley turned on the charm and coaxed three simple hamburger steaks out of them. We sat at a table in the far corner of the room and went over tactics and where Lennie's lies would take him next. "This guy is a worm," Erin said. "I have no sympathy for creeps like him."

She ticked off his offenses on her fingers.

"First he messes up the crime scene. Then he panics and he's got to manufacture a cover-up, so he destroys evidence. He's not guilty of perjury yet, but he will be if I give him a little bit of rope. What else can he do now but keep up the lie?"

She stared into the dark place under the table. "I'm gonna destroy that bastard."

"They'll never sit still for that," Parley said. "Not in a hearing to suppress."

"You can bet me. Whatever else he is, Gill's a political animal and he doesn't want to go to trial on Lennie's flimsy shoulders. I've got a hunch we can win this thing right there in the hearing."

She looked up at me. "I'd like you to go in with us. You don't need to say a word, just sit behind me in the courtroom and give Lennie the evil eye. I think you've got his number."

I was uneasy even in that role, but she lifted her wineglass. "Here's to tomorrow. And the beginning of the end for deputy whatever."

39

Lennie was sitting sullenly in the courtroom when we arrived that morning. The judge's court reporter was leaning over his box looking bored. We were all early; no one else was yet in the room, but Lennie squared his shoulders, filling out his police jacket, and looked back at us. "What's he doing here?" he said gruffly, and the court reporter smiled playfully and took down his words.

"Mr. Janeway is my investigator," Erin said. I faced them all and smiled.

"I didn't ask you that, I know who he is. What's he need to *investigate* in here?"

"You never know." Erin smiled pleasantly.

"You never know *what?*"

"When some great lie that needs investigating will surface."

"Are you trying to fuck with me, sister?"

"No way. I wouldn't do that for a hundred million dollars."

Two doors opened suddenly. The bailiff came in from chambers, and from the hall I heard Ann Bailey's voice. She and Gill came down, nodded crisply, and sat on the bench across from us. Our witness, Hugh Gilstrap, was right behind them, and he took a seat in the row behind us.

Lennie stared back at the photographer and he looked pale. He jerked his thumb my way. "I don't want him here."

"I'm sure you don't want any of us here, including yourself," Erin said. "Too bad you don't get to pick and choose."

Lennie pointed a trembling finger. "Listen, sister, don't you screw around with me. You hear what I'm saying?"

"My goodness, Deputy, that sounds like a threat."

"Lennie, please," Miss Bailey said, wincing.

"I don't know what the hell these people think they're gonna prove. Everything I did was by the book. *Ev-ry*thing."

"Then you won't mind telling us about it," Erin said.

"It's all in my report. This hearing is bullshit."

"That may be, but it's one of the trials of life, you'll just have to put up with it."

"Lennie," Miss Bailey said softly. "Remember what we discussed."

"Some people you just can't coach," Erin said. "They are the great uncoachables. No matter what you tell them, they're always going to be a wild hair."

"Listen to that shit," Lennie said. "That's exactly what I'm talking about."

Now Gill leaned forward and looked Lennie in the eyes. He spoke so softly that only Lennie could hear him, but he was intense, and when he was finished, Lennie sat glumly and silently. Erin was right, I thought: he's a loose cannon, ready to blow up.

I heard another shuffle and the sheriff arrived with Laura. She sat with us and he joined the prosecutors. The bailiff said, "All rise," and the judge came in.

The judge sat, then we sat, and he looked over at the prosecution's side of the bench. "Where are your witnesses, Mr. Gill?"

"Mr. McNamara is only interested in Deputy Walsh, Your Honor. If we brought them all in, this hearing could run half a day. We could have done that, but the testimony from the preliminary hearing won't change. We're trying to save the court's time."

"Mr. McNamara?"

"That's fine with us, Your Honor."

"All right then. Let's get going."

Miss Bailey rose and called Lennie, who raised his hand over the Bible and was sworn.

What followed was ten minutes of routine, almost pedantic questioning: *Where were you when you first got the call? Where was the sheriff and why wasn't he in the office?* Lennie lied about that, covering the sheriff's ass by saying he wasn't sure.

What did you do right after the call came in? How long did it take you to get up the hill to Mrs. Marshall's house? Did you knock on the door? When did you decide it would be proper for you to enter the premises?

"I looked in through the open door," Lennie said. "I could see that something bad had happened. Mrs. Marshall was sitting at the table with blood on her dress. There was a gun on the floor."

Gill leaned over and whispered something to Miss Bailey. She furrowed her brow, obviously annoyed. "One minute, please, Your Honor."

The judge looked away and drummed his fingers on the bench. Miss Bailey and Gill were locked in some kind of disagreement for most of a minute. In the end, Gill made his point more forcefully and Miss Bailey, frustrated, said, "Okay, tell us what you did next."

The remainder of Lennie's testimony was almost to the letter what I remembered from the preliminary hearing. Everything sounded proper to hear him tell it. He had gone step by step, discovering things in their correct order. Miss Bailey gave Gill another look and said, "That's all."

Erin rose slowly and came forward. "You say you looked in through the open door and saw Mrs. Marshall at the table with blood on her dress. You say there was a gun on the floor. And you could see all that from the front doorstep?"

"Most of it, yes."

"How much of it?"

"Enough of it."

"What specifically does that *mean*, Deputy? Keep in mind, please, that we have all been up there, we have all looked in through that front door. If you'd rather do this the hard way, we can all go up there right now and see just what's visible from the front door."

Lennie seethed in his hotbox.

"Isn't it true that you went inside without seeing anything?"

"I sure didn't go up there on a blind. I knew something bad had happened."

"How did you know that?"

"Because of the *phone* call, isn't that obvious? She didn't call the sheriff's office to find out the time of day or directions down the mountain. What would you think?"

"What I'd think isn't the point here, I didn't enter the Marshalls' house." Erin moved around the room, looked out the window, and came back to her spot. "What did she say when she called?"

"Her husband had been murdered."

"Is that what she said?"

I saw Miss Bailey give a slight headshake across the table. Lennie turned and we stared at each other for a few seconds. "Make him stop that, Judge," Lennie said.

The judge gave me a stern look. But he said, "Just answer the questions, Deputy."

"The question was," Erin said, "did she say her husband had been murdered?"

"Maybe that wasn't it exactly."

"It doesn't have to be exact, here and now. Just the true gist of it. There's a tape, as you know. We can get the exact wording later if you can't remember it now."

"I'm trying to recollect."

"Take your time."

"She said there'd been a shooting. Her husband had been shot."

"Yes, that's what the tape will show. There had been a shooting. For all you knew at that moment, it had been an accident. Isn't that right, Deputy?"

"I knew it hadn't been any accident."

"From what, just the sound of her voice?"

"That's right."

"From your vast experience and the sound of her voice."

"Don't you belittle me," Lennie said, and Miss Bailey closed her eyes.

Erin smiled. "I certainly don't mean to, Deputy."

Miss Bailey came up from her chair. "Your Honor, these personal attacks —"

"Just ask the questions, Ms. d'Angelo."

"How many shootings have you investigated in your career, Deputy?"

"I know what guilty people sound like."

"That must be a great talent in your line of work. So the answer to my question is what? Fifty? . . . Ten? . . . Two?"

"You know we haven't had many shootings here."

"The answer then is none. Is that right?"

"The woman was hysterical."

"I'm sure she was. Her husband had just been killed." Erin looked at her notes. "All right, you got up there, the door was open, you went inside and found Mrs. Marshall at the table. Is that it?"

"Something like that."

"Well, if it wasn't *exactly* like that, Deputy, would you please tell us what was different about it?"

"I'll have to refer to my report."

"I have a copy of it here. Do you want to look at it?"

"No, I remember now."

"Then tell us, please."

"I called in through the open door. Nobody answered, so I went in. Hell, for all I knew Marshall might still be alive, bleeding to death in there."

"So you went on in. Were you armed? Did you take out your weapon?"

"You better believe it. It's easy for you to ask sarcastic questions here in this nice warm courthouse. You try going out alone to a scene like that and see how you like it."

"So you walked in on Mrs. Marshall with your gun drawn."

"And I was right, wasn't I? Her husband was dead at her feet and there wasn't any ifs or maybes about it."

"No, there weren't. And you immediately assumed that she had done it."

"Well, he had two lethal wounds, so I knew right off he didn't do it to himself. Nobody else was there."

"Nobody you saw. Tell us what happened then."

"I spoke to her. She looked up and said, 'I shot Bobby.'"

He said this smugly, with a smirk of victory, as if he had just put the biggity-ass, hotshot lawyer in her place. Erin nodded and said, "I understand you spent some time down at the station trying to get her to confess. Now you're telling us she'd already confessed, is that correct?"

I glanced at the prosecution table, expecting an objection that never came.

"She gave me a verbal confession, first words out of her mouth."

"And at the station you were trying to . . ."

"Get her to sign it, what do you think?"

"Without a lawyer present to protect her interests."

"I had already read her her rights — twice, in fact. Once up at the house, once in the jail."

"Which no one but yourself saw or heard."

"Freeman was there when I gave her her rights the second time."

"Freeman being the old jailer."

"That's right."

"So she gave you this spontaneous confession at the house. Did she repeat that at the jail?"

"Yeah. Not to me, but —"

"Why do you suppose not?"

"Someone had arrived and told her not to."

"Ah. Who might that have been?"

"You know who it was."

"You mean the photographer, Mr. Gilstrap, is that correct?"

"Yeah," Lennie said with obvious reluctance.

"Good thing he was there, wasn't it?"

"Good for you maybe; it gives you something to chew on. But lemme tell you something, lady, what he did was totally off-base. He was interfering with an officer of the law in an official duty. Whatever he says, I'd take with a grain of salt if I were you."

"Thank you, officer. He'll give us his version shortly."

"He'll say I'm lying. Are you calling me a liar?"

Miss Bailey leaned forward. "Lennie —"

"God*dam*mit, I don't have to sit still for that shit."

"Let's assume somebody was lying," Erin said. "You're saying it was Gilstrap, is that correct?"

"I'm saying what I just said. Nothing more, nothing less."

"I think you're saying a good deal more

than that, Deputy. In fact you know exactly what Mr. Gilstrap observed that day."

"I know what he *thinks*."

"He's here to testify to what he saw. Under oath, sir, as you are."

"Don't talk to me that way. I don't lie."

"He thinks you sealed up the house and left —"

"Now *that* is bullshit."

The judge picked up his gavel. "Sir, you will not use gutter language in my court-room."

Lennie stared ahead as if he had heard none of this. Erin leaned over into his line of vision, and in that moment there were just the two of them locked in a battle as old as time. "Are you going to tell us you did not seal up the crime scene and leave Mrs. Marshall's children inside?"

"That's a fuckin' lie."

The gavel rapped; the judge roared something about contempt. Lennie said, "It's a lie, it's a lie, it's a goddamned lie. Read my lips and go to hell." Erin said, "Your Honor, may the record reflect that the witness appears to be enraged by this line of questioning and that his attitude toward me is one of extreme hostility."

"So ordered."

"You've gone a bit pale, Deputy," Erin

said. "Would you like some water?"

"You just go to hell." He looked at Gill, then at Miss Bailey, and finally, at last, at the judge. In a watery voice, he said, "Your Honor . . ."

Softly, Erin said, "May I just ask a few more questions, Your Honor?"

And the judge, in his steely voice, said, "Go on."

Go on, fry the bastard.

"Are you people gonna sit still for this shit?"

Miss Bailey rose from her chair. "Your Honor . . ."

"Hey," the judge said, motioning her down. "He rigged his own sail."

"Did you seal up the house," Erin said, "and *then* go back up there —"

"*No!* . . . No, I did not!"

"— and while you were there the second time, did you destroy every blood trace that that kid had put on the walls *after* you left them in there —"

"You . . . are . . . outta . . . your . . . fuckin' . . . mind."

"All the bloody little fingerprints —"

"No, goddammit, *no!*"

"All the smears on the wall —"

"I'm not saying another word to this bitch."

450

"What did you do with the bloody police tape with the fingerprints all over it?"

"You looked at the crime scene photos. You see any tape with blood on it?"

"I'm talking about the other tape, Officer Walsh. The original tape you used to seal the room before the kid got in there and messed it all up."

"That never happened."

"Let me suggest, Deputy, that you did return to the Marshall house. And at that time you discovered that the children had smeared blood on the walls and had even handled the police tape with their bloody hands. And let me also suggest that when you saw what they had done, you destroyed that police tape and replaced it with a fresh one, and that you also washed all the smeared blood and handprints off the walls. Isn't it true that this is in fact what you did."

Lennie looked at the DA. "She's gone crazy. She's gone fuckin' nuts."

Erin smiled at him, not unkindly.

Lennie looked imploringly at Miss Bailey. "What the hell are you doing to me? We're supposed to be on the same side, for Christ's sake! How can you let her do this?"

"Better now than at the trial," Erin said. "Right, Miss Bailey?"

"I wasn't *talking* to you, goddammit! Can't you understand English?"

"Your honor, I would once again ask that the record reflect —"

"Fuck you! Fuck you all!"

Suddenly he got up and pulled open his jacket, and for just a moment his hand came to rest on his gun. Everyone in the room tensed. Miss Bailey said, "*Jesus* Christ, Lennie, what are you doing with that gun in here?" Lennie whirled, kicked over the chair, shattered it against the wall, and stalked out. We all sat and stared at one another, and for a moment no one knew what to say.

The judge recovered first. "I want a warrant sworn out for that man's arrest," he said to the sheriff. "Then you get out there and find him."

"Yes, sir."

He looked at the two sides. "Is there any reason why I shouldn't rule right now on the motion to suppress?"

Gill stood and said, "Well, Your Honor, I would respectfully request a continuance until Deputy Walsh is found and we have a chance to assess his bizarre behavior here today."

"What's to assess?" Erin said. "It's clear that his entire investigation is tainted and his testimony has been full of lies from the beginning. So while they're assessing things, our client continues to sit in jail based largely on the word of a man who did everything but pull a gun on us all."

"I'm inclined to agree," the judge said.

"At least, let us find him, Judge," Gill said.

"I'll give you till the middle of next week," the judge said. "I'll be out of town till next Wednesday. If Deputy Walsh has not been produced by then and brought in here as a prisoner, unarmed, I will suppress his entire testimony."

"Thank you, Your Honor."

The judge got up and went into his chambers.

Gill cleared his throat. "I think we might be willing to look at a lesser charge. What would you say to man one?"

"She killed him in the heat of an argument," Miss Bailey said.

"Whoever killed him might've done that," Parley said in a soft, corrective tone.

Whoever it was had killed him, then shot him again for good measure. Miss Bailey was right about one thing: that was indeed hot blood at work. Erin smiled, gracious now, and said, "Of course we're obligated to take your offer to our client. But there's

453

no way I could advise her to accept such a thing."

Of course they knew that too. No one asked what the defense would suggest, but at some point Erin, in her softest voice, told them anyway: "C'mon, guys. How about dropping these charges and letting her get back to her children?"

40

We headed toward the Christmas season on a high note. Lennie had disappeared. The Wednesday deadline came and went; the judge threw out all of Lennie's testimony, and there was a mood of celebration at lunch that day. "Essentially this leaves them with no case," Erin said.

She hoped that afternoon for word from the district attorney that the charges were being dropped, but it didn't come. "It's starting to look like they intend to string us along till the fat lady sings," she said for my ears only. "I still think they've got to dismiss, but until they do I've got to prepare for trial." In mid-December Miss Bailey was conspicuously everywhere. She personally conducted all the interviews yet again in her rugged determination to salvage their case. We saw her in the stores and hustling across the street from the saloon where Bobby Marshall occasionally drank and bought the boys a beer. I ran into Hugh Gilstrap downtown and learned that she had been out to see him twice that week. But the case was as cold as the high mountain passes, and with every passing day it got colder.

Erin spent long hours alone, reading case law and making notes, and at night she and Parley went over and over the people's case. At least once a day she went to the jail and visited with her client for an hour or more. "Mostly we go over the same stuff," she told me. "Occasionally she remembers something new, but never very much and nothing of any value." I asked if they had ever been able to talk about their old days, and Erin said yes, they had finally broken through that ice. "So how are you with her now?" I asked, but she shrugged and said, "I still don't know. I'm still uneasy. She's eager and I'm distant, and I guess that's how it's going to be, at least for a while." But I could see that she wanted something, some final answer to an enigma that had been on her mind for more than ten years.

I passed my time covering the same ground Miss Bailey was raking over: I talked to people, I went over the scene, I combed through the town and called Rosemary in Social Services and wandered in the hills above Laura Marshall's house. I made out-of-state phone checks daily, trying to pin down where the Preacher and the Keeler boys might have run. I called booksellers cold: dealers in Arkansas and other places where Kevin Simms, also known as Earl Chaplin, had been known to live, and in Oklahoma, which the Keelers had once mentioned was their home base. I figured they had gone to ground. The Preacher would open a bookstore somewhere well off the beaten track; he'd sell off what stock he had and he'd dream of bigger things. Maybe somewhere, someday, he'd try another scam.

Near the end of the week the answer popped up from an ABAA bookseller, some man I had never seen or heard of in far-flung Texas. The elusive Kevin Simms had come into his bookstore yesterday, asking questions about the walk-in traffic in that part of town. "He says his name's William Carroll. He's looking at a vacant store about a block away," the fellow said. "He talks like he's already made up his mind." I thanked him and left him with a warning: "Don't buy any of his signed stuff, no matter how cheap he makes it. And please, whatever you do, don't tell him we had this conversation. He may be a witness in a murder investigation."

I reported this to Erin and she made

notes, taking down the fellow's name, address, and phone number. The way the case looked now, Kevin Simms and the whole issue of signed books was irrelevant. But she had a subpoena prepared for Earl Chaplin, aka Kevin Simms or William Carroll, perhaps doing business in Huntsville, Texas. She wasn't sure yet whether or how to use this. "We'll have to spring it on him fast to keep him from taking off again, and we'll need grounds for his arrest if we want to assure his appearance. And those two buffoons who worked for him: God knows where they are now."

If they weren't with him in Texas, I had their addresses in Oklahoma and the plate number for that truck. I had found the name of their insurance company — there was no claim on file as of last week. "I can't find any evidence that they actually towed the truck in — I think they may have just left it up there, in which case it'll sit there at least till the road opens again in the spring, and maybe forever."

"If we can keep it simple, we'll be better off," Erin said. "They've got to prove she did it and we've got to counter whatever evidence they put on. Her confession is their big enchilada. That's it in a nutshell, and Lennie's the unshakable millstone around their necks. If they can't find him and they can't get past that, what do they do?"

They asked for a continuance, a move Erin vigorously opposed. There was a hearing in the judge's chambers and His Honor came down with unexpected grit on our side. The woman had been sitting in jail, for God's sake, separated from her children since October. Fish or cut bait.

They dropped the charges a week before Christmas.

Erin's law firm had given her a long leash and she wasn't expected back in the office till mid-February. "You can go on back to Denver if you want to," she told me. "I know you've been itching to get away from here and I don't blame you. But I think I'll stay around for a few days."

Laura had asked her to, she said: "There are some things we need to tidy up, a bunch of legal odds and ends and money matters. She's only now beginning to realize how much this thing may wind up costing her."

And there was still the old stuff between them, all the things that Erin had avoided and now needed to face. "I didn't just come out here to get her off, I've always known that, even when I wouldn't say so. It's hard for me to make even you understand why she was so important to me in those old days. Have you ever had a friend like that? . . . She's just never been out of my mind. I believe there's an answer to us, somewhere in that head and heart of hers, and now I want to find out what that is, for my own peace of mind."

Sure, I understood that. "I'll stick around too, if it's all the same to you; give you something to warm your feet on at night. And my store's doing fine; Millie says I should take off more often. Denver'll still be there when we get back."

By Christmas week the streams had frozen over and the kids were out skating, building snowmen and ice forts. At one house south of town, a row of tiny igloos was going up on each side of a long driveway. The snow that year was just short of sensational. There hadn't been much recorded in Denver so far, but here in the mountains, and particularly in Paradise, there were drifts as high as a car, a wonderland for kids and even for old duffers who appreciated a good snowball fight. Back-country skiers were flooding into town.

Within a day of her release, Laura rented a house in town for herself and the kids. She planned to have her place recarpeted and remodeled so that maybe they'd be able to go up there again without those constant reminders of what had happened. But when all was said and done, she thought she would sell the place, pay her legal bills, take the kids and move somewhere out of state.

"I think I need to get a new start," she said more than once after her release. "Paradise just has too much old baggage attached to it."

I thought her words contained a hint, a hope that perhaps she wanted Erin to say, "Why don't you move back to Denver?" But that invitation didn't come quickly or easily, and at the moment Laura took pleasure in what she had avoided when Bobby had been alive. She pushed back her reclusive nature and was seen almost every day on the streets, wandering into shops, talking to people, walking with her children. "She's taking the pulse of the town," Erin said, "trying to see whether people are suspicious, and how they are with her." In the afternoons she and Erin walked the town together: Laura would come by, and Parley or I, sometimes both of us, would babysit the kids while she and Erin went out alone and tried to rediscover themselves in a free world. I never asked what they talked about: it was Erin's business, but at night, when we were alone, she volunteered glimpses of it. "We haven't talked much about the old days yet. It just doesn't come up. I think she wants to have some kind of ongoing relationship but I'm not sure yet what that might be. Today she talked again about moving back to Denver."

Score one for the old Janeway and his hunches. But where it would go from there was anybody's guess.

For her part, Erin still didn't know what she wanted. "Maybe I still love her," she said one night. "But I've pushed her away for so long, I denied not only her existence but her right to exist in my mind. And yet she was always there. Even after all these years I'd find myself suddenly thinking of her. I'd be in court and I'd have a momentary lapse in my concentration, like a cat had just crossed my path, and I'd stop and think about it and it was always her. Her face would come floating up out of nowhere, and sometimes I was almost certain she was back there in the crowd, watching me."

"Do you think you could be friends again?"

"I don't know. Not like we were, I don't think. But life is strange, who knows how the ball bounces? Suddenly out of the blue she'll say something that makes me laugh, and we'll almost be like those long-lost sisters we were."

I had still not heard her say Laura's name: it had always been "her" or "she" when we talked, "Mrs. Marshall" in court. But I didn't mention it again.

As the holiday approached, Laura was looking radiant: she had had her hair done up and had splurged on some new clothes for herself and the kids. There was almost an air of freedom about her but not quite. "She understands that murder charges are dropped without prejudice," Parley told me one evening. "They can still refile them, and I think they intend to, somewhere down the road. They'll always have the Lennie problem to deal with. They'll need new evidence, a stronger case than they have right now. But I know they're not satisfied the way it is."

The judge was fairly well pissed at the way the case was frittered away, Parley said. "He wants Lennie in his court." Gill remained his usual distant self, but Parley knew after talking to Miss Bailey that he had been right, that they were trying to gather information for a case down the road. "Ann's like a lot of women I've known," he said, "she's stubborn to a fault."

Parley's best guess was that Lennie had left the state: "That damn fool has gone as far away as his truck will take him." Me, I wasn't so sure of that. I had a hunch Lennie was still around, and every day I walked the streets and talked to people in gas stations and shops, the waitress in the café, the old people who sat bundled in the park on the strangely warm snowy days and watched the kids at play. I asked everyone I saw: I left Parley's phone number and asked them to call me there if they saw or heard anything.

We had planned an old-fashioned afternoon dinner at Parley's house on Christmas Day. Erin would cook it, Laura and the kids would come over around noon, and we'd spend the afternoon watching *It's a Wonderful Life* on video and listening to Christmas music. "This'll be the first time I've had a Christmas tree since Martha died," Parley said. "I should always do this at Christmas; I ought to have one every year, even if there's nobody but me to enjoy it." Erin smiled and said, "Yeah, you should," but later, in the kitchen, she told me he never would. "There's nothing worse than trying to fake good cheer when you're really alone. A tree would drive me crazy if I were him, getting old alone, with nobody really close around me." A little later she said, "I've been considering asking him if he'd like to move into Denver. I think I could get him a job in the firm. I know I could. We always need help, and he could work as little or much as he wanted to."

That afternoon the three of them went for a walk while the turkey cooked. Erin had pointedly invited Parley to join them, leaving me alone to watch the kids. The big front room was full of toys, which delighted the twins even as they went through them all for the tenth time. Jerry and I sat alone watching them. Laura had bought him some new clothes and a fine-looking watch, which alternately seemed to fascinate and bore him. He and I drank eggnog, which he loved coated with cinnamon and spices, and I talked about the world that, so far, he had seen only in movies. I watched his face as I talked and I thought I saw real comprehension there.

His eyes were soft and doelike, and at some point I put on *Hondo,* another of the films we had rented, and watched him as it began to play. He sat transfixed in front of the set, and when the credits came up, I said, "You like John Wayne, Jerry?" Instantly he took up a paper and began to write. I let him do this undisturbed until he had filled the page, then I asked if I might see what he had written. He handed it to me without expression, and it was line after line of John Wayne's signature, all perfect replicas as if the man's ghost had floated into the room and done it himself. I handed him another sheet and said, "Can you do Alfred Hitchcock, Jerry?" and in an instant he had scrawled Hitchcock's signature, with the little Hitchcockian fat-man caricature attached to the end of the name. "That's fine," I said, "that's great. Let's see what you can do with a few more." I thought of the books, which had been released by the DA and were now stacked in Parley's back bedroom; but I didn't want to get up or disturb anything, so I scanned them in my mind and softly said the names of the authors I remembered — Leonard Bernstein, Paul Whiteman, Robert Frost — and with each name I instantly got back what looked like a perfect signature on the paper. I remembered some of the Preacher's books and said the names, and some of them worked and some of them didn't. "What about Andy Warhol, Jerry?" I said, and almost before I got the name out he had scrawled Warhol's name and had added the famous tomato soup can. He had begun to go down the page, line after line of the same signature, but then I heard a laugh outside and a bump on the porch and I said, "That's enough for today," and I reached for the paper and took it gently when he handed it to me. I folded it and put it away as the door opened and Erin came in.

"Well," Laura said, "what've you two been doing all afternoon?"

"Just hangin' out, watchin' movies."

I nodded at Jerry and said, "This is a good kid you've got here."

"He sure is." She tousled his head. "He's my boy."

The turkey came out of the oven at four o'clock and we ate at the big dining table in a room that had been dark for years. Erin offered a toast, "To new beginnings," and four glasses clinked lightly. Outside, the snow had begun again: we could see it fluttering past the windows as darkness fell over the town. Parley had lit the fireplace and it roared mightily as we ate and talked and shared an occasional laugh. "Parley's considering moving to Denver," Erin said at one point, and Parley shrugged. "I will admit that it sounds exciting," he said. Laura said she had already made her decision: "I can't live here anymore. This was never my place." She didn't mention her dead husband by name, but we all got the point. It had been his house, his town, his choice to live here. "I'm going to put the house up for sale next week," she said. "The kids'll be better off in the city, with real schools and others their own age. I think they've had enough of me as a homeschool teacher."

She was motivated to sell it, she would be willing to dicker the price, she wanted to be far away from Paradise and its little minds before the season turned.

"At the same time, don't be foolish," Erin said. "This land alone will be worth a fortune in a few years, and you don't want to give it away."

"I know that. But I can't live my life based on what may be, either. Besides, as I think you all know, I've got some pretty steep legal bills."

Erin said nothing.

"I may move somewhere I've never been before," Laura said a few moments later. "Seattle maybe. I've always liked the rain."

Erin nodded and they looked at each other across the enormous gulf of that tabletop. Laura said, "You think that's a good idea?"

"I think what makes you happy is what's good."

"I don't know what happy is," Laura said.

"Then maybe it's time you found out."

There was a moment just after dinner: Erin and Parley had cleared away the dishes and taken them into the kitchen, and the kids were playing in the far hallway. Laura and I moved past each other at the end of the table, and suddenly she reached over and hugged me tight. "Thank you," she whispered. "I know how much work you did for me. God knows where I'd be without you."

Even more suddenly, she stood on her toes and kissed me hard on the mouth. I felt her tongue and I pulled back instinctively and stammered, "Uh, Laura . . ."

"Mistletoe," she said, pointing over my head. "But I guess I'd better leave you alone before Erin comes in here and gets the wrong idea."

The evening passed uneasily. I had the feeling of something afoot that hadn't been there before. At nine o'clock, late by Paradise standards, the telephone rang.

"It's for you," Parley said.

I went into the hall and picked it up.

"Mr. Janeway?" A woman's voice.

"Hi, who's this?"

"It doesn't matter who I am. You've been going around town, asking about Lennie Walsh. You still interested?"

"Sure I am."

"Well, he's still here. I saw him night before last."

"Where?"

"Up at the end of Main Street, right on the edge of town. He was talking to old Freeman Willis . . . you know, the jailer."

"You're sure it was him."

"Oh, yeah. Listen, I've got my reasons for wanting that son of a bitch to get whatever's coming to him. He hasn't made many friends in this town. But I'd rather not get directly involved in whatever happens. Just a word to the wise."

"Thank you," I said, but she had already hung up.

41

Erin sat still and said nothing while I put on my coat. "I'll be back in a little while," I told her, and I hurried out before any of them had a chance to ask any questions.

One thing about a jail: Christmas, Easter, or the Fourth of July, it never closes.

Freeman was sitting behind the big desk with his feet up, playing sheriff. He jumped when I came in, as if I had caught him robbing a poor box, and his feet clattered on the floor.

"Oh, it's you."

"Hi, Freeman."

He came around the desk and sat in the perp's chair looking guilty.

"I thought maybe you and I could have a little talk."

"I got nuthin' to say to you."

"That's okay. You can tell it to the DA instead."

"Tell what to the DA?"

"How a good country boy like you became an accessory to a crime."

"The hell you talkin' about?"

I sat across from him and looked into his face. "Hey, Freeman, no matter what you think, I am not your enemy. I have no wish to see you go to jail."

Alarmed now, he said, "Why would I go to jail?"

"Aiding and abetting a criminal was a crime itself, last time I looked."

"You talkin' about Lennie?"

I nodded solemnly, avoiding the temptation to be sarcastic. "Lennie's got himself into a mess, Freeman. And you two were seen together two nights ago, here in town."

We stared at each other and I smiled, not unkindly.

"I know you don't think he ran in here and quit his job just because he suddenly got bored with it," I said. "I know you're smarter than that, Freeman," but in fact I knew nothing of the kind.

"Who said he quit his job?"

"Then where is he?"

A long moment passed. Freeman rubbed his grizzled chin and tried to look away. I did look away, striking a pose of infinite patience. I read the WANTED circulars on the wall and avoided saying the obvious: that soon Lennie would be up there in the rogues' gallery with Elmer Trigger Adams and Henry Scott, notorious flasher and tit-tweaker, who had moved on to buggery, child molestation, kiddie porn, and other monkey business. *I wonder how you'd look up there in that company, Freeman.*

"Lennie says you're trying to sandbag him."

"That's about what I'd expect Lennie to say. In fact, I don't care anything at all about Lennie. You can believe that or not, Freeman, it's no skin off my nose, but if you crawl into bed with Lennie Walsh, you'll live to regret it."

I waited. "You were seen the other night, talking to Lennie," I told him again.

"Who says?"

"Never mind that. Somebody reliable, I'll tell you that much. What'd you boys have to talk about so seriously?"

"Nothin'. He just wanted me to give somebody a message."

"Who might that be?"

"I can't tell you that."

"What was the message?"

"I don't know." He looked into my doubtful eyes. "I'm tellin' ya, I don't know. It was a sealed-up letter."

"I see. Did you deliver it?"

"Why wouldn't I? Lennie never did me no harm."

I shrugged. "I'm looking for a killer, Freeman. If that happens to be Lennie, and you go down with him . . ."

I let that settle on him. Softly I said, "Murder's serious business."

"What's it got to do with me?"

"I think Lennie knows something about it."

"Well, he didn't tell me where he was going."

"I see."

"He didn't. I'm not lyin' to ya."

"I think you know where he went anyway."

I pushed back as if to leave.

"Wait a minute," Freeman said. "Listen."

I pulled in close again and I listened.

42

Fourteen hours later I was rolling gingerly along what looked like a rutted turn-of-the-century logging road. It had taken most of the morning to rent the Jeep; I had to wait till the guy decided to open and do the paperwork, and now as I went higher, I felt the tension growing like a knot in my belly. There was a feeling of death in the air: it's always that way when a standoff is in the works and you don't know what the other guy is capable of. The way so far was just as Freeman had said: a nearly impossible road unfit even for horse and mule teams, with deep holes in both ruts that kept me rocking back and forth and in the worst places tilting precariously to one side and then the other over yawning rocky valleys. The cabin was just below timberline, surrounded by a few scrawny, mutant-looking trees and some hardy underbrush. Far below I could see the remains of an old mining town, a collection of ruins that twisted around smaller mountains along what was probably a snow-covered dirt road. Beyond the range was Paradise, socked in now as a storm system moved in from the west. I could see it coming seventy miles away, a swirling gathering of black clouds and snow moving slowly across the rugged landscape. I came over a crest and saw a higher mountain just ahead, and one to the north beyond it. *You'll know you're gettin' close when you see them two peaks,* Freeman said. *You follow the road on up the ridge, past what's left of an old mine, and right after that you'll come on the cabin all-of-a-sudden-like. You'll have to walk or crawl them last two hundred yards. You could make it in a Jeep, but he'd see you comin' and I wouldn't wanna be you if he does. Lennie is a crack shot with that deer rifle.*

He looked worried. *Don't let 'im know it was me you got this from. He'll know anyways; he ain't stupid, and he ain't talked to nobody else.*

I'll cover for you, Freeman, I said. I tried to mean it, but he wouldn't say more than that; he froze and shook his head, afraid he had already put himself in jeopardy, probably wishing that he'd said nothing at all.

Before starting out, I had retrieved my own gun and it was snug under my left arm. But I knew Lennie's deer rifle would beat it at a distance hands down, and there was a good chance he'd be watching.

I stopped and got out; looked over the terrain and imagined Lennie out there, cunningly hidden. No fooling around now, no silly games as we'd done on the slope across from the Marshall place. In plain fact I didn't know what to expect from Lennie. He had talked a bad show, but I had met others like him, dozens of badass hoods who had talked and were dead now because they had messed with the wrong guy or hesitated at the wrong time. Three of them were in the ground by my own hand, and I wasn't anxious to add to that dark tally. But here the odds were on Lennie's side and I knew that as well. That fact alone made me too ready to shoot first and ask questions later, and I still couldn't pin him with anything more than intentionally screwing up a crime scene and lying about it.

I still didn't know. I had had one quick glimmer and a growing hunch that whatever had happened, for better or worse, the answer went through Lennie.

Hunches, instincts, glimmers: all converging in a game of life and death.

But it was more than a hunch now. I moved on, keeping my head below what his line of sight would be from the ridge, and I skirted it with the gun in my right hand, held down at the ground as I walked. There was a path, but it was rugged, cutting across the face of the hill, apparently to the top of the mountain a mile downrange. Much farther than I wanted to go on my belly. For now I picked my way along, dropping off the path whenever I sensed too much open space across the gulch. I knew there would come a time, and it was coming up quickly, when I'd have to dare the hundred-yard final approach across what was essentially open terrain or lie down and wait for the darkness, many hours away. My sense of things told me I didn't want to do that. The storm that was coming would be wicked, especially here at the top.

I had almost reached the ridge when I saw the roof of the cabin peeking above the hill. I stuck my gun hand inside my coat and started on a perpendicular path across the face of the mountain. Ten minutes later I eased up the ridge and saw the cabin just below. Parked behind it was Lennie's truck, and beside that, two freshly cut stacks of firewood.

I sat on the ground and thought about everything, starting long before the murder of Laura Marshall's husband and going right up through this morning. And I looked over the ridge and watched for any sign of life.

There was no life.

The truck sat cold and untouched.

There was no smoke coming from the chimney.

Nothing.

I stood and surveyed the cabin from the top of the ridge. I watched every window for a glimmer of the rifle and there was nothing.

I faced my fear and sucked it up. Started across the open ground. My feet went noiselessly in the fresh, uncrusted snow, which gathered in the wind and whipped across the rocky mountaintop like tiny white dervishes. Once I had decided to go, I went: didn't stop or slow down; just walked straight to the edge of the cabin and stood there getting my breath.

Maybe he's sleeping, I thought. But slowly the truth dawned.

The cabin had a cold, empty feeling to it. No cheery windows steamed warm from his fire.

No fire. Not a sound from inside; only the wind out here.

He wasn't there.

Could be a trap.

I eased around the corner. The door

facing the range was open, billowing gently in the wind. From there I could hear the rhythmic squeaking of the hinges. I went to the door and peered inside.

Nothing.

It was a simple hunter's cabin; crude, one big room with a smaller room off to the right and a bathroom on the left; both doors open, light shining in from windows beyond.

I moved quickly now, sensing the worst. Went into the bedroom and rifled through his closet, rummaged through his dresser, such as it was, looked in the desk/table that had been pushed aside in some kind of haste.

A few papers; nothing current, nothing valuable. Lennie wasn't much of a writer, letters or otherwise.

On a whim I tossed his bed; I slapped down the pillows and then turned the mattress. Under it was a sealed yellow business envelope.

I sensed its importance; I could feel it burning through the paper. I tucked it under my arm and moved back out into the big room, went to the doorway, looked out over the distant mountain range.

The door to Lennie's truck was open, like the cabin. Not a good sign.

I moved across what yard there was. Came around the edge of the truck, and there was Lennie, sprawled grotesquely across a seat drenched black with his blood. He stared up in disbelief. One shot had ripped his throat out. The other had got him between his wide-open eyes.

Suddenly I knew what had happened, should've known all along. I tore open the envelope and looked inside and felt a sudden deep chill. It went from my gut up my backbone to my numbing brain. I had made a horrible misjudgment at the start of this case. I thought of Erin and I trembled, and I felt my knees buckle in fear as I slipped quickly down the ridge to the Jeep. I dropped the keys in the snow and roared my anguish at the dark sky as I scrambled frantically to find them.

43

The fear doubled as I rolled dangerously down from the mountain. It doubled again before I reached the edge of town.

I fishtailed into Parley's street thinking, *Oh, God, please, pleeeeease let them be here.* But Parley came out on the porch, looking anxious.

"You seen the ladies?"

"They left here almost four hours ago. I thought they were just goin' for a drive."

He came down from the porch and looked in through my open window. "This is a bad storm coming. All the stores downtown are closing early. This town's gonna be socked in good tonight."

"Where are the kids?"

"I got 'em inside."

"Good. I'll go out and see what I can find."

"Laura knows this country. She knows what can happen when it turns ugly."

"It's probably fine, Parley."

I watched him in my rearview mirror till the swirling snow blotted him out.

The sky over the town was already black; only a few people were on the streets, shopkeepers hurrying home. The snow had just begun, but in the time it took me to sit at a stoplight, it welled up and crusted on my windshield.

I stopped at the house Laura had rented. One quick look around the empty building and I headed out of town.

I started uphill to the Marshall house. If they weren't there, then what? Sit down in the snow and go slowly crazy. Run around in circles chasing my tail.

There was nowhere else to look.

Of course she would know that. She knew everything.

I sensed her cool mind. I felt her tongue, heard her laugh.

Mistletoe.

And there was my own smug voice in the afternoon darkness. *Laura, you are the worst liar I've ever seen.* With those words, barely knowing her, I had pronounced her innocent. *You are the worst liar.* But what if she had been the best?

What if she had coldly decided to kill Bobby and blame Jerry? What if she had killed Bobby in a sudden rage, then confessed and manufactured evidence of her own cover-up; what if she had played that dangerous game, putting herself in the crosshairs of a murder probe and rolling the dice on her ability to lie her way out?

Jerry did it, she whispered at last to that dumb klutz Janeway. *Jerry shot Bobby.*

I had dragged it out of her and so I was ready to believe her.

The land went white and the sky turned black. An almost garish look had come over the earth, like nothing I had ever seen. Not quite day, not yet night. My worried mind had begun to drift and I found myself thinking of that line about Cathy in *East of Eden.* I think of it in troubled moments like this one. I revisit all the crimson-streaked crime scenes in my head, the bloody walls, the throats slashed open, the brains blasted into a door; and all I see is carnage done for nothing more than the hell of it. It took a writer, not a cop, to bring the answer into its clearest focus. Steinbeck said, *I believe there are monsters born in the world to human parents,* and that line has stayed with me all these years. Now it seems to define my old life. I was the guy who tracked down the monsters. Experts, pundits, social scientists — whatever they call themselves today, those boys don't ever want to admit there's such a thing as pure mean-as-hell evil, but I know better, I've seen its grim handiwork. There are in fact monsters. Sometimes they can snooker and charm us and that makes them even more monstrous. As a cop I was supposed to counter them in court with nothing more than the facts of a case. No ivory-tower textbook opinions, no attitude, no mumbo-jumbo psychobabble; I wasn't the one with the $800 suit and the PhD in Everything: I couldn't coolly analyze from afar and then fly in, a hired gun on expense account, and snipe at the truth. My own testimony must be limited to the physical evidence — what I had seen, what I had found, what I knew and had meticulously recorded; what I could prove. I'm probably hopeless, stuck in my cop mode till the day I die, but I will never understand how we can pardon an animal who rapes, then cuts off his victim's hand and sits calmly smoking, watching her bleed to death. How can we say he was crazy then but now he's well, what kind of doctorate covers wisdom like that, and who cares if he is? Who cares if his mother beat him every day with an ironing cord when he was five? I'll grieve for the child he was and lock up forever the monster he has become. All I know is I will never trust his sorry ass on the street again.

These were the cheery thoughts that chased me up the hill.

The hill was a nightmare of blowing snow . . .

So easy to get disoriented and go off the road, especially hurrying with fear in my heart. I passed the turnoff where Lennie had gone that day to watch me from the far slope, and my Jeep sloshed and skidded uphill into the last half mile.

No tread in the snow, no tracks. There wouldn't be, of course, if they had come up hours ago. It didn't mean a thing, it didn't mean anything, it meant nothing, nada, nothing, zip . . .

I turned in to the road leading back through the trees to the house. I could see a hint of it now: the house, materializing through the trees and the blowing snow.

Looks deserted.

My heart sank.

But this means nothing.

Means nothing how it looks.

Lying to myself, maybe just warning myself to be careful. *As if I need it.*

I got as close as I dared in the Jeep. Stopped, got out, snuggled the gun inside my coat. Began to move, just off the road: through the trees, up the hill into the teeth

486

of the storm. The house became clearer, more sharply defined.

Looks dead.

Lousy choice of words.

How it actually looked was abandoned. Except for the wildly blowing snow, it would have looked like a still painting.

Then I saw the faint light . . . half a breath later, a wisp of smoke from some room on the far side of the house. *Somebody's here, all right . . . somebody . . .*

I know everything that happened . . . don't know why but that doesn't matter now . . .

I felt a chill in my heart. *Doesn't matter why. Doesn't matter . . .*

Now there was no thought of stop, be careful, wait awhile. I crouched low and zigzagged like a foot soldier in enemy territory, up the slope to the road. I hurried along it to the yard.

Around the porch I went . . .

. . . quickly, carefully . . .

Around another corner to the lighted window.

Laura stood in the kitchen, not five feet away. She was alone, humming some melody to herself. I couldn't hear it through the thick winterized walls; I got just a sense that she was humming and that was enough. She had a soft, idyllic, almost dreamy look on her face. She looked peaceful and contented . . . happy . . . almost frighteningly calm.

No sign of Erin.

No time to plan or worry about it. Just go.

I went quietly up the back-porch steps, crossed the porch to the back door, looked inside through the door glass.

Nothing.

The room was just as I'd seen it through the window. Everything shipshape, everything cool, except there was no Erin and now there was no Laura.

Fresh coffee dripped from the percolator.

The coffee dripped and the clock ticked. I could see the pendulum hacking away at the pieces of life and the black liquid dripping like blood into the pot.

I tried the door. It eased open with a slight creak.

Quickly I crossed the room, heels down first to minimize noise. I left pools of water on the floor from my shoes.

The hell with it; nothing's perfect.

I flattened myself against the wall. Listened.

Nothing. Not a sound anywhere in that big house.

I had an urge to call out their names.

Stupid . . . stupid . . .

. . . no noise . . .

. . . not a sound . . .

But I was already vulnerable. She knew I was there.

She had seen me or heard me; one way or another she knew. Why else would she do such a quick disappearing act?

She had stood in her kitchen singing softly, knowing I was there as if she had eyes in the side of her head. I relived that moment and saw her eyes shift slightly my way and a small smile tremble upward at the corners of her mouth.

Christ, I was demonizing her.

What if I kill her and none of this is true? She walks into the room and before she can say, "Hi, Cliff, what're you doing up here?" I blow her away. She's innocent, it's all in my mind, she's done nothing and I kill her. She reaches for something in her apron and I kill her where she stands. Then it turns out to be nothing, her hands were wet and she's drying them and I killed her. How could I live with that? I've killed men but she's a woman and that makes it worse. So I'm a flaming sexist idiot asshole; it damn well is worse that she's a woman, just thinking about it makes my skin crawl. I never shot a woman but of course I won't just blaze away like some stupid Rambo clone, my training and instincts are strong and I know better. But what if I hesitate and she kills me instead? Remember Lennie. Remember Bobby Marshall. And where oh where is Erin?

I eased around the door and into the hall. Almost pitch-dark from here on: a faint gray light at the doorway to the death room. I flattened myself against the wall and inched my way along it, feeling in the dark for unseen things.

My leg touched something and it fell in the hallway. A clatter went up and I froze there. I scrunched down and felt for whatever it was.

A poker.

Damned strange place for it. No fireplace within two rooms of here.

She had left it for me to knock over.

I waited.

Nothing.

Waited.

Nothing.

I moved across the hallway in the dim gray light and sank into the darkness on the other side. Felt my way toward the light, carefully now . . . carefully.

I heard a bump. One . . . dull . . . bump . . . somewhere ahead.

I tensed against the wall. My gun had

come up instinctively, the barrel cold against my cheek. I watched the light for a full minute but there was no movement, no break in the solid gray square, no more noise . . . until, suddenly, I saw her.

She had darted noiselessly across the hall: I saw her silhouette against the window for just that instant, but it was a moment quickly frozen and then gone. A moment when she stopped and turned and I swear she was looking straight at me.

She scurried back into the dark places like a cockroach.

Should've gone after her; now the moment was lost.

Can't hurry, can't get careless. She knows this house far better than I do; she knows every part of it and can pop up anywhere — behind me in a doorway I didn't know existed and can't see in the dark; or ahead, where I expect her but not where she really is. I try to remember but it's spotty . . . didn't know about this alcove I'm passing, didn't see it till I was almost abreast of it: she could easily have slipped in there, might be hiding there even now in the darkest part of it.

Got to assume she's armed. No room for mistakes.

I moved slowly down the hall.

Slowly, carefully, easy . . . the best thing I

can do for Erin is not get myself killed looking for her.

I eased past the crossing hall to the door of the library, now stripped and empty of books. I stood almost flush with the doorway, looking into the death room with peripheral vision, unwilling to risk my head in a full frontal view. I could see on through from there, the same scene I had come upon that first night with Parley but now so enormously changed. Everything beyond the house was going from deep purple to coal black with fierce flecks of white snow swirling across it. I turned my head and glanced back into the library. Nothing there but the black. I eased around the corner into the death room, keeping my back flat against the wall and the gun ready. Somewhere I could see a light, like a candle or a lantern a room away. It was on the side porch, I saw as I came closer, a flickering candle on the glassed-in porch. I knew I was in the greatest danger here: one false step, getting lured by the light, stepping away from the shadows, any mistake would be fatal. How could I not go? But the only way was straight ahead.

It's a trap.

It's a trap.

But I've got to take the chance.

Go fast! . . . Be a moving target.

I lurched onto the porch, crouching against the wall.

Erin lay on a cot a few feet away. Between us was a small table with two candles lighting the room. I scrambled across to her, blew out the candles, and threw my arm across her body.

She was strapped down and covered with heavy blankets.

I felt her face. It was hot, sweaty. I felt the pulse beating in her neck. I put my face against hers and softly said her name. I fumbled with the ropes and got them loose.

Then I felt another, and another . . .

Half a dozen knots on top, more underneath. I picked at them and slowly worked them free.

Erin moaned softly as if she'd been drugged. I thought of the coffee, dripping in the pot. *We were sitting in the kitchen having coffee,* she said in my mind. *That's the last thing I remember.* This wasn't rocket science. Now I had to get her out of there.

"Laura." At last she had said her old friend's name. I felt her take a deep breath and I heard her say it again. "Laura . . ."

"Don't talk."

"Cliff . . ."

"Shhh."

I had to get her off the cot. She was a sitting duck.

"Come on," I whispered. "Try to sit up."

The cot squeaked. I squeezed her arm. "No noise now. Quiet . . . quiet . . ."

Slowly I got to my feet. I stood in a crouch. At some point I thought I could see beyond the porch. On three sides the swirling snow; on the other the interior of the house, a black place made only slightly less black by the indirect light trickling through from the kitchen. I could make out where the doorway was, I could almost see the room and the hall beyond it wrapped in pitch-blackness; I could see the black hall, which must mean I was seeing the light, as faint as it was. I could see across the porch and somewhat into the house. I knew I could see a little better, I was sure I could, as my eyes adjusted more to the dark.

I could see the hall, definitely a lighter shade of black, I thought. But what was definite; what was real?

The corners of the room seemed to emerge murkily. I crouched absolutely still till my muscles began to ache. Then I moved, slightly; I stood up straighter and convinced myself that, wherever Laura was, she wasn't in this room.

I waited. Watched.

Nothing.

She wasn't in this room. So I believed, after an eternity of crouching.

I got my arm around Erin and pulled her off the cot . . . an inch at a time.

Now we were against the wall, deep in a pocket of darkness, and we huddled together in the black corner. The wind howled around the house and there was an occasional bump from somewhere. Might be a limb blowing down on the roof . . . maybe a load of snow falling and hitting something . . . or was *that* noise just now something closer, inside the house, a room away? The building creaked in the wind. The glass above my head seemed to be rattling in its sash, and beyond it the snow whirled past like a giant white cyclone.

I knew one thing: the house was getting colder. No heat had been turned on; whatever we had was coming from that one distant fireplace. By morning, if we were still here, the fire would be out and the house would be like an icebox. I had worn my heavy winter overcoat and I drew Erin inside it. She squeezed my hand and we moved along the wall.

One . . . step . . . at a . . . time.

I heard another bump. Erin hitting the wall, probably with a heel or an elbow.

Hush, I thought. *Oh, please, hush.*

I heard her sigh and I said it was okay. But it wasn't okay, it would never be okay till we were out of there.

"Can you run?"

"I don't know . . . I don't . . ."

"When we get outside, we'll have to make a run for the car."

"I feel sick."

"Hold tight to my arm."

"I'm sorry, I just . . ."

"Don't worry, I'll wait for you. As long as you need me."

"Where're we going now?"

"Out of here. Down the slope to the car. Is there a door out of this porch?"

"I don't know. It would probably be locked."

"Did you come in this way?"

"No . . . no. Oh, God, I feel sick."

"I'll wait for you. However long it takes I'll be here."

I felt her sag against me. An ice age passed. At some point she said, "It's not going to get any better. Let's go."

The shortest way was out the front door. We moved slowly into the hall and turned right. Backs against the wall we went to the end. "Hold still," I whispered, and I tried the door. It was locked.

"We'll have to go back through the house."

I gripped her arm and eased down the wall toward the kitchen. *No noise now, no noise.* "Stay behind me," I whispered.

I peered into the house.

O black night. Blacker than black.

Now I saw why. The light had been turned off down in the kitchen, plunging the whole interior into this blacker-than-hell midnight.

I couldn't see anything, not even the blowing snow beyond the windows. This was how it would be from now on, groping along an inch at a time, going by feel and memory. I inched down the wall, holding Erin with my right hand and my gun with my left, easing along it toward the kitchen. A sudden slight change in the air told me I had reached the crossing hall. I felt for the opening with my hand and there it was, yawning into eternity. She's there, I thought: that's where she'll be, and we stood for another eon trying to wait her out. But nothing moved, nothing changed, nothing happened.

"Come on," I whispered, and we hurried across, again sinking against the wall on the other side.

I stopped for a breather. "Almost there," I said, but in plain fact I didn't know what we almost were. I took a step and that goddamned poker fell again, clattering like ten ghosts screwing on a tin roof.

So. She repropped it.

Clever, diabolical, while all I had been was blind, stupid, unthinking, stupid.

I stood somewhere south of the kitchen, feeling stupid and alone.

Gotta go.

I squeezed Erin's hand and took a step. Another. Another . . .

In this way we reached the threshold of the kitchen.

One more room to cross. But then I heard a noise: not behind me . . . ahead . . .

Something bumped.

"That wasn't me," Erin said in my ear.

"Mmm-hmm."

A footstep.

She's getting impatient.

This time the noise was softer, closer.

She's coming.

She's coming.

She's here.

She's in the next room over from the kitchen.

She's here, just across the room.

She's here in the kitchen with us . . .

"Hi," she said.

44

"I know you're in here," she said.

She crossed the room and disappeared into the far side of it, but for those few seconds I could see her shape and track her movements. I could have shot her then, but of course I couldn't and of course she would know that. The advantage of the moment was hers. She had taken off her shoes; she made no sound as she walked, but then she disappeared again into the murk and the house settled back into that eerie quiet, broken only by the pounding of the wind. She'll go crazy after just a little of this, I thought, I can outlast her. But time passed and nothing happened.

Had she gone farther back into the house or was she still nearby in some black hole of her own? I squeezed Erin's hand. *No noise now . . . not even a soft sigh to give her a hint that we are together or where we might be . . .*

I pictured vast sheets of ice moving across the land, thousands of years apart. I saw asteroids pounding the earth, sending tidal waves rolling toward us.

I thought about what I knew and tried to imagine why.

She's insane. That's the easy answer.

Too easy. Far too simple, much too pat.

If she's a monster, she's not like Steinbeck's monster. No, and she's not like those real-life monsters, Bundy and Gacy and Dahmer, either; there are so few women like that, it's not worth the time it takes to think about them. Serial savagery is like poaching, it's almost exclusively a male sport. Unless she's some kind of freak with bodies buried all over this mountaintop, she is far more typical of women who kill than any of those monsters. There's a strong personal motive for what she does, I'd bet four of my best books on it: the two sweetheart Raymond Chandlers, my cherry Grapes of Wrath, *and the signed Richard Burton. If she kills once, others may follow, but they too are personal, not random. She has no inherent bloodlust; if no one offends her, we may never hear of her again. Bobby had been personal, an accumulation of long resentment; maybe it hadn't even been premeditated. Lennie too was personal, though we don't yet know how. Something he said, perhaps, in that angry moment captured on Jerry's sketchpad as he looked through the doorway. Erin would also be personal, maybe a grudge of such long standing that even she can't understand it anymore. I don't want to kill her but I have a bad feeling about any probable outcome.*

Erin's voice, close now: "Let's talk to her."

"No way."

"What can it hurt?"

Are you kidding? You must still be under the influence of that dope she gave you if you can even ask such a thing. "Not a word," I whispered. "Not a sound."

Let her stew.

Suddenly, somewhere out in the void, she sneezed and laughed irrationally. "This is ridiculous," she said, just above a whisper. "What's wrong with you two?"

She sneezed again. Sneezes come in twos, but this time there was no laugh and her voice was louder. "What's the matter? You're treating me like some kind of leper."

A long, quiet moment passed.

"What's wrong? What's going on here? Can't we even talk?"

She's beginning to crack.

"Talk to me.

"Talk to me," she said again, some time later. But she was the one who talked.

"None of this would've happened if it hadn't been for that stupid deputy. Trust me, Erin, you'd have killed Bobby long ago if you'd had to live with him, you'd have shot him dead, fed him rat poison, cut his throat in his sleep. I thought about it a hundred times over the years. At first it was a shock that I could even think such a thing. But I saw the whole thing one morning in a vision over my cornflakes and bananas. I remember thinking, *What if Jerry killed him?* What if Jerry did it? They wouldn't do anything to him, we'd both be home scot-free.

"When it finally happened, it was over so quickly I couldn't believe it. I shot him in an argument that flared up before either of us saw it coming, it was just, oh, *Christ,* it was an accumulation of stuff that had been building up for years until finally I had had it. There was his gun on the chair; I picked it up and, *wow!* Bobby Marshall was the most surprised fellow in the state."

She laughed, a crazy schoolgirl giggle. "So what the hell, I did it, there he was. But that deputy was such an idiot, then McNamara came, and after a while everything was unreal, and it almost seemed like I hadn't done anything at all.

"Jerry did it."

I heard her breathe, a deep shivery sound just across the room. Her voice in the void was like velvet.

"Jerry did it."

She sniffed. "I am the victim here, not Bobby."

She sighed. "You were always my idol, Erin. Still are. I'll bet you didn't know that. You need to know how I've been quietly admiring your life and career for years. Anytime you won a big case, I kept the press accounts, I cut them out and put them in a scrapbook. Would you like to see it? I can get it out for you and turn on the lights. Just say the word. I know you'd be as impressed with yourself as I've been; how could you not be? I know you would never collect your own press accounts, you'd never stoop to such vanity. You've always been better than that, but not me, hey, I'm not above it. I loved seeing you excel and accomplish things. I know her, I would say to myself; she's a very good friend of mine. I'll bet I know things about you that you yourself don't know, or have forgotten. I'll bet you don't know how I've watched you at work. I can make myself up to look like an old woman and I've done that; maybe a million times I've driven to Denver and sat in the back row of some courtroom, watching you work. I drove all the way to Rock Springs for that water case you were on. And I always think, *Damn, she is so good, she's so smooth and quick,* and I'm so proud to have you for my friend. I've always been proud of you, Erin. I've been waiting for years just to tell you that."

She coughed. "One day in Rock Springs you looked straight at me. Our eyes met and I thought, *She sees me, she knows, in a minute she'll come over here and say, 'Don't we know each other?' and I'll say, 'Of course we do, dear,' and everything'll be all right again.* But it never was, was it?

"Does it matter to you, what I've just said? Do you care? You must not or you'd say something. I know you're awake, I heard your voice back here. I didn't give you that much sugar in your coffee, just enough when you started to realize what had really happened here, when I could see it in your face.

"I was only trying to *explain* something to you, but I could see that you . . .

"I could see it . . . I saw it in your face."

She moved and something bumped. "I wouldn't hurt you, Erin. You can't believe I'd do you any harm. All I wanted was to find something I thought I had lost forever."

I heard her move. Again I saw her shadow against the windows; again she dropped low and disappeared into the dark places.

"Jesus, I wish you'd talk to me. Don't shut me out like this. You've been doing that for so long, how long do I have to pay for that silly thing I did all those years ago? I wish you'd talk to me about it. I know I could get you to understand if you'd just . . .

"Talk to me . . .

"*Talk* to me.

"*Please.*"

I heard her tremble in the dark. Her breath came out in a shivery gush.

Now a touch of anger rippled through her voice. "It wasn't all me, you know. It wasn't like I set a trap for Bobby just to hurt you. You know I would never do that. He's got to have some responsibility in what happened. Takes two to tango, but you, you could never forgive either of us. Just a word from you would've made all the difference in my life. Just something easy like 'Hey, I understand' or 'It's okay.' Is that asking so much? You could do that now. It would be easy just to say you understand. Then we'd be okay again. Just like old times. Just like old times, Erin. Just . . ."

I squeezed Erin's arm. *Not a word . . . not a sound.*

"I love you, Erin. I always have."

She sniffed.

"You were so good to me when we were kids. Remember that day we met, when those brats were jeering at me at recess? How you stood up to them all and told them off? You didn't care if they ostracized you, you didn't need those creeps. I always admired that. Still do. And I've been waiting years to tell you.

"Years . . .

"A lifetime.

"You were so much better off without Bobby. Actually I did you a favor if you only knew it. You have no idea how maddening he was, like some pissy old woman, he picked and fussed over everything. I couldn't cook, couldn't make love, there was always you; you were always there between us; there were always those subtle little reminders, and some not so subtle. Someone like me finds that pretty hard to take. It would've been so easy to resent you . . ."

She sighed. "If I just hadn't loved you so much."

Her voice broke. "Oh, Erin, I've always loved you. Why won't you believe me?"

A long silence.

"Men," she said contemptuously. "They mess up everything. You think that one you've got now is such great shakes, but don't bet your farm on it. He kissed me, you know. Right there in McNamara's dining room he kissed me hard on the mouth. I'll tell you something, Erin, you cut to the heart of it and your precious Janeway is no better than Bobby was. They all think with their cocks."

I squeezed Erin's arm. I heard Laura sniff and saw her move opaquely across the room. Suddenly she screamed. "God *damn* you, *SAY* something! *Say something!* Don't just sit there in the dark and judge me with that superior silence! Who in the *hell* do you think you are?"

I felt Erin tremble against me. I squeezed her tight.

"I'm sorry. God, I'm sorry, I didn't mean that. Of course I didn't mean it. I can never stay mad at you. But now you've got to talk to me, that's why I brought you up here. Just a few words to say you understand and it's all okay. I'll tell you how it was with Bobby and me and you'll thank your lucky stars I took him away from you.

"That's what I'll do, I'll tell you about Bobby. And you'll be surprised. You may've thought he was God's gift to women . . ."

She laughed without humor, a dry

chuckle. "He was a nightmare to live with. All he cared about was those *God . . . DAMN . . .* books!

"From the moment he found out what Jerry could do, he had a one-track mind. We laughed at first when this little boy could sign all this stuff and it looked so real."

Again she laughed. "It was fascinating to watch him. All he had to do was see a signature and it rolled out of him. You should see what he does with Beethoven and Mozart. But Bobby wasn't stupid enough to fool with that. Bobby said, *We'll stick to the new stuff, the stuff nobody questions.* You don't have to know about papers and inks to put some movie star's name in a book. Jerry could do it with a modern pen, and we laughed, God, how we laughed. But then Bobby began selling this stuff and it wasn't funny anymore. He knew this bookseller from Arkansas and they made this alliance. The guy would bring up some books, give us a lot of money, and take away the signed ones, no questions asked. We could live forever out here on the money they brought us.

"But we fought. We fought all the time. I'm telling you, he'd have driven you nuts. He was so *damned* controlling. It was his way or the highway.

"He asked me for a divorce. Fine by me. But then he said, 'I'm taking Jerry,' and everything unraveled.

"*I'm taking Jerry.* Of all the nerve. Where was he when that kid was nothing but trouble and hard work? Where was he then?

"Jerry meant nothing to him except as a money machine. So we fought. And it got worse and worse . . . kept getting worse until that day in a fit of anger I had to kill him.

"Tell *me* he's gonna take Jerry!"

Softly, a moment later: "He got what he asked for."

Her voice settled into a quiet drone. "So I killed him. I killed Bobby."

I heard her move. The floor creaked.

"I killed him and here was Jerry, waiting to help me like some gift from heaven. Jerry's always been so anxious to help me. He always wants me to be pleased with what he does.

"This is what you've got to understand. Jerry *wanted* to help me.

"He seemed to be speaking to me. *Say I did it,* he said to me. Nobody will know.

"Hey, don't sit out there in silent judgment like that. I told you Jerry talks to me, didn't I tell you that? So what if he doesn't

509

speak? I know what he wants; I know what he's trying to say.

"*Tell them I did it.* That's what Jerry wanted.

"But then I thought, nobody will believe it. So I would confess instead, let my lawyer discover on his own what Jerry had done. Everybody goes home happy.

"Was that clever? Only that deputy knew what really happened. Another one who got what he asked for. He wanted me to pay him to get out of town — ten thousand dollars so he could run away and not be an . . . not be . . . not . . .

". . . an embarrassment."

She sighed. "So he wouldn't embarrass me in front of you.

"Actually it was cheap at ten grand. I've still got Bobby's book money, all the money he got from that preacher, it's hidden away where I can get at it. You know I'd never kill anybody for money, not even that stupid deputy. When I tell you, you'll understand. Just say yes. Erin? Just say you want to hear it and you want to understand. That's all that matters to me now, that you understand what happened."

More time passed. Suddenly she said, "I want you to know everything. That's all I want, *then* you'll understand it. I know you'd have done exactly what I did, there's never been any real differences between us. Just understanding."

So this was Laura's story of Lennie's sorry death. When he went back up to the house to get the kids that day, he had found Jerry in the bedroom with the twins, shivering and clutching a sketchpad. It never occurred to Lennie to look at what Jerry had drawn. He found it much later, under the backseat of his police car. Jerry had drawn two pictures of the shooting: Bobby in his last living moment, his face showing realization and sudden terror . . . and the killing itself . . .

"Me shooting Bobby," she said.

But Lennie wasn't happy with his ten thousand. "He took my money and then said, 'Oh, hey, didn't I tell you, that was just the down payment.' If I wanted what he had to sell, I had to ante up a lot more money. So fuck it, I killed him and took my money back. You should've seen his face when he knew what was coming. What a surprise. He begged and whined for his miserable life, he said the pictures were out in the truck. So we went out there and guess what, no pictures. And I shot him just like Bobby, on the spur of the moment."

She coughed. "Tell me he's gonna take Jerry."

I heard her moving again. She had come closer and now she faded back. I could see her melting into the inky woodwork.

"Erin? . . . Talk to me . . . where've you gone?

"Where've you gone?

"Where are you? Damn, I need you now more than ever. Say something."

What happened next was almost unbearable. The room melted into nothingness and for ten thousand years there was only the sound of the wind. I felt Erin trembling under my coat and I drew her as tight as I could. Laura made no more moves, no sound until the last minute, when she cracked wide open.

"Erin?

"Say something. Say something. Talk to me.

"*Erin . . .*

"*Talk to me.*

"*Talk to me!*

"*Erin? . . . Erin! God damn you, Erin, you fucking TALK TO ME!*

"*You better talk to me. If you know what's good for you . . .*

"*What makes you so fine? What makes you better than me? You've always thought you were better than me.*

"Say something!

"SAY SOMETHING!

"YOU TALK TO ME RIGHT NOW!"

Suddenly the lights went on: she had reached the wall and the room flashed yellow-white like dynamite had gone off in her hand. She was standing about five feet away. I saw the gun for perhaps three seconds. She said, "I'll always love you, Erin," and, "Good-bye," and I remember thinking in that moment, *She's going to kill herself.* But when she brought up the gun, it wasn't herself she shot. I heard the explosion and felt the incredible violence as the slug ripped into me. It flattened me against the wall and took my breath away. I knew right away it was a bad one, it had gone through most of me and hit my spine, I could feel the sensation going out of my hands and feet, and in the same half second she fired again and I felt Erin jerk over backward with the pain; she groaned out three words, "My God, Cliff," and rolled out of my arms. Laura took three giant steps and loomed over us; I heard her gun click and at last then I shot her, knocking her backward across the room, into the glass door, shattering it in the gale of blowing snow.

45

I saw red. I opened my eyes and the flashing red lights told me we were heading down the hill in an ambulance.

When I opened them again, I was in a white room, and the doctor standing over me looked grave. I heard him say I had lost all my blood, every drop of it had leaked out in the snow. But that had to be a dream because nobody can live any time at all without at least some blood.

A young nurse peered over my bed and said hello.

"Where am I?"

"You are in intensive care at CU Medical Center in Denver."

I didn't ask how I'd gotten there. I flexed my fingers . . . moved my toes, then my head. "It's all there," the nurse said. "A little stiff but all apparently in working order."

"Where's Erin?"

"Lie still," said the nurse.

"What about the woman who was with me?"

"She's here too."

Again I said Erin's name and the nurse went for a doctor, who came in a few minutes later. "You're a lucky man. A fraction of an inch to the left and you'd be paralyzed."

"How's Erin?"

"Your friend is doing as well as can be expected."

"Don't bullshit me, Doctor . . ."

There was a moment when I thought the worst. He's not answering my question because he doesn't want me to know the truth, I thought. I gripped the sides of the bed and tried to pull myself up.

"He's getting upset," the nurse said. "Maybe we should . . ."

"Should what?" I said. "All you people need to do is just be straight with me."

The doctor leaned over my bed. "Lie down there and listen to me. Your friend is in grave condition. We almost lost her twice last night. She is very serious."

She had been shot above the left breast. The shot had missed her heart by the same thin whisker, almost exactly the margin as the one that had missed my spine. Two blood transfusions had temporarily improved her outlook, but she was still critical. "We are doing everything we can for her," the doctor said.

I asked if I could see her. "Maybe in a

while," the doctor said. "We'd have to roll your bed down the hall, and right now she's unconscious; she wouldn't know you're there anyway."

I couldn't help thinking of Hemingway and his death scene in *A Farewell to Arms*. This was going to be like that. She was dying and there was nothing I could do for her. I had used up all my luck that other time with Trish, and now there was none to call up for Erin. I looked over at the window and it was raining like that scene in the book. Rain, the symbol of all things bad.

"I'm going in to see her," I said.

"You can't yet."

"I'm going. You can either help me or get out of my way."

The doctor called an orderly and they decided not to restrain me. They wheeled my bed down the hall and into her room.

She looked dead to me. Her face was pale and she had tubes running everywhere. Her eyes were shut tightly, her breathing . . .

"She's not breathing," I said. "Do something, for Christ's sake, she's not breathing."

"She's very weak," the doctor said.

"She's not breathing."

"This is why I didn't want you to come in yet. The fact is, we don't know what's going to happen with her. We're doing everything we can."

"Can you save her?"

"I don't know. I wish I could tell you that but I can't."

They've got to save her, I thought. They've got to.

They will save her.

But the Hemingway illusion would not go away. I kept seeing that rain falling on the window and I couldn't shake the notion that I had used up all my luck that night years ago with Trish.

"You should go back to your room now," the doctor said.

"No, I want to be here."

I had a good grip on the foot of Erin's bed. He couldn't make me let go so they left me there and I watched over her till she died.

I jerked out of the dream. Across the way her eyes blinked open . . . just slits . . . enough to know I was there and who I was. I raised my finger in a *Hi there* motion and she saw it and she knew.

The next face I saw was Parley's. He sat and we talked for a few minutes.

They had found Bobby's autograph books — *hundreds* of dealer catalogs with vivid facsimiles — but no one ever found the money Laura claimed to be hiding.

"This was the most screwed-up case anybody could imagine," he said. "I feel like it was my fault as much as anybody's. I was the one she snookered."

"So was I."

"But I was the one that led to all the others. Then mistakes were made and made again on every level. I don't think we ever *could've* resolved this in a courtroom."

It was Erin who had called him that night from the house . . . Erin who had saved us. All I could do was roll over and play dead, but somehow, through some massive gut-check and a deep well of strength, she had crawled over and got the phone off the hook. "I thought you were both goners when I got up there with the doctor," Parley said.

But I have tough genes and so, apparently, does she.

Evening came and she was hanging tough. I ate my chicken soup stuff in her room and Parley sat with me, talking. I could feel myself gaining strength almost by the hour.

The sheriff had found Laura in a snowdrift behind the house. She had crawled down the back steps and died there, her hand sticking grotesquely out of the snow, still clutching the gun.

Laura is my cross to bear and I carry it alone.

At the Rocky Mountain Antiquarian Book Fair the following summer a dealer from Kansas came up with the novel *Laura*, so scarce it might almost legitimately be called rare. The book was hardly a perfect copy, but at twelve hundred it was a steal. I knew I could blow it out of my shop in a few hours. I stared at the jacket, and in the heroine's face I saw what I could not have seen in Burbank. She looks almost like the real Laura, I thought: the hair is different, the mouth, the eyes . . . all different. Everything was different, and yet there was something about that pulpy dust jacket that reminded me of what I'd rather forget. The Laura of the book was heroic; I knew with one phone call I could double my money on her. But I didn't want her in my store, not even for a little while.

I felt an arm on my shoulder. Erin said, "Is that a good one?"

"No."

"Must be at least pretty good at that price."

She didn't say anything more about it, but she did touch the paper where the title was, and in her fingers I sensed a wave of feeling. Too many people she had cared about had betrayed her, and all I could do was make sure that I would never be one of them. The dealer saw us looking at the book and he drifted over and asked if we could use it. "I could do a little better," he said, but I thanked him and moved on.

I saw a signed Cormac McCarthy, priced right and thus scarce. The reclusive McCarthy signs little and his early books get a premium, but I passed on that as well. I have a different feeling about signed books now, and I have quit dealing in them unless I know the dealer well or witness the signature myself.

That afternoon I ran a slow mile and vowed to burn a candle until I could do it again, double-time, without pain. That night Erin and I went out for our long-delayed dinner at The Broker.

The days and weeks passed.

Time is our mortal enemy but it's also the great healer. We never talk about Laura, never mention her name, though we do keep tabs on the kids. They are now in good foster homes and the twins are being adopted. Jerry remains an enigma even to the experts. He had combinations of abilities that none of them had ever seen in a single subject, and later that year, with diligent encouragement and coaching from a young teacher, he began to talk. He has a good, rich voice, but almost as soon as he said his first words, his savant skills went into a slow fade. This is what sometimes happens when a mute savant learns to talk. So I read. So they say.

Don't ask why. Might as well ask why they are in the first place. One door swings open; another closes forever.

Today Jerry can talk but he can't draw a straight line or write his own name.

The mysteries of the human mind are far beyond my comprehension.

ABOUT THE AUTHOR

JOHN DUNNING, winner of the Nero Wolfe Award, is the author of three Cliff Janeway *Bookman* novels: *Booked to Die*, which instantly became a hotly sought collectible; *The Bookman's Wake*, a *New York Times* Notable Book of 1995; and the *New York Times* bestseller *The Bookman's Promise*. Dunning was for many years host of the weekly Denver radio show *Old Time Radio*, and has written extensively about radio, including a novel, *Two O'Clock, Eastern Wartime*, and a nonfiction book, *On the Air: The Encyclopedia of Old-Time Radio*. Dunning also owned and operated the Old Algonquin Bookstore in Denver and now does his bookselling online. He and his wife, Helen, live in Denver, Colorado. Visit his website at www.oldalgonquin.com.